Robert Hauser is a retired cardiologist who lives in Minnesota with his wife, Sally. This is his second book and first novel. The first book, *Heart Stories*, recounts his career in medicine and the incredible progress that was made in the prevention and treatment of heart disease.

For my mother, Georgia Mae Benham Hauser, who inspired my love of history and the pioneers who made our country.

Robert Hauser

BLOOD SUMMER 1862

AUSTIN MACAULEY PUBLISHERS™
LONDON * CAMBRIDGE * NEW YORK * SHARJAH

Copyright © Robert Hauser 2023

All rights reserved. No part of this publication may be reproduced, distributed, or transmitted in any form or by any means, including photocopying, recording, or other electronic or mechanical methods, without the prior written permission of the publisher, except in the case of brief quotations embodied in critical reviews and certain other non-commercial uses permitted by copyright law. For permission requests, write to the publisher.

Any person who commits any unauthorized act in relation to this publication may be liable to criminal prosecution and civil claims for damages.

This is a work of fiction. Names, characters, businesses, places, events, locales, and incidents are either the products of the author's imagination or used in a fictitious manner. Any resemblance to actual persons, living or dead, or actual events is purely coincidental.

Ordering Information
Quantity sales: Special discounts are available on quantity purchases by corporations, associations, and others. For details, contact the publisher at the address below.

Publisher's Cataloging-in-Publication data
Hauser, Robert
Blood Summer

ISBN 9798889102854 (Paperback)
ISBN 9798889102861 (Hardback)
ISBN 9798889102885 (ePub e-book)

Library of Congress Control Number: 2023917858

www.austinmacauley.com/us

First Published 2023
Austin Macauley Publishers LLC®
40 Wall Street, 33rd Floor, Suite 3302
New York, NY 10005
USA

mail-usa@austinmacauley.com
+1 (646) 5125767

I am grateful to the many authors and researchers whose books and publications provided the historical context for this novel.

Prologue

The President of the United States escaped the disease-ridden swamp of summertime Washington. Home at last for a much-needed rest, Thomas Jefferson relaxed in the quiet splendor of Monticello. It was July 1807, and he was approaching the last year of his second term. The tall patrician looked forward to the day when he would retire from government service and devote all his attention to the care of his five-thousand-acre estate.

His one appointment that day was scheduled for noon, when John Jacob Astor, a wealthy New York City businessman, would arrive for lunch. The visit was unofficial. They would discuss Astor's proposal for establishing a fur trading network west of the Mississippi. This was a topic of particular interest for Jefferson. He was concerned that the land he acquired from France in 1803 was dominated by foreigners, who had longstanding relationships with the region's Indian tribes.

The previous evening, John Jacob Astor arrived at the Albemarle Inn in Charlottesville, a few miles from Monticello. He traveled by coach from New York via Philadelphia and Washington. His thoughts this morning were entirely focused on his meeting with the President of the United States. Astor knew that he and the author of the Declaration of Independence came from very different backgrounds and shared little in the way of culture or philosophy.

Astor was born in Walldorf, Germany. His older brother, George, had left Walldorf for London, where he became a skilled builder and seller of fine musical instruments. In 1780, he joined his brother's thriving business. It was an ideal apprenticeship for young Astor, who mastered the English language and acquired the manners and cultural attitudes of upper-class British society, an attribute that would serve him well in the years ahead.

The Astor brothers expanded their musical instrument business. Despite their success, John Jacob was drawn to America. He was inspired by letters from Henry, his other brother, who sailed to America as a Hessian mercenary. A year later, Henry deserted the army, married, and became a successful butcher in New York City. He wrote lengthy letters to his brothers in London, describing life in America after the Revolutionary War.

Henry's descriptions of the New World ignited John Jacob's imagination. He booked passage on the *North Carolina* and boarded the ship for Baltimore in November 1783. After a rough voyage, he arrived in New York City in late March.

Astor went to work for a fur trader, and began importing his brother's musical instruments. They sold briskly. While his musical instrument business was doing well, he continued to eye the fur trade. That trade was spurred by the popularity of beaver hats. It was the felt derived from the soft, barb-like underfur of the beaver that was in great demand by hatters in Europe and North America.

Astor built a fur trading network in upstate New York. Within three years, he had a system of loyal Indian trappers and white agents. In 1800, he dispatched a ship loaded with furs and Hawaiian sandalwood to China, where he traded them for silk and spices. By 1807, Astor was accumulating such wealth that a few of his contemporaries thought he must be crooked. He became America's first millionaire. Along the way he acquired New York City real estate and cultivated influential friends in government, finance, and high society. It was one of those friends who had arranged his appointment with Jefferson.

Two large black Irish draft horses drew his white barouche carriage up the 857-foot mountain where Jefferson began building Monticello in 1770. As he exited the carriage, Astor heard a Chinese gong announce the noon hour. He was met by a formally attired servant—one of Jefferson's two hundred black slaves—who ushered him into the Entrance Hall.

Jefferson emerged from his private rooms and strode across the hall. His sandy red hair was graying, but his lean frame moved easily. He, too, wore a blue coat with gold buttons, although it appeared worn and a bit threadbare; his pale breeches were a corduroy material, and his gray-worsted stockings were spotless, though worn.

"Welcome to Monticello, Mister Astor," he said, extending his right hand. "I hope I haven't kept you waiting."

Astor stepped forward and grasped the president's outstretched hand. "Not at all, Mister President. I am very grateful for this opportunity to meet you. Your home is magnificent."

"Thank you. And we are still building, Mister Astor," Jefferson replied. "Unfortunately, I have little time, as you can imagine."

"Yes, of course," Astor replied. "The troubles with the British must weigh heavily on you."

"Indeed, Mister Astor. That, and the situation in the new territories. Our country, our nation, is growing…rapidly. But there are many strangers—foreigners—on our land." Jefferson paused, expecting Astor to comment.

When the New York businessman only nodded, Jefferson continued, "I understand you may have some ideas regarding the new territory?"

"Yes, Mister President," Astor replied. "That is precisely why I am here. The present, ah, situation, should I say, suggests that we—the United States—should strengthen our grip on domestic markets. I have a proposal—"

"Excellent," Jefferson interrupted. "But first we shall dine."

As they made their way through the Entrance Hall to the dining room, Jefferson paused by the artifacts that Lewis and Clark had brought back from their expedition. Jefferson glanced at Astor, who was examining an Indian war shield.

"I hope we can find peaceful ways to cooperate with the natives, Mister Astor. We will need their land for settlement. Not just yet, but soon. Already people are crossing the Alleghenies into the Old Northwest Territory east of the Mississippi, as I'm sure you know."

"Indeed, sir," Astor replied as he turned to face the president. "I trade along the Ohio River and the Great Lakes. Settlers are coming in increasing numbers, year after year, and I fear a major confrontation with the Indians is not far off. The white farmers wish to clear and fence land and plant crops. Indians farm in a limited way and, as I'm sure you know. They prefer to hunt and trade."

Gently Jefferson grasped Astor's elbow and led him toward the dining room.

"A few years ago," he said in his soft voice, "I wrote General Harrison a private letter. In it, I suggested we should encourage the Indians to learn to farm, as we practice it."

"I'm afraid that may be quite difficult, Mister President. I've lived among the Mohawk in New York. I cannot see an Indian hunter or trapper taking to the plow. They view planting as work for women, not warriors."

"You may be correct," Jefferson agreed, "but the alternative is an endless conflict between the white man and the Indians. No one wants that. We have to find ways for them to adapt to our way of life."

The two men entered the dining room and sat at either end of the wide table. A black servant offered Astor a platter containing guinea fowl and ham. Astor chose the guinea fowl. Jefferson said, his crisp voice almost a whisper, "You should try the ham, Mister Astor. It's from Meriwether Lewis's mother. She sends us a few of her very special hams every year. One of my favorite dishes."

Astor nodded. The servant placed a slice of ham next to the guinea fowl.

The two men ate in silence until Astor said, "Mister President, my compliments to Madame Lewis. The ham is exceptional. Would it be possible to purchase one or two?"

"I will have several placed in your carriage, Mister Astor," Jefferson replied. "A gift from Monticello."

"Thank you, sir. I will reserve them for very special occasions."

When they finished, Jefferson stood and said, "Let us continue our conversation in the parlor. It is cooler there. I will ask William to bring us tea."

The two men entered a high ceiling room contiguous with the east Entrance Hall. A harpsichord was in one corner, and Jefferson's violin rested on a table near the fireplace.

Astor observed, "I see music has a prominent place in your home. I believe the harpsichord was made by Jacob Kirkman in London."

"In fact, Mister Astor," Jefferson replied, "I believe I purchased the harpsichord through you twenty years ago."

Jefferson motioned to a pair of chairs by the window.

"Let us sit where there is a little breeze, Mister Astor. And please continue."

Astor spoke with a very slight accent.

"As I see it, Mister President, the challenge is the peaceful settlement of our country's land from the Mississippi west to the Pacific. By settlement, I mean American citizens living and working on land that they own and farm— or put to other productive uses. It means that the federal government must control its territories and determine how they will be governed. Otherwise, foreign interests will shape the destiny of the western United States."

Jefferson asked, "What do you intend when you say that our government should control its territories?"

"As a sovereign nation," Astor replied, "the United States has every right to enforce its laws, collect taxes, and regulate trade. I do not intend that the federal government should preempt or otherwise restrict the rights of each state."

"Certainly," Jefferson said. "But what of the Indians? The various tribes believe the land is theirs and are unwilling to vacate it. You have lived among them. How do we open our territories for settlement without first accommodating the natives who already live and hunt on the land that we—the United States—claim to be part of our sovereign nation?"

"I'm a businessman, Mister President. I believe there is a practical solution."

Astor stood and extended both arms, his palms open. "Battling the natives will be such a hazard for settlers that I doubt many will try. And those who do will fail or be massacred—"

"Pardon the interruption," Jefferson said, "but I'm quite aware of these problems. What I need are solutions."

Astor sat down and leaned forward, facing Jefferson, resting his elbows on his knees.

"Mister President," he spoke softly, "I would like to establish a series of trading posts along the Missouri River, across the mountains, and on to the Columbia River to the Pacific. I would also like to build trading posts in Detroit, Mackinac Island, and Prairie du Chien in the Wisconsin territory. These facilities will provide the goods the Indians desire, including food to get them through the winter and supplies they require for trapping.

"Instead of relying on the French, British, or Spanish, the Indians will trade with my company—the American Fur Company—because we will live among them and provide better quality goods at a lower price."

Astor sat back in his chair and said, "I am willing to risk all that I own to make this enterprise—the American Fur Company—succeed."

Jefferson nodded his understanding, and said, "I do favor driving out foreign interests, particularly the British. But how will your trading posts avoid conflicts with the Indians and foreign traders—the British and French-Canadians?"

"They will require government protection…"

"What sort of protection?" Jefferson shot back.

"Troops, forts—and sheriffs to enforce the law."

William entered the parlor carrying a new sterling silver tea service. He placed it on a mahogany teacart.

Jefferson rose and asked, "Would you like tea, Mister Astor?"

"Yes, please," Astor replied.

As he prepared the tea, Jefferson said, "We'll discuss 'protection,' as you call it. But first, I am going to tell you my plan for settling the territories. What I am about to say to you is very confidential, Mister Astor. I would not want it to become general knowledge."

He looked directly at Astor and waited.

Quickly, Astor said, "You have my word, Mister President. I will not repeat what you confide in me. Not even to my wife."

Jefferson handed a cup and saucer to Astor and sat down, stirring his tea with a silver spoon.

"Our goal is to live in perpetual peace with the Indians," Jefferson began. "We want to cultivate an affectionate attachment from them, by everything just and liberal, which we can do for them within the bounds of reason, and by giving them effectual protection against wrongs from our own people, including traders like you—no offense intended."

"None taken, sir," Astor interjected.

"As you may know, Mister Astor," Jefferson continued, "while the land the Indians occupy is part of the sovereign United States, our law has long recognized that North America was Indian property when our forbearers arrived here from Europe. Consequently, since that day, we have negotiated contracts and treaties—legal agreements—to transfer ownership from Indian property holders to white settlers.

"Today, only the United States government may purchase land from the Indians. Individuals and states are preempted from buying Indian property. We did not seize the land, as a conqueror would. No, we—that is, the federal government—have, and will continue, to purchase land from the Indians."

"I understand the point," Astor said. "However, what incentives do the Indians have to sell? And what if they do not want to part with their property?"

Jefferson sipped from his teacup and replied, "The Indians east of the Alleghenies are already suffering for lack of game to hunt for their subsistence and for furs to trade for necessities. This situation is also beginning to affect the tribes in Ohio, Kentucky, Indiana, and south to Georgia and Florida."

"Wherever the settlers go, the land will be fenced in, converted to agriculture, and the Indians will no longer have game to hunt or trap and provide them with the necessities to survive."

Gesturing with his right hand, Jefferson continued, "I can see the time—perhaps a hundred years from now—when the United States is one vast farmland, stretching from the Atlantic to the Pacific and from Canada to the Gulf of Mexico. This, I believe, is our country's destiny." Jefferson paused.

"More tea, Mister Astor?"

Astor held up his hand. "No, thank you, sir."

Jefferson's voice became forceful: "We wish to draw the Indians to agriculture and spinning and weaving. The latter they should take up with great readiness, because they fall to the women, who gain by quitting the labors of the field and moving indoors. When the men begin to cultivate a small piece of land, they will perceive how useless their extensive forests are and will be willing to pare them off from time to time in exchange for the goods and the implements they require for their farms and families.

"I am not naïve. The Indians will need some prodding. Otherwise, they will continue to do what they have done, quite successfully, for centuries. They are living in the United States, on their property, but they do not see it that way. They do not believe that any person owns the land. Rather, they feel that the land belongs to everyone—and to no one. For the Indian, personal land ownership is an abstraction—if you understand my meaning…"

"I do, Mister President," Astor replied, "but how do we convince the Indians to sell their land if they have no sense of property?"

Jefferson smiled and replied, "First, we will allow our trading houses to provide credit to the Indian leaders—the chiefs and other influential individuals. They will have everything they need to farm in the summer and hunt in the winter—all purchased from our trading houses on credit. When they are unable to pay their debts, which is inevitable, we will offer to settle their obligations in exchange for their lands.

"It will be entirely legal, of course. The Indians will agree to live and farm any land we reserve for them. The government will pay them an annuity based on the value of the land that they vacate and sign over to us by treaty. The annuity will be applied to any debts that the tribes have with the trading houses—or the government. The natives should not want for anything, even if their crops fail or if they are unable to support themselves through hunting and trapping."

Jefferson gestured with his right hand for emphasis and continued, "I think it is a generous policy, a peaceful approach if you will. We will be doing them a great favor. Otherwise, there shall be endless conflict, between the Indians and the settlers and, unfortunately, with the federal and territorial governments. Naturally, we will have to protect them against lowly predators—crooked traders, speculators, and the like."

Jefferson bowed his head slightly and said, "Please forgive my monologue, Mister Astor. What are your thoughts?"

Astor cleared his throat and said, "An enlightened approach, Mister President, but permit me to ask: Will the trading posts be operated by the federal government? Will you expand the number of government factories President Washington created to trade with the Indians?"

"The government-run fur factories—trading posts—were President Washington's idea. The goal—at the time he made the decision to create them—was to counter intrusions by the British from Canada and to give the Indians a better option than the private traders who were taking advantage of them with whiskey, exorbitant prices, and shoddy goods."

Jefferson stood and gazed out the window. On the lawn were two black slaves trimming one of the cherry trees.

Turning back, he continued, "Washington's idea was well-intended, but the fact is the Indians are not doing business with our federal fur factories. There are many reasons for this. One is their location. Many factories are too distant from where the Indians live and trap. It takes days to transport their furs to them. Another is the utter lassitude of the people who run this federally subsidized enterprise."

Astor asked, "I take it, then, that you will abandon the federal factory program?"

"That will be a decision for my successors," Jefferson replied.

"What I will do is support private efforts, such as yours, by building an army and navy capable of asserting the sovereignty of the United States in our territories and by defending our citizens and their property from foreign intrusion or illegal activity of any kind. Of that, I can assure you. If you establish a network of trading posts for your American Fur Company, as I encourage you to do, our military will do its best to protect them."

These were the words Astor had traveled so many miles to hear. He did not want or expect Jefferson to approve, much less underwrite the American Fur Company. What Astor needed, and Jefferson promised, was a military presence that only the federal government could provide.

There was one more topic to be discussed.

Astor said, "A related issue is the British and French-Canadian traders, who continue to inflame the Indians against the settlers and the United States."

"What do you have in mind?" Jefferson asked.

"Drive them out. Expel them from American soil," Astor replied.

"That may be difficult, Mister Astor. And far beyond what the government can do now or in the near future. We are heading for a conflict with the British. If not a declared war, at least a war in every other sense. I do not want to divert our military to tasks that can be dealt with later. We simply do not have the resources. What I will propose to Congress is a policy whereby the federal government must license all traders in U.S. territory."

The Chinese gong sounded four times. The afternoon was waning.

Jefferson picked up his violin and brushed its dark wood with the soft cuff of his cotton shirt.

"Government," he observed, "is like a fine instrument, to be played with precision, and not too loudly. Our government—our country—is young, strong to be sure, but all the same as an adolescent boy finding his way. Eventually, we will be the dominant bull, and no one—not even the British—will want to be in the same field with us, absent our invitation."

***

Captain Robert Benham limped uncomfortably from his log cabin to the birch rocking chair he had fashioned for himself when he lived in Kentucky. Now, in July of 1808, he was in the twilight of his adventurous life and enjoyed sitting under the elegant old elm tree that he had spared thirteen years ago while clearing land on his six-hundred forty-acre farm southwest of Lebanon, Ohio. The government awarded Benham this land for his service in the Revolution and Indian wars.

He sought the warmth of the summer sun and scooted the chair out from under the tree's shade so that its healing rays fell directly on his thighs. Gradually, as he sat there in the sun, the icy, uncaring aches that gripped both hips seemed to melt away like lard in a skillet. It was at moments like these, that Captain Robert remembered the bullets striking his legs that afternoon on the Ohio River so many years ago, in the autumn of 1779...

It was the fifth year of the Revolutionary War. Captain Benham was a Continental Army officer serving as the commissary under Colonel David Rogers, a Virginian who commanded an expedition to New Orleans to collect gunpowder and cannonballs that Congress had acquired from the Spanish government.

Benham and fifty-two men embarked in two keelboats from Fort Pitt in Pennsylvania. They navigated down the Ohio and Mississippi rivers to the Arkansas River where the Spanish had constructed a fort. There Rogers learned that the munitions were no longer in New Orleans but had been transferred upriver to Saint Louis.

"A bit of a cock-up."

Rogers's expedition rowed and poled upriver to Saint Louis where it loaded forty fifty-pound kegs of gunpowder, two tons of lead, and two cases of flintlock rifles into the two keelboats. They replenished their food stores and headed up the Ohio River toward Fort Pitt.

This segment was the riskiest of their journey, and a third keelboat with two dozen soldiers joined them from Fort Nelson near Louisville to provide added protection. The new keelboat also carried a few civilians, six British prisoners of war, and a dozen kegs of rum.

Indeed, there was danger ahead. The British had recruited Simon Girty, a tough Scots-Irishman, to lead a large force of Indians against settlers in the Ohio River Valley and Kentucky. The object was to divert the American army from attacking Detroit. Girty was a turncoat who had deserted the colonials at Fort Pitt the year before.

He had lived many years with the Seneca and Mingo, and he had strong ties to other tribes in Ohio and Kentucky. The force he assembled included over one hundred Shawnee and Wyandot warriors. Among them was a young Shawnee, a boy named Shooting Star, who had not yet celebrated his twelfth birthday. History would know him as Tecumseh.

Girty's scouts spotted Rogers's three boats slowly ascending the Ohio River. They sent word that the boats were heavily laden with cargo. Girty resolved to set a trap. Thirty years later, sitting in his rocking chair, Captain Benham could still visualize, in great detail, the band of Indians gathered on the edge of a sand bar near where the Licking River flowed into the Ohio River across from Cincinnati.

The Indians had just crossed the river in a canoe and were armed with muskets and painted for war. Colonel Rogers believed that he was duty-bound to intercept the war party before it could attack settlements in the area.

Benham counseled Rogers to ignore this small group of Indians and continue upstream; after all, their mission was to deliver the desperately needed munitions to Fort Pitt.

"Colonel," Benham said, "we've been gone for a year and know nothing about the situation here. Let them go!"

"No, Captain," Rogers replied, "we are soldiers first. It's our duty to engage the enemy wherever we find them!"

Rogers's men readied their rifles as the boats headed toward the sloping banks of the Licking River. When the bow struck the muddy bottom, Rogers leaped from the first boat and pointed his sword toward the Indians, who were whooping loudly as they ran into a dense grove of trees a hundred yards south of the river.

Without hesitation, Rogers shouted, "Follow me!" and charged after the retreating Indians.

Benham muttered to himself, "This is stupid—there's no need for this." Nevertheless, he checked his flintlock, climbed the riverbank, and joined the all-out pursuit.

They were midway to the grove of trees when volleys of rifle fire erupted from the tall grass ahead and on both sides. The gunfire was followed by shouts and screams from more than a hundred Indian throats as they charged out of the trees and underbrush toward the colonial soldiers.

Colonel Rogers and a dozen soldiers fell immediately. Three bullets hit Benham; one struck his right thighbone, the second lodged behind his left knee, barely missing the popliteal artery, and the third tore through his left buttock. He fell to the ground holding his rifle. With great effort, he managed to crawl under a fallen tree and disguise his hiding place with branches and leaves.

The battle was brief and bloody. The Indians overwhelmed the few soldiers who managed to get off a shot. They killed the wounded and took their scalps. A half dozen soldiers leaped into the Licking River and swam to the opposite shore. A platoon of Indians started to pursue them, but Girty diverted them to secure the expedition's boats and the valuable munitions they contained.

In less than half an hour, Rogers and most of his men were dead. The gunpowder, rifles, and lead intended for the depleted Continental Army would soon be in British hands. As an unexpected bonus, Girty found a chest of Spanish silver coins worth thousands of British pounds. It was a fortune that he would secure for himself.

Clouds and the late autumn sun cast long shadows over the field of slaughter where Captain Robert Benham lay wounded and in hiding. Rogers and at least forty-five of his men lay dead. Girty released the British prisoners. They spared the five American civilians, who appeared well-to-do and would likely attract a healthy ransom.

A cold, desultory drizzle and brisk northwest wind began at twilight. The change in weather was, in hindsight, a blessing, because the Indians abandoned their search for survivors to seek the warmth of their fires. The rum they captured would help ward off the cold.

The throbbing pain in his legs kept Benham awake during the night, together with paroxysms of shivers that sought to warm his body and fight off the chill of an early winter. Around dawn, he fell asleep and did not wake until he heard a faint rustling nearby. Benham brushed away the leaves and twigs that camouflaged his hiding place under the tree.

The clouds were low flung and thick. There would be no sun this day. He felt the hunger in his belly and thrust his hand into his deerskin pouch, where he kept dried corn and salted jerky. It was empty. "Damn," he groaned. '*How careless of me,*' he thought.

Thunder sounded off to the northwest. Benham had a premonition that this would be his burial place. His wife, Elisabeth, would never know what happened to him. So, too, his sons, Peter and Isaac. They were home in western Pennsylvania, where he had left them two years ago. God, he was tired of being away from home!

The rebellion had made so much sense then, and now it seemed destined to fail. The British were too powerful, and they and their Indian allies were everywhere. How did General Washington and the remnants of his army persevere? It seemed that victory was beyond their grasp, that freedom from the British Crown was an unrealizable dream.

His legs were on fire.

He fought back a moan and said to himself, "Take the pain, take the pain."

Cold rain came in a torrent, filling the cavity in the earth that held his body. Benham shivered uncontrollably. Toward noon the rain stopped, and the agony of his wounds lessened. Still, he could not move his legs, and he was hungry.

"Can anyone hear me?" a voice said. It was a familiar voice, but Benham was hesitant to respond. The enemy might be nearby, and that would be the end of him and whoever was calling.

Finally, after several more anguished shouts, Benham said, "For God's sake, man, shut your mouth. The bastards may hear you!"

"Is that you, Captain?" the man asked frantically. "Have you been hit, sir?"

"I'm hit in both legs," Benham replied, "I can't move. Who are you?"

"I'm Patrick Knotts, sir, Private Knotts. I'm shot. Both shoulders. Can't move my arms. Not at all, sir. Can you hear me, sir?"

"Yes, Private, I'm right under you," Benham replied, thrusting his hand out from beneath the tree. "Can you kneel?"

"No, sir, my arms aren't working. I might not be able to get up if I did."

Benham sheathed his knife and dragged himself out from under the tree. It was the first time he had moved in a day and a half. He was a strong, well-muscled man who was unaccustomed to physical limitation.

His father had him working in the fields before he was five and by the age of eleven, he could handle the horse and plow, thresh wheat, hunt and trap, and do most chores a man had to do to live on the frontier. His mother taught him to read, write, and count money before she died when he was thirteen. Now, severely injured in hostile country, he would have to summon all that was within him to survive and return home.

Private Knotts said, "I think they've left, sir. I went down to the river. The boats are gone too. Colonel Rogers is over there." He pointed to a tangle of saplings and brush. "He's dead. Shot in the belly. I think he must've lived awhile, 'cause he has his scalp."

Benham sat up and rested his back against the tree. "I've forgotten. What's your first name, Private?" he asked.

"Patrick, sir," Knotts replied.

"Mine's Robert. Call me 'Captain' or 'Robert,' as you please, Patrick. You have your legs, and I've got my arms. We must work together if we're going to make it out of here. First, see if our dead have anything that we can use—food and supplies the Indians haven't taken. Use your feet to kick it this way. While you're gone, I'll get my rifle ready. Sooner or later we'll have to hunt for food. Understand?"

"Yes, sir—Captain," Knotts replied. He was relieved to have an order to follow.

"Good. Get going. It'll be dark in a few hours."

At Benham's side was the Pennsylvania long rifle that his father purchased in 1762 from a German gunsmith in Berks County. The spiral grooves in the bore imparted a stable trajectory for the spinning round ball, which markedly improved the rifle's accuracy.

A sharpshooter like Benham could hit a small target at two hundred yards, a threefold improvement over a smoothbore musket. The rifle's stock was polished maple. In 1776, Benham had carved in it a single word—'Independence'. He loaded gunpowder and a round lead ball and shifted his body so the sun would not disturb his aim.

While Knotts was scrounging, Benham examined his wounds, using his hunting knife to cut away the remnants of his leggings. A shard of bone protruded through the skin of his right thigh. The wound was red and blue gray.

Carefully, with his fingers, Benham pulled on the bone, which came out freely, followed by a gush of dark red blood. Using both hands, he squeezed his thigh and expressed more old blood and particles of shattered bone. There was no pus—yet. He decided not to cover the wound.

"Leave it open," he whispered to himself. "Let it weep."

A second bullet had struck his left leg behind the knee, which looked like an overripe tomato. Benham probed the entry wound with the tip of his knife and encountered the round ball that had lodged between two tendons. He knew that infection was inevitable if the ball and debris of his clothing remained in the wound. So, using the knife, Benham enlarged the opening in his skin.

He cleaned the index finger of his right hand as best he could, and inserted it into the hole, digging out the lead ball with his fingernail. The pain was excruciating, but the ball was out, and a brisk flow of bright red blood followed.

Benham let it bleed; he knew fresh blood was a cleanser and had healing powers. After a few minutes, he tore the collar off his cotton shirt, rolled it into a ball, and pressed it against the wound, tying it in place with a strip of deerskin from his leggings.

As Benham finished dressing the wound, he heard a faint rustling coming from the brush to his left. Slowly he reached for his rifle and pointed the barrel in the direction of the noise. He took slow deep breaths to calm the pounding in his chest. Suddenly a bare brown foot stepped on the barrel of his rifle. He looked up and saw the handsome face of a tall young Shawnee brave looking down on him. He had large dark eyes, unusual for an Indian. Both men remained silent and motionless.

Benham thought: *He will tomahawk me and take my scalp. He considered calling out to Private Knotts, but what could he do with paralyzed arms?*

Seconds passed. The young brave smiled, leaned down, and took Benham's rifle.

Examining it, the Indian said in finely accented English, "Your rifle has a name—'Independence'. My name is Shooting Star. I will hunt with your rifle."

As he turned to leave, Shooting Star said, "Tell your white man over there that he's making many sounds."

Benham looked in the direction that Knotts had taken. When he turned back, the young Indian was gone. Benham thought: *Why did he spare me?*

A half hour later, Knotts reappeared, kicking before him a dozen items, mostly sacks of jerky and canvas bags containing wool blankets, clothing, and eating utensils.

"Captain, the bastards took the lead pouches and powder horns," Knotts said.

"The rifles are gone too. The fuckers did awful things to our soldiers, sir." Knotts began to sob.

"All right, Patrick," Benham said. "God will have to look after them. They served their country. Now we must find a way to survive and get home."

"Where's your rifle, Captain?" Knotts asked.

Benham told him about the young Shawnee, then added, "Now we must find a way to survive without a rifle to hunt."

One by one, Benham examined the sacks and bags. He divided the jerky with Knotts. It was enough to satisfy their hunger for now, but soon they would need to trap rabbits and squirrels. The blankets were a godsend. The cold northwest wind was gaining strength, blowing swirls of brightly colored leaves about them. They would not build a fire tonight lest an unfriendly eye see the flame and smoke.

When he finished, Benham said, "Patrick, I want you to check my ass."

Somewhat bemused, Knotts replied, "Pardon, Sir?"

Benham rolled onto his right side and pulled down his pants. "My ass got shot. What does it look like?"

Knotts bent over and examined the jagged wound in the Benham's left buttock. It was about four inches long and held a large purple gelatinous blood clot.

"Doesn't look too bad, Captain. Flesh wound, no bleeding, and it looks like the shot went right through."

"Okay," Benham said, "now let me look at your shoulders. Sit here on the tree next to me."

Knott had the powerful chest musculature of a man who had rowed and poled keelboats. His gunshot wounds were nearly identical. A bullet had pierced the ligaments and cartilage below each shoulder joint and exited out the back. Neither arm bone seemed broken but the joints were dark purple and severely swollen.

"I don't think any bones are broke," Benham said slowly. "I'll put both your arms in slings, so the shoulders stay quiet. You'll rest easier."

"Whatever you say, Captain," Knotts replied.

Using his knife, Benham fashioned two linen slings out of the clothing Knotts had gathered from the dead soldiers. By sunset, Knotts' arms were suspended in slings, fully immobilized.

"Thank you, sir. Feels much better. I'm obliged to you, sir."

The two men wrapped themselves in wool blankets. Benham rested against the tree and Knotts sat on the trunk next to him. Benham fed Knotts. They chewed on jerky and drank water from wooden canteens. The odds of surviving were still long.

Compared to yesterday, though, their chances had improved, provided they continued to work together. If one became incapacitated, the other would surely die…

Elisabeth Benham left the cabin and approached her husband, who had been sitting in his rocking chair for the better part of an hour.

"Are you feeling poorly?" she asked. "I've never known you to sit so long."

"Just thinking," Robert replied.

"About...?"

"Kentucky, during the war, when Girty's war party ambushed us. Every time my legs ache, it reminds me of that day."

"It was thirty years ago, dear."

"Yes, but it's still fresh in my mind, every minute of it. Patrick Knotts and I barely made it out. If that boat had not picked us up when it did, we would have died, what with winter coming on. Starved or froze to death."

Elisabeth said, "We haven't heard from Patrick since he joined General Harrison in Indiana."

Robert looked up at Elisabeth, arching his eyebrows, and asked.

"Remember when Patrick and I started the ferry? From the Licking across the Ohio River to Cincinnati—after we left the army?" Robert asked.

"Our dock was near the riverbank where we were ambushed in seventy-nine."

He paused and coughed deeply and coughed again.

"We did well for a couple of seasons, 'til Absalom Martin began his ferry service. What a character he was—hair as white as snow, and tall and skinny. Good man, though, hard-working and honest. There wasn't enough traffic for two ferries, so Patrick rejoined the army, and we moved up here. Cleared this land and built our cabin."

Smiling, he stroked Elisabeth's arm and took her hand.

"No time for that. You better get ready," Elisabeth said. "The boys are taking you to the Golden Lamb this afternoon. General Harrison has invited you to meet him."

"I know," Robert growled. "Probably about Tecumseh, or his brother, that so-called Prophet. I tell you, there's goin' to be trouble. The British are stirring the Indians again, just as they did in seventy-six."

"Whatever the general asks of you," Elisabeth said forcefully, "don't you sign up for anything that takes you away from home. You've done your part, God knows, and your body is in no shape for a fight."

Elisabeth placed a hand on her husband's shoulder; his skin was pale despite all the hours he spent in the sun.

"I don't like that cough. You should stop smoking, Robert. Throw that pipe away."

The Golden Lamb was a popular meeting place for politicians and the military. A rough-hewn sign painted with the picture of a yellow lamb distinguished the two-story log inn on Lebanon's broad main street. Jonas Seaman and his wife, Martha, an excellent cook, had built the Golden Lamb Inn in 1803. The inn had a reputation for clean rooms and a comfortable tavern. Martha served deer, bear, wild turkey, and apple butter to her guests at a long maple table.

William Henry Harrison arrived at the Golden Lamb on horseback from the territorial capital, Vincennes, a journey of nearly two hundred miles over Indian trails and buffalo tracks. He was thirty-six, the son of Colonel Benjamin Harrison V, a wealthy Virginian who had signed the Declaration of Independence.

In 1803, President John Adams selected Harrison to be the first governor of the Indiana Territory. The appointment occurred after Congress passed Harrison's land reform bill that would allow settlers to purchase small plots of land at reasonable prices on good terms. At last, thousands of families could afford to buy farms in the Northwest Territory.

Robert Benham entered the Golden Lamb and found Governor Harrison seated at a table with a young officer. Harrison and Robert Benham met while both were serving under General 'Mad Anthony' Wayne.

Extending his hand, Benham said, "William, good to see you. It's been too long."

Harrison was astonished by Benham's appearance. Unlike the robust and vigorous frontiersman he had known six years before, the man before him was thin and frail. His deep brown eyes were sunken, and his hair was thin and graying. Surely, he was suffering a sickness.

Harrison rose from his chair and said, "Robert, wonderful to see you, and thank you for coming."

The men grasped forearms.

Turning, Harrison said, "Allow me to introduce my aid de camp, Lieutenant Peter Sprong of Virginia."

Benham introduced his sons, who quickly excused themselves. Lieutenant Sprong also removed himself so the two old friends could meet privately.

"How are you, Robert?" Harrison asked from across the table.

"Been better, as you can see," Benham replied. "No meat on me anymore, and I've got no appetite to speak of. The old wounds hurt most days. I'm an old stallion, William, off my feed and waiting in the pasture for sundown." He reached inside his coat and removed a pipe and tobacco pouch.

"How's Elisabeth?"

"She's well. Spends most of the day looking after me. God knows I don't deserve such a woman."

He paused, looked down at the pipe in his hand, and asked, "What about you, William, what brings you here?"

"Anna has been at our home in North Bend for two months. She's worried about the farm and the distillery and how they're being managed. I'm here to straighten things out." Harrison paused and asked, "Are you hungry, Robert? How about a plate of Mrs. Seaman's best?"

Benham nodded and signaled the bartender. "Jackson, we'll have the Golden Lamb special," he said.

Harrison looked into Benham's dark eyes and said, "I want to talk to you about Tecumseh, Robert. I understand you've spent some time with him and his brother, I believe his name is Tenskwatawa—they call him the Prophet. What can you tell me?"

"What version do you want?" Robert asked. "Long or short, or something in between?"

Harrison grimaced, his long face darkening. "The French have been troublesome, but it's the British who will be at our throats soon. My nightmare is a coalition between Tecumseh's Indian confederacy and the British in Canada. Somehow, our government must neutralize the Indians, and prevent Tecumseh from aligning all the tribes into a single confederacy. If these tribes come together and are armed by the British, then bloody hell will visit every white man and woman in the Northwest Territory."

He paused, and dropped his voice an octave, "So, Robert, I need to know the details. Most important, what do you think?"

Jackson placed a platter of meats and potatoes between them. Harrison unrolled a finely monogrammed deerskin pouch that held a silver fork, knife, and spoon; they were made in England and were given to him by his father. Benham had a carved wood pocketknife whose handle contained a steel blade and a three-prong fork; it was his fiftieth birthday present from Elisabeth.

Harrison was hungry. He speared two slices of bear meat and one of venison.

Benham took a small piece of venison and half a baked potato.

He began, "Tecumseh is by far the most impressive Indian I've ever met. Quite the physical specimen—the kind of man who commands attention by his presence alone. Men stop talking when he enters a room. Women consider him godlike. He's tall for an Indian. His voice is deep, and he knows how to captivate an audience with words and gestures. Highly intelligent, a born leader, no doubt about it…"

"How often have you seen him?" Harrison interrupted as he stabbed a potato with his fork.

"Three times," Benham replied. "The first was in '79 when I was with Rogers on the Ohio River. We got ambushed on the Kentucky shore by Girty and his Shawnees. Remember that fiasco?"

"Everybody in the army does. Rogers lost his whole command and all that ammunition. Got some civilians killed too. Stupid. I'd forgotten you were there. Go on…"

Benham continued, "Tecumseh was a youngster then—his name was Shooting Star—and you could see that he was going to be special. Anyway, I was on the ground, shot in both legs and completely helpless. Tecumseh could've taken my scalp. Most any warrior would. Instead, he told me in perfect English that we were making too much noise. Then he took my rifle and left."

Harrison finished chewing a piece of bear meat, and said, "You've always been lucky, Robert. I recall you dodged death again with St. Clair in Ohio. Keep going…"

Benham coughed and wiped his mouth with a dark bloodstained handkerchief. "The next time was fifteen years ago when I was living in Kentucky. He and his one-eyed brother---Tenskwatawa—were hunting and wanted to trade some pelts for gunpowder. I didn't need the pelts, but we talked in front of my cabin for an hour or so. I recognized him from the time he let me keep my scalp. Couldn't mistake those eyes. But I didn't say anything, and he didn't either."

"Eventually, Elisabeth invited them to share our dinner. I was impressed with how he handled himself—very polite, quick mind. His brother was an odd one, though. Didn't say much. Wore a patch over his right eye. Their father was a Shawnee war chief by the name of Puckshinwa, and their mother was a Creek.

"Some say she had mixed blood—her mother or grandmother was the daughter of a wealthy southern planter in Georgia or the Carolinas. After they left, I told Elisabeth that Tecumseh would be chief someday."

"And the last time?" Harrison asked.

"Last summer. He was passing through on his way south to Georgia. He knew we had moved up here and wanted to thank us for the hospitality at our farm in Kentucky. He gave Elisabeth a nice mink pelt. She invited him to stay for dinner. An interesting two hours."

Harrison put down his knife and fork and leaned back in his chair.

"What did he say?"

"Tecumseh spoke mostly about his brother, the one-eyed ne'er-do-well they now call the Shawnee Prophet. I'm sure you know more about the Prophet than I do…"

"Perhaps," Harrison said, "but go on."

"Until four years ago, Tecumseh's brother was a drunk. Couldn't feed his family. Abused his wife and children. Was dependent on Tecumseh for food and shelter. One night he got drunk and fell into the fire in his lodge. His wife thought—maybe hoped—that he was dead. They pulled him out. He didn't appear to be breathing, so they began to prepare him for burial. Then his eyes flickered, and he sat up, staring, like in a trance. He described a nightmare where drunken men were condemned to life in prison and torture.

"After that, he became a different man. Gave up whiskey and preached a vision for his people. He said they should reject the white man's ways, return to their roots, and restore their native culture. That's when they began calling him the Prophet, so he changed his name to Tenskwatawa. For the next three years, he traveled among the tribes, not just the Shawnee, but others, like the Delaware, Miami, and Mingo. From what I hear, the Prophet attracted quite a following, overshadowing Tecumseh."

Benham paused and sipped from his tankard of ale. "I heard the Prophet met with you at Vincennes. Is that true?"

"Yes, I'm surprised you know," Harrison replied. "It was only two weeks ago. He professed his intention—and that of his people—to live in peace. Lieutenant Sprong, whose speaks Shawnee, kept a record of the conversation."

Harrison reached inside his jacket and withdrew an oilskin pouch containing a small leather-bound book.

Handing the book to Benham, Harrison continued, "I trust you can read his handwriting."

Benham held the book at arm's length and sighed, "I'm afraid my eyes can't see writing this size. Can you read it for me?"

Harrison retrieved the book and began, "The Prophet said, 'It is three years since I have practiced a new system of religion…At first, the white people and some Indians were against me, but I only wanted to introduce to the Indians the good principles which the white people practice…I heard that you wanted to hang me, but I want you to know that it is our intention to live in peace…

"Both of us are warriors, but we should turn away from war and attend to our children and live side by side, each people living according to their customs…I ask that you prevent the sale of liquor to Indians…Unlike white people, we do not know how to use whiskey…I hope that you can promote our happiness and give us a few necessaries, such as needles, flints, hoes, and powder so we can hunt meat and feed our families'. "

Harrison replaced the book in the pouch and looked inquiringly at Robert. "Well?" he asked.

Benham responded, "I believe the Prophet is sincere, inasmuch as he's trying to help his people. But the Indians are being destroyed by disease and whiskey, and the flood of white settlers threatens them. Dozens of tribes are squeezed into land that only one tribe hunted twenty years ago. Game is disappearing as that land is overhunted. We know this. These are facts. Tecumseh knows it too. He understands that time is running out for him and every Indian east of the Mississippi."

Benham leaned forward and whispered, "I guarantee you this, William. While his brother is preaching peace, Tecumseh is planning war, all-out war, a fight to the finish. He's recruiting every tribe within a thousand miles, from Georgia and Florida to Indiana and up north beyond the Mississippi into Canada. His goal is to field an army of ten thousand warriors in an all-out effort to rid his land of every white man, white woman, and white child."

Benham's sons entered the tavern.

Peter said, "Sorry to interrupt, Father, but it's getting late in the day. Unless you want to stay here overnight, we should head home."

Harrison said, "Robert, please stay, be my guest. There's so much more to talk about…"

Benham's tone was apologetic, "Thank you, but Elisabeth expects me home, and she's alone."

He looked at Peter. "Get Jupiter ready. I'll be with you in a few minutes."

Turning to Harrison, Benham said softly, "If I were you, William, I would get the militia up to strength. Tecumseh won't be ready for a year or two. You have time to strengthen your army, and fortify Vincennes."

Tecumseh slowly approached the Benham cabin on horseback. He was alone. The summer sun was just above the horizon and a swarm of mosquitoes danced in the twilight.

Not wanting to cause alarm, he decided to dismount and sit cross-legged in front of the cabin, hoping that eventually someone would emerge and understand his peaceful intentions. After half an hour, he heard voices from the direction of the road to Lebanon. Minutes later he recognized Robert Benham on horseback, accompanied by two younger men whom he did not recognize.

Tecumseh stood, extending open hands, a sign of peace.

Benham paused as he entered the clearing in front of his home. The tall man before him was silhouetted against the setting sun. His son, Peter, unslung his rifle and cocked the hammer.

"I can't see your face," Benham barked. "Identify yourself!"

"I am Chief Tecumseh," the mysterious man replied. His deep, sonorous voice implied no threat.

Cautiously Benham edged his horse closer, until he saw the chiseled features of the most handsome man he had ever seen. Indeed, it was Tecumseh, principal war and civil chief of the Shawnee, brother of the Prophet, and champion of Indian independence.

"Welcome, Tecumseh," Benham said, as he dismounted. "These are my sons, Peter and Isaac." They dismounted and stood behind their father, holding their long rifles.

"Captain Robert," Tecumseh said, "I'm alone and would like to speak with you. I'm sorry to inconvenience you and your family. Should I return in the morning?"

The evening was warm, and the fading sun and nearly full moon eerily illuminated the clearing around the cabin.

Benham turned to his sons.

"Tell your mother that Chief Tecumseh is here, and please bring a chair from the cabin."

Pointing to the rocking chair under the elm tree, Benham said, "Chief, please be seated. This is a good time. We can talk here."

Long ago, Tecumseh had stopped wearing European dress. Instead, he wore a traditional fringed deerskin shirt that extended to his knees, form-fitting leggings, and plain leather moccasins pierced with red and blue tinted porcupine quills. Tied about his head was a scarlet silk scarf that contrasted with his shoulder length pitch-black hair.

At his waist were a silver-mounted pipe tomahawk and sheathed steel knife with a carved bone handle. This was the image Tecumseh had carefully crafted to remind his people of the past, before their land had been contaminated by white men and their foreign ways.

Peter Benham brought a chair from the cabin and placed it in front of Tecumseh, who was seated in the rocking chair.

"Mother is cooking," he said to his father, "she would like Chief Tecumseh to join you for dinner. Isaac and I should get on home."

Isaac took the reins of Benham's horse and said, "I'll unsaddle Jupiter and turn him out."

"Thank you. Will we see both of you Sunday?"

His sons nodded, and together replied, "Yes, Father," before disappearing into the dusk.

As Peter and Isaac left them, Benham turned to Tecumseh and said, "I've been blessed with a fine family, Chief. Both my sons are excellent farmers. They married good women too."

Tecumseh said, "They have your blood. I can see that. And Madame Benham's too. How much land do they have?"

"Each has a hundred and sixty acres north and west of here. The government granted me six hundred and forty acres ten years ago."

"I know of the land you received from the Father in Washington," Tecumseh said. "It was the result of the treaty signed at Greenville in 1795, after General Wayne defeated the tribes at Fallen Timbers. I did not meet with General Wayne. And I did not sign that treaty."

"Yes, Chief. I know you didn't sign the treaty that opened Ohio for settlement."

Tecumseh was silent for a moment, as if organizing his thoughts.

"Captain, the chiefs who signed the Greenville treaty had no right to do so. Their thumbs should be cut off. They did not speak for us. They sold land they had never seen, much less hunted or planted. Those chiefs did not own it, or live on it." Tecumseh leaned forward, his voice rising, "The Greenville treaty is not legitimate. This land is not rightfully yours. It belongs to the Great Spirit."

It had been a long day for Captain Robert Benham. His meeting with Harrison was tiring and now he was confronted by an angry Shawnee chief who could break him in half if he wanted. He reached into his jacket and removed the pipe and tobacco pouch.

He said, "Chief, I'm going into the house to light my pipe. Come with me, if you like."

Smiling ruefully, Tecumseh said, "I don't want to disturb Madame Benham. I trust you will not return with your rifle."

Limping, Benham walked to the cabin. Elisabeth was bending over an iron pot hanging in the fireplace, stirring a stew of venison, potatoes, and carrots. As usual she wore her blue striped linen apron and a ruffled white cotton cap. She was five feet three inches in height and light as a feather. Her dark eyes were set below thick eyebrows and her delicate nose turned up slightly. She had a wide mouth and dimpled chin.

When Robert first saw her, he thought she was part Indian, a mixed breed, but in fact she was Black Irish. Her mother was descended from a Spanish sailor who was shipwrecked on the Irish coast after the English defeated the Spanish Armada in 1588. Whatever her ancestry, Robert was smitten with Elisabeth from the day he watched her sashay across the courthouse green in Freehold, New Jersey.

As he entered the cabin, the pleasant aroma surprisingly evoked a brief wave of nausea. He paused for a moment, then asked, "When will dinner be ready?"

Elisabeth turned and saw the pipe in Robert's hand.

"Give me that thing!" she ordered. Without a word he handed it to her.

"Have you lost your senses!" she said sternly. "Smoking when you spend half the night coughing!"

As always, her anger was brief.

"Now, what does Tecumseh want, and how was your meeting with Harrison?"

"I expect Tecumseh is looking for the same thing Harrison wanted—my opinion about the opposition," Benham replied. "I'm going to tell Tecumseh what I told Harrison—the truth, or at least the facts as I know them."

"Well, ask him to dinner. I would like to hear also."

"Are you ready, then?" Robert asked.

"Yes, go fetch him," Elisabeth replied as she set the oval mahogany dining table that she inherited from her grandmother, who had bought it before the family moved to New Jersey. The table had survived multiple moves, first to western Pennsylvania and then to Kentucky and finally to their farm outside Lebanon.

Robert returned with Tecumseh.

"Welcome to our home again, Chief Tecumseh," Elisabeth said. "It's good to see you again."

"Thank you, madame," Tecumseh replied, smiling. "I didn't mean to impose on your hospitality."

"No imposition at all. Please sit here," Elisabeth motioned to a chair to Robert's right at the head of the table. Elisabeth sat nearest the fireplace and across from the Shawnee chieftain. She blushed inwardly when she looked at Tecumseh. '*He is magnificent,*' she thought to herself. Why is so difficult for me to behold him?

Robert poured water from a clay pitcher into Tecumseh's cup and said, "There is much concern on the frontier, Chief. Many settlers have endured attacks and thievery by members of the tribes west and north of here. Some of the perpetrators are Shawnee. Governor Harrison is quite concerned."

"And some of the murderers are white men disguised as Indians!" Tecumseh retorted. "They want to enrage the white militias against us."

Tecumseh waited for the captain to reply, but Benham remained silent, his eyes fixed impassively on the Shawnee chief. Seconds passed, then Tecumseh smiled thinly.

"I know that you met with Harrison today, Captain. Few things occur on my land that I do not know."

"Your land?" Robert asked, as he chewed a piece of venison. He swallowed and looked inquiringly at Tecumseh. "I take it that we are having dinner here, in our home, on your land?"

"Yes, that is true, Captain. But I am grateful for your hospitality and friendship. I promise that your farm and the farms of your family will not be disturbed as long as I am the chief of the Shawnee."

Benham weighed Tecumseh's assurance and responded: "Your brother—the Prophet—recently told Governor Harrison that he wants peace for his people. Is that your belief also?"

"Yes, I want peace—under certain conditions," Tecumseh replied.

"Peace can come after all white settlers return the land they have stolen from the Great Spirit. Peace can come after the Father in Washington stops the sale of whiskey to my people. Peace can come after the white trappers stop hunting our beaver, elk, and buffalo."

"You must know, Chief," Benham retorted, "that the Father in Washington—President Jefferson—will never order American citizens to abandon Ohio, or any land that has been legally purchased by the government from the Indians. You must know that. He will insist that Governor Harrison enforce the Treaty of Greenville."

Smiling, Tecumseh replied, "Yes, I do know that, but before we continue, I would ask Madame Benham if I may have another plate of her excellent stew?" He looked at Elisabeth in a way that reminded her of Peter and Isaac when they were boys.

Caught unaware, her face reddened, and she dropped her eyes. "Yes, of course," she whispered.

Turning to her husband, she asked, "More for you, Robert?" He shook his head, "No, thank you. I'm content."

When Elisabeth left the table, Tecumseh said, "Captain, are you troubled by your flesh?"

At first, Benham did not grasp his meaning. Comprehending, he replied, "Oh, my weight. Yes, I seem to be thinning out."

"I hope it's natural," Tecumseh said with empathy in his voice, "and not an evil spirit."

Benham yearned for his pipe at moments like these. For what he was about to say, he needed the comfort of its stem and the biting acid taste of the tobacco juice. For some reason, it calmed him, made him more reflective and confident.

Creasing his forehead, Benham said, "Chief, I suspect you want to know what I told Governor Harrison today." Not waiting for a reply, he continued, "I will tell you, without betraying any confidences."

Elisabeth set a fresh steaming plate of venison stew in front of Tecumseh. He turned to Robert and said, "Yes, I would like to hear what the governor had to say. Before you begin, though, I want to tell you what I believe is happening."

Benham waved his hand, "Go ahead…"

Tecumseh swallowed and said, "The Father in Washington—President Jefferson—is a clever man. He defeats us in battle, and when our women and children are starving, he buys our land for little money, in the form of goods and livestock. We cannot live on what we receive each year. So, we go in debt to the traders, who are in league with the government agents who distribute our goods. We see only a part of the annual payment because they go to the traders to settle our debts—and line their pockets.

"What occurs next is precisely what your government expects—and wants. The poorer tribes sell more land so they can survive. That's what the Kaskaskia did three years ago, when they were starving and needed seed and livestock. They sold much of Indiana—land that did not belong to them—to Harrison who was acting on behalf of the United States."

Tecumseh sat back in his chair and looked kindly at Elisabeth.

Turning to Robert, he said matter-of-factly, "The Father in Washington controls us, Captain. He sends his armies against us, reduces us to dependents—beggars, desperate people—and poisons my brothers with whiskey."

The two men stared at each other, expressionless.

Tecumseh said, "Now, please tell me about your talk with Harrison today."

Benham sighed and said, "I told Harrison that your goal is to drive every white man back over the Appalachians. Including, may I say, Elisabeth and me, and our family. To do this, you must raise an Indian army that can challenge and defeat our regular army and the local militias. In fact, your Indian army will have to be the largest force ever assembled in North America.

"You will have to recruit the major tribes in the Northwest Territory, as well as the tribes in the south and west and to the north into Canada. These are the Delaware, Miami, Potawatomi, Ottawa, Kickapoo, Dakota, Ojibwe, Cherokee, Choctaw, Chickasaw, and Seminole. You will have to convince their tribal leaders, as well as their people who live in dozens of villages."

"But that is only half the challenge," Benham continued. "The essential part is supplying them with munitions—lead and gunpowder—and food. Food not just for your warriors, but food also for your families, to sustain them while your army is fighting my country. The only way for you to do that is to ally yourself with the British, because there will be no American traders or government factories to supply you or your warrior army with the necessities."

Slowly, deliberately, Tecumseh placed his fork on the plate in front of him and slid his chair away from the table. He glanced at Elisabeth, who was captivated and frightened by her husband's words.

A war of such magnitude, she knew, would consume the fragile frontier for years. She knew also that thousands would die, while others would lose everything they had struggled to acquire and build. Elisabeth was less worried for herself and Robert than she was for the safety and future of her sons and grandchildren.

Benham continued, "The Shawnee fought on the side of the British during our War of Independence. Many of your kin died for King George."

Benham paused and extended his arms, "How did he reward your loyalty and sacrifices? How did he treat his allies? Instead of returning the lands that the Crown had purchased from you during a hundred and fifty years of British rule, the King surrendered it all—every acre—to us, the United States of America. He left you nothing, not a thimble full of soil or an ounce of gold."

Benham pounded the table with his fist. "The British condemned you and your people to a life of hardship and poverty!"

Tecumseh's face was impassive, his hazel eyes darkening, and his body tense. The anger inside him was stirred by the captain's choice of words and, far worse, by the knowledge that he spoke the undeniable truth. For him, this Shawnee leader, the difficulties before him, however ominous, were simply mountains that he had to climb.

Had to climb because there was no alternative, at least for him, the warrior chief. He wanted the Benhams to understand this, if only to make clear how desperately he and his people wanted to bring back the way of life that bonded them to the land and the spirits of their fathers.

Calmly, Tecumseh said, "The Father in Washington wishes us to become like white men—to be farmers, blacksmiths, carpenters, and storekeepers. He wants us to learn the ways of your God and be good Christians and to send our children to your schools.

"Many of my brothers have done these things. They've learned your language, they wear your clothes, and they attend church on Sunday. I know a few who have plantations in the south and own black slaves. There are others who raise cattle, grow corn and wheat. A few are prospering."

Tecumseh hesitated, dropped his voice, and continued, "But they are not happy—even though some of them have all the things most white people want. I ask myself, Captain, why are my brothers not satisfied with this new life?

"They have food and shelter and do not fear the winter. They have enough food so they can trade for goods from across the water. No longer do they have to hunt many moons to find game. Their children attend missionary schools and are learning your language and religion. They could be teachers, doctors, lawyers—"

"Yes, they could be," Robert interrupted, "and you could lead them! If you chose to do it…"

"Perhaps, Captain, but that is not the point."

Benham raised his right hand.

"Wait, let me finish. Rather than lead your confederacy to war with the white settlers and the Father in Washington, you could encourage your people to live a different way, become educated, learn new skills, become self-reliant, and bury the tomahawk."

"Tecumseh," Benham pleaded, "no other man can do this. You have the power, the influence, the ability to reshape the lives of not just the Shawnee but all the tribes. I believe this to be true."

For a moment, Benham thought *he had convinced Tecumseh. But the chief demurred.*

In a low voice, he said, "My brothers who have assumed your ways are not content with their new life. They return to their tribes when they are not working. They shed their English clothes. They pray to the Great Spirit and to the spirits of all living creatures, whose powers we have revered forever. Our strength, Captain, comes from nature. Your home is your cabin and your fields. Our home is the earth beneath our feet, where the sun shines, and the rain falls. We are not attached to a plot of land or things.

"When I was young, my family moved many times. The Shawnee shared land with other tribes. White people do not share land. Every white man wants his own piece of land, to fence in and keep others out. This is not our way. To think that Indians can be like you is foolish. Perhaps someday our spirits will change, but that is not what we are today."

It was far past sunset, and the crickets were in full chorus. The candlelight flickered off the faces of the two adversaries, who did not want to fight each other.

After minutes of silence, Robert Benham said, "I think you and Harrison should meet in council, to see if there is a way to avoid a war. There is no harm in talking, and there may be an opportunity for the Father in Washington to consider your grievances. He may find solutions that you and your people can live with."

Tecumseh nodded and asked, "If I did this, would you be there?"

Benham looked inquiringly at Elisabeth.

Elisabeth spoke firmly. "Robert, I don't think you can travel. You do not have the strength. I would say yes if the council was held nearby."

"Elisabeth is right—of course. I will write Harrison and tell him that you and I have talked and that I have suggested a meeting between the two of you. And that I would like to attend if it is not too distant. Would you agree, Chief?"

Tecumseh replied, "Yes, Captain, I agree. I trust your intentions, but there will be many native voices at the council, not just mine. My brothers and I want peace, though. We will listen."

"I understand," Benham replied.

Tecumseh stood and said, "I have something for you. It's on my horse. May I get it?"

"Of course."

Tecumseh returned, carrying a rifle in both hands. Benham recognized it immediately.

"I present you---with your 'Independence,' Captain Robert."

Benham took it and ran his fingers over the stock. "This was my father's."

He looked at Tecumseh with grateful eyes. "Why didn't you kill me that day?"

Tecumseh glanced at Elisabeth and returned Robert's gaze. "I had never killed a man before, and I, as a young warrior, did not want my first kill to be a helpless cripple, as you certainly were." Tecumseh smiled, placed his hand on Robert's shoulder, and said, "I'm happy it turned out this way."

On November 13, 1808, Captain Robert Benham wrote a letter to General Harrison:

Dear William,

I trust you resolved the difficulties that brought you to Cincinnati and have returned to your duties.

I had occasion to speak with Tecumseh at my home after you and I met at the Golden Lamb. He has agreed to a council with you to see if there may be a path to peace in the disputed territory. As you are aware, Tecumseh and his confederacy reject the Treaty of Greenville, but I believe there could be a middle ground that may be acceptable to our government and the chiefs. The alternative is a war that will be long and bloody, and that will not resolve the major differences between the natives and us.

As you know, I have been fighting the Indians most of my life. I have seen terrible acts committed by them against our settlers, including women and children. I have tracked down dozens of Indian thieves who stole our horses or raided our homes. There have been many times when I was so angry that I wanted to kill them all and rid them from the frontier.

Then, too, I have observed the violence we have done to them on the battlefield, in their villages, and to their women and children. When we steal from them, their pleas for justice are ignored. When we hunt on their lands, the poachers are never punished. You and I both know that the treaty goods we send to our agents are often never distributed to the Indians.

William, as I see an end to this life, my view of our world is changing, or at least it is clearer. We tell the Indians that they must adapt to our ways. This approach, I believe is going to fail. Instead, in keeping with God's teachings and the spirit of the Declaration of Independence, we should find a way to accommodate them. By this, I mean we should be tolerant of their culture and traditions, and allow them to live as they choose, provided they are respectful to their neighbors and obey our laws. Otherwise, I fear, there will be many bloody summers ahead.

Your Humble Servant, Sir
Robert

A month later, Robert Benham, a soldier of the Revolution, died of consumption. Tecumseh was killed by Harrison's army at the Battle of the Thames on October 5, 1813, when the British Army deserted him.

Chapter 1

The five young Swedish farmers arrived in New York City aboard the *Merry Widow*, a three-masted sailing ship that crossed the Atlantic in four weeks. It was a long, stormy voyage, and a harbinger of things to come.

It was June 1858, and they were the vanguard of the 17-member Lindquist and Eriksson families who were seeking land and a new life in America. Sweden in the mid-nineteenth century faced a severe shortage of tillable land. Most farms were an eighth the size they had been in 1750.

The reason was simple: families divided and redivided their land among their children and grandchildren. Now subdividing their farms was not an option, because smaller parcels would not support a family. Most members of the present generation would have to leave the family farm and seek employment as laborers, factory workers, or servants.

For many, a life without land of their own was unacceptable. Land was equity. Without land, the future was tenuous and subject to the vicissitudes of government and the economy. Thus, the elder Lindquists and Erikssons decided to risk their comfortable life for the opportunity to secure a future for their children.

Their destination was Minnesota where there was virgin farmland available for settlement. The five young men were charged with the task of purchasing land and building cabins. They would be joined by the others after their farms in Sweden were sold.

The Swedes found a decent boarding house where they slept on the floor in a single room and shared the outhouse with a dozen guests. They were unused to crowds, congestion, and the clamor of hundreds of people struggling to survive each day. Around them was a neighborhood where trash and dead animals were abandoned in the streets and the inhabitants were undernourished and unwashed.

Johannes Lindquist, the oldest, said, "We're getting out of this cesspool as soon as we can find a train to take us west."

On the second evening, Elliot Lindquist met Julia Svenson, a Swedish midwife from Stockholm. She was traveling to Chicago to join a clinic where she would practice and teach midwifery. Julia left her family home because she felt imprisoned by the prevailing conventions of the day.

Nineteenth-century Swedish women remained under the guardianship of their husbands. The word she thought but did not dare to utter publicly in Sweden was 'repression'. Julia believed that America was a land where she could breathe the oxygen of freedom. She would not be a doll in any man's house.

They sat on the back step of the boarding house.

"My family's farm is forty kilometers east of Gothenburg," Eliot said. "It's productive but my brother, Johannes, would inherit the land. It's too small for more than one family. So, my father and his two cousins decided to sell their farms and go to America. They sent me and my three bothers and cousin here to find enough land to support three families. We're heading to Minnesota tomorrow."

He turned to Julia, "Why are you here? Where are you going?"

Julia had thick auburn hair drawn back into a bun. Her fair skin was flawless. Oval blue-gray eyes, her most prominent feature, were set below a high forehead. She replied, "I accepted a midwife position at a Swedish clinic in Chicago. I will be a midwife and teach aspiring women to deliver babies."

"Why here, why America?" Elliot asked.

"Freedom," Julia replied. "Freedom to practice the way I think is best for both mother and the baby. We are very constrained in Stockholm. Even the church gets involved. I read about the clinic in Chicago and some of the progressive things they are doing. That's where I'm going tomorrow."

Elliot looked into her eyes and realized that he did not want to lose this woman. Quickly, he said, "I and my three brothers and cousin will be taking the train to Chicago. You should join us. We will be your escorts. It would be safer for you as a, uh…"

"A woman?" Julia said evenly.

"Yes. As an unaccompanied woman. This is new country for all of us. There might be bad people…"

Julia's expression softened. She looked away, considering Elliot's offer. Indeed, she would be more comfortable traveling with people she knew. These were good Swedish farmers.

Extending her right hand, she said, "That's very thoughtful. Yes, I would like that."

The Hudson River train from Harlem would take the Swedish immigrants to Albany, where they would board a New York Central express to Cincinnati on the Ohio River. From there, they would change trains and take another railway northwest to Chicago on the southwestern shore of Lake Michigan. The route would take them through the Hudson Highlands, Utica, and Buffalo in upstate New York before turning southwest into Pennsylvania and Ohio.

The weather on the day they boarded was mild with clear skies and a westerly breeze. Julia sat next to Elliot on a hard wooden bench bolted to the floor of their passenger car that accommodated twenty-four people.

Opposite them, across the aisle, were Elliot's three brothers, Johannes, Gustav, and Lars, and his cousin, Robert Eriksson. They occupied two benches facing each other. All that they owned were in satchels and sacks around them. Unseen around their waists were money belts containing silver and gold coins.

The coal-burning steam locomotive struggled to average fifteen miles an hour as it pulled the three full passenger cars through the Hudson Highlands. The hills and mountains on either shore were emerging from the morning mist. The train made multiple stops: Peekskill, Poughkeepsie, Hyde Park, and Tivoli.

By late afternoon, it arrived at Greenbush on the eastern shore of the Hudson River opposite Albany. It was here that the passengers traveling west left the train and took a ferry across the Hudson. The first railroad bridge to span the river would not be built for another decade.

The six Swedes disembarked from the ferry and walked to the Albany train station, where they boarded the New York Central express to Cincinnati.

As they waited for the train to depart, Julia said to Elliot, "I'm glad you invited me to accompany you. I feel quite safe. It would have been more difficult and much less pleasant alone." She glanced at him and quickly looked away.

Smiling, Elliot replied, "We like having you with us. It keeps us on our best behavior." Briefly he considered taking her hand but did not. "We have a long night ahead," he continued. "I can rest on the floor so that you can lay down here on the bench."

"Thank you," Julia said, "but I'll be fine sitting here." She looked out the window.

The sun was setting, and passengers scurried to board the train in the twilight. One was an attractive, fashionably dressed woman with a large suitcase who was helped onto the train by a conductor in a spotless chocolate-brown uniform. Another was a young boy, who had a piece of bright yellow paper pinned to his green wool jacket; he waved goodbye to an elderly couple, who were obviously distraught at his departure.

The conductor waved a red lantern, signaling the engineer that the train was ready to depart. The passenger car lurched as the locomotive began to move. In minutes, they were out of Albany and heading west to Schenectady, where the train was scheduled to arrive before midnight.

Johannes had purchased bread and cheese in Albany. He cut slices for everyone and passed around a blue enamel pail full of delicious dark ale. The men quickly consumed the bread and cheese. Julia ate food she had prepared at the boarding house. Everyone enjoyed the ale, and soon the pail was empty.

The food and especially the ale had their mellowing effects. The men were soon asleep despite the jostling and clatter of the metal wheels on the uneven tracks. Julia lost her struggle to stay awake; she rested her head on the window. Around 11:00 p.m., she awoke when the train pulled into the Schenectady station. Her head was resting against Elliot's shoulder.

Julia sat up and blurted, "I'm sorry, Elliot, I didn't mean…to disturb you…" Then she realized he was in a deep sleep.

"Oh my," she whispered to herself. The flickering light from the kerosene lamps illuminated his face. Unlike his brothers, Elliot was clean-shaven. His blond hair was combed straight back. He had long, dark eyebrows and a slightly curved nose above a full mouth and prominent chin with a shallow cleft. Altogether he was a fine-looking young man, Julia thought—not precisely handsome, but quite attractive in a manly way.

"He has a very nice smile," she said to herself in Swedish.

A young woman appeared in the doorway of their car carrying a scarred brown suitcase. She was looking for an empty seat. Julia waved to her and pointed to the vacant bench where Elliot was resting his feet. The woman lifted her suitcase over Elliot's outstretched legs and managed to sit on the bench opposite Julia without disturbing him. Julia saw that the woman was pregnant, quite pregnant in fact, probably in her eighth month.

Julia peered out the window. It was as dark as pitch. She saw the conductor waving the red lantern from the platform of the third car. The train began to move. The clattering resumed, and within minutes she was asleep, again resting her head on the window.

The train made good time and did not stop until it reached Utica, a town in the Mohawk Valley that was a significant waypoint for the Underground Railroad. Escaped slaves from the South passed through Utica on their way to Canada and freedom.

The piercing glow of the early morning sun woke Elliot as the train left Utica. Julia was asleep, her head on his shoulder once more. Opposite him was a new passenger, a pretty young woman who was sleeping with her head tilted back, eyes closed and mouth slightly open. Across the aisle were his three brothers and cousin; they, too, were asleep, sitting upright. Behind them, a man was snoring fitfully.

The New York Central express train headed toward Whitesboro, three and a half miles west of Utica. It was using one of two tracks and was a half hour behind schedule. The engineer decided to make up for the lost time and throttled up. Ahead, approaching from the west, was a fast freight train on the other track; its boxcars were carrying cotton bales destined for Utica's textile mills. Both trains arrived simultaneously at the wooden railway bridge over Sauquoit Creek, a northward-flowing tributary of the Mohawk River. It was 6:30 a.m.

The combined weight of the speeding trains overwhelmed the bridge's rotting timbers. The bridge fractured, collapsing the tracks into the creek. The first passenger car separated from the locomotive and hurled downward. It struck the bridge's stone abutment and exploded as if it blown to bits by dynamite. The second passenger car followed and was crushed against the rear of the first car.

Elliot was catapulted up and out of his seat in the second car. His forehead struck the roof's center beam, splitting his scalp and knocking him unconscious. Minutes later, he awoke. Cries of pain and a chorus of moans greeted him. What had happened?

Gradually, Elliot's vision refocused and emerged from the blackness. He tasted blood in his mouth. The corpse of a male passenger—the snorer—was draped across his chest. Elliot was able to move his arms and legs. He rolled the dead man off his chest, knelt on his hands and knees for a moment, then slowly stood. He was light-headed and slightly nauseated; the tunnel like vision returned briefly. Choking dust saturated the air. Blood from his lacerated scalp flowed down the left side of his face. He ignored it. Where were his brothers? Where was Julia? She had been sleeping next to him.

The passenger car was twisted on its side and tilted downward toward the creek bed. Most benches had been torn from the floor and flung about, creating tangled barriers obstructing the aisle and doors. Bodies were everywhere, some moving, others still. A few passengers were trying to help the injured. One of them was Johannes.

Elliot called out, "Johannes! Johannes!"

Johannes struggled to his feet. His face was pale and mottled. He coughed and said, "Gustav is hurt bad. He can't move his legs. Lars is looking for Robert."

Elliot climbed over a bench and grasped Johannes's hand. His older brother was a powerful man, like their father. Elliot knelt beside Gustav. Crusted, dark red blood fouled his brother's hair.

"I can't move my legs," Gustav moaned. "My back must be broken." He tried to sit up, but Elliot stopped him, saying, "Rest quiet, Gus. Moving could make it worse."

Abruptly the passenger car shifted and settled. Elliot looked up at Johannes. "We may sink into the water soon," he said. "We should get Gus out of here."

The brothers gently slid Gustav onto a slab of wood from a broken bench. They lifted the makeshift stretcher and stepped through a gap in the side of the wrecked passenger car. Outside, two men were standing in the shallow creek. One was the train's conductor, the other a young man in a bloodstained blue army uniform.

The conductor pointed to a patch of sand on the western shore and said, "Take him over there!" He and the young soldier clutched either side of the stretcher. The four men brought Gustav out of the creek bed and placed him on dry ground. Elliot removed his coat and placed it over his brother.

Johannes said, "I'm going back to find Lars and Robert. You look for Julia."

Gustav glanced up at Elliot, who was reluctant to leave his injured brother. "I'm okay," Gustav said. "Go find her."

Elliot saw the full extent of the train wreck as he waded back to his passenger car. The locomotive had derailed on the far side of the bridge. Steam was escaping from its ruptured engine. Behind it, the first car was a tangle of wood, bent iron, and glass shards.

The second car, partially immersed in the creek, was splintered, and crushed on either end. Miraculously, the third car was upright on a portion of the bridge that had not collapsed. The eastbound train carrying freight had plunged into the creek. Its cars had broken apart, disgorging the cotton bales destined for Utica.

Elliot reentered his passenger car and shouted, "Julia! Julia!" There was no reply. He and another man cleared a path forward, removing broken beams and belongings. Three stunned but uninjured passengers—a man and two women—were set free from the wreckage. Elliot helped them to their feet. Behind them, another man said, "Here, I'll take them out."

Elliot continued his search for Julia. They assisted four more passengers before uncovering the body of a woman lying face down. Elliot turned her over. She was an older woman who was dead, nearly decapitated, her head disarticulated from her spine and attached to her torso by the skin and ligaments of her neck.

Johannes reentered the car. He said, "No sign of Lars or Robert." Twenty minutes later, Elliot and Johannes had searched the entire car, removing the injured and another dead woman. Johannes said, "They must have made it out. We should see to Gus."

"You go back to him," Elliot said. "I'll go to the opposite bank and look for the others."

Elliot jumped into the creek and waded to the east bank. As he climbed out of the river, he saw the back of a woman with auburn hair. It was Julia. She was on her knees under a large oak tree. Extending out on either side of her were the legs of a woman who was lying on the ground. Elliot approached, unsure of what was happening.

Then he saw the pool of bright red blood staining the soil around Julia. Stretched out in front of Julia was the young pregnant woman who had boarded the train in Schenectady. Julia was holding the woman's newborn baby, who had delivered just minutes before Elliot arrived.

As he knelt next to her, Julia exclaimed, "Oh, Elliot, thank heaven you're here! She's bleeding terribly. Go for help!"

Elliot ran up the hill to the road beside the fallen bridge where passengers from the train had assembled.

He shouted, "Is there a doctor here?" No one responded.

A woman stepped forward and in accented English said, "I worked at a hospital in Germany. Can I help?"

"Yes, yes, please come with me," Elliot replied.

Julia had tied the baby's umbilical cord but had no instrument to cut it. The placenta, a hunk of magenta-red tissue, was lying on the ground. Protruding from the woman's birth canal was a fiery red ball, her uterus, which had turned inside out and was streaming blood. The mother was unconscious, her skin was ashen and cold to the touch. She was in shock and near death.

"Elliot, do you have a knife?" Julia asked.

He had a folding pocketknife that his father had given him for his sixteenth birthday. Elliot removed it from the pocket of his trousers, opened the polished steel blade, and handed it to Julia. It was razor-sharp, and quickly severed the baby's umbilical cord just beyond where she had tied it with one of her shoelaces.

The German woman said, "Give the baby to me."

Without a word, Julia lifted the tiny baby—it was a boy—into the woman's arms. He began to cry. His translucent skin had streaks of white vernix that had protected him while he floated in his amniotic sac. The woman wrapped the baby in her wool shawl.

Julia, frantic at the mother's bleeding and exposed uterus, said, "I've never seen this. I've heard about it. But I've never seen it." She grasped the uterus in her right hand and pushed it into the mother's birth canal so that it was inside her pelvis and no longer inside out. The flow of bright red blood seemed to slow. Next, she pulled back her long dress and, using Elliot's knife, sliced a section of cloth from her petticoat and tore it into smaller pieces. These she used to pack the cervix and birth canal as firmly as she could.

Exhausted, Julia sat back and considered what to do next. The mother, in a coma, was as white as her underclothing. Julia felt her wrist for a pulse: it was hard to find, barely detectable. She turned to Elliot and said, "Please ask if there is a doctor or hospital nearby." He nodded and left.

The German woman placed the baby in Julia's arms, removed her coat, and gently placed it over the mother.

She said to Julia, "My name is Emma. I worked at a hospital in Cologne. I can see you have some experience."

"I was a midwife in Stockholm," Julia replied. "I've heard about the uterus coming out during childbirth, but I've never seen it. I'm afraid we're going to lose her." Gazing down at the baby in her arms, she continued, "Thank God. He looks healthy." She paused and extended her hand, "I'm Julia Svenson."

"And I'm Emma Strohmeyer."

By nine o'clock in the morning, a stream of horse-drawn wagons and buggies from neighboring farms and villages converged on the collapsed bridge. The magnitude of the tragedy stunned the onlookers. Dead bodies and debris floated in Sauquoit Creek. The injured were lying on its banks. The wrecked and ruptured locomotives continued to disgorge steam. Survivors huddled near the road, and a few were trying to help their fellow passengers.

One of the first to arrive was Dr. William Warren, who had been returning to Whitesboro after delivering a baby at a nearby farm. Immediately he moved among the injured, seeking to identify those whom he could help the most.

He performed a tracheotomy—an opening in the windpipe—on a man who could barely breathe due to blood clots from a crushed nose that blocked his airway. Next, he splinted and dressed a woman's compound leg fracture that she suffered after being thrown from the first passenger car.

There were victims whom he could not help. The boy in the green wool jacket had been thrown through a window with such force that it unroofed his skull, exposing his brain. The note on yellow paper pinned to his jacket read, 'My name is Charles Engel. I am going to Cincinnati. My parents will meet me at the station. My grandparents are Elmer and Barbara Engel of Utica'.

The fashionably dressed woman who had boarded in Albany was crushed like an insect, fracturing her breastbone so that her chest was flailing. She was barely conscious, her face swollen and purple, as she tried futilely to get oxygen into her lungs. Mercifully, their suffering would end soon.

Elliot found Dr. Warren attending to a girl with a simple arm fracture.

He ran to him and said, "Sir, we need your help. A lady just delivered, and she's bleeding badly!" The doctor followed Elliot. The unconscious mother was lying inertly on the ground by the creek. Julia, her hands and clothing crusted with blood, was kneeling next to her. Emma Strohmeyer was holding the newborn swathed in her shawl.

At first sight, Dr. Warren thought the mother was dead. Without uttering a word, he knelt and placed an ear on her chest. "She's alive," he said softly, a hint of amazement in his voice. He turned to Julia and asked, "Tell me what happened?"

Julia recounted how she helped the woman escape from the wrecked passenger car.

"She was complaining of pain in her lower abdomen, where she was struck by something during the crash. Then she went into labor. The baby came quickly, followed by the afterbirth. She began to bleed, and her uterus came out! It was inside out, like a glove!" Julia began to weep.

"I've never seen this, and I didn't know what to do." She paused, regained control, and continued, "So I pushed the uterus back in and made sure it was right. Then I packed her cervix and birth canal with cloth from my petticoat. The bleeding stopped, but I'm afraid I was too late…"

Warren patted Julia's shoulder, "No doubt the accident caused it. I know of it happening to a woman who was kicked by a horse. You did the only thing you could do. I would've done the same. We'll take her to Whitesboro, where I have my office. The hospital is in Utica. I doubt she will live."

Everyone looked intently at the face of the unconscious woman before them. After a minute of silence, Elliot said, "Doctor, my brother has a broken back—he can't move his legs—he's across the creek, on the other bank."

"Bring him to the road, up there." Warren pointed to a collection of horse-drawn wagons. "We'll take him with us to my clinic in Whitesboro."

A man shouted from the direction of the bridge.

"Elliot! Elliot!"

It was Lars. He was with Robert. They ran down the bank.

"We thought you were dead!" Lars said. "Where's Johannes and Gus?" Then they saw the blood on Julia and the woman lying motionless on the ground. Elliot explained what had happened and what they were going to do with the woman and Gustav.

The four men, followed by Julia and Emma, carried the woman up to the road to where Dr. Warren had commandeered a wagon belonging to the farmer whose infant son he had delivered that morning. They placed her in the wagon. Lars and Robert crossed the creek and, together with Johannes, brought Gustav over to the wagon. Dr. Warren mounted his horse and led the immigrants and the makeshift ambulance toward Whitesboro.

It was noon, and the sun was bright and warm in a cloudless sky. Dr. Warren rode next to the wagon driven by Johannes. He considered what he could do for the unconscious woman in the wagon, if she survived the day. And what he might be able to do for young Gustav who likely had a spinal cord injury that could paralyze him for life.

The Swedes had lost most of their belongings, but not the gold and silver coins secured in the money belts around their waists. Emma Strohmeyer, riding in the wagon with the newborn baby, would not meet her relatives in Cincinnati as planned. And Julia Svenson, walking next to Elliot, would be late to Chicago and the community where she was to serve as a midwife and teacher.

Still, they felt anxiety only for Gustav, who was helpless and in pain. At least, everyone else in the group had survived the horrific accident without serious injury. Tomorrow or the next day, they would decide who would continue to Minnesota and who would remain behind with Gustav. Already Johannes was formulating in his mind the letter he would write to his parents back home Sweden.

Dr. Warren's clinic was a single room with two beds, a small window, fireplace, and an unfinished oak desk. A white metal cabinet held his surgical instruments and a menagerie of bottles containing herbs and other medicines. The clinic was attached to a wood-frame house with a single large room that served as a kitchen, dining area, and living room. Crude stairs lead up to a loft where Warren slept. Behind the house was a well, and further back in the yard was an outhouse.

Warren told Johannes and Lars to carry Gustav into the clinic and place him on the floor next to the large fireplace.

"Keep him on the wood plank just as he is now," Warren ordered. Then he examined the young woman. She was unconscious, cool to the touch, and her pulse was thready.

He turned to Julia and said, "There's nothing we can do for her now except keep her warm." Warren eyed Elliot and Robert. Pointing to the clinic door, he said, "Take her in there and put her in one of the beds. I'm going to see what I can do for Gustav."

Gustav's spinal cord had been injured in the accident. The recommended treatment was nonsurgical. Most patients like him suffered bladder paralysis and urinary retention that often caused fatal infections. So treatment consisted of regular bladder catheterizations and long-term nursing care to prevent bedsores and pneumonia. It was a grim injury, and for this young man, it would mean complete dependence on his family for the rest of his life, however long or short it may be. Warren resolved to give Gustav an option.

"You are Gustav?" Warren said as he knelt beside him.

Gustav looked up, "Yes, sir—Gustav Lindquist—you can call me Gus, if you like."

"Can you move your toes for me, Gustav?" Warren asked as he removed the blanket.

"No, sir. I can't move my legs either. Hardly any feeling in 'em."

Warren took out his pocketknife and began to slash open Gustav's trousers.

A voice behind him said, "Let me help you, doctor." It was Emma Strohmeyer. "I'm a nurse."

Quickly the two of them splayed Gustav's trousers. Using a straight pin, Warren pricked Gustav's skin from ankle to waist on both sides. "Do you feel this?" Warren asked as he moved the pin from one leg to the other.

Gustav shook his head. "I don't feel anything, sir."

Warren sat back on the floor, grasping his knees. Johannes, Lars, and Emma Strohmeyer surrounded him, listening.

"Here's the situation, Gus," Warren began. "Your lower spine has been injured. The vertebrae are the bones surrounding the spinal cord. One or two vertebrae are likely broken, and pieces of bone and tissue are compressing the spinal cord. The choices are to do nothing, or do surgery with the hope—and I emphasize hope—that I can do something to relieve the pressure. If we're going to do surgery, I think we should do it now. It's entirely your choice."

There was silence. Gustav looked inquiringly at Johannes.

Johannes asked, "What if you don't do surgery?"

"In all likelihood, he'll be paralyzed for the rest of his life," Warren replied. Then looking at Gustav, he said, "But even if I do operate, Gus, you might be paralyzed, permanently, and there's a chance the surgery will kill you."

Again, there was a nervous silence. Finally, Gustav glanced at Johannes and turned his head toward Warren. "Do it, doctor. Do the surgery. I don't want to live like this if—if there is any chance—any chance at all."

Johannes knelt next to his brother. "I think you're right, Gus. That's what I would do if I were you."

"I can assist you, doctor," Emma Strohmeyer offered. "I had surgical experience in Cologne."

"Very well," Warren said. "First we need to position Gustav so I can operate."

Gustav was lying on the same slab of wood that Johannes and Elliot used to remove him from the wrecked passenger car. They had to turn Gustav over so that he lay prone—flat on his stomach without placing any mechanical stress on his spine. Warren told Johannes and Elliot to go to the lumberyard in town and get a similar slab of wood.

Meanwhile, Warren inserted a rubber tube into Gustav's urinary bladder; the urine was clear, free of blood. Then he and Emma rolled three sheets and positioned them under the wood slab holding Gustav. When Johannes and Elliot returned, they placed the second board on top of Gustav, covering his chin, chest and abdomen.

Next, they tied the ends of the sheets tightly around the boards so that Gustav was completely immobile. Then the men turned Gustav over, so he was lying face down. They positioned him on the dining table, and removed the first slab, exposing Gustav's back. Emma cut away Gustav's shirt.

Warren was ready to do the operation, but first he had to anesthetize his patient. He asked, "Mrs. Strohmeyer, are you familiar with chloroform?"

"Yes, doctor, I am," Emma replied. "We used it in Cologne. Quite often, though I didn't administer it myself."

"I'll need you to stand at the head of the table and drip the chloroform onto this cloth when I tell you." He handed her a clean white handkerchief.

"Yes, sir."

"Gus," Warren said. "I'm going to place a handkerchief over your mouth and nose, and you are going to inhale some fumes that will make you sleep—it will take about five minutes. Okay?"

"Yes, sir," Gustav replied.

"Good. Now, take deep breaths…"

When Gustav was asleep, Warren took a shiny steel scalpel and made an eight-inch incision down the middle of his spine.

Andreas Lindquist was surprised to see Erik Moberg when he opened his front door. He invited his parish pastor into the parlor and asked if he would like tea.

"No, thank you," the pastor said briskly. "I have a letter for you from America that was delivered to the church. It's from your son, Johannes, and it appears to have been sent from a town in New York State some months ago."

"Thank you, pastor. Please, come in." Andreas said, and took the letter. As he opened it, he called to his wife Lena who was in the kitchen. "Lena, the pastor is here with a letter from Johannes. Come here, please."

Lena, a little breathless, was removing her apron as she entered the parlor. "Hello, pastor. Did Andreas offer you tea? Please do have a seat."

"Andreas offered tea, and I declined," the pastor replied softly. "I'll stand if you don't mind."

Andreas opened the envelope and began to read. After a few sentences, he sat down and put on his reading glasses, his face darkening.

Alarmed, Lena said, "Andreas, please read it aloud. Your expression is frightening me."

"I can leave, if you wish," the pastor said.

"No, no," Andreas replied. "You should stay. Please hear this. It is dated May 11. 'Dear Father and Mother,'" Andreas began: "'I have troubling news. Yesterday, our train out of New York City crashed when a bridge collapsed. Many people were killed. Others were terribly injured. Gus was one of them. His back was broken, and he could not move his legs. He was treated at the accident by Doctor Warren of Whitesboro, New York, and a nurse from Germany who was traveling with us."

"Dr. Warren did surgery on Gus's back this afternoon. He removed pieces of bone that were pressing on his spinal cord. Gus will have to be still for three months. He will be staying in Dr. Warren's clinic. We're building a bed frame for him so we can turn him without straining his back. Elliot, Lars, and Robert were bruised but otherwise unhurt. We are staying in a boarding house in Whitesboro near Dr. Warren's clinic'."

Lena began to weep. The pastor placed a hand on her shoulder.

Andreas asked, "Are you all right? Should I continue?" Lena nodded and sat next to her husband.

Andreas continued reading, "'The question is what we should do next. I decided to leave Lars here with Gus while he is recovering and continue our journey to Minnesota with Elliot and Robert. Oskar Nilsa is expecting us this summer, and we do not want to miss the chance to acquire the land he said was good for farming west of Minneapolis. We'll arrive there by July. I'll return for Gus and Lars after we complete the land arrangements. Father, my suggestion is that you and Mother wait until you hear from me. I have asked Julia Svenson—she is a midwife from Stockholm—to write to you about Gus's condition. Your loving son, Johannes'."

Andreas folded the letter and placed it back in the envelope. He stood and embraced Lena.

"I should go to Gustav," he whispered. "It was I who sent our boys to America." He turned to the pastor. "Thank you for bringing the letter. I hope you will keep this confidential, at least for now."

"Of course, Andreas. I'm sorry about Gustav. The congregation and I will pray for him." The pastor shook their hands and left.

Andreas sat next to Lena and said, "I may be gone a long time. I want you and the children to stay with A. P. and Britta."

"No, Andreas, this is my house, and I am quite capable of taking care of it myself. I refuse to burden them. I'll let them know if I need help."

"But…" Andreas began to object.

"No," Lena interrupted. "I won't discuss it further. I'll be here with Sarah when you come home—whenever that is."

"I won't argue," Andreas sighed. "Your mind is made up. I know what that means." He paused and stood. "We should visit Olaf and A. P. and tell them what has happened. I'll harness Old Dan to the buggy. Please ask Sarah to join us."

It was late in the afternoon when they returned from their cousins' homes. A. P. wanted to go with Andreas to America, but Britta put her foot down.

"No, A. P.," she exclaimed, "you, Olaf, and the boys will have to work Andreas's farm as well as ours."

A. P. looked at Andreas, hoping he would have a solution.

"Of course, you're right, Britta," Andreas said, avoiding A. P.'s stare.

A. P. grimaced slightly. Accepting his fate, he asked, "How long do you think you'll be gone?"

Andreas replied, "It being August now, I may not return 'til the spring."

Olaf said, "We'll get your crops in. The Karlssons and Andersons will help too."

Britta smiled and said, "Lena and I are as good in the fields as any of you. Don't you worry, Andreas, we'll take good care of things."

Andreas said, "I'm sorry to leave you with so much to worry."

Lena replied, "Andreas, it's worth it. Our boys must have their own farms. Otherwise, we will leave them nothing—and they will have nothing."

Britta sighed. "Yes, Andreas, we need the land."

The Whitesboro boarding house where the Lindquists were staying was owned and operated by Herman Stein and his wife, Hilda. They were German immigrants from Frankfurt who had fled in 1847 after Herman was arrested and briefly jailed for protesting the presence of Prussian and Austrian soldiers in their city.

"I could see the handwriting on the wall," Herman recalled. "Prussia despised the freedoms we had in Frankfurt, and we were about to be brought to heel. So we left, along with many other Frankfurters."

The Steins' boarding house was comfortable, and Hilda was an excellent cook. Herman, who had been a wheelwright in Frankfurt, had a growing business building sturdy wheels for the wagons that were in high demand by people emigrating west. They hosted a party the night before Johannes, Elliot, and Robert were to leave for Minnesota. Julia Svenson, Dr. Warren, and Emma Strohmeyer attended, as did Lars and Gustav, who was carried into the dining room on his wood stretcher and positioned on sawhorses next to the long table.

"Welcome to our feast," Herman said when everyone was seated. "Mrs. Stein and I have enjoyed having you with us, and we look forward to your brother staying with us until he can travel."

"Don't forget us," Julia said, smiling. "Mrs. Strohmeyer and I will be with you as well, at least until we can make our arrangements."

"Yes, yes, of course," Herman replied. "And the baby too. Does he have a name yet?"

Julia glanced at Dr. Warren. "I thought we should name him William, after the good doctor here."

Warren shifted in his chair, clearly uneasy. "I regret we couldn't save his mother…"

Julia gently placed a hand on Warren's arm. "We—you—did everything possible for her."

From his stretcher, Gustav said, "Doctor, we owe you our gratitude. For everything you have done. I think the name William is very appropriate."

Elliot, sitting next to Julia, said, "It's settled, then. Mr. Stein, the answer to your question is 'William'."

"Do we know anything about his mother's family?" Johannes asked.

Julia replied, "I went through her belongings. There were letters from Sweden addressed to Greta Nielsen in Schenectady. That's where she boarded the train. I assume that was her name."

Everyone waited for Julia to continue. When she did not, Emma Strohmeyer, a little impatient, asked, "Who were the letters from?"

Uncomfortable, Julia continued, "Apparently the letters were from her mother who lives in Hassela in Hälsingland—"

"Where's that?" Herman interrupted.

Johannes replied, "Hassela is about four-hundred kilometers north of Stockholm, in the middle of the country." Herman nodded.

"Go on, Julia," Elliot said.

"I do not believe that Greta Nielsen was married when she became pregnant. Her family arranged for her to emigrate to America and live with a family in Schenectady."

"Why was she on our train?" Elliot asked.

Julia replied, "I'm not certain. There was also a letter from an Eric Andersen who lives in Minnesota, in a settlement called Chisago Lakes. It seems some settlers are living there from Hassela. He proposed marriage, even though obviously they had never met. Perhaps Greta was on her way there."

Dr. Warren cleared his throat. "We should let him know what happened."

Julia said, "I posted a letter to him this morning. And I sent a letter to her family."

"Good," Whipple said. "And how is the wet nurse working out?"

"Quite well," Julia replied. "She's very kind, and William is putting on weight."

"I've sent inquiries to the orphanage in Utica," Whipple said, "hopefully they will accept William soon."

Julia placed two fingers on her chin. "Oh," she said, "doctor, I wasn't aware you were going to do that…"

"Is there an alternative?" Warren asked.

"I was thinking of taking him with me—to Chicago."

Taken aback, everyone, especially Elliot, stared at Julia in silence. Then Hilda Stein entered the dining room with plates of beef and potatoes. Herman had poured home-brewed beer for each of his guests. He stood when his wife appeared with the food.

"Now then, I would like to propose a toast," he said, "to these three young men who will leave us tomorrow to find a new home—and land—in Minnesota. If I were younger, I would go with you. We wish you every success and a safe journey!"

The four Swedes arrived in Minneapolis on July 4, 1858, amid a downpour. They had traveled by train and steamboat from Whitesboro to Saint Louis and north, again by steamboat, to Saint Paul. All of them would remember the beauty and sheer vastness of the country they passed through.

Minneapolis was on the brink of becoming a boomtown. A suspension bridge had been built across the Mississippi River, connecting Minneapolis on the western shore to the Township of Saint Anthony. Sawmills were thriving on the waterpower provided by the Saint Anthony Falls, the only major waterfall on the upper Mississippi.

Fifteen miles to the east was Saint Paul, the state capital, built at the confluence of the Mississippi and Minnesota rivers. A few miles south of both cities was Fort Snelling, constructed in 1820 to protect river traffic and trade from foreign intrusion, particularly the British and Canadians.

They struggled through the muddy streets. Their boots were caked with mud when they arrived at the Nicollet House on Washington Avenue. It was a newly constructed limestone four-story hotel with a hundred guest rooms, and a saloon on the first floor. It had been open for just six weeks. After cleaning their boots, they entered the lobby and were met by the pleasant smell of fresh pine and paint.

"This place looks spendy," Robert said, looking around. "Maybe there's a boarding house…"

"Well, let's find out," Johannes replied. He went to the desk where a smartly dressed clerk greeted him with a hint of disdain.

"Yes, sir?" the clerk asked snottily.

"How much would a room be for the three of us?" Johannes asked.

"I'm afraid we have no rooms available," the clerk replied proudly. "We are fully occupied. The hotel's grand opening dinner is tomorrow, and a great many people have come to town for the celebration."

"Is there another hotel in town?" Johannes asked politely.

The clerk pursed his lips and clicked his tongue. "I'm afraid you will have great difficulty finding a room anywhere. Minneapolis is a hectic place right now. You might try the Winslow House hotel in Saint Anthony across the river."

The three men started to leave when a distinguished man arose from a lobby chair.

Folding his newspaper, he said, "Gentlemen, I might be able to help you." He extended his hand to Johannes. "My name is John Pillsbury." Johannes shook his hand and introduced him to Elliot and Robert.

"I have a warehouse in Saint Anthony," Pillsbury said. "It has a room with two beds. You're welcome to stay there for a few days. If you wish."

Johannes looked at Elliot and Robert, who nodded. "Thank you, sir—Mister Pillsbury—we accept, and we are willing to pay…of course."

"No need for that," Pillsbury said, and then asked, "what brings you to Minneapolis?"

Johannes told Pillsbury that they hoped to find farmland and prepare it for their families back in Sweden. He recounted the train accident and Gustav's injury.

Pillsbury said, "I'm sorry to hear about your brother. I hope he recovers quickly. I know there is excellent farmland available north of a town called Hutchinson. It's about sixty miles west of here. The government wants $1.25 an acre. How many acres do you need?"

"We're thinking around three hundred," Johannes replied.

"That would be $375, and of course you will need money for implements, seed, and so forth."

Quickly, Robert said, "We can manage that." Surprised, Johannes and Elliot looked at Robert with raised eyebrows.

Pillsbury smiled and said, "Excellent, Robert. Excellent. Here, I'll write a note to the warehouse superintendent. His name is Charles Fish. He's a good man to know. Charles has relatives who farm in Acton, near where you may be purchasing land."

Pillsbury asked the hotel clerk for a pen and paper and composed the note.

He handed it to Johannes and said, "You can take the bridge across the river to Saint Anthony. The warehouse is just north of the bridge, on the river, and it has my name on the sign. Well, good luck, gentlemen." They shook hands.

As they were leaving, Pillsbury said, "By the way, your English is quite good. That's a big plus for newcomers."

As they stepped into the greasy mud of Washington Avenue, Elliot said, "Our mothers would like what he just said. All those dull, long and boring English lessons after school!"

The rain had lessened, and they headed for the suspension bridge. The bridge had been built in 1855 by two investors who charged a toll to cross it. A half hour later they stood in front of Pillsbury's two-story fieldstone and wood warehouse. Johannes knocked on the door with the sign 'Office' nailed on it.

A short, stocky man wearing a stained leather apron answered. "What's your business?" he asked in a not unfriendly tone.

Johannes asked to see Charles Fish.

"Mister Pillsbury sent us."

"I'm Fish," the man said.

Johannes handed him Pillsbury's note.

"I see," Fish said after reading it. "Come with me, gentlemen, and I'll show you the way. It's on the first floor."

They walked through a cavernous two-story room filled with all sorts of hardware, farm implements, and other goods. The place smelled of oil, leather, and soap. Light and fresh air entered through windows high on the pine walls. A few wooden buckets scattered on the stone floor were collecting water leaking through the roof.

Pointing to the buckets, Fish said, "Mister Pillsbury won't be happy with that. This building and that roof are less than a year old."

At the far end of the building, Fish opened the door of a room with two beds and a crude dresser.

"Here it is," Fish said. "One of you will be sleeping on the floor. The window opens and lets in a nice breeze when there is one. I've slept here myself, during busy times. It's comfortable, but from time to time, it can get loud on the street when the saloons close."

"Where's the toilet?" Elliot asked.

"We don't have one. You can use the outhouse behind the saloon next door and bathe in the river. It's cold but the water is pretty clean. Keep an eye out for logs floating down to the sawmills." Fish paused and eyed the small packages they were carrying. "It doesn't look like you brought much with you."

Johannes said, "We lost most of our belongings in a train wreck. That was a month ago, in upstate New York. We need to outfit ourselves. Any suggestions?"

"You'll find just about anything you need on Main Street across the river, or here in Saint Anthony. If you don't mind my asking, what are you doing in Minneapolis?"

Johannes sat on the edge of a bed and removed his hat. The others did the same. "We are here to purchase land and start farming," Johannes began. "We are meeting up with Oskar Nilsa, who has a farm near Lake Waconia. He wrote to us that there's good land available in Acton Township. That's where we're headed."

"I know Acton," Fish said. "It's been getting settled since the 1851 treaty with the Dakota. Land's a bit spendy, though." Fish waited for a response. When there was none, he continued, "So you're going to meet this Nilsa fella and head up to Acton?"

Johannes replied, "Yes, we will leave here as soon as we get supplies and figure out how we're going to get there."

"The best way is by horseback if you're traveling light. Lake Waconia is about thirty-five miles southwest, and Acton is another forty to fifty miles northwest from there. You can lease horses at Dell Livery."

"What route should we take to Lake Waconia?" Elliot asked.

"I would take the Watertown Road west to Long Lake," Fish replied. "There's an inn there if you want to spend the money. I've stayed there—the food's good. Anyway, keep going west on the Watertown Road. Once you're through the big maple forest, head south. It's about twenty miles. Or you can go all the way to Watertown and then go south to Waconia. It's a big lake, not as large as Minnetonka, but big enough to find easily."

"We need a map," Robert said.

"I have a map you can have. And you'll need rifles too," Fish said. "For hunting and protection. Mostly for protection."

"You mean the Indians?" Elliot asked.

"Not just the Indians. They've been fairly quiet this year. But there are white men, mostly half breeds, and all sorts of frontier trash who'll rob ya of everything you got. If you're carrying gold or silver, I'd put it in the bank before you leave."

"We appreciate your help, Mister Fish," Johannes said.

"Look," Fish replied, "since you're new here, tomorrow I'll take you over to the Mister Pillsbury's bank and Diamond's general store. It should have about everything you need. Then we'll go over to Dell and get your horses. You should be able to be on your way in two or three days."

They arrived at Oskar Nilsa's farm four days after departing Minneapolis. Oskar was chopping wood when they rode up to the hill on a narrow path from the lake. His neat three-room log house had a lean-to shed on either side for storage. Behind it was a sizable barn of wood and fieldstone and a smokehouse.

July was the month when the hay was being cut and put up for the winter to feed the livestock. Already Oskar and his family had fashioned two big haystacks in fields north and west of the house. The gray surface of the haystacks disguised the fresh-cut green grass they held inside.

The three men followed Oskar into the house where they met his wife, Inga. She was a big woman with a jolly face, and her girth dwarfed Oskar, who was wiry and a little solemn. Their two sons, Liam and Lucas, were working in the fields. It was noon, and Inga was preparing the midday meal.

Smiling and speaking Swedish, she said, "Welcome, welcome. How was your journey?"

Johannes replied, "The only problem was the mosquitoes and gnats."

"Oh, sure," Inga said, "the mosquitoes are nasty this year. Oskar and the boys use bear grease, but I can't stand the smell."

"I see you have new rifles," Oskar observed.

"Yes," said Elliot. "We met Charles Fish in Minneapolis. Said we'd need them for hunting and protection."

A tall, well-muscled young man appeared in the doorway. It was Liam Nilsa, and he was holding an Enfield 1853 rifle in his right hand.

Oskar said, "Liam, these are the men from Sweden I told you about."

Liam nodded and said, "Pa, there's three Indians out by the barn. I don't recognize 'em."

"Where's Lucas?" Oskar asked.

"He's with the oxen in the south pasture. Taking out stumps."

Oskar said, "I'll see what they want." He strapped on a holster with a Colt revolver, checking to see that it was loaded. Signaling for Liam to follow, he left the house and approached the three Indians standing in front of the barn.

One of them stepped forward, holding up his hand in a gesture of peace. He was the oldest of the three and dressed in a mishmash of Indian and

European clothes. Oskar recognized him: it was Running Bear, a minor chief of the Mdewakanton Dakota tribe that lived on the reservation along the Minnesota River. With him were White Bear, a young brave, and Yellow Dog, who was carrying an old musket.

Speaking in broken English, Running Bear said, "Sir, we come in peace. My people are hungry. They starve. The traders at the Redwood Agency won't give food. No money. Can we hunt here?"

Oskar looked at his son. "What do you think?"

"It's okay with me, Pa," Liam replied. "The Dakota have been short of food since spring."

Oskar turned to Running Bear.

"It's okay you hunt my land. Just today." Pointing to Liam, he continued, "If you want to hunt again, ask him. Come to the house. I give you deer meat for your wigwam."

The three Indians followed Oskar and Liam to the smokehouse, where they gave them a haunch of venison. Running Bear, grateful, offered a bracelet of red and blue beads. Oskar placed it around his wrist.

"Good hunting, chief," Oskar said.

As the three men disappeared into the woods, Oskar said, "Don't tell your mother, but I'm concerned. It's one thing for a man to be hungry. It's another when he sees his family starving. Not good. Not good at all. Keep your rifle close. Tell your brother. Tomorrow I'm going with the Lindquists to see Jesus about his land."

It was late afternoon, and the sun was retreating. Robert Eriksson was riding in front of his cousins and next to Oskar when they came to a rise in the prairie overlooking a long narrow lake that was surrounded by wetlands rich with monarch butterflies and red-winged blackbirds. Meadowlarks were plucking crickets from the timothy.

Flat grassy fields extended to the west, where groves of oak and maple trees created vast green canopies. To the north and east were stands of black ash, pine, and basswood mingling with an assortment of shrubs and wildflowers. The land here was flatter and more open than the Nilsa farm.

A flock of Canada geese circled the four riders and settled on a narrow bank beside the lake.

Johannes said, "This could be Sweden. Oskar, where are we, exactly?"

"Near Acton Township, over there," Oskar replied, pointing east. A pheasant burst from the underbrush and startled his horse. Oskar swung his finger to the northwest. "Jesus Garcia's place is just over there."

The log cabin was a rough, unfinished structure that had two windows and a crude door. Fields to the west and south of the cabin had freshly cut hay neatly arranged in small haycocks, awaiting transport to a fenced-in haystack that was taking shape beside a long shed. To the north was a meadow where cattle grazed.

Sitting on a chair in front of the cabin was a giant of a man who was bald, shirtless, and smoking a long pipe. He stood when the four men emerged from a grove of maples.

"Hello, Oskar!" the man shouted. "I wasn't sure you were coming."

Oskar dismounted and shook the leathery hand of Jesus Garcia. "This is Johannes and Elliot Lindquist and their cousin, Robert Eriksson. They're from Sweden. Looking for land to settle."

Jesus slapped the back of his neck.

"Goddamn mosquitoes," he exclaimed. "Worse now with the sun going down." He shook the hands of the three Swedes as they dismounted, and said, "I'll get some chairs from inside, and we can talk."

"Thank you, Mister Garcia," Johannes replied.

As everyone sat, Jesus said, "I've been getting the hay in the past week. I got no help, so it's been slow. Too hot for the oxen, too."

Oskar said, "Last week our oxen got so hot and thirsty they bolted to the lake, and darn near pulled my wagon loaded with hay into the water!"

Jesus turned to the young men and asked, "How much land are you lookin' for?"

Johannes replied, "We thought 300 acres, but that would be tillable land. With lakes and wetlands, we should probably double that—so 600 is what we're thinking now."

"I got 640 acres. Most of it never farmed. I've lived here eight years—since '51. Got this land from the government because I fought in the war down in Mexico. I built this cabin. Married an Ojibwe woman. She got the pox and died last year."

Jesus paused and shook his head, then continued, "I'm from Arkansas and don't want to spend another winter here. You can have all my land, the cabin, my tools and implements, and the animals for a thousand dollars."

"What animals do you have?" Elliot asked.

"A cow, some cattle—all steers—and half dozen or so chickens."

Looking around, Robert asked, "Do you have a barn?"

"Nope. There's an outbuilding behind those trees and a walk-in shed."

Scratching his chin, Elliot asked, "What do you do with the cow and chickens in the winter?"

"Bring 'em into the cabin. Helps keep it warm."

The men smiled. Oskar, unperturbed, continued, "If that doesn't suit you, you should be able to build a nice barn before it turns cold in October."

Oskar left for home the following morning, and the Lindquists rode the property with Jesus. It had been surveyed, and Garcia had the boundaries well marked with stakes. Robert estimated that at least 475 acres were suitable for crops.

Johannes thought there was plenty of timber for four good cabins with barns and assorted outbuildings. Elliot was pleased that a buffalo trail suitable for a wagon ran along the northern edge of the property; it connected east fifty miles to Watertown and west twenty miles to Willmar.

In the late afternoon, they returned to Jesus' cabin and sat down to discuss terms.

Robert said to Jesus, "I think we should pay you top dollar for the land we can farm. That would be 475 acres at $1.25 an acre, or $593.75. Let's say $600. The rest of the land is worth a couple of hundred dollars. We're prepared to pay you $800 for everything."

Jesus lighted his pipe and stretched his legs out on a stump.

"You know," he began, "the war in Mexico took most of the men in my company. Not to fighting, but to sickness." Pointing to his left shoulder, he continued, "I got shot through here at Monterrey in '46 and damn near lost my arm."

He stood and pulled down his trousers; on his right hip was a jagged reddish-purple scar.

"This was shrapnel from a canon at Buena Vista in '47. I got blood poisoning and damn near died." He sat down again, looked directly at Robert, and said, "This land is what I got for four years' service. I'm not giving it up for less than a thousand dollars."

A distant rumble from the northwest signaled the approach of a summer thunderstorm. Wind gusts disturbed the swarms of gnats that were orbiting in the fading sunlight.

Johannes glanced at Elliot and Robert, and said to Jesus, "We'll pay you the thousand, but you have to stay the winter with us. We're new to this country, and from what I hear just surviving a Minnesota winter is no small feat. None of us have ever hunted or trapped. You can teach us. And you can help us build a new cabin and barn. In the spring, we'll pay you, and you can go home to Arkansas."

Jesus sat forward and tapped his pipe on the stump. "How do I know you have the money? What guarantee do I have that you'll do what you say? I need assurances."

Robert and Elliot looked quizzically at Johannes, who said, "I understand. We'll pay you $750 now and $250 in the spring." Johannes paused and looked at Robert. "Robert will be going home to Sweden to bring our families here. He—"

"Why me?" Robert interrupted.

"Because Elliot and I are older, stronger—and healthier," Johannes replied.

"But—" Robert blurted.

"That's my decision." Johannes locked eyes with Robert, who looked down and nodded grudgingly.

Turning back to Jesus, Johannes continued, "The four of us will ride to Minneapolis. That's where we have our gold in a bank. When you sign over your land, we'll pay you $750 in gold. We'll buy horses, supplies, and a wagon. Robert will leave for the east, and we'll come back here. In the spring, you get $250 in gold."

Jesus liked being paid in gold. The territory had gone through a financial crisis in 1857 when many Minnesota banks failed, and their paper became worthless. Jesus stood and extended his hand to Johannes, "I accept your offer. It's fair—all around. There's a land office in Minneapolis. We can transfer the deed there."

That evening, Jesus took the Lindquists over to the Long Lake, where they caught a dozen walleye. They cooked them over a fire in front of the cabin. They feasted on pan-fried walleye, sweet corn, and green beans from Jesus's garden. It was the best meal they had had since leaving Whitesboro.

Afterward, Johannes took Elliot and Robert aside.

"Robert, you will go to Whitesboro and see Gus and Lars. I hope they can come here in the spring. Then you'll find a ship to Gothenburg. It may take a year for our families to sell their farms. The goal is to have everyone here two years from now."

Elliot asked, "Don't you think we need more land if each of us is going to have his own farm? While we were riding the western boundary, the land west and north looked quite good."

Both Johannes and Robert nodded. "You're right," Johannes replied. "We need more land, but first Father and Mother must sell their farm. Same for the Erikssons. Otherwise, we won't have money for more land, and all that we'll need to farm and for our homes."

Robert said, "We can use the deed on this land for collateral."

"You mean to borrow the money?"

"Yes," Robert replied. "We won't see land at these prices very long. Let's purchase as many plots as we can use, even if we don't farm them right away."

"Robert's right," Elliot said. "Let's talk to Pillsbury when we're in Minneapolis."

Johannes removed his hat and combed his thinning hair with his fingers.

"Okay, say we borrow the money. How do we pay it back?"

"With the wheat, we'll grow," Robert replied. "Those new flour mills in Minneapolis will need wheat and plenty of it. So does the rest of the country. We'll grow what crops we need to live. Wheat will be our cash crop. That's how we'll pay off the loan."

Elliot and Johannes looked admiringly at Robert with a new appreciation for his intellect. His father, Olaf, was correct: Robert had a big brain.

The maple leaves were just beginning to turn when Robert Eriksson arrived in Whitesboro. He walked to the Steins' boarding house from the train station. His long journey had taken him by steamboat from Minneapolis to Pittsburgh via Saint Louis and Cincinnati, and on to Whitesboro by several trains. The bridge over Sauquoit Creek had been rebuilt during the summer. It had been six months since the terrible accident.

When he entered the Steins' house, Robert found two men sitting in the parlor. One was Gustav, and the other was his uncle, Andreas Lindquist. He was tall, big boned, and had a Dutch-style beard and dark penetrating eyes. His formidable appearance concealed his generous nature.

Astonished, Robert was speechless. Andreas rose and crossed the room.

"Robert! So good to see you!" They shook hands and embraced.

"What…what are you doing here?" Robert stammered. Before Andreas could answer, Robert turned to Gustav and exclaimed, "You're sitting, Gustav! Can you walk?"

Gustav, smiling broadly, and grasping a pair of crutches by his chair, replied, "Yes, with these." He rose, leaning on a crutch, and stood upright.

"Soon, he won't need those," Andreas said. "And Robert, you look very fit. How are my sons?"

Robert said, "They're well, in Minnesota, on our new farm. Sit and I'll tell you."

They were just seated when Lars entered. He greeted Robert warmly and sat on the couch next to his father.

Robert recounted their journey to Minneapolis and their ride to Lake Waconia and on to Acton with Oskar Nilsa. In graphic detail, he described the six hundred forty acres they had purchased from Jesus Garcia, and the three days they spent in Minneapolis transferring the deed and paying Garcia in gold.

Andreas asked, "Don't you think you should have looked at other lands first? You might have found something just as good for less money."

"Uncle," Robert replied patiently, "we rode a hundred miles and saw a lot of land. The land we purchased was the best we saw. It has fertile soil and is fairly flat, with good drainage—ideal for crops like hay, corn, oats, and wheat. There's a spring-fed lake with fish, and plenty of trees for lumber—pine, maple, ash, basswood."

Robert paused and appeared a little uneasy.

He cleared his throat, and continued, "In fact, we bought more land—another six hundred forty acres—for $700. Its west, next to our plot."

Astonished, Andreas asked, "Where in the Lord's name did you get the money?"

"We borrowed it—took out a loan. Used the deed for the land we bought as collateral. And we entered an arrangement with a man named Pillsbury, John Pillsbury. He loaned us the money—$1,000—at 3 percent a year. Far better than we could've gotten from a bank. In return, we agreed to give him an option to purchase all the wheat we produce for the next fifteen years at a ten percent discount to fair market rates." Robert paused and looked straight at Andreas.

Sunlight shone through the parlor window. Andreas raised his hand to shade his eyes and arose from the couch to close the drape. The parlor was now nearly dark. He remained standing and rested a forearm on the mantle above the fireplace. "So now we have twelve hundred eighty acres of uncleared land that has never been plowed or cultivated in any way—"

Robert broke in, "There's about forty acres producing hay."

"All right, that makes twelve hundred forty acres of uncleared, virgin land. Correct?"

"Yes, sir," Robert replied.

"I gather Johannes and Elliot agreed with all this?"

"Yes, sir, of course."

"I assume that you can repay the loan anytime you wish?"

"Yes, sir, but Pillsbury's option to buy our wheat would still apply." Robert sensed correctly that Andreas was warming to what they had done. At least, he was not visibly angry.

Andreas asked, "Did you acquire horses? Or implements?"

"We bought two draft horses, two young oxen, and two wagons in Minneapolis. Pillsbury's warehouse sold us six scythes, five axes, chisels, an anvil, and carpenter tools. We bought seed to sew in the spring, and enough food to get three men through the winter."

"Who is the third man?" Lars asked.

"Jesus, Garcia. We bought his 640 acres. Part of the arrangement was for him to stay on until spring—so he could help build a cabin and barn, and show us the traps, and where to hunt."

The room was silent as the three men processed what Robert had told them. Andreas turned to Gustav, "Are you ready to travel?"

Gustav hesitated, tightened his mouth, and stared at his hands.

Noting his brother's discomfort, Lars asked, "What is it, Gus?"

Gustav looked up at Andreas, and said, "Pa, I want to stay here and study medicine with Doctor Warren. He said he would be happy to take me on. And I would live in his house. It would take two years before I was qualified to go out on my own. Then I could join you in Minnesota, as—as a doctor."

The tall, imposing Swede regarded his son, who was the most reflective of his children, and perhaps the most caring. Undoubtedly the accident and the disability had prompted him to rethink his life. To be a farmer anywhere was hard, but to be a pioneer farmer on virgin land was brutally difficult. Survival itself was not a given. A farmer had to do everything for himself and his family: it was a life of endless labor compounded by the uncertainty of weather, infestation, and disease. Given his injury and likely disability, perhaps it would be best for Gustav to be a physician. Best for him and for his family.

Andreas sat down next to Gustav, placed a tender hand on his shoulder, and said, "If that's want you want, Gus, I'll support you, and I'm sure your mother and brothers will too. I want you to know, though, that we're going to keep a piece of land for you if you change your mind."

"Maybe I'll live there and build a clinic, as Doctor Warren has here."

Smiling, Andreas said, "Maybe you will."

Robert asked, "What happened to Julia Svenson and Emma Strohmeyer?"

Lars replied, "Oh, they left about three weeks after you. They took the train to Cincinnati, where Emma was meeting her family, and Julia was going on to Chicago. They left their addresses. Said they would write to us here when they got settled."

"Did Julia take the baby—William, I believe?" Robert asked.

"Yes, she did," Lars replied. "And she took the wet nurse with her. It seems William was a colicky baby, and Julia wasn't sure she could find fresh milk during the trip. That Julia is quite a woman…"

"And an excellent nurse," Gustav broke in. "She didn't leave here until she knew I was going to be all right."

Robert said, "Elliot was smitten by her the moment they met in New York. Acted like a puppy dog around her."

Though he did not express it, Andreas was pleased with the initiative shown by his sons, including Gustav, and his nephew Robert. They were confronted by challenging situations and dealt with them. Their youth and optimism allowed them to risk purchasing additional land. Would he have done the same? Probably not. Certainly not at his age, or perhaps ever. He was anxious to sail to Sweden and return to America with the entire family as quickly as possible. More than anything, he looked forward to seeing their new land in Minnesota.

Chapter 2

Three hundred miles south of Whitesboro, Chief Little Crow of the Mdewakanton Dakota Sioux was in Washington, DC, attempting to retrieve what the federal government owed his tribe in southern Minnesota. He was the leader of a twelve-man delegation intent on recovering the compensation that the government promised them in the treaties of 1837 and 1851.

By these treaties, the six thousand Mdewakanton Dakota Sioux had surrendered twenty-four million acres of land east and west of the Mississippi River. In return, they received $1.6 million. A portion of the money would go directly to white traders to settle Indians debts. Congress also insisted that the Indians live on a twenty-mile-wide reservation along the northern and southern shores of the Minnesota River.

This land, the Great Father in Washington promised, would be theirs forever. After paying off the traders, the balance of the $1.6 million would be paid in the form of an annuity that the Dakota Sioux would receive from the government every summer.

Little Crow, resplendent in a calico hunting shirt, stood before Charles Mix, the commissioner of the Bureau of Indian Affairs. Mix, a career government bureaucrat, sat at the head of the table in a small second-floor conference room. The recently completed castle-like red sandstone Smithsonian Institute was visible on the Mall from the window behind Mix. Three assistants, including an interpreter, were seated to his right, and an elderly clerk was busy recording the names and titles of the attendees.

Commissioner Mix's agenda was quite different from Little Crow's: he wanted the Dakota Sioux to cede the northern half of their reservation along the Minnesota River in exchange for the promise of cash and preferential treatment for those Indian leaders who were willing to abandon their native ways.

Little Crow was a classic Indian figure. His tan, leathery skin and high cheekbones framed a broad nose and full lips above a square jaw. Though imposing, he did not appear belligerent. His eyes were friendly. Indeed, Little Crow sought accommodation, a nonviolent way to settle the differences between the Dakota and the Great Father's government: this was the deathbed advice that his father had given him.

"Commissioner Mix," Little Crow began, "we are here in this council today to retrieve what was promised us in 1837 and 1851. Without the money you owe us, we cannot feed our women and children. My people have been reduced to beggars. The little money we have does not pay the high prices that the traders demand."

Little Crow extended his hand and turned to a member of his delegation, John Other Day, who gave him a roll of papers. "Here," Little Crow continued, "is a list of your government's obligations based on the treaties of 1837 and 1851. After each obligation is a notation specifying what you have paid us and what is due." Little Crow laid the papers on the table in front of Mix.

Without looking at the documents, Mix handed them to the clerk and said, "Chief Little Crow, the money you refer to is in a safe place in the Great Father's bank. It will be delivered to your people when it can be applied properly…"

Little Crow had painted a blue circle around his left eye: he found that it mesmerized his audience and focused their attention on him.

"You actually mean," Little Crow interrupted, "when you can pay off the traders with as little as they are willing to accept! Meanwhile, we can get no credit to buy food and clothing, or the implements or seed we need to farm the land that is now ours!"

Charles Mix knew Little Crow's reputation as a skilled orator and crafty politician. Despite the Dakota chief's inability to read or write English, Mix could see that Little Crow had detailed knowledge of the treaties' provisions.

"Chief Little Crow," Mix began, "I compliment you for being so keen and well prepared. My staff will review these documents, and we will schedule another meeting—another council—to present you with our reply. In the meantime, we will provide you with money for your meals and hotel. Of course, the money will be deducted from the balance we owe your tribe."

Little Crow's anger receded. He liked Washington and, in fact, enjoyed the theater and mingling with dignitaries at various social events. The previous day, he and his delegation met a Turkish military entourage and observed an artillery demonstration by the U.S. Army. This evening he was scheduled to attend a gala dinner for the upper crust of Washington society. Little Crow welcomed a few more days in this city.

After weeks, not days, of waiting, Little Crow and his delegation finally returned to hear Mix's response. Little Crow was stunned to hear that the Great Father had no intention of redressing the Indians' grievances. Instead, Mix wanted to discuss the land the Dakota occupied on the northern shore of the Minnesota River.

Little Crow stood and said to Mix, "It seems that we, the Dakota Sioux, own nothing. We had, we supposed, made a complete treaty in 1851, and we were promised a great many things—horses, cattle, flour, plows, and farming utensils, and land to live and hunt on." Scowling, his voice rising, he concluded, "But it now appears that the wind blows it all off…"

Mix saw his opening: "Chief Little Crow, you are living on that land because the Great Father allows you to do so. If you agree to abandon the land north of the Minnesota River, the Great Father will give you and each of your chiefs an eighty-acre farm on the south shore. You will also receive money and supplies. It's your decision: either you give it, or the Great Father will permit the Minnesota government to take it."

On June 19, 1858, after months of delay and Mix's threats, Little Crow and his delegation signed a treaty ceding their reservation's lands on the northern bank of the Minnesota River to the Great Father in Washington. This land would be sold to settlers and speculators.

The proceeds from the sale would be used to pay off the debts the Indians owed the local traders; the balance, if any, would be delivered to the Dakota people. Tribal leaders would receive eighty-acre farms on the river's south bank. The rest of the Dakota people would get nothing.

Little Crow and his delegation returned to their homes along the Minnesota River. The news they signed a treaty transferring Dakota land on the north shore of the Minnesota River to the Great Father angered many tribal members. To help offset the negativity, Little Crow falsely inflated the amounts of money and quantity of presents the Dakota would receive. He indicated the Dakota could receive $200,000 for their land, as well as gifts and goods. Expectations rose, and for a time, Little Crow's position in the tribe was secure.

But the US Senate failed to act on the treaty, and with the onset of winter it became clear that no payments from Washington would be forthcoming. Little Crow took the brunt of the blame. He was displaced as the speaker for the Mdewakanton band. It could have been much worse: a group of young warriors wanted to kill Little Crow, but they were dissuaded by Red Owl who had emerged as a talented and influential leader.

By 1859, Little Crow no longer attended councils. He had lost the respect of his people.

Meanwhile, change was occurring within the Dakota Sioux reservation, and it was the result of a white man's initiative. Joseph R. Brown was a former fur trader, Democratic politician, and land speculator who had been appointed Indian agent to the Dakota Sioux in 1857.

Brown was married to a woman of mixed blood and had lived among the natives for thirty years. Like Henry Sibley, Brown sympathized with the Dakota's plight and helped engineer their treaties with the federal government in 1851 and again in 1858.

Indeed, it was Brown at Traverse des Sioux in 1851, who convinced the Dakota chiefs to sign a document acknowledging their debts to the traders and authorizing direct payment out of the money the federal government promised for the Dakota's land. One could say that Brown, like so many white men of that era, played both sides—Indian and government—to serve their political and financial self-interests.

However, when he assumed the duties of Indian agent, Brown devoted himself to ending the Dakota's dependence of federal annuities and the white hired help who did most of the farming and skilled work on Indian land. He did this by convincing Mix to release the money owed the Dakota and then using that money to reward Dakota men for doing farm labor and learning new skills.

Brown wanted the Indians to be paid, not because the government owed it to them but because they earned it. He also built schools, hired teachers and offered to train Indians in the essential trades so that they could live independently and be assimilated into what is now called mainstream America.

It was a noble effort, and by the end of 1858, the number of acres under cultivation doubled on the reservation south of the Minnesota River. Houses were built on five-acre lots. Many Indians adopted European dress, cut their scalp locks, and pledged to abstain from alcohol. From the funds Mix released,

Brown bought oxen and cows and gave them to Dakota men who were willing to join his program named 'Improvement Sioux'. It was so successful that Brown ran out of animals. Soon, traditional villages began to disappear, and in their place were small Indian communities with farms and brick houses.

Like the Shawnees decades before, many Dakota leaders were disturbed by the changes taking place around them. It was not so much the farming but the adoption of white man's clothes and hairstyles, and their growing disregard for native culture. By 1860, many traditional Dakota villages were shrinking rapidly.

Even though the Senate had yet to ratify the 1858 treaty, the Dakota Sioux's land on the northern bank of the Minnesota River was quickly occupied by white settlers, who numbered over a thousand by 1860. Discontented Dakota hunters slaughtered the settlers' livestock and destroyed farm property. Brown was forced to use his funds to compensate settlers for their losses.

The Dakota's disenchantment escalated in 1860 when the US Senate finally ratified the 1858 treaty. Instead of paying Agent Brown's recommended five dollars an acre, the Senate approved just thirty-six cents per acre or a total of $96,000. Given the two-year delay, during which the Dakota had continued to live on credit, the entire payment for their 266,000 prime acres on the north shore of the Minnesota River was sent to the traders to settle Dakota debts. The Indians did not receive a penny.

Nearly a half century earlier, on February 27, 1803, Jefferson penned a letter to William Henry Harrison. In it, he wrote, "To promote this disposition to exchange lands which they have to spare and we want, for necessaries, which we have to spare and they want, we shall push our trading houses, and be glad to see the good and influential individuals among them run in debt, because we observe that when these debts get beyond what the individuals can pay, they become willing to [settle their debts] by a cession of lands."

Thomas Jefferson's land policy had come home to the Dakota Sioux. Only now the Dakota had no land to spare, and they were completely dependent on government annuities and the willingness of the traders to extend them credit during bad times.

After the election of 1860, Democrat Brown was replaced as Indian agent by a Republican, Thomas J. Galbraith, a politician with little knowledge of Indian ways. He distributed goods and money primarily to the Indians who farmed, while the Dakota who continued hunting received less. Consequently, the Dakota community became even more divided, and the hunters began to attack their brothers who farmed.

This native civil war escalated to the point where U.S. Army soldiers were stationed on the reservation to enforce an uneasy peace between the two factions. In the midst of all this, Red Owl, Little Crow's successor as chief, died suddenly.

The discredited Little Crow did not step into the leadership vacuum. Instead, like so many of his tribe during the winter of 1860–61, he was preoccupied with survival. Cutworms had destroyed much of the corn crop, and food of any kind was scarce on the reservation. Famine was on the horizon, and many Dakota families fled to the Big Woods, where they hunted and waited for spring.

Chapter 3

The sale of their land in Sweden took longer than anyone anticipated. Andreas Lindquist and A. P. and Olaf Eriksson refused offer after offer until finally they got what they believed their farms were worth. That was in the winter of 1859–1860, and they remained on their land, as renters, until they could arrange passage for everyone to America.

After two and half weeks at sea, the families arrived in Boston in early March 1861, thankful to be on solid land after a tempestuous voyage across the north Atlantic. From Boston, they traveled by train to Erie, Pennsylvania, where they boarded a Great Lakes steamer to Chicago. There they took a train to Saint Paul and arrived on April 13, 1861.

Unbeknownst to them, the American Civil War had begun the previous day when Confederates under General P.G.T. Beauregard fired on Fort Sumter in Charleston Harbor. It would affect these new immigrants in ways no one could foresee.

They were met at the station by Johannes and Robert, who had been in town for three days awaiting their arrival. It was a joyful reunion. The families stayed overnight in Saint Paul and set out early the next morning in two covered wagons for Minneapolis. Andreas, A. P., and Olaf each purchased a covered wagon, two draft horses, and a pair of oxen.

After two nights at the Nicollet House, which the senior men thought far too expensive, the convoy of five wagons with fifteen passengers set out for their new home north of Hutchinson.

Minnesota was growing rapidly in 1861. Already it had two hundred thousand people, twenty times the state's population a decade earlier, and a large majority of them lived on eighteen thousand farms. There were dozens of banks and retail shops, and numerous small businesses were popping up in cities and towns around the state.

Three-quarters of new Minnesotans were Americans born in New England, New York, and the lower Midwest. Germans and Irish were the largest immigrant groups, followed by the British, Norwegians, and Swedes. While the state had chartered several railroads, little track had been laid, and transportation to the interior was by horse or ox drawn vehicles or river boats. By 1860, the telegraph had appeared, and over a thousand steamboats were docking annually at Saint Paul.

Late in the afternoon, Elliot and Lars spotted the dust cloud stirred by a train of wagons.

"It must be them!" Elliot shouted. They mounted their horses and galloped to welcome their family. Since acquiring the property almost three years ago, the four young men had built three houses and three barns of fieldstone and logs, cleared, fenced, and plowed 160 acres, dug wells, and added three cattle sheds. Andreas, A. P., and Olaf were impressed with their sons' accomplishments.

Each family—the Lindquists and two Eriksson clans—would have 360 acres to farm. Common property would include the Long Lake and land not suited for crops. Gustav would join them in the summer after completing his medical training under Doctor Warren. They would build him a cabin and clinic near the road to Watertown.

Already small towns and villages were appearing along the much-anticipated western railroad: Waverly, Dassel, Litchfield, Grove City, Kandiyohi, and Willmar. Almost all the land around them had been purchased or granted. New settlers were arriving every week. Gustav should have plenty of patients.

The following day Elliot asked his father to walk with him to the barn. When they were out of earshot, Elliot said, "Pa, I met a woman, a midwife, from Stockholm in New York. She was with us when the train wreck happened. She helped Doctor Warren care for Gustav…"

"I know," Andreas said. "Lars and Robert told me about her. You were, uh, interested in her…I believe her name is Julia Svenson—a good Swedish name."

"That's right. I asked Julia to marry me, but she wasn't ready. Now she's in Chicago at a Swedish clinic, I think…"

Andreas smiled and placed a hand on his son's shoulder.

"Why are you telling me this? Shouldn't you go to Chicago and bring her here?"

"I may be gone for a month or two," Elliot said apologetically.

"We can manage. You know that she adopted the baby whose mother died after the accident?"

"Yes, Robert told me. The house will be crowded until I can build a place of our own."

"That's not a problem. Let's tell your mother. I think she'll be pleased."

Chicago in the summer of 1861 was beginning to suffer from the loss of trade as the result of the Civil War. The flow of goods and foodstuffs to and from the southern states was abruptly terminated. Businesses suffered and many went bankrupt.

Eventually, government orders for war materials and new markets in the west would offset these losses. But that was in the future, and when Elliot arrived in June, many Chicagoans were out of work.

Elliot went to the address Julia had left in Whitesboro. He found the remains of a building that evidently had burned to the ground some time ago. The nearest church was Immanuel Lutheran three blocks away. There he spoke to the pastor, who did not know Julia but referred him to a Swedish clinic south of the Chicago River.

Julia Svenson was folding dressings and absently watching passersby on bustling Lake Street. Across the way, she saw a handsome, clean-shaven man carrying a brown canvas bag. The man reminded her of Elliot Lindquist. He was looking at a piece of paper and seemed to be scrutinizing her building. Now he was crossing the street, dodging horse-drawn buggies going in opposite directions. As he got nearer, she said out loud, "Bless me, it is Elliot!"

She opened the door to the clinic and stepped onto the boarded sidewalk. Waving her hand, she shouted, "Elliot, Elliot!"

Grinning, he came to her and gently grasped her hands.

"So good to see you, Julia. It's been three years. You look wonderful. How are you?"

He was taller and more muscular than she remembered, and he had lost his boyishness.

"I thought you were in Minnesota. What are you doing in Chicago?"

This was not a time to be obtuse or subtle.

He hesitated briefly, smiled gently and replied, "I came to Chicago to find you...You are the only reason I'm here."

Julia's first impulse was to run into the clinic. Instead, she looked up at this blond Swede. His unblinking blue eyes were locked on hers. She had had many suitors since arriving in this city. A few of them were quite well-to-do, offering her a life of ease and security. Others were kind and dependable Scandinavians. But none of them had sparked her interest or affection.

In a faintly scolding tone, Julia said, "I wish I had known you were coming."

"I was afraid to write."

"But why?"

Elliot removed his hat.

"You may have told me not to bother."

"Oh, I see. You mean that now you're here, it may be more difficult for me to say no."

"Julia, I've loved you since that first day we met in New York. I want us to marry and have a family. I've thought of this—you—every day for the past three years. I came here because I wanted to tell you in person. If you say you don't want me around, I'll take the next train back to Minnesota."

Flustered, Julia stammered, "Elliot, I'm very flattered, but I...I have to get back to clinic. Where are you staying?"

"Nowhere, yet."

Julia pointed down Lake Street.

"My boarding house is right around the corner—by the saloon. It's much better than that pigsty in New York. I know it has a room to rent. Go there, and come back at six o'clock. We can have dinner and talk."

Elliot began to leave when Julia said, "And bring William with you. He's at the boarding house with his nanny."

Elliot moved into the boarding house. The three of them had dinner that evening and every evening for the next two weeks. When Julia was free from her midwifery, they took three-year-old William down to Lake Michigan or to one of Chicago's small parks.

William had blond hair and a cherubic face, and he called Julia 'Jucy' and Elliot became 'Andy'. On several occasions, they watched US Army troops parading down Michigan Boulevard. The war was going badly for the Union, and President Lincoln had issued another call for volunteers.

Elliot accompanied Julia when she delivered babies at night, especially in poor neighborhoods. Most of the homes and apartment buildings were constructed of wood. Crowding and poor sanitation were a given, and it was not unusual for a seven or eight-member family to be living in one room.

It was after midnight when they were returning to the boarding house after a particularly prolonged labor and complicated delivery. Julia said to Elliot, "You are so patient—and kind. Thank you for helping. I couldn't have carried that pail of water up all those flights of stairs. And the mother was so heavy. I couldn't have delivered that baby without you."

"I just like being with you," Elliot said matter-of-factly, and kept walking. Julia stopped. Elliot turned and faced her.

"Did I say something…wrong?" he asked.

Julia stepped forward, placed her midwife bag on the sidewalk, and looked up at him. "How long will it take us to get to your farm in Minnesota?"

Elliot was perplexed. "What are you asking…saying?" he replied.

"I want to spend the rest of my life with you. I want that very much."

Minnesota's harsh winter climate, with its subzero temperatures and heavy snowfalls, meant that farmers had to put up enough hay to feed their livestock until they could graze in the spring and the first cut of hay could be harvested. In 1861, hay was cut using scythes, a long thin crescent-shaped blade attached at an angle to a snath. This design allowed a farmer to cut a wide swath in one swinging motion.

The men were in the fields swinging their scythes when Elliot, Julia, and young William arrived at Andreas's farm in early July. Every fifteen or twenty minutes, they would stop to sharpen their scythes with a whetstone that each man kept in the back pocket of his trousers. Andreas, A. P., and Olaf were working together; their rows were perfectly straight.

Johannes, Lars, Robert, Carl, Rolf, and Gunnar were in a different field; they worked faster, but their rows were a bit crooked, which could throw the oxen off track when the hay was ready to be loaded.

Lena Lindquist welcomed her son and his bride.

She picked up William, and said, "You're going to be a big one, I can tell. Thank heaven, we have a cow with plenty of good milk."

Turning to Julia, she said, "I understand his mother was Swedish."

Julia nodded and replied, "She was very pretty. It was a shame what happened to her."

A bearded man appeared in the doorway. It was Gustav. His dark beard was thicker and longer than the last time Elliot and Julia saw him in Whitesboro. The three of them embraced.

Elliot said, "Gus, looks like you've recovered completely!"

Gustav held up a cane.

"I take this along just in case, but mostly I do without it." Turning to Lena, he asked, "Mother, can we sit here at the table?"

"Yes, yes, of course," Lena replied, "and I have my kalops stew ready for your dinner." She went to the large fireplace and stirred the fire under a kettle.

Gustav explained to Elliot and Julia that he was opening his practice and expected to be making frequent outcalls that would take him away from the clinic. Would Julia be interested in covering the clinic when he was gone? Would she want to be a midwife in the practice?

Julia beamed. "I would like that very much." Turning to Elliot, she asked, "What do you think?"

Elliot, thoughtful, replied, "It would be fine, but who will take care of William when I'm in the fields and you're at the clinic or delivering a baby?"

"I'll take him with me," Julia replied, "the same as I did in Chicago."

Troubled, Elliot said, "The problem is the distances here are so much greater than they were in the city. And then there's the winter. I want you to do this. But I want you and William to be safe."

Andreas, bootless and soaked in sweat, entered the house and removed his stained straw hat. He saw Elliot and Julia.

"I thought that was you! Welcome, Julia! I'm Andreas. I would hug you, but I'm not fit to hug a hog!" He extended a large, calloused hand, and Julia took it in hers.

"Elliot has told me so much about your family, Mister Lindquist," Julia said respectfully.

"Please, I'm Andreas to my family—or Papa or Pa, or…Anyway, this is my afternoon break." He sat at the table next to Gustav. Lena brought him a mug of steaming coffee, as she did every day at this time.

"Julia," Andreas said after sipping the coffee, "thank you for all you did for Gus."

"Your sons took good care of me, too," Julia replied.

"How's the hay, Pa?" Elliot asked.

"Good mix—timothy and clover—considering it's wild. Thank heaven it's dry—we haven't had rain for three weeks. Hope we can get another cut in before winter. We'll need it. Each of those Percherons your uncles bought will eat fifty pounds a day."

Andreas finished his coffee and stood.

"I must get back to work. We should finish this field by dark. Tonight I want to talk about the house and clinic we're going to build for Gustav after the hay is in." Speaking to Elliot and Julia, he said, "Maybe we should build a house and barn for you close to Gustav. There's good farmland up there. And Julia might want to help Gustav in his clinic."

Elliot and Gustav chuckled, and Julia smiled. "Did I make a joke?" Andreas asked.

"No, Pa," Elliot replied. "We were discussing that when you came in. Building our place near Gus makes sense."

"I see. We'll discuss it tonight after dinner. And tomorrow you, Elliot, can get to work fencing the haystacks."

Chapter 4

Many Dakota Sioux chiefs and their families joined the Improvement Sioux program. They lived in houses, farmed, wore the white man's clothes, attended Episcopal missionary services, and sent their children to government schools. They also abandoned traditional Indian ceremonies and cultural activities.

The Great Father in Washington and his Indian agent, Thomas J. Galbraith, were pleased with these 'enlightened' Dakota tribesman, who were trying to adapt to the white man's ways. Predictably, the Improvement Sioux Dakota received more food, goods, and money from the Indian Agency than the Dakota hunter band—the 'blankets'—who preferred chasing game, living off the land as their ancestors did, and worshipping the Great Spirit, Wakan Tanka.

Although Little Crow supported the hunters, he recognized that the winds of change favored the Dakota farmers. Thus, he decided to forsake the hunters and join the Dakota farm community. In effect, he decided to adopt the white man's ways.

He attended Episcopal services, dug a cellar for his brick house, and installed a stove. All these changes he had rejected only a few years before. While the Lindquists and Erikssons were building their homes and barns sixty-five miles north, Little Crow was completing his transition to a new culture and lifestyle.

As Galbraith's policy of favoring Dakota farmers became widespread during the summer of 1861, secret lodges of young warriors—the 'soldiers'—formed throughout the reservation. These soldier lodges fiercely opposed Galbraith's efforts, and they were furious with their tribesmen who submitted to his policies. They became the underground, the resistance fighters who were angry with the loss of their hunting grounds and the hunger suffered by their women and children.

Oskar Nilsa was prescient when, in 1858, he said, "It's one thing for a man to be hungry. It's another when he sees his family starving." As the winter of

1861–62 approached, these unhappy men became dry tinder, awaiting a leader or a spark to unleash hell on every white person west of the Mississippi.

By November, the Lindquists and Erikssons had laid out four farms, complete with log houses and barns. Gustav had his log cabin with an extra room that was his clinic and surgery. The harvest yielded enough hay to feed the livestock until spring, and each house had a root cellar filled with vegetables, apples, berries, and meat. All this was achieved despite a rainy fall that tainted the last cut of hay.

On this chilly morning, Lena could hear Andreas, Johannes, and Lars chopping wood in front of the barn. Already they had neatly stacked two stories of wood. Now they were splitting two oak trees that Olaf and A. P. hauled in from uncleared land to the west. The rough lumber would to be used for crafting a long sled for use during the winter.

Shortly after noon the men entered the house for stew and coffee. They sat quietly at the long table without removing their coats and wool caps. No one spoke until A. P. finished his meal and said to Lena, "Your kalops has always been the best in all Sweden, Lena."

"I brought my spices with me. Andreas wasn't happy about it, but my kalops recipe needs those spices."

"I was wrong—I admit it," Andreas said.

A. P. lighted his pipe and leaned back against the wall. "We should finish the sled in a couple of days. After that, we should get to work on a water tank."

Olaf cleared his throat and said, "I saw four Indians today. Probably hunters. They were crossing my front pasture just after sunrise. All of' em were carrying rifles."

"What direction?" Johannes asked.

"Southeast," Olaf replied. "Probably headed back to their reservation. They were emptyhanded. No game."

"I wish we knew more about the situation down there," A. P. said. Turning to Robert, he asked, "you've been here three years. Have you ever had any trouble with the natives?"

"No," Robert replied quickly. "We've heard of thefts and trespassing, but no violence."

Lena stopped collecting plates from the table and said, "I think we should take precautions."

"Such as?" Andreas asked.

"Locks on the doors and windows. The women should be taught how to shoot a rifle. We should have some kind of signal to warn of trouble. A place to hide. Seems like common sense, doesn't it?"

"Mother's right, Pa," Johannes said. "With winter coming, we're going to be isolated for months. It could be hard just keeping in touch with each other. If food is short on the reservation, we may get some hungry visitors."

"All right, then. A. P., Olaf, do you agree?" Andreas asked.

"Yes," they replied in unison.

Andreas continued. "We won't be able to get locks or any kind of hardware 'til spring. Olaf, you're our best carpenter. Can you figure a way to secure the doors and windows of our homes?"

Olaf replied, "Sure, that should be easy enough."

Andreas turned to Johannes. "You're in charge of being sure everyone knows how to load and fire a rifle—and clean it. Set up a target for them to shoot at." Andreas paused. "It would be even better if they learned to shoot by hunting. Instead of wasting shot and powder on target practice, we could bring in venison and bear meat for the smoke house."

"What about a warning signal?" Lena asked.

"Two shots. Close together," Andreas replied. "Followed by a third shot further apart. Bang-bang—bang. That means the rest of us will grab our rifles and come as fast as we can." He looked at everyone at the table, one by one. Each understood.

"One more thing," Andreas said. "Keep a pistol and ammunition in your root cellars. It's a good place for the women and children to hide." He turned to Johannes. "Be sure the women know how to handle a pistol."

The door opened. It was Gustav. "Afternoon, everyone," he said, and pulled off his wool cap. "I came over to tell you that I had my first patient this morning!"

"Who? Where from?" Lena asked.

"Per Anderson's daughter-in-law from down south. She went into labor yesterday. When the baby didn't come, he brought her up here. Heard about me from Oskar Nilsa."

"What did you do?" Lena asked.

"Actually, I didn't have to do a thing. The baby was breech—legs rather than head coming first. I sent Per to fetch Julia. I was ready to perform a caesarian section when Julia arrived. She examined the woman and said I should wait. Julia did some manipulations from below, told her when and how to push. It took an hour, but the baby's head finally delivered. Mother and baby are fine."

He sat down next to Elliot. "Your wife is very skilled."

"I know," Elliot said. "I watched her deliver dozens of babies in Chicago."

"Where's the baby's father?" Lena asked.

Gustav replied, "He's a soldier in the First Minnesota, somewhere in a hospital near Washington. Per said he was wounded last July. They haven't heard from him for a while. I'm sure they will get word to him that he's a father now."

"The war isn't going well for the Union," Elliot observed. "When I was in Saint Cloud last week, the paper said Lincoln has appointed a new general by the name of McClellan. The First Minnesota has taken a lot of casualties."

A. P. said, "Many of our neighbors are joining up. Some farms are going to be short of help."

Lena looked at her sons.

"I don't want any of you getting ideas of glory in a uniform. You're needed here."

Andreas stood and adjusted his coat. "Back to work. The days are getting shorter."

A foot of snow was on the ground outside Chief Running Bear's tepee. The bitter cold of January had descended on his village with the full moon. He knew the winter would be colder than usual because the woodpeckers were nesting together rather than in separate trees.

To preserve his body heat, Running Bear, as his ancestors had done for generations, wore many layers of clothing. The inner layers were a buckskin shirt and leggings, a fur vest, and a bearskin belt around his waist that served as an insulated seat cushion.

Over this he draped a finely decorated buffalo robe that hung from his shoulders to the ground. On his head was a fur cap of muskrat and raccoon with an erect eagle feather.

Unlike white settlers, he and most Dakota men welcomed the winter. It was a time of peace because warriors stayed close to their villages. It was easier to track game in the snow and fish through the ice.

During the long hours of darkness, men would pass the pipe, tell stories, and plan springtime raids on the Chippewa. Running Bear enjoyed the tribal fellowship and sense of common purpose that evolved during the time they spent talking around the fire.

However, the winter of 1862 was different. More than ever, the Dakota were deeply troubled by the white man's invasion of their country. The traditionalists among them were most disturbed by those in their tribe who deserted the village for a farm, who wore white man's clothing, and who no longer honored the Great Spirit. Their land and their customs were going or already gone.

The land had been forfeited in treaties that none of their leaders completely understood. Worse, these same chiefs, like Little Crow, received special treatment, including cash payments and perks that were nothing less than bribes. And often these chiefs were the members of who were abandoning their people and becoming farmers and church goers. The Dakota suffered a leadership vacuum when leaders were most needed.

The Dakota Sioux were starving. They were eating roots and berries. Already many had eaten their dogs. Not even those who farmed escaped the famine that descended during the winter. The annual harvest had been poor.

Reservation administrators had funds, but instead of providing food they insisted on building schools and purchasing books. The traders refused to advance the Indians more credit, but they sheltered and fed the native women who slept with them.

Running Bear sat on a thick red blanket. Beside him was White Eagle, the seventeen-year-old son of Little Dog and grandnephew of Big Thunder. Behind them were Running Bear's wife, Weayaya, and their fifteen-year-old daughter, Mina.

They were preparing the venison that White Eagle had brought them for dinner. The young man was reputed to be the best hunter of his generation. "He thinks like a wolf, and he can run like an antelope," Little Dog once remarked.

Ostensibly, his visit was to pay his respects to Chief Running Bear. In fact, he had been attracted to Mina since the previous summer.

"Where did you find the deer?" Running Bear asked.

"Across the river," White Eagle replied.

"Were you on a settler's land?"

"Yes."

"Did you have permission to hunt there?"

"No, I didn't ask."

Running Bear absently adjusted his buffalo robe and turned to face White Eagle.

"I've always asked permission to hunt on a settler's land." His voice was not harsh, but the note of disapproval was unmistaken. "You should share your kill with the settler. To show respect."

White Eagle said, "Chief Running Bear, no one in our tribe has enough to eat. I have given meat from my kill to every tepee. There's none left. And you taught us that no one owns the land. It belongs to all of us. Why must I ask permission to hunt anywhere?"

Running Bear nodded. "What you say is true. Our tradition was to share the land with each other—that is, within our tribe. Our fathers and their fathers honored that principle, and it strengthened the bond between us. Together we defended our land from our enemies, especially the Chippewa, and we never took more from the land than we needed."

White Eagle raised a hand and began to speak, but Running Bear cut him off.

"Listen, my son. Many summers ago, Chief Little Crow signed a paper with the Great Father at Traverse des Sioux. The land that was once ours was exchanged for money and supplies and the promise of an annual payment that would sustain us. With it, we could buy food, clothing, tools, and other necessities at the traders' stores.

"After the treaty was signed, the Great Father sold or gave our land to white settlers. It is their land now, and no longer ours. If we wish to hunt their land, we must ask, or there will be trouble."

White Eagle was not in agreement, but he held his tongue. Running Bear was a chief, an elder, and the young man would not risk offending him. Instead, tomorrow he would sit with the young warriors—the 'soldiers'—in the lodge they had built away from the village to discuss the dire situation on the reservation.

It was there that White Eagle was beginning to have a voice. His skills as a hunter and trapper were admired, especially by the older men. However, he had yet to draw the blood of an enemy.

After minutes of silence, Running Bear asked, "White Eagle, why do you not speak? One way or other?"

"I will do as you say, chief," White Eagle replied. "I will ask permission before hunting a settler's land."

"You are troubled, though. Are you not? You sit with the young men in that lodge in the woods. Yes? Where I have not been invited. And listen to that hot head, Red Cloud. And perhaps to others who have wild ideas?"

"That's true," White Eagle responded. "There's great unrest, chief. The men we looked up to, like Little Crow, have betrayed us, and they no longer have a voice. And those we respected, like Red Owl and Shakopee, are gone with the Great Spirit."

Running Bear listened as White Eagle detailed the struggles he and his generation were grappling with, seemingly alone, and without any sign of resolution. A gust of cold wind swirled around the tepee, amplifying the forebodings that were twisting in Running Bear's gut. He was forty-five years old, and for years he had been a minor chief.

Did he have the emotional and physical strength to lead the Dakota in opposition to the Great Father? Would his voice be heard, and would his words be accepted? Even if he could ascend to leadership, what would he do? What choices would he make? He did not know.

Weayaya and Mina brought plates of roasted venison and dried corn. They sat behind the two men. White Eagle turned slightly so he could see Mina. Their eyes met and their expressions softened.

Mina's mother saw and understood the language their bodies were speaking. She would talk with Running Bear in the morning. Too many young women in their village were becoming pregnant without a husband. Tribal mores were fracturing as life became harder and the tribe splintered into factions defined by privilege, poverty, and lifestyle.

Many women were lying with white men—soldiers and traders—at the Redwood or Yellow Medicine agencies in exchange for food or whiskey. Their mixed-breed offspring were embarrassments to the tribe.

Weayaya asked White Eagle, "What will you do in the spring?"

White Eagle replied, "I will help my mother with the planting. Then I will join the men going west to hunt. I will visit my sister, on the James River. She married a Lakota who has a horse. I hope he will help me catch a pony so I can hunt the buffalo."

Mina asked, "You will be gone much of the summer?"

White Eagle nodded and said, "There is little to hunt around here. Last fall I tracked north and east and did not see a single deer or turkey. On my way back, I passed near the Long Lake. There are more houses, and the fields are being cleared for planting. We used to hunt and fish around the Long Lake every summer. Now that belongs to white settlers. If our tribe is to have enough meat next winter, we must hunt bigger game, like the buffalo. We can't survive on squirrels and rabbits."

White Eagle speaks well,' Running Bear thought. And what he said was true: without game, the Dakota are dependent on the traders for food, except for the small crops of corn and beans each family grows. The Dakota's annual payment from the Great Father in Washington would not arrive until the summer.

Rumors were circulating that the Great Father's war with the southern gray coats was very costly, and that the US government's gold was almost gone. Reverend Bates at the Yellow Medicine Agency said that the annual payment may be cut in half, and it might be paid in paper greenbacks rather than gold coins. Would the traders accept greenbacks? Or would they keep their warehouses locked?

Running Bear noticed that White Eagle and Mina were glancing at each other quite often. He would speak to Weayaya in the morning.

The winter of 1861–62 tested every neuron and fiber of the Lindquist and Eriksson families. Feeding and watering the animals was painful when temperatures plunged below zero, and often it was twenty below and especially brutal if the wind was blowing from the northwest. The wells froze. So, too, did their water tanks. Three or four times a day someone had to break the ice with an ax so the animals could drink.

A sudden January blizzard nearly trapped Johannes and Andreas on Long Lake where they were fishing through a hole they drilled with an auger. They made it back to the cabin because Lena had had the good sense to fire the rifle every few minutes to guide them through the blinding snowstorm.

The cold was one thing, but endless days of little or no sunlight combined with hours of confinement sapped their energy and exposed fraying nerves. Minor irritants threatened to become major conflicts. They were moderated only by the knowledge that the families' survival depended on tolerance and cooperation.

On Christmas Eve, the Lindquists visited Robinson Jones and his wife at their store and post office, where they met Howard and Ann Baker and their two children. Mrs. Jones had been widowed the previous year when her husband died suddenly during the fall harvest, leaving her with two children. Robinson took them in, and they married three months later. The three families celebrated the holiday with roast turkey, smoked ham, and a chocolate cake.

During January and February, the Lindquists and Erikssons visited each other as often as they could. They shared the dwindling supply of vegetables, fresh fish caught in Long Lake, and the little deer or bear meat the men trapped or shot. To save water they bathed once a week from a common bucket, and the men did not shave.

No one washed their hair because it was too difficult to dry; instead, they 'dry cleaned' it with powdered soap. They used chamber pots at night or when the weather was too bad to use the outhouse; at times, the stench forced them to open a window or door and suffer the cold.

In the middle of March, they had a respite. The skies cleared and the temperature was above forty degrees for a week. As the snow melted, patches of green appeared in the fields. The men repaired and sharpened their farm implements, cleaned and oiled the harnesses and collars they would use for plowing, and chopped enough wood to last them into May.

Well water flowed freely, allowing the women to do laundry and scrub down their cabins. Lena warmed water over the fire, kicked everyone out of the cabin, and took a luxurious bath in the washtub.

Andreas and Elliot drove a wagon to Willmar and bought sugar, flour, apple butter, soap, and an old newspaper. They learned that the Civil War was going badly for the Union except for a general by the name of Grant, who had captured two Confederate forts in Tennessee. The Third Minnesota Volunteer Infantry was in Kentucky and had yet to see serious action.

They returned from Willmar late in the afternoon. A mile from Elliot's cabin, they heard a roar behind them that sounded like a locomotive. A minute later they were overtaken by a blinding wall of sleet and hail. Lightning streaked across the darkened sky followed by bone-shaking thunder. The sleet turned to snow; the temperature dropped well below freezing. Elliot leaped off the wagon and walked ahead so his father could keep the two horses on the narrow track.

At Elliot's cabin, they found a note from Julia. Around midday she had gone to Gustav's clinic to examine an expecting mother who was spotting. She had William with her and should be home for supper.

"I hope she is there and not out in this weather," Elliot said.

Andreas nodded and said, "Get some blankets. We should go to Gustav's."

Gustav's cabin and clinic were less than a mile away, but the snow accumulated so rapidly that they had to abandon the wagon. Fortunately, they had snowshoes and were able to leave the wagon behind and lead the horses to Gustav's barn. They arrived as the sun was setting.

No one was at the clinic or in the cabin, but a note on the clinic door read, "Clinic will be open tomorrow."

"There's nothing we can do now," Andreas said. "Let's put the horses in the barn, and we'll stay the night in the cabin. I have a key."

If it had been daylight, they would have noticed tracks in the snow leading to the barn. When Elliot opened the barn door, he heard a rustling above him in the hayloft. *'Probably an animal,'* he thought. Then he smelled smoke.

"Somebody's in the loft, Pa," he whispered to Andreas. Both men drew their Colt pistols.

"Come out of there!" Elliot shouted. "Show me your hands!"

A few seconds passed. The figure of an Indian appeared at the edge of the loft, his arms extended, his hands empty. Elliot motioned for the Indian to come down. He wore a fur cap with an eagle feather and a brown wool coat decorated with beads, leggings, and boots. A long knife was sheathed at his waist.

Elliot had learned some basic Dakota language during his three years in Minnesota. "What are you doing here?" he asked.

The Indian replied, "Away from the wind."

"Why are you on this land?" Elliot asked impatiently.

"I hunt," the Indian replied.

"Who said you could hunt here?" Elliot asked forcefully.

"The white medicine man said I could hunt here this morning."

Andreas turned to Elliot, "Ask him if he's seen anyone." Elliot spoke to the Indian. They exchanged words for a few minutes. Andreas was growing impatient when Elliot relayed what the Indian told him.

"His name is White Eagle. Lives on the reservation south of the river. He saw Gustav leave this morning with a woman and a child in the buggy. It must have been Julia and William. They were headed east."

Andreas studied White Eagle. The Indian looked him straight in the eyes.

"Okay," Andreas said. "Tell him he can stay in the barn, but no fire. He can come to the cabin for food."

During the night, the temperature rose, and it began to rain, melting most of the snow that had accumulated the previous day. White Eagle left at sunrise to return to his village. His belly was full for the first time in many moons. The white settlers had given him venison and corn. He would remember their kindness.

That morning Elliot took the horses and retrieved the wagon while Andreas remained behind hoping that Gustav and Julia would return. They did not. The two men set out in the wagon, heading east along the old buffalo track.

The going was slow because the wheels sunk into mudhole after mudhole. By midafternoon, they had traveled barely seven miles. Then, off in the distance, they spotted a lone rider coming toward them. It was Gustav.

Elliot urged his team of horses to increase their pace, but the wagon made slow headway. They waited impatiently for Gustav to reach them.

When he was within shouting distance, Elliot bellowed, "Where's Julia and William?"

Gustav did not reply immediately.

Finally, as he got closer, he said, "They're at the Berg's farm. They're fine. We got there before the snow. Delivered twin boys. Stayed the night."

Elliot's relief left him speechless.

"Where's your buggy?" Andreas asked.

"Left it at the Bergs. Have to get back to the clinic. Buggy wouldn't have made it in this muck." His voice was weary. He had not slept for two days.

Elliot said, "We'll fetch Julia and William. And bring your buggy back."

"Thanks, brother," Gustav replied. "I don't know what I would do without Julia. She's taught me more about delivering babies these past months than I learned in two years at Whitesboro."

Elliot nodded.

Andreas said, "There was an Indian in your barn by the name of White Eagle. You know him?"

"Yeah," Gustav replied. "I told him he could hunt my land yesterday. His village is starving. The government hasn't given them their annuity yet. And the traders won't advance them any more credit. Bad situation."

Elliot said, "We went to Willmar yesterday before the storm. Didn't see a deer or turkey. Might as well be on the moon."

As he snapped the reins, Andreas said to Gustav, "I'll see you this afternoon with your buggy." The wagon lurched ahead, heading east toward the Berg farm. When they arrived, Julia was helping Nancy Berg with her newborn sons, and young William was napping on the couch. The sun had appeared, and the remaining snow was melting rapidly, leaving vast pools of water in the flat field next to an impressive two-story barn.

Karl Berg helped the men attach Gustav's buggy to the wagon, and the four Lindquists set off on the two-hour return journey to Elliot's farm. On the way, they enjoyed a westerly breeze that hinted of spring. William romped in the wagon, playing hide and seek with his mother, who was resting under a blanket on a soft bed of straw.

Thankfully the April snowstorm was winter's last blast. The following Sunday the family gathered at A. P.'s farm to discuss the upcoming planting season. Rather than work individually, they decided to pool their labor and animals and work their fields collectively. They would plant vegetables—peas, potatoes, tomatoes, squash, sweet corn—and larger crops of feed corn, oats, and barley.

Robert argued for two fields of wheat. He called it a 'money crop', meaning it would generate cash to help pay off the loan from Pillsbury and perhaps purchase more horses and machinery. The older men—Andreas, Olaf, and A. P.—were skeptical of Robert's plan.

But Johannes, Lars, and Elliot thought their future—and their families' future—was wheat. Certainly, they would grow what they needed to feed their families; however, they were excited by the raw opportunity this rich land proffered the men and women who were willing to work and take risks.

Flour mills were beginning to flourish in Minneapolis along the river, and more were being built, because the Union Army needed food, and a lot of it.

Armies marched faster and fought better when its troops were healthy and their bellies full. In addition, the growing tide of settlers coming to the Midwest would need flour. The main risk was not the market, but rather the possibility their wheat crop would fail.

After much discussion over dinner, the family agreed to Robert's plan and placed him in charge of the wheat crop. The newspaper Andreas and Elliot procured in Willmar had a story about two farmers in southeastern Minnesota who were planting wheat with success. Robert read and re-reread it and decided to visit them. Two weeks later he returned with a wagon loaded with enough seed for both spring and winter crops.

By the end of May, he and the Lindquists planted thirty acres. The soil was moist, and the temperatures were in the high sixties and low seventies. Soon the seedlings sprouted, and the fields turned from dark brown to yellow. Meanwhile, the older men and women planted the other crops.

It was backbreaking labor, but all of them welcomed the opportunity to work outdoors after such a long winter. They were in the fields every day at daybreak and did not quit until the sun was low on the horizon.

Once the seeds were in the ground, the men turned to other tasks. They cleared more land, fenced additional pastures, and expanded their cabins and barns. Gustav added a room to his clinic where he could perform surgery.

Elliot built a bedroom for William. Lena insisted on an indoor privy and private room where she could bathe. When the other wives saw what Andreas fashioned for Lena, they, too, demanded their husbands do the same.

By the middle of August, the Lindquists and Erikssons were expecting a bountiful harvest, and their farms were beginning to look and feel like the ones they left in Sweden. The wheat field appeared abundant and was nearly ready for the scythe.

Gustav was busy in his medical practice, Julia had taken on a young woman who wanted to be a midwife, and Robert was organizing transportation to take their first wheat crop to the market in Saint Cloud.

On Saturday, August 16, the Reverend Luke Henning arrived at the farm of Andreas and Lena Lindquist. He was an itinerant Lutheran preacher who arrived in Minneapolis from Pennsylvania the previous fall and wintered in a half dozen towns along the Minnesota River. He traveled north and west during the spring and summer, holding services in homes and villages along the way.

Lena invited him to stay for dinner. She was not particularly anxious to get involved with the Lutheran church again, but she was curious for news. The reverend had much to tell. He told Lena and Andreas that the Dakota reservation was in a bad way. People were starving to death, even in the middle of summer. An untold number had died during the winter.

The warriors were angry with the members of their tribe who were farming and getting more government assistance as a reward. There had been violence, but few US Army soldiers were available to keep the peace on the reservation.

The unrest was further aggravated by the delay in the government treaty payments, which the Dakota needed desperately to buy food and other necessities.

The reverend said, "The traders won't open their warehouses until they get payment for the goods the Indians have purchased on credit since last summer. When he heard this, Little Crow told the Indian agent, Thomas Galbraith, that the Dakota may have to take their own way to keep from starving. He said that when men are hungry, they help themselves." He paused and looked straight at Andreas.

"To me, Little Crow was warning there could be trouble---violence against not just the traders but all white men. You should lock up at night and keep your rifles nearby."

The reverend's news unsettled Lena. After he left, she urged Andreas to ride to the other farms and urge their sons and the Erikssons to take precautions. He refused.

"Lena," he scoffed, "there are more important things to do. Last week George Whitcomb rode through on his way to Litchfield. He said the young Dakota men were always threatening trouble. It's all talk. They wouldn't dare lift a hand against a white man."

Chapter 5

The following day, Sunday, August 17, four Dakota men were returning from the northern Big Woods where they had found no game. They were hungry and angry. While following a trail southeast to the Minnesota River, they came across a homestead in Acton Township where one of the Indians found a nest of hen eggs.

One of his companions cautioned him not to take the eggs because they belonged to a white man, whereupon the Indian crushed the eggs and shouted, "You're afraid of the white man!"

Insulted, his companion replied, "I am not afraid of the white man, and I will kill him to prove it!"

The eggs belonged to Robinson Jones, who operated a combination store and post office. At the time, his wife was visiting the farm of her son by a previous marriage a half mile away. Jones was looking after their two adopted children, a fifteen-year-old girl and her eighteen-month-old brother.

The four Indians entered Jones's store and demanded liquor. Jones, who knew the men, refused. When they became angry, Jones, in an apparent attempt to protect the children, invited the Indians to accompany him to his stepson's farm.

The stepson was Howard Baker. He and his family had celebrated the previous Christmas with the Lindquists. In addition, a young couple from Wisconsin by the name of Webster was living temporarily in a covered wagon near the farmhouse while they searched for land to buy.

When Jones and the Indians arrived, Mr. Baker, Mr. Webster, and Mrs. Jones were standing in front of the house talking. Mrs. Baker was in the house with the youngest child, and Mrs. Webster was in the wagon.

The Indians appeared friendly, and casually challenged the white men to a shooting contest. Each of the men, except Webster, took turns firing at a target. The white men were better marksmen, and they won easily.

As the white men celebrated their victory, the Indians quickly reloaded their rifles. Jones recognized what the Indians were up to and began to shout the alarm. But a bullet struck his windpipe, and he fell to the ground, suffocating in his own blood. The Indians fired three shots in near unison, killing Baker instantly and mortally wounding Webster.

Mrs. Jones, screaming, was bludgeoned to death with a tomahawk. Ann Baker and one of her children hid in the root cellar. The second Baker child went unseen nearby, and Mrs. Webster was out of sight in the covered wagon. Both women and the two Baker children survived and fled north to a neighboring home.

The four Indians resumed their journey southeast toward their village. As they passed Jones' store, they murdered the fifteen-year-old girl, Clara Wilson, and left the eighteen-month-old boy unharmed. For some reason, they took no whiskey or weapons from the store. Next, they stole a team of oxen and four horses from a farm in Kandiyohi County.

Late in the evening they arrived at their village and told their soldiers' lodge that they killed five white people in Acton Township. News of the killings spread like wildfire and large group of Dakota warriors set out to Chief Little Crow's home several miles away.

Little Crow heard them coming and stepped outside his house. As he listened to the young men recount the slaughter, Little Crow knew that the white settlers and the state and federal governments would seek a terrible retribution for these callous murders.

As he saw it, there were three choices: turn the four men over to the authorities, flee west with the entire tribe, or wage war with the goal of driving the white man out of Minnesota and across the Mississippi.

Surrendering the four Indians for hanging would be traitorous, an unconscionable act. But to flee? Where? With no food or money? Yet, to fight was to invite disaster for the Mdewakanton Dakota and any Indian in the territory.

White men, be they soldier or civilian, would not discriminate between a Dakota warrior or his woman or child, or a member of another tribe. All would be punished and suffer deprivation. Many would die.

At first, Little Crow attempted to dissuade the warriors.

He said, "You may kill one—two—ten, but the white men are like locusts, and you are only a small herd of buffalo. You will die like rabbits in the winter when the wolves are hungry."

Little Crow soon realized he could not restrain these warriors. They were angry and their blood was too hot for rational thinking. In the eyes of many, he was a diminished leader, a chief who had been compromised by the white men and their lies and half promises.

After all, it was Little Crow who signed the treaties that confined the Dakota to a strip of less fertile land along the south bank of the Minnesota River. He did not live in a tepee but rather in a frame house, as did many of the Dakota farmers who emulated the white settlers. Little Crow once said he rejected Christianity, but that very day he had attended services at the Episcopal mission.

A warrior stepped forward and pointed his rifle at Little Crow.

"You are a coward!" the warrior shouted.

The words stung, not because he was afraid to fight but because they reminded Little Crow that he was a fading leader who no longer spoke for his tribe. War could allow him to reclaim his status as the speaker for the Mdewakanton Dakota.

Little Crow agreed to join them.

Assuming the posture of war chief, he raised a clenched fist and shouted, "We must attack at dawn tomorrow! Before the alarm is sounded! We will strike the Redwood Agency first!"

The warriors cheered wildly; a few discharged their rifles. "Don't waste your powder!" Little Crow implored. "Save your lead for the traders!" He sent riders to nearby Dakota villages to rouse every warrior for an attack on the Lower Sioux Agency in the morning.

White Eagle waited at the edge of the woods surrounding his village. It was dusk on the banks of the Minnesota River. In the morning, he would join the war party attacking the Lower Sioux Agency. They would kill every white man, white woman, and white child.

The August sun was drifting below the horizon, and the swarming mosquitoes pricked the exposed skin of his back and legs. He barely noticed them. His entire body was consumed with one purpose: to lay with Mina, the first-born daughter of Running Bear.

The passion had gripped him from the moment Red Cloud had selected him to scout ahead of the war party. The prospect of danger and death had kindled in him an all-consuming desire to copulate. It was neither love nor lust: it was a basic instinct, a warrior's drive to procreate before going into battle.

Mina emerged from her father's lodge. She was fifteen years old and a virgin. Her long black hair and amber body were freshly washed and faintly scented with the flakes of wildflowers. That morning White Eagle had asked her to meet him in the woods at sunset. She had known him all her life. They had played together as children, and she had watched him become a man. Tomorrow, Mina feared, White Eagle would risk his life for her and their people.

Something stirred within her. What was this strange feeling? Mina's hunger and fear dissipated. Instead, she felt an urgency, a desire to be with White Eagle. Tomorrow their world would change forever, and the future, any future, was as uncertain as the seasons. A hot wave flowed through her body, sharpening her senses, and focusing every impulse and desire on what she would do tonight.

Silently, White Eagle led Mina deep into the forest of red and silver maples. The moon was full, and their shadows followed them to a dry creek bed. A young deer, startled by their approach, bolted and leaped away. Mina stopped and looked up at White Eagle. Gently, deliberately, he drew her to his body.

They made love. It was painful, but Mina did not cry out: she could feel his warmth within her, and her body shuddered. The explosive tension that gripped White Eagle's body vanished and his muscles relaxed. She moaned softly as he left her.

They laid there, in the moonlight, aware of each other, knowing they could not linger very long. Running Bear would be asking for his daughter. Mina raised herself up on an elbow and looked down on White Eagle. Abruptly the tears began to flow.

She struggled to stifle a sob. He encircled her with his arms and held her tightly for many minutes. A cloud obscured the moon. Enveloped in darkness, they did not speak for fear of disturbing the moment.

The cloud moved east and once again the moon shone brightly. A chorus of crickets and katydids comforted them. Then an owl screeched, and a coyote howled. White Eagle sat up. What was that sound? He heard it again, a faint rustling behind him.

He unsheathed his knife and turned. Not ten yards from him stood a young black elk, as startled by the encounter as White Eagle.

"What is it?" Mina whispered.

Looking down at her, White Eagle replied softly, "Hehaka." When he looked again, the elk was gone.

"We should go back now," White Eagle whispered. "You go. I will take another path."

He helped Mina to her feet. He embraced her, knowing this may be their last time together.

That night, as Mina slept in her father's lodge, White Eagle's seed penetrated the ovum that was entering her womb. At this instant of fertilization, their son was conceived. His Dakota Sioux name would be Running Bear, after her father.

Early the next morning White Eagle mounted the black pony he borrowed from Red Cloud and set off for the government's Lower Sioux Agency alone. The sun was barely visible on the horizon.

The Lower Sioux Agency included a two-story stone warehouse built in 1861. It contained the food and supplies that the Dakota desperately needed. But the Indian agent, Thomas Galbraith, would not distribute food or supplies without payment.

On this Monday morning, there was optimism among the traders because it was rumored that more than $71,000 in gold coin would arrive at nearby Fort Ridgely later that day. This was the long overdue annuity money that the federal government owed the Dakotas for turning over their land in 1851 and 1858. '*At last,*' the traders thought, '*they could safely extend credit to the Indians.*'

The tension between the Dakota Indians and one particular trader, Andrew Myrick, had been building all summer. The Dakota were starving.

Myrick refused to sell them food on credit, stating, "So far as I'm concerned, if they're hungry, let them eat grass and their own shit."

It was the first full year of the Civil War, and the government was intent on defeating the Confederacy. Meeting its treaty obligations to the Dakota nation was a low priority, a commitment that would have to wait. The land where the Dakota hunted and gathered rice was rapidly disappearing as it was cleared for settlement and farming.

The growing white population competed with the Dakota for game, and the deer, elk, and buffalo, which had fed the Dakota for centuries, were scarce. Likewise, the Indians had fewer furs to trade for food. They were desperate, and many were dying of malnutrition. Poverty, starvation, and hopelessness was driving them to violence.

Many of the eighty or so people around the agency that morning worked in the trading establishments as clerks or cooks. Others labored in the fields, and a few were teachers, missionaries, and carpenters. Around 7:00 a.m., a brief thunderstorm caused many to take shelter.

As the rain passed, a large band of Dakota warriors appeared on the road, carrying an assortment of rifles and shotguns. They wore buckskin leggings and loincloths. Some had colorful beaded bonnets decorated with eagle feathers. Their faces were painted for war, and they were led by Little Crow. Quickly they split into smaller groups and surrounded the four trader stores and the agency building.

James Lynd happened to be standing in the door of Myrick's new store. He was one of the store's clerks and a former member of the Minnesota State Senate. When the Indians approached, Lynd was puzzled by their appearance.

One of them, a warrior named Plenty of Hail pointed his rifle at Lynd and shouted, "Now I will kill the dog that would not give me credit!"

He shot Lynd, who slumped dead in the doorway. He was the first casualty of the Dakota Sioux War.

White Eagle joined the war party a few minutes before the thunderstorm struck. He carried a rifle and farmer's scythe. Little Crow told him to stay behind on the road and intercept any whites trying to escape.

When the sky cleared, White Eagle watched the other warriors attack the agency. There was a flurry of gunshots and bloodthirsty screams. His attention was drawn to a white man crawling out of the second story window of Myrick's store. It was Myrick himself, trying to escape the Indians who had killed Lynd and his cook, Fritz, an old German immigrant.

Myrick ran toward White Eagle. He was unarmed and frantic. White Eagle gripped the scythe and swung it wildly as Myrick passed him. He missed. Abruptly Myrick halted, arched his back, and fell to the ground. He had been shot in the spine but was still alive.

White Eagle stood over him and raised the scythe. Myrick watched wide-eyed as White Eagle brought the scythe down, burying its finely honed blade in his chest, splitting his breastbone and heart in half like a melon. As he looked down on Myrick's lifeless body, another Indian thrust manure into the trader's mouth and seethed, "Now, you eat dung!"

The Dakota Sioux War had begun. Little Crow said it would not end until all the white intruders had been killed or driven from their lands west of the Mississippi. They began by burning the Agency's buildings. Only one wood structure, a kitchen, would remain standing.

As the smoke billowed skyward late into the morning, word spread to surrounding communities and farms that the Indians had massacred government workers and civilians. Settlers loaded their families into wagons and fled toward Fort Ridgely, twelve miles southeast of the Agency on the north bank of the Minnesota River.

Very few white settlers had weapons of any kind. Many were intercepted by the rampaging Indians who killed defenseless people---men, women, children, infants---as they sought the safety of the fort.

Later they would be found on the road and in ditches, bloated and decaying in the summer sun. Their horrible deaths would be described in communiques and newspapers, fueling a sustained outcry for revenge.

The first terrified settlers arrived at Fort Ridgely around 10 a.m. They informed its commander, Captain John Marsh, that the Indians had attacked the Lower Sioux Agency shortly after sunrise and were ravaging the countryside.

Marsh, a veteran of the Battle of Bull Run and an attorney in civilian life, hastily assembled forty-six soldiers and marched southwest toward the Minnesota River, where he planned to cross on the ferry and quell the uprising.

He left nineteen-year-old Lieutenant Thomas Gere in charge of the fort. Gere was ailing with the mumps, but he deployed his twenty-two men in a defensive line facing south. Before departing, Marsh sent a rider to recall Lieutenant Sheehan and his company of fifty men who departed the previous day for Fort Ripley in northern Minnesota.

On the way to the river, Marsh encountered terrified settlers heading for the safety of the fort. Most of them had crossed the river on the ferry from the south shore. They spoke of death and destruction at the hands of the Indians who were looting and burning homes and slaughtering anyone in their path.

One of the refugees cautioned Marsh that the Indians far outnumbered his command, and he should not cross the river to the southwest side.

Marsh ignored this warning and continued to the river. They passed flaming houses and barns and found murdered civilians and the Redwood ferryman lying in the road. When he and his troops arrived at the ferry, they found a Dakota named White Dog was standing on the opposite bank. He appeared peaceful and told Marsh through an interpreter that there was no trouble on the south bank and the soldiers could cross.

Then a sergeant spotted Indian ponies fording the river upstream. Before he could sound the alarm, rifle fire erupted from the trees across the river and from thickets on both banks. It was an ambush. Half the soldiers, including the sergeant, were killed. Marsh drowned while attempting to lead the remnants of his command across the river. The surviving men scattered, leaving behind twenty-four dead comrades.

At dusk, the first survivors of Marsh's command returned to Fort Ridgely with news of the ambush and Marsh's death. Lieutenant Gere knew he was in a tough spot, and the situation was even more daunting because he was now responsible for hundreds of civilians, mostly women and children, who sought safety in the fort.

First, he dispatched a letter to the town of Saint Peter, asking for reinforcements. Then he deployed a thin picket line around the fort and nervously patrolled the post through the night, wondering what Little Crow and the other Dakota chiefs would do next.

The following day began with a glorious sunrise. Andreas Lindquist, unaware of the conflict in the south, milked the cow and returned to the cabin. Lena was in bed, still asleep, her nightgown above her waist. Andreas stood by the bed, fixated by the triangular mound of reddish hair between her thighs. He resisted the temptation to lay beside her. Instead, he shook her awake. She groaned and reluctantly opened her eyes. "Go milk the cow," she whispered and rolled onto her side, exposing the curve of her bare buttocks.

"I have, my sweet." He paused and gently sat on the bed, placing his hand on her shoulder. "There are two Indians by the smokehouse," he said.

"They're hungry," Lena replied.

"I'm not sure. They're acting peculiar."

"How do you mean?" Lena asked, abruptly sitting up.

"They're walking back and forth, as if they can't make up their minds what to do."

Lena turned and looked at her husband. "Tell them to leave."

Andreas cleared his throat. "Alright."

"Do they have weapons?" Lena asked.

"Both have rifles," Andreas replied. "And their faces are painted black and red. I have not seen that before."

Lena stood and wrapped a cloth robe about her shoulders.

"Wake Johannes and Lars! Quickly, now!" She went to the window. "I see them. They're not thirty feet from the house! Andreas, get your rifle!"

It was too late. The two Dakota warriors, Black Beaver and Silver Moon, burst into the cabin and shot Lena through the heart as she grasped a knife to defend herself. Desperately, Andreas reached for his rifle above the kitchen table, but a bullet from Silver Moon's rifle entered his left ear and exited through his forehead.

Asleep in the loft, Johannes and Lars were awakened by the blast that killed their mother. Johannes struggled into his trousers as Silver Moon's shot entered Andrea's skull.

"Jävla skit!" he exclaimed and leaped from the loft onto the cabin floor. He saw the Indians in a flash as he rolled onto his side and began to stand. It was his last conscious act. Johannes's cervical spine was severed by Silver Moon's tomahawk.

Lars leaped from the loft onto Silver Moon's back. They fell to floor next to Johannes's lifeless body. The Indian's tomahawk was loose on the floor. Lars grasped it. As he raised it to strike, he was shot dead by Black Beaver.

Gustav Lindquist stood outside the door of his brother's cabin. He hesitated. It was a beautiful, serene morning, and he was reluctant to disturb Elliot and Julia. But he needed Julia's expertise. That morning, a young woman and her husband had come to the clinic from their farm near Saint Cloud.

She had been in labor for twenty hours, and it was not going well. Gustav could hear the baby's heart beating much too fast, like the wings of a hummingbird. The mother was so exhausted that she was becoming indifferent to the labor pains.

Gustav knocked and entered. He found Elliot stirring the fire, and Julia was holding William as if the youngster were an infant. Julia was singing to him in French.

"Frère Jacques, frère Jacques, dormez vous, dormez vous, sonnez les matines, sonnez les matines, din din don, din din don…"

Julia looked up.

"Gustav." She sang his name. "How nice to see you."

"Hi, Bro," Elliot said, turning away from the fire. "What brings you here this fine morning? Err. Let me guess…"

"I apologize," Gustav stammered, turning to Julia. "I'm very sorry. I have a patient…"

Julia placed William on the floor. He promptly jumped into Elliot's arms. "Don't be sorry, Gustav," Julia said. "You have a patient?"

"A young woman in labor, at the clinic. She's not doing well…"

Julia stood, "Then we should take a look, shan't we?"

"Thank you. I'd be most grateful if you would," Gustav, relieved, looked at Elliot, who nodded.

Julia touched Elliot's arm. "Shall I take William with me?"

"Yes," Elliot replied. "I'll be bringing hay in with Olaf. Robert and Carl are in Saint Cloud."

When Elliot arrived at Olaf Eriksson's farm, Britta and her daughter, Ester, were washing the breakfast dishes. Ester was fourteen, very pretty, and taller than her mother.

"Olaf's in the barn getting the horses ready," Britta said. "We haven't seen your father or brothers. They're usually here by this time."

Elliot turned and looked east along the trail that led to the Lindquist farm. No riders were in sight. But he saw a group of men on foot leave the trail and enter the cornfield about two hundred yards away. They were Indians.

"Britta," Elliot said briskly, "there's maybe a dozen Indians in your cornfield. I'm going to see what they're up to. Might be stealing."

Elliot took Olaf's shotgun from the rack above the fireplace. Once in the cornfield, he knelt and listened. He heard the rustling of leaves and stalks as the Indians came nearer.

When they were ten yards away, Elliot abruptly stood and lowered the shotgun, pointing it directly at a tall Indian whose face and body were painted with black and red stripes. Behind him were eight Indians, also painted, who swiftly darted to either side and behind. Elliot was surrounded. The lead Indian raised his tomahawk.

Britta heard a shotgun blast coming from the cornfield. She ran to the barn to find Olaf, but he had heard the shot, too, and was sitting on one of the horses.

"Elliot went into the field after some Indians!" she shouted. "He took your shotgun!"

Olaf slapped the horse's rump and headed for the cornfield at a gallop. He was unarmed. As he approached the edge of the field, four Indians with rifles emerged and fired in unison. Olaf was struck in the chest and shoulders and fell to the ground, unconscious. A fifth Indian stood over his motionless body and shot him in the face with a shotgun stolen from the Lower Sioux Agency.

Terrified by the shots, Britta grabbed Ester by the hand and ran behind the barn where they burrowed under a haystack. Unfortunately, they left a clear trail that was easy to follow by experienced hunters. As the two women gasped for breath, lying face down under a mound of hay, two pairs of hands grasped Britta's ankles and ripped her from her hiding place.

She screamed, "Hjälp! Hjälp!"

The Indians did not waste time: the tall one named Lazy Dog buried his hatchet in Britta's skull. Ester, out of sight beneath the haystack, did not move or make a sound. This prehistoric reflex saved her.

The Indians set fire to the house and barn, slaughtered the cow and oxen, and set out to the northwest toward the farm of A. P. Eriksson.

A desultory shower soaked the ground around Elliot Lindquist where he had lain unconscious. The Dakota warrior had battered him with the butt of his rifle and left him for dead. Elliot recalled discharging his shotgun in the air in a misguided attempt to frighten the Indians. He would not make that mistake again.

Slowly, painfully, he rolled onto his back and allowed the rain to wash away some of the dark blood and dirt caked on his face and neck. His tongue felt the jagged edge of a chipped incisor. He coughed and spat a piece of tooth and scarlet clot. Through swollen eyes, he saw the gray sky overhead, stippled with dark clouds.

As the mental fog cleared, Elliot remembered Britta and Ester. What happened to them? And to Olaf? He rolled onto his stomach and, using his good right arm, struggled to kneel. He paused; his balance uncertain. Minutes later he was able to stand, wobbly for sure, but he could put one foot in front of the other without stumbling. He searched the corn rows around him for the shotgun, but the Indians must have taken it.

When he emerged from the cornfield, Elliot saw the smoldering ashes of the house and barn.

"Good God," he gasped. Then he saw Olaf's body on the ground, his face decimated by the shotgun blast.

Elliot wept. "I'm sorry, Uncle. It's my fault! It's my fault!" He looked away and walked toward the mound of glowing embers that had been the barn. There he found the body of Aunt Britta, that sweet, gentle woman who did not have a mean bone in her body.

"Oh, Aunt Britta," Elliot cried aloud. "I shouldn't have left you here…This is all my mistake!" Out of the corner of his eye, he saw movement from the haystack. He drew his knife. Ester's face appeared, covered with hay and dirt. She was quietly sobbing.

"Cousin Elliot!" she cried, "I thought it was you!" Then she saw her mother on the ground. Kneeling, Ester took Britta's hand in hers and rocked back and forth. "Why did we come to this place! I want to go home! I want to go back to Sweden!" She looked pleadingly at Elliot.

Elliot knelt on the ground and placed his arms around her. She looked up at him.

"Where's Pa?" she asked.

When he grimaced and did not reply, she said, "He's gone too? He's gone too!" Elliot nodded and sighed, "You don't want to see him, Ester."

It was early afternoon. The Indians had killed all the livestock except the horse Olaf was riding when he was shot. Elliot saw it grazing in the south pasture as if nothing had happened. The bridle and blanket were still in place. Elliot thought of burying his aunt and uncle, but his left arm was practically useless. He would take Ester to Gustav and Julia, and then ride to his parents' home and warn them—if it was not too late.

After killing Merrick at the Redwood Agency, White Eagle joined the horde of Indians burning the buildings and looting the warehouses. When they finished, he and five warriors from his village decided to head north, where there were farms and villages to plunder and plenty of white people to kill.

They collected rifles, ammunition, food, and horses from the looted Lower Sioux Agency and set out in the early afternoon, heading northwest. White Eagle rode the striking black pony whose most distinctive feature was a white face.

News of the attack on the Lower Sioux Agency spread rapidly. The settlers were in a panic. They fled their homes in wagons and on horseback, leaving behind everything they owned. Toward sunset, White Eagle and his band intercepted two wagons filled with a dozen Norwegian immigrants, including women, children, and babies.

They killed all but one, mercilessly, and adorned themselves with jewelry and clothing taken from their victims. The sole survivor was a young woman, Astrid Hansen, who had been walking between the two wagons. When the attack came, she slipped off into a ditch with thick tall grass where she listened to the agonal sounds of her family's last moments on earth. The indelible images of White Eagle and his white face horse were indelibly burned into her memory.

The following morning, White Eagle and his gang rode northeast, in the direction of Gustav Lindquist's home and clinic. As they exited a dense forest of giant maple trees, a buggy appeared on the trail, heading east. In it were three people: a man, a woman, and a child with blond hair.

White Eagle recognized the man—it was Dr. Lindquist, the 'medicine man' who had allowed him to hunt his land the previous winter. White Eagle spoke sharply to his companions. "Let them go!" he barked. "He helped me in the winter. He is a medicine man."

Gustav and Julia saw the five mounted Indians. They did not know about the uprising or the terror and carnage spreading across southern Minnesota. Their only concern that morning was the woman in labor at the clinic.

Gustav said casually, "I know that Indian on the black and white horse."

When they passed over a rise, a cloud of smoke was visible on the horizon ahead. "My God!" Gustav exclaimed. "It's my house---my clinic!"

Minutes later they found the house and clinic in flames. Gustav charged into the burning clinic and dragged the smoldering body of the pregnant woman outside and went back in for her husband. Julia knelt next to the woman as Gustav pulled the burned body of her husband out of the fire. Both had been shot with arrows, stabbed, and scalped.

Gustav said, "They probably died before the fire was started."

Julia cried, "Who did this. Who would kill a woman in labor?"

"It must have been those Indians we saw," Gustav replied.

"Why didn't they come after us?" Julia stood and looked back in the direction they had come. No one was on the road, but off in the distance, there was black smoke.

"Gustav, look." She pointed to the plume of smoke drifting southeast with the wind.

"That could be my cousin's farm." He shaded his eyes with his hand. "Yes, it must be!"

Julia said, "The Indians. It's the Indians!"

"Why are they doing this?"

Julia replied, "They've been starving since winter. They're hungry, and angry. And they want their land back."

During that afternoon and evening, wagon loads of farmers and their families arrived in New Ulm downriver from Fort Ridgely. Some carried the bodies of men, women, and children who had been killed or wounded by rampaging Indians. The community was thus alerted of the Dakota Sioux uprising. Immediately, they began to organize a defense.

All able-bodied men were formed into companies and placed under the command of Captain Jacob Nix, a German immigrant from Bingen on the Rhine where he had been an officer in the Freikorps. The Turner Society, a local social and political club, provided citizen sharpshooters who had excellent rifles.

New Ulm was perched on the high ground between the Cottonwood and the Minnesota Rivers southwest of Minneapolis. Its eight hundred citizens were mostly German immigrants. That night, an assortment of residents and refugees from surrounding farms sought safety in New Ulm's three brick buildings. Nix had the men build barricades, and he inspected their weapons, an assortment of shotguns, rifles, and pistols. There was a meager supply of ammunition, especially bullets, so they melted lead during the night.

About the time Andreas and Lena Lindquist were murdered—a group of men armed with rifles and shotguns left New Ulm on a rescue mission west of the town. They found death and destruction everywhere: men, women, and children, massacred in their homes, in their barns, and in their fields. Some had been shot, others hacked to death and dismembered.

Smoke was everywhere: burning houses and outbuildings, granaries, and smoldering haystacks. The rescuers found people hiding in the woods and wetlands; these survivors had escaped the terror that befell their relatives and neighbors. Many were women and children, and many bore wounds they sustained before escaping their attackers.

Little Crow's 'army' of three hundred warriors had split and splintered. Some of them remained near Fort Ridgely, others decided to attack individual farms like the Lindquists', and a mounted band of one hundred braves headed for New Ulm. They arrived around midafternoon. The rescue parties that had been dispatched that morning had not returned, so the town was thinly defended by Captain Nix and forty armed men who were positioned behind the hastily constructed barricades.

One of New Ulm's citizen defenders was Frederick Fritsche, who had a 160-acre farm on the north side of the Minnesota River about two miles from New Ulm. Fritsche's father had brought his family to the United States to escape the unsettled conditions in Germany after the 1848 revolution.

When Fritsche learned of the attack on the Redwood Agency, he brought his family into New Ulm and joined a group of farmers from Nicollet County who called themselves the Lafayette Company.

The Indians first set fire to three houses and a brewery outside town. Then they attacked the barricades, firing rifles, shotguns, and arrows. The first person killed was a twelve-year-old girl, an only child, who had heard the shots and ran into the street looking for her mother.

Nix dispatched messengers to recall the rescue parties. While awaiting their return, he was shot in the left hand and lost his ring finger. The Indians attacked from the south and northwest. They were unsuccessful because the rescue parties arrived just in time and were able to fight their way into town and man the barricades. Nix's reinforced command repelled repeated assaults. Toward evening, the Indians withdrew during a heavy rainstorm. The first battle of New Ulm was at an end.

Elliot rode northeast toward Gustav's home. Ester sat behind him, her arms encircling his waist. His injured left arm hung nearly useless at his side; the searing pain had morphed into a gnawing ache. The sun overhead amplified the dry August heat.

When they reached higher ground, the smoke from Gustav's home was visible on the horizon. Elliot spurred his horse to a canter. Off to his right, a group of Indians emerged from a grove of pine trees. In front, on a black and white horse, was White Eagle, whom Elliot recognized from their encounter in April during the blizzard.

There was no point trying to outrun them. Elliot pulled up and watched as they approached at a gallop. Three of them were armed with rifles and two carried shotguns. Defenseless, Elliot knew his survival would depend on White Eagle. Quickly they surrounded him. White Eagle seemed to be the leader. He saw Elliot's injured arm.

"How you hurt?"

"Your brothers, White Eagle," Elliot replied evenly. "Killed my aunt and uncle and left me for dead."

"Where will you go?" White Eagle asked, motioning northeast.

Holding up his left arm, Elliot replied, "To the medicine man's house. Fix this."

"You go. Quick. With the woman. Much trouble coming."

Elliot turned toward Gustav's home, smacked his horse with the reins, and galloped away. After a quarter of a mile, without losing a stride, he turned and saw the Indians heading west, toward Kandiyohi.

At sundown on Tuesday, Minnesota Governor Alexander Ramsey crossed the river from Fort Snelling to the palatial home of Colonel Henry Sibley, who was commissioned in the state militia at the start of the Civil War.

Earlier that day Ramsey had learned of the attack on the Redwood Agency, and Marsh's defeat and death at the ferry crossing. Ramsey wanted Sibley to mount an expedition against the Indians with the troops available at Fort Snelling, mostly untrained recruits in the Sixth Minnesota Regiment.

The fifty-one-year-old Sibley was skeptical. Would he be independent of the regular army, or would he have to battle the federal bureaucrats as well as the Dakota Sioux? Taking pen to paper, Ramsey wrote out his instructions and bluntly assured Sibley that he would receive no interference from the military or the politicians.

Sibley was still lean, but his hair was thinning, and he wore the permanent look of a worrier. On this day, there was a lot to worry about: in addition to four companies of raw recruits, he found that his command had no tents, no camping equipment, no rations, and very little ammunition. Most of his soldiers had outdated rifles that were incompatible with standard US military bullets.

Nevertheless, he detailed a quartermaster to round up supplies, loaded his men on a steamboat, and headed up the Minnesota River toward Fort Ridgely. Along the way, he collected about a hundred civilian volunteers, including a group of armed riders from the Cannon River valley under Alex Faribault, a trader who once worked for Sibley.

Sibley encountered streams of refugees fleeing for their lives in the towns of Belle Plaine and Saint Peter. They described, in gruesome, graphic detail, the brutal acts committed by the Indians. Sibley and his men were outraged: they vowed to show no mercy. Most white Minnesotans would share their anger and desire for revenge. Governor Ramsey would tell the state legislature that his goal was the wholesale slaughter of the Dakota Sioux.

"If any shall escape extinction," he said, "the wretched remnant must be driven beyond our borders."

The newspapers echoed his wrath; one editorialist implored, "Exterminate the wild beasts!"

A sixty-year-old hunter, Jack Frazer, told Sibley that he had come from Fort Ridgely, where over two hundred women and children had taken refuge. The fort's thin garrison was besieged by a large group of Dakota under Little Crow.

Sibley and Little Crow knew each other from the treaty negotiations at Traverse de Sioux in 1851, when the Dakota ceded much of southern and western Minnesota to the United States in exchange for cash and an annuity. Little Crow was the first chief to sign the treaty, and Sibley was a significant beneficiary. As a creditor, he and other traders would receive a large share of the money the Dakota were promised for their land.

While Sibley wanted to relieve Fort Ridgely, he did not have the men or supplies to do it. Moreover, he was suddenly responsible for hundreds of refugees seeking safety in Saint Peter. Consequently, the troops at Fort Ridgely would have to defend the post with what they had until Sibley's command was ready to march and fight.

Fort Ridgely was no fort at all. It did not have a stockade, and its buildings were not easily defensible. Indeed, this army post was a collection of wood and stone structures sitting exposed on a bluff overlooking the Minnesota River valley.

It was flanked by wooded ravines that provided perfect cover for an attacking force. Worse, it did not have a well, and its ammunition was stored in a magazine outside the u-shaped perimeter of buildings that surrounded the parade ground.

Little Crow had wanted to attack the fort Monday afternoon after Captain Marsh's ill-fated sortie. But he was overruled by the other chiefs who instead sent their warriors to raid New Ulm, where there were unarmed people to kill and valuable goods to plunder.

When the assault on New Ulm failed Tuesday afternoon, the chiefs asked Little Crow to lead them against Fort Ridgely. He was eager to do so. The warrior in him had returned. His blood was up, his mind focused on killing, as it had been decades before when his tribe fought the Chippewa. His spirit, too, was lifted, because once again he was the war chief who would lead his people out of their nightmare.

Within Fort Ridgely's warehouses and armory were supplies of food and clothing and ammunition that could sustain the Indians for weeks while they battled the white men. There were horses, too, and cattle and oxen. Little Crow knew all this; what he did not know was that there was also $71,000 in gold coins, the tardy annuity payment the Dakota had been waiting for since spring.

Fort Ridgely's garrison was now under the command of Lieutenant Anthony J. Sheehan, a twenty-eight-year-old Irish-born farmer from southern Minnesota who had volunteered for service at the outbreak of the Civil War. He and fifty men from Company C of the Fifth Minnesota Regiment were on their way to Fort Ripley in northern Minnesota when Captain Marsh's urgent appeal recalled them.

They arrived Tuesday after a brutal forty-two-mile overnight march from their encampment south of Glencoe. Sheehan took over command from young Lieutenant Gere and ordered the construction of breastworks. Later that day more men arrived, including a group of the newly organized Renville Rangers, and a dozen armed volunteers from Saint Peter. In just a few hours, the number of Fort Ridgely's defenders had increased sixfold to 180 men. While hardly a bastion, it was no longer as vulnerable as it had been the previous day.

Shortly after noon on Wednesday, August 20, Little Crow divided his force of four-hundred warriors. Half circled the fort to the northeast, and sheltered out of sight in a ravine. Meanwhile, Little Crow diverted Sheehan's attention by assembling a group of warriors to the west of the fort, well beyond rifle range. When he thought his two hundred warriors east of the fort were in position, Little Crow signaled them to attack with a volley of three rifle shots.

The Indians burst from their concealed position in the ravine. Firing their rifles, they charged the thin picket line of soldiers guarding the fort's eastern boundary. Two soldiers were killed, and the others retreated.

It appeared that the Indians would overrun the fort. But Lieutenant Sheehan quickly wheeled his troops around and formed a battle line across the path of the advancing Indians. Sheehan's men fired into the onrushing mass, killing a few attackers and wounding others. Staggered, the Indians halted and fell back to the ravine.

The fifty or so troops in Sheehan's battle line took cover behind buildings and a crude barricade they had constructed the previous evening. The two sides exchanged rifle fire, mostly without effect. The Indians shot flaming arrows into the fort's wooden buildings. Fire erupted in the officers' quarters, but it was quickly extinguished.

Little Crow, recognizing that the surprise attack from the east had failed, ordered an assault from another ravine leading to the southwest corner of the fort. Other Indians spread around the fort's northern perimeter. Soon heavy rifle fire enveloped Sheehan's command.

As is true of most battles, a pivotal moment arrived. And one man's actions would prove to be critical. Sergeant John Jones commanded the fort's artillery. He was thirty-nine years old, an Englishman by birth, and a wounded veteran of the Mexican War. Bearded and heavyset, Jones was a stickler on training and discipline.

On this day, he was not merely defending the fort: his wife and three children lived on the post in a log cabin behind the stone barracks. If the Indians prevailed, Jones knew his family would be slaughtered.

Jones's three batteries of six-pounder cannons and twelve-pounder howitzers were attended by crews that could load, aim, and fire rapidly. They were assisted by civilian volunteers who had artillery experience. As the Indians emerged from the southwest ravine, Jones's battery fired round after round of canister, spraying the battlefield with lethal lead balls. The warriors had never been exposed to artillery fire before, and they fell back in fear and confusion. Jones and his crew had repelled the most dangerous assault of the day.

The other two batteries were positioned on the northern corners; they, too, directed fire at Little Crow's warriors attacking from the north and east. When the Indians occupied an old stable on the northeast corner, Sheehan ordered the artillery to level the building. It burst into flames after the second shell ignited the hay. Once again, the attackers retreated.

Although random fighting continued into the late afternoon, Jones's artillery so demoralized the Indians that they broke off the fight before sunset and returned to Little Crow's village. Little Crow and the other chiefs realized that the next assault on Fort Ridgely demanded a larger and better coordinated force.

Within the fort, Dr. Alfred Muller, a native of Switzerland, was attending the wounded, aided by his wife, Eliza. They would not lose a single wounded man, a credit to their skill and caring. Elsewhere, the stress of events caused a few pregnant women to go into premature labor; one of them was Sergeant Jones's wife, whose baby was stillborn. Many men and women who had taken shelter in the fort became civilian volunteers, helping the sick and wounded, cooking, delivering food and water to the soldiers, and making rifle cartridges.

Midnight marked the end of the third day of the Dakota War. It began to rain. During the downpour, an eerie wailing was heard to the west, outside the fort. Lieutenant Sheehan, thinking it was an Indian deception, fired a shot from the howitzer in the direction of the sound. It continued. Finally, he sent a patrol to find the source. They found a disoriented and distraught white woman who had lost her entire family. Her plight was shared by hundreds of refugees who huddled in the stone barracks of the still-vulnerable Fort Ridgely.

Late Tuesday afternoon, Elliot, and Gustav found the bodies of their mother, father, and brothers, lying where they had been murdered early that morning. Julia comforted the two men as they knelt sobbing in the congealed pools of dark magenta blood.

She quietly covered the bodies with bedclothing. Ester and little William were still in the wagon outside. Julia told them what had happened and brought them in. Elliot reached out and took Ester's hand; she began to cry, but there were no more tears to shed. William, sucking his thumb, stared silently at the shrouded bodies.

Minutes passed before anyone spoke.

Finally, Elliot said, "The bastards who did this…it must be the Indians…the same ones who killed Olaf and Britta. My God!" He stood and placed his good right hand on Gustav's shoulder.

Gustav moaned, "They died instantly. You can see that, from the wounds…They didn't suffer much."

"We should bury them," Julia said. "Before we leave…"

"Where're we going?" Elliot asked. "We'd be safer staying here tonight. I'd be surprised, Julia, if our place is still standing. And it's safer to keep off the roads."

Suddenly Gustav turned toward the door and placed his index finger to his lips.

"Shh," he whispered. "I heard something."

Elliot drew the Colt revolver from his belt and slowly opened the door. He raised the revolver and stepped outside. Unsheathing his knife, Gustav stood and motioned for Julia to sit on the floor behind the table with Ester and William. They heard muffled voices.

Elliot stepped through the door with two men.

"It's Robert and Carl."

Robert entered and saw the bodies on the floor.

"Oh, my God," he sighed. "Your family too."

The four men buried Andreas, Britta, Johannes, and Lars in graves next to a large sugar maple tree a hundred yards from the house. When they finished, Elliot said a brief prayer.

The sun had set, and clouds obscured the sickle moon. They stood beside the unmarked graves. It was so dark they could not see each other's faces. Minutes passed while they stared at the four mounds of earth in heartbroken silence. Julia joined them with Ester and William.

Finally, Elliot said, "Four years ago, my father and mother told us that we were going to America. They were prepared to risk everything for us so that we would have our own land—so that we would have a future." He paused, then continued, "Tomorrow we will bury my aunt and uncle. They, too, came here to secure a future for their children. And we do not yet know what's happened to A. P. and Elsa and their family." He paused once more as melancholy embraced him.

When he resumed, Elliot's voice was firm with conviction, "So now this land has our blood on it. Not just our sweat, but our blood. We must do everything we can to be certain this land will remain in our families…forever. No matter what it takes."

"Amen, cousin," Robert said.

"Amen," Gustav repeated.

Carl placed his hand on Elliot's shoulder and said, "I'm with you. We all are."

Julia was silent. She thought, "What I think would not matter now."

Three miles west of the Lindquist homestead, White Eagle and the nine members of his marauding band sat around a fire contemplating what to do with their two captives, Elsa and Ruth Eriksson. Earlier that day they killed Elsa's husband, A. P., and her sons, Rolf and Gunnar, as they were working in the fields. And they had set fire to the house and barn and slaughtered all the animals except for the Percheron.

They decided to take the two women to Little Crow's village. There they would be held captive with other women and children who could be ransomed for money or goods. White Eagle said, "Tomorrow we will join Little Crow's soldiers." And, to himself he said, "I will lie again with Mina."

The Dakota Sioux uprising spread up and down the Minnesota River valley. Hundreds of white families abandoned their homes and farms and sought safety anywhere it could be found. Fort Ridgely was overflowing with refugees, and the soldiers there were advising newcomers to seek shelter elsewhere.

Some went to New Ulm, others to Hutchinson, and many just kept moving east. Most had left everything they owned behind, and many of them would never return, preferring to abandon their homesteads rather than face terror and live in constant fear. Their land would pass to people who were willing to risk their lives and the lives of their families to make it their own.

On Wednesday morning, they buried Olaf and Britta on a knoll behind the barn. Their graves were sheltered by a grove of tall peachleaf willow trees and wetlands that extended south to Long Lake.

Afterward, Elliot, Julia, Gustav, and the two children went to their homes and salvaged what they could from the ashes. There were a few utensils, tools, and surgical instruments that survived reasonably intact. Remarkably, they found a heat-rippled photograph of Elliot and Lena that was taken before they boarded the ship to America; this they would treasure forever.

Meanwhile, Robert and Carl went to their uncle's farm and found the mutilated bodies of A. P., Rolf, and Gunnar. They did not find the remains of A. P.'s wife, Elsa, or his daughter, Ruth. Thus there was a chance they may be alive, possibly prisoners of the same Indians who had killed the men and torched the house and barn. Where would the Indians take them? To a village on the reservation? Or would they hold them to rape or ransom, or to use as shields in a future battle?

Late that afternoon, the survivors of the Lindquist and Eriksson families returned to Andreas and Lena's farm—the only homestead with its buildings still intact. Exhausted, they sat around the long table where many meals had been served and where so many plans had been laid. Those were the bygone days of optimism, of the joy of being in America, and of the knowledge that their land would support their families for generations. How quickly their lives and futures had changed.

Now life was all about survival. And it was not just surviving the Indian violence. They had to bring in the harvest to make it through the winter. Soon the hay would be ready for cutting, the corn for picking, and the wheat had to be scythed and transported to the mill.

At last, Julia said, "I'll see what's in the root cellar and try to make us some dinner. Elliot, please bring in some water and build a fire."

Julia managed to prepare a decent stew, using Lena's spices. They ate in silence, too despondent and fatigued to fashion a conversation. William was the hungriest, and he gobbled every morsel. Ester only nibbled, her appetite s by the blackness that enveloped her.

When they finished, Elliot, sitting at the head of the table in Andreas's chair, said, "I think we should go to Hutchinson tomorrow. We're not safe here."

"What about the crops, Elliot? We have to get the hay in…" Robert asked.

"I'm thinking we get Julia and the children settled in Hutchinson and come back," Elliot replied.

Gently Julia placed her hand on Elliot's forearm and said, "The devil with the crops, Elliot. We've lost most of the animals, so we won't need as much hay next winter as you did the last." She glanced at each of the four men.

"Your lives are more important than corn or wheat. We'll survive somehow, but not with any one of you dead or crippled! The land's not going anywhere. It will be here after this trouble is over." Picking up her plate, she stood and looked down at her husband.

All eyes shifted to Elliot. He smiled briefly and nodded his agreement. "You're right, of course." Turning to Robert, he asked, "What about the wheat?"

"I bit down on a few kernels last Sunday," Robert replied, "they were still a little chewy. And the seeds aren't bowing. So we can let the wheat dry down for a while." Robert nudged Carl with his elbow. "What do you think?"

Carl Eriksson was his brother's opposite. Big and sturdy with red hair and beard, he could have been a mythical Viking except that he was temperate and slow to anger. "The wheat's not near ready," he replied. "I think it'll be another two weeks."

Gustav listened to his brother and cousins. The conversation was a replay of many such discussions he had heard growing up in a farm family. Weather, crops, seed, soil, and markets: these were the topics for hours of serious talk around the dinner table. It was part of every son's education. Gustav would miss hearing Andreas, Olaf, and A. P. engage in friendly and often vigorous agrarian debates.

When the talk drifted to chit-chat, Gustav said matter-of-factly, "We should look for Elsa and Ruth."

Elliot pushed his chair back from the table and crossed his legs. "How do you propose we do that?"

"Well, for starters," Gustav replied, "we can get word to the army or militia. Give 'em their names and tell them what happened. I could follow the army as it puts down this uprising. If Elsa and Ruth are alive, the Indians may give them up to save themselves. Besides, the army may need a doctor for the wounded."

Again, the men looked at Elliot, who was staring at Gustav, obviously weighing his brother's proposal. It was true that Gustav would never be able to do heavy labor in the fields; his legs had never fully recovered after breaking his back. In that sense, he would not be missed. Elliot asked himself: What would my father say in this circumstance? He did not know. He glanced at Julia.

She took the cue and said, "I think what Gustav says is reasonable. We owe it to Elsa and Ruth---and their family."

That settled the matter.

Elliot said, "When we get to Hutchinson tomorrow, Gustav will go to the authorities and see what can be done."

Then he turned to Robert and Carl, "We'll bury your family in the morning."

Chapter 6

He was the son of Enapay and Tika and they named him Tawachi. But for all his life he was Chaska, the Dakota Sioux name for first-born son. After the treaty of 1851, Enapay moved his family from their village north of the Minnesota River to the ten-mile-wide strip of reservation land south of the river. There Enapay took up farming and built a frame house at La qui Parle with the help of Reverend Stephen Riggs, a Presbyterian missionary from Ohio who moved to Minnesota with his wife Mary in 1837.

Chaska worked in the fields next to his father, planting corn and potatoes. In the spring and fall, they fished, hunted ducks and deer, and gathered wild rice. Life, however, was difficult for all Dakota. Many of the fine government promises codified in the 1851 treaty were not kept at all or were only partly fulfilled. While Chaska's family rarely experienced hunger, most of the tribe was undernourished because the government failed to deliver the promised food for winter or the seed for planting in the spring.

During the winter of 1854, Enapay was killed near Fort Ridgely while visiting his cousin Little Crow. The perpetrators were Chippewa who were seeking revenge for a raid by Dakota warriors on their village in Mille Lacs. Their target was Little Crow, who was slightly wounded, but Enapay was caught in the crossfire and fatally shot.

Soldiers from Fort Ridgely captured seven of the Chippewa raiders and incarcerated them at the fort. A mob of angry Dakota men tried unsuccessfully to storm the fort and kill the Chippewa, who were eventually released and returned to their village.

Young Chaska took his father's place as head of the family. Abruptly he was responsible for his mother and sister. At the age of sixteen, he was nearly six feet tall, well-muscled, and his broad smile reflected a friendly nature. His black hair was cut short, and he usually wore a collarless long-sleeve cotton shirt, trousers with braces, and leather boots.

On the Sabbath, Chaska and his family attended religious services. Afterward they mingled with local Christian Dakota, missionaries, and mixed bloods. All of them were attempting to build a peaceful, sustainable community.

A month after Enapay's death, Reverend Rigg's home burned down when his young son accidentally set fire to the dry hay that insulated the root cellar. The fire spread to other houses and buildings and within an hour all the mission's wood buildings, including Chaska's home, were piles of glowing coals and ashes.

Only the adobe church was spared. Almost immediately they started clearing the rubble and fashioning materials for rebuilding. It was a slow process: the one whipsaw was all they had to make boards and timbers, and they were too remote to receive meaningful help from other Christian missions.

The decision was made to abandon La qui Parle and move closer to the Upper Sioux Agency at Yellow Medicine. This they did during the summer, creating a new settlement down river that they named Hazelwood. Log cabins were built, and by fall the Christian Dakotas declared themselves the Hazelwood Republic.

Its members were farmer Dakotas who spoke English and adopted the white man's dress. They were designated a separate band by the Indian agent. Chaska and his family were delighted to join this forward-looking community whose goal was to be self-sufficient and independent of government annuities.

During the next seven years Hazelwood grew and prospered. Log cabins were replaced by frame homes. The Hazelwood Republic was governed by a president and elected officers. Many Dakota Christians applied for Minnesota citizenship. A mission boarding school was built, and teachers recruited. Although he was just a teenager, Chaska was invited to attend council meetings.

When Chaska turned twenty, he was given a Bible by the American Board of Commissioners for Foreign Missions upon the recommendation of Reverend Riggs.

As he handed the book to Chaska, Riggs said, "I hope you will set aside time every day---and particularly on the Sabbath---to read. I recommend you begin with the New Testament. Mrs. Riggs and I read the Bible aloud every Sunday afternoon, and then we select two or three verses to discuss over dinner. You are welcome to join us if you wish."

Not only did Chaska join the Riggs on the Sabbath, but he also taught a Bible class for the children of Hazelwood. He was especially fond of the Gospels: Matthew, Mark, Luke, and John. In each book was told a teaching or an incident in the life of Jesus Christ.

Matthew spoke of the Resurrection when angels rolled back the boulders covering the opening to the Savior's tomb; Mark traveled with Apostle Paul and stayed with Apostle Peter while he was in prison; Luke told of the Savior's birth, information he probably obtained from Mary herself; and John wrote of John the Baptist and Jesus's divine nature as the Son of God.

While Chaska had sexual relations as a youth, he privately adopted a life of celibacy at Hazelwood. Teaching on the Sabbath was his passion. Each week he prepared a new lesson based on his readings of the Bible and discussions with Reverend Riggs and other missionaries. By 1862, he was teaching the New Testament at the boarding school.

There he met Dr. John Wakefield and his wife Sarah who were considering enrolling their two children. Dr. Wakefield was the Upper Sioux Agency physician. The hefty Sarah was unusual for a white woman because she learned the Dakota language and often visited with Dakota women in their villages and wigwams. She told Chaska that she hoped he would teach the Bible to her children when they were old enough.

Shortly after noon on Monday, August 18, Chaska was riding to Yellow Medicine when he was overtaken by four mounted Dakota men painted for war and led by Hapa, his brother-in-law.

"Join us, Chaska!" Hapa shouted. "We're going to kill all the whites at Yellow Medicine!"

Chaska reined his horse. It was obvious they had been drinking whiskey. He shouted, "Why do you want to do this?"

"We're at war!" Hapa replied, slurring the words. "Little Crow attacked the Lower Agency at Redwood this morning. Killed 'em all. Traders! Missionaries! Every white face! We'll do the same at Yellow Medicine!"

"That's madness, Hapa!" Chaska shouted. "You've had whiskey, you're not thinking straight. You'll die! And turn the whites against us all!"

As his three companions galloped off, Hapa grabbed Chaska's rein. "When we join up with Little Crow, there is no one who can stop us! Now is the time to take back our land! Make up your mind! Now! Are you with us? Yes or no?"

Reluctantly, Chaska replied, "I'll ride with you."

The two men cantered toward Yellow Medicine. In the distance, on the road, they spotted a wagon drawn by a team of horses heading southeast. Hapa urged his mount to a gallop and Chaska followed. Within minutes, they overtook the wagon. It was driven by George Gleason, a clerk at the Lower Agency warehouse.

Sitting behind him was Sarah Wakefield holding her infant daughter Lucy and next to her was four-year-old James. They had departed Yellow Medicine at the behest of Dr. Wakefield who thought his family would be safer at Fort Ridgely while he remained at the Upper Agency. On the way, they learned from a trader that a group of Mdewakanton Dakota had killed people in the Big Woods. Indians at both agencies were in council to decide if they should attack all whites and either kill them or drive them from the Great Spirit's ancestral lands.

Upon hearing this, Sarah implored Gleason to return home. He chided her, saying the real danger was behind them. Yet the road was strangely empty. Ordinarily they should have encountered riders and wagons, but none were seen for over an hour. And it was eerily quiet. The more Sarah pleaded with Gleason to turn back, the more steadfast he became.

"Mrs. Wakefield," he said, "I will never drive you anywhere again." When they saw black smoke on the horizon, Gleason breezily dismissed it as a prairie fire.

Sarah's fear was escalating when Hapa and Chaska rode up. For some reason, Gleason halted the wagon. Without a word, Hapa shot him in the shoulder. He fell backward into Sarah's lap, where Hapa shot him again in the belly. Terrified, the horses reared up, catapulting Gleason out of the wagon onto the ground. Then the horses bolted and galloped a hundred yards before Chaska managed to bring them under control.

Chaska recognized Sarah, who was trembling uncontrollably.

"Mrs. Wakefield," he said, "that Indian is drunk. His blood is up. Do not speak. Let me do the talking." He leaped from his horse onto the wagon and, taking the reins, steered it back to where Gleason was writhing on the ground clutching his belly.

Gleason exclaimed, "Oh my God, Mrs. Wakefield!" Instantly Hapa raised his rifle and killed him with a single shot to the head.

The two children clutched their mother and began to cry. Their high-pitched shrieks unsettled Hapa. He pointed his rifle at Sarah and shouted, "She must die! The children too! All whites are better dead!"

Chaska inserted himself between Sarah and the barrel of Hapa's rifle. Quietly, he said, "No, Hapa, she is the wife of the Yellow Medicine doctor, who helps us. We will take her and the children to my home."

Hapa stared silently at Sarah, and slowly lowered his rifle. "You can do what you want. I'm going to Yellow Medicine." He stepped back and turned, as if to leave. Suddenly he re-cocked the rifle, took aim at Sarah's bosom, then pointed the barrel skyward and pulled the trigger. Sarah fainted. The children resumed their shrieking.

Hapa grinned, mounted his horse, and galloped north screaming, "Aaagh! Aaagh!"

Sarah moaned, opened her eyes and sat up with Chaska's assistance. Still sobbing, she did her best to comfort her children.

Chaska said, "I will take you to my house in Hazelwood where my mother and sister live. But it may be too risky to stay there. I will ask Little Paul."

Little Paul was Paul Mazakutermani, an articulate Christian Dakota at Hazelwood who in the days ahead would organize the Dakota Peace Party and devote himself to protecting the white women and children captured by the rampaging Dakota warriors.

He advised Chaska to abandon his house at Hazelwood and take his family and Sarah Wakefield and her children northwest to Red Iron's village. Chaska collected his mother and sister, and the six of them arrived at Red Iron's village the following morning. For the next six weeks, they would live in a tepee.

Chapter 7

News of the slaughter at the Lower Sioux Agency reached Hutchinson Monday afternoon. A teacher, William Pendergast, resolved to defend his town against an attack by the Indians. He formed the Hutchinson Guards and began to recruit volunteers by circulating an agreement to be signed by men willing to enlist.

Pendergast was twenty-nine years old, and he had traveled from New England to Minnesota in 1855 with the Hutchinson brothers, who were members of the Hutchinson Family Singers, a popular four-part harmony group that toured the country. The brothers were staunch abolitionists, and they championed other causes, including temperance and women's suffrage. The town they founded was on the Crow River, sixty miles west of Minneapolis. Pendergast became Hutchinson's first teacher and also served as probate judge.

At first, few men responded to Prendergast's call for volunteers. Most of them simply wanted to load their wagons and flee east to the safety of Minneapolis and Saint Paul. But three women wanted to stay and defend their town.

They were Julia Ells, Ellen Pendergast Harrington, and Sarah Harrington, and they appealed to the men to stand and fight. Their resolve emboldened Hutchinson's citizens, and soon the Hutchinson Guards was signing up volunteers, gathering weapons, and building a stockade.

The Lindquists and Erikssons arrived in Hutchinson late Friday afternoon. Their two wagons were drawn by oxen, followed by Gustav in the buggy and Elliot riding his Percheron. Their twenty-mile journey was slowed by heavy summer downpours that turned the dirt road into a muddy bog.

Along the way, they saw more farms that had been looted and burned. They encountered no Indians because Little Crow was assembling a large force to resume the attack on Fort Ridgely.

Hutchinson came into view as they descended the bluff above the town. It was bustling with activity. Log houses were being dissembled so the beams could be used for the stockade. A rectangular trench had been dug, and ten-foot log beams were being inserted vertically to form the stockade's walls.

They halted next to the stockade. Elliot spoke to a distinguished man in collarless white shirt and high-waisted trousers who appeared to be in charge of the work party.

"Pardon, sir," Elliot said. "We just came in from up north. Indians killed most of our family. We'd like to shelter here."

"I'm William Pendergast." They shook hands. "I'm sorry to hear of your loss. Terrible, just terrible."

Elliot introduced the rest of the family, and asked, "Is there a convenient place for our wagons, sir?"

A young woman in a brown dress with wide pagoda sleeves came rushing up to Pendergast and said, "Sorry to interrupt, William, but there's a Captain Whitcomb over there on the other side of the stockade with a wagon full of muskets and ammunition from Governor Ramsey. He's headed for Forest City, but I think he should leave some of those weapons with us. Will you speak to him?"

"Yes, of course," Pendergast replied and, gesturing toward the wagons, said, "Mrs. Ells, may I introduce the Lindquist and Eriksson families. They're looking for a place to stay in their wagons."

Mrs. Ells said, "I'll take care of them while you deal with Whitcomb."

Pendergast nodded. "Good, thank you."

"I'm Julia Ells, and my home is over there. You can park your wagons in my yard. There should be plenty of room. I would then ask you men to sign on with the Hutchinson Guards. William Pendergast is the sergeant."

By sundown, the Lindquists and Erikssons were camped in the Ells' yard, and the horses and oxen were turned out to graze. Julia Ells's husband, David, invited them into the house for a glass of switchel, and it was here that Elliot, Robert, Gustav, and Carl formally became members of the Hutchinson Guards.

They signed the agreement in the presence of William Pendergast, who said, "The stockade is finished. We're posting guards around it. You will have guard duty. Two hours on, four hours off. Captain Whitcomb left us thirty-one new rifles and a thousand rounds of ammunition. Each of you will be given a rifle. Do you know how to use it?"

"We do," Elliot replied, "but it would be well for us to have some instruction in case we are not familiar with the particular model." Pointing to Gustav, Elliot said, "My brother Gustav is a physician, and Julia is a midwife. Perhaps they can be of some help."

Pendergast said. "Excellent. Excellent! Gustav, I'll introduce you to Doctor Benjamin. He's an Englishman. Brought his family into the stockade today. And Mrs. Lindquist, many expectant mothers have come into town the past few days. They may well need your skills."

Fifty miles south of Hutchinson, Fort Ridgely was overcrowded with civilian refugees and the soldiers and volunteers were bracing for another attack. After beating back the first assault on Wednesday, Lieutenant Sheehan focused his anger on the civilian volunteers and the few soldiers who had deserted their posts during the fight. He lined them up on the parade ground and gave them such an irreverent tongue lashing that it startled even the most profane among them.

By Friday, Sheehan's defense was better prepared. He demolished some outbuildings that the Indians might use for cover during an attack. He organized rifle squads and assigned them to defend a specific sector. And he ordered the sergeants to shoot any man who deserted his post.

Inside the fort's magazine, brave and tireless women were making cartridges and molding bullets, and a creative blacksmith was fashioning rodlike shells that made a terrifying screeching sound when fired from a rifle.

Sheehan's most pressing problem was water. The Indians had fiendishly polluted both springs north and south of the fort. Sheehan decided to dig a well in the parade ground, a task that should have been done when the fort was built. It took more than twelve hours, but by 2:30 a.m. Friday morning, it was completed, and water was flowing.

Little Crow assembled a large force of eight hundred warriors, which now included a few Indians from the Sisseton and Wahpeton tribes. Early Friday morning they left Little Crow's village and arrived at Fort Ridgely around noon. The plan of attack was identical to the failed assault on Wednesday except that there were twice as many warriors. As before, the signal for the attack was to be a volley of three rifle shots.

The Indians were waiting for the signal when a rider appeared from the northeast. It was Eliphalet Richardson, a white militiaman from Glencoe who wanted to know what was happening at Fort Ridgely. A warrior, Wahehna, shot him off his horse and then killed him with two more shots as the Richardson tried to crawl away.

Many Indians thought these three shots were the signal to attack, and they charged the fort. Others either did not hear the shots or were not yet in position. Thus, once again, Little Crow's assault was disjointed.

The attack would succeed if all Little Crow's warriors could charge the fort at once. In hand-to-hand battle, the sheer number of attackers would have overwhelmed the fort's defenders. But a coordinated attack was prevented by the confusion created by the three shots that killed Richardson and by the artillery and rifle fire that splintered the mass of Indians assaulting the fort from the north and east. So, early in the battle, Little Crow lost the advantage of superior numbers.

Around four in the afternoon, Little Crow concentrated his forces in the southwest ravine. A member of the Renville Rangers spotted this activity. Many Rangers were mixed bloods and had volunteered to serve in the Union Army. This Ranger told Sergeant Jones he was certain that the Indians were about to charge their position. Jones hurriedly loaded his artillery pieces with double-shotted canister and shells containing lead balls.

Only minutes later, hundreds of Indians charged out of the southwest ravine and breached the four-foot-high wood barricade. The Rangers fell back behind the artillery, firing their rifles and shotguns. Then Jones gave the order for the artillery to open fire. The cannister and shot decimated the Indian's front ranks. Many brave warriors were killed instantly, cut to pieces, and many more suffered mortal wounds.

With their momentum broken, the warriors retreated. Jones continued his cannonade, and Sheehan's soldiers and the Renville Rangers advanced, firing their rifles and driving the Indians back to the ravine. Not only was Little Crow's second attack a failure, but he was wounded and taken from the battlefield.

Although neither side knew it, this day's assault on Fort Ridgely would be the last. Little Crow and the other chiefs realized they could not overcome the fort's canons with the flesh of their men. They shifted their strategy and redirected their strikes to two towns that did not have artillery: New Ulm and Hutchinson.

Blood matted Elsa Eriksson's blond hair. Her scalp had been split when an Indian with a knurled ear struck her with the blunt end of his tomahawk. When she awoke, lying on the ground, her head was in the lap of her daughter, Ruth, who was crying.

She sobbed, "Mother, they killed father, and Rolf, and Gunnar."

Gradually, Elsa's senses returned, and she saw black smoke billowing into the cloudless sky.

"What, what did you say?" she asked her daughter.

"The Indians killed father and Rolf and Gunnar!" Ruth repeated. "They're lying out there, in the wheat field. And they set fire to the house and barn."

"Min Gud," Elsa said in Swedish.

"Min Gud." Hugging her daughter, she released a torrent of tears.

White Eagle stood over the two women. At first, he was inclined to kill them, as he had done to so many white people during the last forty-eight hours. His hesitancy was due, in part, to weariness: the adrenaline had subsided, and with it his lust for blood.

Also, illogically, White Eagle thought that sparing these women might stand him in good stead with the white men if for some reason the uprising failed. Or he may be able to exchange them for something of value. He gestured for the women to stand. They would be his hostages.

White Eagle and his companions had collected a lot of stolen property. They had three wagons loaded with a variety of items: firearms, tools, furniture, china, food, and a piano. Now they had two captives. It was time to remove the loot to their villages on the south bank of the Minnesota River. There they would unburden themselves and rejoin Little Crow.

The Indians set out, heading south. Elsa and Ruth sat in the lead wagon, their hands and arms tightly bound by strips of deerskin. The road was littered with items that settlers had discarded as they fled to safety: bedsteads, chairs, pots, and clothing. They passed by the mutilated bodies of a family—a white man and woman and two children—lying in a ditch. Flies swarmed about the corpses. The smell of decomposing flesh caused Ruth to vomit. Her captors laughed.

Elsa, fearful of making a sound, cried inwardly. Her family was shattered. No one had anticipated the violence. Who or what had angered the natives? Why did they kill A. P. and her sons? Where were they taking her and Ruth? She resolved to save her daughter. It began to rain; now they could shed tears without being noticed.

On they went, through the summer downpour, until sundown when the Indians stopped by a creek. White Eagle gave the women water and a small pot of dried corn mixed with molasses. After they finished, he tied their ankles to a wagon wheel.

In the gloom of evening, the mosquitoes became more numerous and ravenous; they were especially attracted to the women whose arms were exposed. Elsa was uncomfortable, but Ruth was allergic to the mosquitoes' saliva. Each bite produced a red wheal that itched. Ruth scratched until they bled. At last, White Eagle roughly smeared a foul-smelling grease on her face and arms; it relieved her agony, and she was grateful.

Elsa awoke before dawn. In the blackness, she prayed that the tragedy of the last twenty-four hours was an awful nightmare. Then she heard Ruth mumbling in her sleep. Suddenly Ruth cried out, chilling shrieks that woke the Indians. White Eagle shook her until she awoke and stopped screaming. Her mother reached out and took her hand.

"Ruth, älsking," Elsa said. "We can't provoke them. If we are going to make it through this, we can't be troublesome."

Ruth choked back a sob. "I know…I know."

They arrived at Little Crow's village Friday evening as warriors were returning from their unsuccessful attack on Fort Ridgely. Elsa and Ruth were taken to a crude wood shelter that held two dozen or more white women and children; all of them were captured after the Indians murdered their husbands, fathers, and sons.

The prisoners were a pathetic lot: exhausted, dirty, and terrified. Some had suffered wounds that were festering. A half dozen children were sick with fever and rashes. One woman had given birth to a boy that morning, and another was in labor, attended by an elderly squaw.

Late into the night, Elsa, Ruth, and the other prisoners were aware of furious activity in the village. Tepees were taken down and packed onto horses and into wagons. Warriors, newly armed with stolen rifles and ammunition, were test-firing them.

The sporadic shooting caused fear and confusion. Fights broke out over the ownership of plundered goods. Around midnight a new group of prisoners— forty women, children, and a few men—were brought to the village in wagons. The woman in labor gave birth to a stillborn girl.

At dawn, Elsa, awake and anxious, watched a large band of warriors, perhaps four hundred, leaving the camp heading east. Their destination was New Ulm. A kind German couple gave Elsa and Ruth some food. At midmorning, the prisoners were herded onto the road. They and most of the village began marching northwest toward the Upper Sioux Agency at Yellow Medicine.

After New Ulm survived the first attack on Tuesday, the town was reinforced by Captain Charles Flandrau and two hundred men from Saint Peter and Le Sueur County. Flandrau, a lawyer in civilian life, had enlisted in the Union Army to fight the Indians.

Additional men came into New Ulm during the next two days, and Flandrau was selected to command the defense. He had over three hundred poorly armed farmers and townspeople. Most had short-range shotguns, a few had rifles, and some had only axes and pitchforks.

Many of the men who came to New Ulm's defense had left their families unprotected on farms or in small nearby communities. When these men realized that their families could be in peril, they returned home with or without Flandrau's permission.

On Saturday, with his force depleted, Flandrau learned that Indians had been spotted coming his way. They were burning farm buildings north of the river in the direction of Fort Ridgely. Flandrau, thinking the Indians were about to attack him from the north, ordered Captain William Huey to take seventy-five men, including a squad from the Lafayette Company, and cross the river on the ferry and patrol the north bank.

Corporal Frederick Fritsche and his men of the Lafayette Company were reluctant to leave New Ulm, where their families and more than a thousand other refugees had taken shelter. But Flandrau insisted, and Fritsche and his men accompanied Huey. After reaching the north bank, Huey's citizen soldiers encountered a dozen Indians and drove them off with rifle fire.

Then they heard shooting coming from New Ulm and returned to the riverbank. A large group of Indians was on the south bank. Outnumbered and cut off from New Ulm, Huey ordered his men to withdraw and march east toward Saint Peter. Exhausted and hungry, Fritsche and the other members of the Lafayette Company were compelled to follow.

Meanwhile, Little Crow's main force approached New Ulm from the prairie west of town. Facing them was a line of citizen soldiers that Flandrau had formed well beyond the barricades. He intended to stop the Indians outside the town, where so many women and children sheltered in buildings and cellars. However, this was a tactical mistake, because his men were in the open, without even a tree for cover. Seeing their opportunity, the attackers yelled a fearsome war cry and charged the exposed defenders. Flandrau's men wavered and fell back, ineffectively discharging their pistols and shotguns.

The Le Sueur Tigers from Tyrone Township did not run. Most of them were Irish immigrants, and they had rifles. They held their ground until outflanked and exposed to enfilading fire. During the battle, the Tigers lost six men, who were fathers to thirteen children.

The Indians could have overrun the town, but they decided to occupy buildings rather than continue the assault. Thus they lost momentum and gave the defenders precious time to recover and man the barricades in the center of town. The battle became fragmented, morphing into individual skirmishes along the barricades and in houses surrounding the town.

Inexplicably, the Indians set fire to the homes and buildings they occupied, a reckless tactic since they lost their cover. Flandrau ordered the burning of all buildings that obscured his soldiers' line of fire. In midafternoon, about sixty warriors advanced behind the smoke and once again charged the town. This time, Flandrau's men did not waver. They met the attack head-on and drove the attackers back.

The fighting died off late in the afternoon and ceased altogether with nightfall. During the night, which was cool and dry, Flandrau told his men to destroy all buildings outside the barricades that could provide cover for the enemy.

Inside the barricades, Dr. William Mayo—the father of the Mayo brothers—and several other physicians tended to the wounded and sick. Disease was spreading among the unwashed refugees confined in unventilated spaces. Unspoiled food was running low, and drinkable water was scarce.

The Indians reappeared in the hazy light of a beautiful sunrise. They fired a few shots at a distance but did not mount an attack. At noon, a relieving force of a hundred men from Saint Peter crossed the river to New Ulm. Among them were Frederick Fritsche and men of the Lafayette Company, who had been cut off at the beginning of the battle. They found their families exhausted but unharmed.

The second battle of New Ulm came to an end. The citizen-soldier defenders had lost thirty-four men killed and sixty wounded. The Indians, having squandered another opportunity, suffered many killed and wounded, but the actual number was unknown.

New Ulm itself was unlivable. Many homes were in ashes; fire destroyed one-hundred ninety of New Ulm's two-hundred thirty buildings. Its tired and hungry citizens loaded the sick and injured and whatever possessions they had into over a hundred wagons and headed for Mankato thirty miles away.

The New Ulm refugees arrived safely in Mankato the following day.

The Indians traveled north, toward the Yellow Medicine River and the Upper Sioux Agency, where they had sent their families and white hostages—including Elsa and Ruth Eriksson.

Chief Running Bear moved his small village north, away from the Minnesota River valley. Like so many older Dakota Sioux, he disapproved of the uprising and was disappointed that such a prominent chief as Little Crow would bow to the warriors' lodges and lead it.

A few of the young men in his village, including White Eagle, had joined Little Crow and were on the warpath against the white settlers. When he learned of the atrocities, Running Bear realized that it was time to seek safety well away from the mayhem.

As he led his village north, Running Bear saw smoke coming from burning homes and farms, and he saw the bodies of white settlers and their children bloating in the summer heat. He realized there would be terrible revenge once the whites mobilized their soldiers. As chief, it was his duty and responsibility to protect his people. But he did not know how he would do this.

Running Bear had hunted often in the Big Woods north of Hutchinson. Game had been plentiful, but the trappers and settlers had overhunted it, and now game was scarce. The many lakes, however, were full of fish—walleye, northern pike, bass, and sunfish. And the lake waters also produced wild rice that was tasty and nutritious. Running Bear always savored the wild rice and molasses dish that Weayaya prepared.

At last, they reached the oval lake where Running Bear had fished so often, even in the winter, when he netted fish through holes bored in the ice. Here the villagers set up their tepees. All about them were tall trees—mostly elm, basswood, and red oak—that sheltered them from the sun and imparted a sense of security. Running Bear told the men not to fire their muskets and disclose their presence. Instead, they would use the bow and arrow for hunting.

Late in the afternoon, Mina was collecting berries when she heard dry brush snapping behind her. She turned and saw White Eagle on his white-faced black pony. He signaled for her not to speak and slid off the horse. Quietly they embraced, and White Eagle led her to a cluster of dogwoods, where they sat facing each other.

"My father is very angry with you," Mina said, her smile becoming a frown. "All of us fear what will happen when the Great Father sends his soldiers to punish the Dakota for what Little Crow has done to his white children."

"We will kill them all!" White Eagle growled softly. "Everywhere, they run like chickens!" He stood, clenching both fists. "Tomorrow, I will rejoin Little Crow. We will attack Hutchinson town and kill everyone!"

Kneeling, he looked into Mina's dark eyes and said, "When this war is over, I will ask Running Bear for permission for us to marry. And I will have my own tribe—warriors like me—and you will be my wife and have many children."

It was only ten nights ago that she had lain with this magnificent young warrior, whom she had loved for as long as she could remember. She could not know that their child, a boy, was forming in her womb.

"Father will never allow you to marry me," she whispered. "But I will marry you anyway, and follow you anywhere, and have your children."

They made love, more passionately than before. As White Eagle climaxed, a salvo of rifle shots erupted from the direction of Running Bear's camp. They heard screams and more gunfire. Mina began to speak, but White Eagle gently placed his hand over her mouth. After a few minutes, the firing stopped, and there was an ominous silence.

White Eagle whispered, "Stay here."

Leaving his pony behind, White Eagle carefully used the abundant foliage of midsummer to conceal his approach to the oval lake where Running Bear had taken his village. He camouflaged himself with grass and leaves and crawled through a wetland to a clearing on the south side of the lake.

He heard volleys of gunshots and angry white voices. Women were screaming and children crying. At the edge of the clearing, he saw a mounted soldier in a blue uniform. Around him were the bloody, lifeless bodies of

Indian men, women, and children, including Running Bear and Weayaya. A dozen soldiers were setting fire to the tepees.

The soldier on the horse bellowed and pointed his saber toward the wetlands where White Eagle was hiding. "See if anyone is in there!" he ordered. Three soldiers raised their rifles and approached White Eagle's hiding place. The young warrior unsheathed his knife. If he had to die, he would draw blood first.

One soldier was in the lead. He had the shoulder stripes of a regular army sergeant, and he was carrying an M1855 Springfield rifle with a long bayonet. White Eagle sprang forward and charged the sergeant, who expertly dodged sideways and swung the butt of his rifle in an arc that caught the warrior on his chin. White Eagle groaned and dropped like a stone.

"Run him through, Sergeant!" a soldier behind him shouted.

"No! He's my prisoner. I'll bet he's one of them that killed those folks at the Lower Agency. The murderin' sonofabitch is goin' to stand trial and hang."

After an hour, when White Eagle did not appear, Mina returned to the lake. There she found her mother and father lying in pools of crimson, congealed blood. Around her were the bodies of the old men, women, and children of their small tribe. The light breeze carried smoke from the blackened remnants of seven tepees. The soldiers had taken everything of value, including all the food. Only a few clay pots remained, and they were empty. White Eagle must have been captured, or his body carried off.

Mina sat between her mother and father and sobbed, her body swaying with the agony of her grief. Toward evening, she dragged the bodies of her parents to a group of tall evergreens and covered them with a layer of wild lavender rhododendrons. It was all she could do. There were no stones or rocks to protect them from the carrion eaters.

She ate some berries and managed to catch a bass with a fishing line Running Bear kept in a deerskin pouch. The fish she ate raw, fearful that smoke from a fire might be seen. At sundown, she sat on a rock ledge by the lake and soaked her feet in the cool water. The air was warm, and there was no breeze.

Eventually she lay back, staring at the stars, wondering what she would do in the morning. I have no food or clothing, she said to herself. I don't know where I am and have no idea where I could find my mother's tribe, if they are still alive. Abruptly, she sat up, and covered her face with her hands, crying disconsolately. '*And,*' she thought, '*I feel different inside.*' What's wrong with me? She laid down again and closed her eyes.

The birds woke Mina at dawn. She caught another fish and cooked it over a fire that she started by expertly twirling a stick between her palms until it produced flame from a slab of dry maple.

The massacre of Chief Running Bear's village was a prelude to the revenge sought by Governor Alexander Ramsey. Soon he would call a special session of the legislature and proclaim that his avowed policy was the wholesale slaughter of the Dakota Sioux. He declared that all Indians, friend or foe, would be forcibly expelled from the state. His anger was shared by most white Minnesotans.

"Do not wait to be hunted by the savages," one editorialist wrote. "Exterminate the wild beasts. Never let it be said that whole settlements were given up to a few lousy, lazy, savages."

Chapter 8

After Colonel Sibley arrived at Fort Ridgely, he dispatched 170 men to bury the dead at the Lower Agency and rebuild the ferry across the Minnesota River. The senior officer was Major Joseph R. Brown, a member of the state militia and Indian agent familiar with the Dakota Sioux.

The detail included Captain Hiram Grant, who commanded a green seventy-five-man company of the Sixth Minnesota Volunteers, Captain Joseph Anderson, a veteran of the Mexican War, who led fifty mounted men of the Cullen Guards and nineteen teamsters and their wagons.

Accompanying them were a dozen civilians, including Nathan Myrick, whose brother's heart had been cleaved by White Eagle's scythe during the attack on the Lower Sioux Agency, and Thomas Galbraith, the Indian agent who that summer had refused food to the starving Dakota.

The ferry crossing was fourteen miles away. The entire route was a scene of horror: decomposing bodies of men, women, and children, and the personal detritus of people fleeing in panic. At the ferry, they found and buried thirty-three men of Captain Marsh's ill-fated command.

The following morning Major Brown and the Cullen Guards crossed the river to the Lower Sioux Agency and buried more victims. Nathan Myrick found and buried his brother. Then they rode to Little Crow's deserted village, where they collected souvenirs from the chief's house. During all this activity, they did not see a single live human being.

Meanwhile, Captain Grant's troops on the north side of the river buried more victims, including entire families. It was a grim task because the corpses were bloated and covered with maggots. One woman and her two children had been shot and thrown onto a feather bed that had been set afire.

At Beaver Creek, they found and rescued a wounded woman, Justina Krieger, who had managed to survive without food. She and her family were members of the Sacred Heart German community. The Indians had killed her husband and two children. As Justina fled from her burning farmhouse, she was shot in the back, stripped of her clothes, and her abdomen slashed. After the Indians left her for dead, she managed to stay alive by eating berries. Grant dressed her wounds, placed her in a wagon, and lead his command eastward to Fort Ridgely.

In the late afternoon, Major Brown and the Cullen Guards rejoined Captain Grant's detail on the north side of the river opposite the Lower Sioux Agency at a place called Birch Coulee, so named because its defining feature was a deep, wooded ravine of white birch. No one had seen any Indians, and the force of a hundred-seventy men made camp by circling their wagons on a swatch of prairie near the ravine.

Captain Anderson of the Cullen Guards, a veteran of the Mexican War, objected to the camp's location. It was, he said, a poor defensive position because attackers could approach unseen from the ravine on the east or behind a knoll to the west.

Major Brown was concerned, but he was convinced the Dakota Sioux were no longer in the area; he thought they had most likely moved north and west toward the Upper Sioux Agency some thirty miles distant. It was sundown, and everyone was bone tired from the day's exertions. They ate some rations, posted ten pickets, and went to their tents to sleep.

The Indians had indeed sent their families to the safety of Yellow Medicine, but the warriors were on the move. One force under Little Crow deployed northeast toward Hutchinson and the Big Woods to block supplies and reinforcements to Fort Ridgely.

A larger group under Gray Bird crossed to the south bank of the Minnesota River, intent on plundering and threatening Sibley's line of supply. Eventually Little Crow and Gray Bird planned to reunite and move southeast down the valley toward Mankato.

Gray Bird spotted the Cullen Guards as it left Little Crow's village heading north. His scouts followed and watched as Anderson's command crossed the river and camped at Birch Coulee.

However, the Indians were unaware of the presence of Captain Grant and his seventy-five-man company of the Sixth Minnesota Volunteers. Thus they believed it would be easy to overwhelm the Cullen Guards with a surprise attack at dawn.

During the night, Gray Bird soundlessly deployed two hundred warriors in a ring around the camp. They occupied the ravine to the east and the knoll to the west and infiltrated the grasslands and sunken marsh to the north and south. The plan was to dispatch the pickets quietly with arrows before charging the camp and shooting the sleeping soldiers.

Just before dawn the horses, which were tied to ropes between wagons, suddenly became restless. An alert cook noticed this and woke Captain Anderson. Minutes later, a lookout fired his rifle at Indians crawling through the grass. In seconds, the camp was receiving volleys of intense rifle and shotgun fire from every quarter.

Almost immediately, thirty soldiers were hit as they sought cover behind the wagons. All eighty-seven horses were shot, and most were killed. Captain Grant ordered his men to use the dead horses as cover while they dug rifle pits with shovels and bayonets. Major Anderson was wounded, as were many others in the Cullen Guard. The wagons were turned over to form a barricade, and breastworks were built with saddles, rocks, and the bodies of the dead.

The wind carried hints of Intense rifle fire sixteen miles east to Fort Ridgely. The sound waxed and waned. Some soldiers at the fort thought it was a brief gunfight, while others believed it was sustained and coming from a battle at the Lower Sioux Agency. Perhaps Grant was in a fight. Sibley sent out a detail of riders from the fort, but they returned after encountering silence and finding nothing.

Then muffled shots were heard once more, and finally, around noon, Sibley dispatched a force of two-hundred-forty infantry with two howitzers under the command of Colonel Sam McPhail, another veteran of the Mexican War. Unfortunately, McPhail moved cautiously, reluctant to deploy his mounted troopers ahead of the main column.

By now, the besieged soldiers at Birch Coulee were short of ammunition—they had been supplied with the wrong caliber bullets—and their water buckets were nearly empty. For some reason, the wagon containing their provisions was left outside the defensive perimeter, and consequently they had no food.

Their attackers, however, were in good shape: they had food and water and the cover and protection provided by the ravine and knoll. *'It was only a matter of time,'* Gray Bird thought, *'before the white soldiers would be compelled to surrender.'*

The sound of firing increased as McPhail's force moved west. About three miles from Birch Coulee, one of McPhail's scouts spotted a group of Indians. Fearing that he was facing a large Sioux contingent, McPhail halted to form a defensive position.

He ordered the howitzers to fire at the Indians; the cannonades did no harm, but the thundering sounds were heard by the defenders at Birch Coulee. Captain Grant wondered if a relief column was on its way, or perhaps the Indians had captured artillery and were about to use it on his troops. The booming stopped, and soon it was forgotten.

The fifty Indians that confronted McPhail created the faux appearance of a large war party. They surrounded his superior force, shouting fierce war cries, beating tom-toms, and firing their rifles. Their theatrical performance so concerned the perplexed colonel that he ordered Lieutenant Sheehan to ride back to Fort Ridgely for reinforcements.

Sheehan was a good choice; he was the hero of the battle of Fort Ridgely and bravely broke through the line of Indians despite his horse being twice wounded. Satisfied that the intimidated McPhail had been neutralized, the Indians left his paralyzed force and returned to the Birch Coulee battlefield.

As the day wore on, the situation in Captain Grant's and Captain Anderson's commands deteriorated rapidly. The Indians continued to fire at them from all sides. Snipers in trees picked off exposed soldiers. The wounded pleaded for water. The bodies of dead soldiers bloated and blackened in the sun. The stench from the slain horses pervaded the camp. Everyone was thirsty and choking on the clouds of dust that wafted over the prairie. And ammunition was very low.

During the night, Captain Grant distributed rifles and what ammunition he could retrieve from the dead and severely wounded. Everyone expected the Indians to attack at dawn and overrun them. Death, they knew, was at hand.

At sunrise, a solitary Indian appeared on a horse carrying a flag of truce. He shouted that any brother in the camp with Dakota blood would be spared. There were nine mixed-blood men. Captain Grant said they could leave if they wished.

When all nine declined to leave, Grant fired at the Indian, missing the man but killing his horse. Angered by this perceived breach of battlefield ethics, the enraged Indians attacked with renewed vigor.

Sheehan succeeded in reaching Fort Ridgely. Immediately Colonel Sibley assembled a relieving force of a thousand men and arrived at McPhail's position by midnight. At daybreak, Sibley advanced the three miles to Birch Coulee just as Gray Bird renewed the attack. At the sight of this large force, the Indians broke off the assault and quickly vanished.

Sibley's relief force found a grisly sight. The dazed, filthy survivors could barely stand. Many of those who tried collapsed to the ground. Some were retching while others simply sat cross-legged, staring at nothing, too exhausted to move or utter a word.

The battle was a terrible defeat: thirteen men dead, fifty wounded, many severely, and eighty-seven horses killed. All but one wagon was destroyed That particular wagon contained Justina Krieger, who miraculously survived the battle despite being grazed by five bullets.

Sibley's men collected the survivors and returned to Fort Ridgely by midnight. During his march to the fort, Sibley considered his situation. He was already being criticized for moving slowly since he had taken command of the army two weeks ago. The debacle at Birch Coulee would only catalyze the storm of criticism that was engulfing him.

He would lament to his wife, Sarah, "The responsibilities of my position are so great that I can't hardly sleep at all." Worse, his self-esteem had been bruised, and he longed to be home.

Before leaving the Birch Coulee battlefield, Sibley left a note for Little Crow attached to a stake.

In it, he wrote, "If Little Crow has any proposition to make, let him send a half breed to me, and he shall be protected…" The note was picked up, but Little Crow did not see it immediately. He was preparing to attack Hutchinson and Forrest City.

Sibley would await Little Crow's reply at Fort Ridgely. And he would offer his resignation to Governor Ramsey.

The Lindquist and Eriksson men signed on with the Hutchinson Guards and joined the townspeople strengthening the stockade. Prairie sod was plowed and cut to reinforce the walls. Three-inch firing ports were bored every four feet. Small blockhouses protected the gates on the northwest and southeast corners. The stockade could shelter two hundred people comfortably.

News of the debacle at Birch Coulee reached Hutchinson on Wednesday, September 3. A group of refugees passed through town heading east. Most were in wagons loaded with their life's belongings. Many were abandoning their homes and farms, never to return.

"I'm not raising my children to be murdered by savages," one woman proclaimed. Another uttered bitterly, "My husband brought me out here from Chicago eleven years ago. Now he's dead. My son too. I can't stop crying. I'll never go back!" A grim mood settled on the town. It was a mixture of dread, determination, and desire for retribution.

In the early afternoon, Captain Richard Strout arrived in Hutchinson with his battered company of sixty-five men from Acton Township, where early that morning they had been ambushed by one-hundred-fifty of Little Crow's warriors. The company consisted of citizen soldiers and a small contingent of new recruits from the Ninth Minnesota.

They fought bravely, but their ammunition was low because some of them had been supplied with the wrong caliber bullets. Facing annihilation, Strout ordered his men to fix bayonets and charge through the Indian line. Many men were wounded, but they made it to their horses and wagons and managed to outrun the Indians during an eight-mile chase.

William Pendergast welcomed Strout and his men. "We expect the savages to attack us any day, Captain."

"I think it'll be tomorrow, Mr. Pendergast. I would bring everyone into the stockade before sunset. And I'd appreciate any aid your doctors can give my wounded."

That evening the Lindquists and Erikssons gathered at their wagons two blocks from the stockade. Julia was cooking supper over an open fire. She and Gustav had spent most of the day at the American House hotel caring for the sick and injured among the refugees and Strout's soldiers.

"We'll sleep in the stockade tonight," Elliot announced. "There was a big fight in Acton today. Near our land. The soldiers were surrounded, but most of them fought through and made it here. They said the Indians are headed our way. We'll probably be attacked tomorrow."

"I heard the Indians are going to attack Forest City," Robert said. "That's what the soldiers from the Acton fight told Pendergast."

"Maybe they're going for both towns," Elliot replied. "I don't know. But we're not going to be surprised again. We've already lost two-thirds of the family to the bastards…"

"Elliot, please watch your language!" Julia interrupted. "The children…"

"Sorry," Elliot replied. "It's just…just…"

Julia reached out and gently placed her hand on her husband's shoulder.

"I know," she whispered. Turning to the others, she said, "There's more meat and corn if anyone wants it."

Without hesitation, Carl passed his empty plate to Julia.

Smiling, she said, "I thought you'd want more. You've been working hard on the stockade all day. Do you think it will be strong enough?"

Carl took the plate and replied, "Yeah, I do. I'm just worried there won't be room for everyone. That's why we should get the family in there before more people show up."

"Pendergast wants us to double the guard at sundown," Robert announced. "We're going to do two hours on and two off 'til dawn. Then two on and four off, sunrise to sunset. I volunteered to be a picket."

"What's a picket, Robert?" Elliot asked.

"I'll be posted a hundred yards out from the stockade. Ten of us will post around the stockade during the night. So the Indians can't sneak up on us. Especially before dawn."

Elliot stood and looked down at Robert. "Might be dangerous, Robert. I don't want to lose you…"

"Thanks, cousin, but I don't plan on getting jumped."

Carl said, "Why don't you get that mean mountain cur that belongs to Mrs. Hansen? Take him with you. He'll hear or smell 'em long before you see 'em."

Robert chuckled, "I'm more afraid of that dog than I am of the Indians."

A distant volley of rifle fire caused everyone to stand and look northwestward. Scattered shots were heard for a minute followed by silence.

Julia looked at Elliot. "What do you think?"

"I don't know. Let's go to the stockade," Elliot replied. "Carl, Robert, bring the rifles and ammunition. Gustav and I will bring the food, water, and bedding. Julia, you and Ester take what you'll need for a couple of days. Bring anything valuable. The Indians will take whatever they can carry."

"What about the horses?" Gustav asked.

"We'll leave 'em tied up," Elliot replied.

"If we lose them, we're going to have a devil of a time with the harvest," Robert said.

"I know. I know. But there's no room in the stockade and our priority is surviving tomorrow."

The evening was warm and humid. As usual, the ravenous mosquitoes became more active at sunset. Inside the stockade, Elliot and Julia sat on a blanket, with little William asleep between them. Next to them were Robert, Gustav, Carl, and Ester, all resting on blankets.

They were the seven survivors of the seventeen Lindquist and Eriksson family members who left Sweden to make a new life in America. The enormity of the tragedy was numbing. Like all farm families, they were closely knit, intertwined, and interdependent. For now, their brains were stunned, their bodies physically exhausted. The future beyond tomorrow was distant and uncertain.

Julia took Elliot's hand in hers and whispered, "I was going to wait to tell you…" She looked down.

"What? Tell me…what?"

"I'm pregnant." She smiled and pressed their clasped hands to her chest. "I wanted you to know in case…in case…"

Elliot kissed her forehead. "We're going to get through this…don't worry. When is the baby…?"

"In the spring. March or April, I think."

"Oh, that's wonderful. I would shout, but…"

"No, don't wake them. There will be another—happier—time."

The nearly full moon cast its light on the stockade. Armed volunteers were on guard at the two gates. Outside were eight men posted around the stockade from fifty to a hundred yards from the walls. They were the pickets, the eyes and ears that would prevent a surprise attack. Three of them had dogs, including Mrs. Hanson's big yellow cur named Billy.

At four o'clock in the morning, Robert and Carl and six other men relieved the pickets. Elliot went to his post in the northwest blockhouse and Gustav stood at a gunport facing southeast. They were armed with the new model 1855 Springfield rifle that fired a .58 caliber minié ball and was accurate up to five hundred yards.

In the early light of morning, a half dozen farmers left the stockade to work in the fields. Captain Strout discouraged them.

"Stay here! If you're attacked, we won't be able to help you."

One of them stopped and said, "I've got to protect my animals, Captain." He held up an ancient smoothbore musket.

"That won't be much help if they rush you," Strout warned. "Maybe you will get one of 'em, and then you'll be dead."

The farmer patted a hatchet in his belt, "I got this, too, Captain. I'll make a fight of it."

Strout shook his head. "You're stubborn, sir. You can replace your animals, but what will your family do if you're killed? Who'll take care of them?"

Without a word the farmer shrugged and walked away.

After failing to overtake Strout, Little Crow assembled his warriors at Cedar Mills on the South Fork of the Crow River ten miles northwest of Hutchinson. More men had joined him during the evening, and now he had a force of two hundred that would be available to attack Hutchinson in the morning. Meanwhile, a smaller band of Dakota would march twenty miles north during the night and strike Forest City in Meeker County on the river's north fork.

Little Crow moved among the young men. It was late in the evening. They were eager to crush the white defenders awaiting them in Hutchinson. They were well provisioned because Strout's troops had discarded supplies to lighten their wagons during the retreat to Hutchinson.

Initially Little Crow was inclined to chastise them for being distracted by Strout's abandoned supplies. But the chief was under pressure. Several days before, an angry and disgruntled group left him and struck out on their own after learning he considered asking Sibley for a truce. Eventually they returned, but Little Crow knew his status was tenuous. So he assured his warriors that he would fight the white man to the death.

Little Crow planned to delay the attack until midmorning. He knew the farmer's habits and mindset. This was harvesting time, and at sunrise they would be drawn irresistibly to the fields. So by midmorning the number of defenders in town would be reduced, and those remaining would be mostly women and old men. But he did not yet know about the new stockade and trench or the resolute and well-armed volunteers of the Hutchinson Guard.

At sunrise, Robert Eriksson focused his attention on the bluffs on the northern edge of Hutchinson. They overlooked the South Fork of the Crow River as it flowed southeast through town. Captain Strout thought the Indians would likely attack from the direction of the bluffs and along the riverbed. On the north side of the river were a steam sawmill, schoolhouse, and home of

William Pendergast. To the south were more homes and the American House hotel that held many wounded soldiers from Strout's command. West of town was a dense and deep grove of trees that stretched from the Crow River south to the Preston Lake Road.

To Robert's right, about seventy-five yards distant, was his brother Carl, who was not only sturdier than Robert, but also an expert rifleman. He was an avid hunter back home in Sweden, and he was delighted when Lieutenant Bremmer distributed the Springfield rifles to the Hutchinson Guard. *'Carl,'* Robert thought, *'was the kind of man you wanted to be next to in a fight.'*

When the expected dawn attack did not occur, more farmers and townspeople left the stockade despite Strout's repeated warnings. Gustav and Julia insisted on tending to the wounded in the American House hotel. Elliot accompanied them, together with three young recruits from the Tenth Minnesota, who were armed with old muskets. Little William was left behind in Ester's care.

At eight o'clock, Strout ordered the pickets to return to the stockade for breakfast. The men who had stood guard most of the night decided to sleep for a few hours. Some went home while others found a quiet place outside the stockade. Altogether, many of Hutchinson's defenders were doing precisely what Little Crow had expected them to do: relax their vigilance and return to their fields and businesses.

Inside the stockade, Robert and Carl had coffee and a thick slice of wheat bread spread with honey. Ester fed William and combed his curly blond hair. Captain Strout walked by and spoke to Robert and Carl. He was medium height with a thick beard typical of the fashion, and spoke with a New England accent.

Given his military rank, Strout had assumed he was entitled to command the defense of Hutchinson. While his soldiers obeyed him, the citizen soldiers of the Hutchinson Guard thought postmaster Lewis Harrington was their captain and often ignored Strout's orders.

Strout said, "When you're finished with your coffee, I'd like you to return to your posts," Robert and Carl looked up and nodded.

"Any sign of the Indians?" Robert asked.

Strout started to reply when rifle shots erupted from the west.

Little Crow led his warriors to the bluffs above Hutchison. His plan was to charge the town and drive its inhabitants south toward the road to Glencoe where he positioned men to ambush them in the open. This tactic always succeeded. Attack, terrorize, kill, loot, and burn.

White civilians rarely stood and fought, and nearly always loaded their wagons and skedaddled. Once they were exposed and on the run, it was easy to overtake them.

Little Crow was surprised when he looked down on Hutchinson from the bluffs. He saw a substantial stockade that was surrounded by a trench. The walls were high and reinforced, and the gates were protected by blockhouses. Armed men and soldiers were standing guard outside. He could not see beyond the walls but assumed more men with weapons were inside. He could see many people walking about town. On the outskirts were unguarded buildings and grazing horses and cattle.

Quickly Little Crow drew back his warriors and held a council with his chiefs.

"They've built a stockade," he said. "And they have many men with rifles. We're not strong enough to attack it."

Several chiefs began to object. Little Crow gestured for silence.

"Hear me out!" he shouted. "We'll surround the town, loot the houses, and burn the outbuildings. Take hostages and torture them in sight of the stockade. We'll slaughter their animals. Get them pissed! Make them very angry! Then they'll come out to fight. When they do, we'll attack, kill them, and burn the stockade. No prisoners, except young women!"

A minor chief, Red Pony, stood and asked, "What if the wašíču refuse to fight?"

"If they don't come out," Little Crow replied, "we'll load the wagons and go to Yellow Medicine. We'll come back when they don't expect us."

Already the first white man had been wounded. He was a farmer, Hiram Brown, who was hit with two buckshot while cutting hay west of town. Those were the shots heard in the stockade. Quickly Strout ordered his troops into the stockade and shut the gates. Still, many civilians remained outside, including Julia, Gustav, and Elliot who were caring for a dozen wounded in the American House hotel.

About nine o'clock, Elliot heard heavy gunfire coming from the north and west. He stepped onto the porch and saw Indians streaming out of a dense grove of trees to his left. They were setting fire to the schoolhouse and sawmill across the river. Smoke was billowing from the windows of the Pendergast home. He had to get Julia and Gustav to the safety of the stockade.

A half dozen warriors stormed the hotel as Elliot was leading Julia and Gustav out the rear entrance. Elliot was clubbed unconscious, Gustav was flung to the floor, and Julia was pinned against a wall and her dress ripped from her body.

Red Pony knelt over Elliot, slashed his cotton shirt, and carved a six-inch flap of skin from the center of his chest. Then he grabbed Gustav by the hair and slashed both cheeks. Streaming blood, Gustav tried to stand but was cudgeled with the flat side of a tomahawk. Julia, sobbing, knew what was about to befall her.

The defenders inside the stockade laid down fire from the ports and blockhouses, preventing the Indians from approaching the trench that surrounded the stockade and nearby cabins. Occasionally an Indian bullet splintered a post, but none found flesh. Strout saw that the Indians had surrounded them and were taking cover in the homes and tall grass and trees west of the stockade.

"The bastards are killing the oxen!" cried one of the Hutchinson Guards. He pointed to the southwest. "And they're hitching the horses to wagons. They're gonna steal 'em!"

Pendergast and Herrington approached Captain Strout standing by the northwest gate.

"Captain," Herrington said, "we can't fight 'em from the stockade. We've got to go out there, and drive 'em off! Or they're going to destroy the town. Kill or steal our animals! We'll have nothing left! We won't survive the winter!"

"That's exactly what they want us to do, Herrington," Strout said. "You want to go out and fight? Leave the protection of the stockade? Good God, man, they far outnumber us! We'll be easy pickings. No, we stay here. That's an order!"

Clenching his fists, Pendergast seethed, "I don't take orders from you, Captain. I'm—"

"My God! Look! They have the Swedes!" The shout came from the blockhouse at the northwest gate. "Oh, Jesus! They've cut 'em…and the woman…the midwife…"

Robert and Carl ran to the blockhouse. Two hundred yards west, next to the hotel, in plain view were three kneeling, naked, fair-skinned figures covered in blood. They were Elliot, Gustav, and Julia. Around them were four Indians gesturing with knives and tomahawks, as if they were about to execute them. They waved their arms and shouted, taunting the white men inside the stockade, daring them come out and rescue the hostages.

The firing stopped as everyone, defenders and attackers alike, were transfixed by the spectacle before them. The rage felt by the white men would never leave them; they would relive it for the rest of their lives. For many Indians, including Little Crow, the scene was sobering. If they lost this war, they would be hunted for the rest of their lives, and their families would suffer terribly.

Carl Eriksson shouldered his new 1855 Springfield and targeted the tallest Indian, who was standing next to Julia. He estimated the range to be close to 200 yards. The air was thick, but there was no wind.

"Carl," Robert said, "what are you doing? It's an impossible shot. You'll get them all killed…"

"Brother," Carl said calmly, "when I fire, hand me your rifle and reload mine." Carl glanced briefly at Robert, took aim, and exhaled slowly. Gently, deliberately, he squeezed the trigger.

The Springfield fired. Not waiting to observe the result, Carl quickly shouldered Robert's rifle, aimed, and fired again.

Carl growled, "Reload, damnit!"

A soldier from the Ninth Minnesota thrust his Springfield into Carl's hands.

Carl's first minié ball hit the tall Indian in the mouth and blew out the base of his skull, killing him instantly. The next bullet struck Red Pony in the neck and pulverized his windpipe and carotid artery; he slumped, dying, onto Gustav. When the third Indian's skull exploded from the third shot, the remaining Indian clutched the naked Julia to his chest as a shield and disappeared back into the dense grove of trees.

The northwest gate opened, and fifteen men led by Pendergast and Herrington charged out of the stockade firing their rifles in all directions. The Indians fell back. Carl and Robert ran to Elliot and Gustav. Both were conscious but unable to stand.

Captain Strout arrived in a horse-drawn wagon and squad of soldiers. Quickly they placed Gustav and Elliot on makeshift stretchers and loaded them into the wagon. Next, they evacuated the wounded from the hotel. Within fifteen minutes, they were back in the stockade.

"Where's Julia?" Elliot asked as he was being lifted off the wagon.

"The Indian took her," Carl replied. "Before I could shoot him. I'm sorry. I just couldn't reload before he grabbed her."

Elliot covered his eyes and groaned.

Robert said, "We'll find her. They'll keep her hostage…to trade or bargain…that's what they're doing."

Little Crow watched the attack from a knoll across the river. He saw Red Pony and three other warriors fall as if they had been shot by a ghost. When the gate opened, Little Crow urged his men to charge the stockade. The few who tried were thrown back by defenders who had emerged from the stockade and taken up firing positions behind logs and fences.

Little Crow crossed the river and urged his men to load the wagons with as much loot as they could hold. "Then burn everything!" he shouted.

For the next hour, the Indians took every movable object from the homes and hotel. Earlier, Sumner's store had been emptied by its owner, who managed to move most of his merchandise into the stockade.

After loading the wagons, the Indians set fire to any building they could without coming under fire. The smoke that rose over Hutchinson was seen by the fifty soldiers of Company H of the Ninth Minnesota, who were bivouacked at Lake Addie eleven miles south. Immediately Lieutenant Joseph Weinman ordered his men to march north. An hour later they were joined by twenty-five mounted militiamen of the Goodhue County Rangers under Captain D. L. Davis.

At four o'clock in the afternoon, Little Crow received a message from his warriors on the Glencoe road south of town. Troops and cavalry, they said, were moving rapidly toward Hutchinson and should arrive within the hour. Little Crow ordered his men to kill any animals they could not take and head west to the Upper Sioux Agency at Yellow River Agency.

Gustav struggled to sit up. His face was covered with clotted blood. He examined his brother's wound. "That should be cleaned, or it'll fester." He touched his cheek. "And I need these cuts stitched."

"I can do it," a young woman said behind him. She stepped forward. "I'm an assistant to Dr. Mayo in Le Sueur."

Gustav extended his hand. "I'm Gustav Lindquist. This is my brother, Elliot."

She took his hand briefly. "I'm Margaret Thompson. Are you the new doctor at Acton?"

"Yes," Gustav replied. "I've been there nearly a year. How did you know?"

"I heard about the midwife who works with you. She's very skilled. We heard about her in Le Sueur. Dr. Mayo wants to meet her."

Elliot said, "She's my wife—her name is Julia Lindquist. The Indians have taken her."

"I'm terribly sorry, Mr. Lindquist. May I look at your wound?" Without waiting for a reply, she lifted the blood-soaked cotton dressing that someone had applied while he was in the wagon. An inch-wide strip of skin and tissue were missing from the center of Elliot's breastbone. Bright red blood oozed from the wound and streaked his abdomen.

"I don't think there is anything to stitch here." She turned to Gustav and asked, "Do you agree, doctor?"

"Yes, I agree. Scar will fill it in," Gustav replied. "It'll take a month."

"I'll boil water, irrigate it, and apply a proper dressing," Margaret said. "Then, doctor, we'll stitch those cuts on your face. I'm afraid they're going to scar."

Gustav grunted, "Not worried about scars."

Margaret said, "I've catgut and needles in my bag. I'll boil the needles and rinse the catgut in alcohol. That's what Dr. Mayo does. He says it cuts down on suppuration."

"I would like to meet Dr. Mayo sometime."

During the next hour, Margaret cleaned and dressed Elliot's wound and sutured Gustav's cuts with catgut. There was no anesthetic, so he felt each stitch as she carefully approximated the edges of each wound. He was impressed by her skill and demeanor, and she was quite pretty.

The crooked-nosed Indian took Julia to one of the stolen wagons, wrapped her in a blanket, and tied her hands and feet with strips of deer hide. The wagon contained plunder from the town, mostly furniture, clothing, crockery, tools, and kerosene lamps.

Also in the wagon was a wretched young Indian woman whose arms and legs were covered with grass cuts and bull thistle scratches. She looked at Julia with sympathetic eyes and offered her a water bag. The water was warm and hard, but Julia drank it gratefully.

As she handed the water bag back, Julia smiled and said, "Thank you." The woman returned the smile, pointed to herself, and said, "I Mina. I speak English. I learn at missionary school."

"Hello, Mina," Julia said. "I'm Julia...Julia Lindquist. Are you a prisoner?"

"I don't know what 'prisoner' is," Mina replied.

"Were you taken---like me?" Julia asked, holding out her bound hands.

"Oh, no. My family was killed by soldiers three days ago. Little Crow found me near Cedar Mills. Brought me here. He knew my father, Running Bear."

Julia watched a plume of black smoke hover briefly over Hutchinson and drift east on a dry wind. She heard random shots from the direction of the stockade and the road south. Fearful thoughts of what might have happened to Elliot and the family caused her heart to race and throat tighten. Every few minutes a sob would break through the calm she struggled to maintain. Her survival, she knew, depended on caution and clear thinking.

In late afternoon, a short, bow-legged Indian climbed into the wagon. Pointing west, he said something in Lakota that Julia did not understand. He climbed into the driver's seat, gathered the reins, and urged the horses to move out. Ahead and behind were more wagons filled with loot.

Every few miles a wagon became mired in a wetlands slough and had to be unloaded to pull it out. Their progress was slow, and the trek was made more uncomfortable by the heat and mosquitoes. The Dakota warriors wanted to put distance between their wagon train and the soldiers that were converging on Hutchinson. So the ragged column continued on until long after midnight, when it finally stopped in a grove of dogwoods by a small stream.

Mina spoke to the bowlegged driver and said to Julia, "He'll free your hands and legs and let us go to the water." After Julia was unbound, she and Mina walked barefoot to the stream in the moonlight. Mina filled the water bag while Julia removed the blanket and washed away the crusted blood from her face, arms, and legs.

As she squatted naked by the stream, an Indian behind her said in perfect English, "You should cover yourself. There are many young bucks around here who'll take advantage."

Julia hastily replaced the blanket and turned to face a tall handsome man in European dress. A rifle was slung on his shoulder, and a sheathed knife was strapped to his chest. He handed her a cloth bundle.

"Put this on," he said. "It's a white woman's dress and underclothing. I'll find shoes for you in the morning. I've left bread in the wagon."

He turned and disappeared into the night.

Mina said, "That was Chaska. It means 'first son'. He's a farmer at Hazelwood and a Christian. My father thought he was a good man. He's peaceful. I don't know what he's doing here."

"His English is very good," Julia observed as she stepped into the white petticoat Chaska had given her. The black cotton dress was slightly large but comforting.

"He went to missionary school, like me," Mina said.

The two women returned to the wagon and ate the cornbread Chaska had left them. Afterward they slept for three fitful hours until the wagon began to move before dawn.

Elliot and Carl left the stockade on horseback and followed the trail left by the stolen wagons. By early afternoon, they overtook the wagons and followed at a distance, maintaining contact on a parallel track north of the column. Their plan was to close the gap at sundown and find Julia, although they did not know exactly how they were going to do this and escape.

The wagons continued to move during the afternoon. Billowing clouds gathered at dusk obscuring the moon and enveloping the wagons in darkness. It would be foolhardy for Elliot and Carl to move in closer, so they dropped back, dismounted, and followed on foot. Around midnight, they heard a commotion ahead. The wagons had joined Little Crow and his warriors on the Minnesota River south of the Upper Sioux Agency. The two men decided to cross to the south bank where it would be safer and where they could rest until morning.

That night Little Crow was given the note Sibley left for him at Birch Coulee. He had it read to him by several mixed-bloods, one of whom was Tom Robertson, the son of the school superintendent on the reservation. Robertson and his family were captives, but Little Crow trusted him. What Robertson told him agreed with what others said. Apparently, Little Crow concluded, Sibley was willing to talk peace.

Little Crow sent a letter to Sibley at Fort Ridgely recounting the reasons for the war and reminding him that they had 150 prisoners, mostly women and children. It was delivered by Robertson under a flag of truce.

Sibley's reply was blunt: "You have murdered many of our people without any sufficient cause. Return the prisoners under a flag of truce, and I will talk to you like a man."

When Robertson returned with Sibley's reply, he found Little Crow's warriors preparing to move twelve miles northwest to Lac qui Parle. Little Crow read Sibley's brusque letter, and penned a reply. In it, he reminded Sibley that the two of them once had a good relationship and they should try to resolve the situation peacefully. Robertson delivered the letter to Sibley at Fort Ridgely.

The following day Sibley replied, "You have allowed your young men to commit some murders since you wrote your first letter. This is not the way to make peace."

At midday, the wagon train arrived on the junction of the Chippewa and Minnesota rivers. Chaska gestured for Julia to step down from the wagon and led her to the river. On the bank were the most forlorn collection of people she had ever seen. The majority were white women and their children. The few men appeared to be mixed blood. Dust caked their faces and clothing. The feet of the shoeless were swollen and bleeding. Their expressions told of exhaustion and fear.

Julia noticed a woman kneeling over a girl lying motionless on the ground. There was something familiar about her. She moved closer.

"Min Gud," Julia whispered in Swedish, "it's Elsa—and Ruth."

Julia and Elsa quietly embraced.

"Oh, Julia," Elsa moaned, "Ruth is so weak. She hasn't been able to eat anything for days."

Julia took Ruth's hand. "Ruth, Ruth, its Julia. Can you hear me?"

Ruth's eyes flickered. She saw the indistinct outlines of a woman's face. Gradually Julia came into focus. "Julia?"

"Yes, yes. Can you sit up?"

"I'm so weak. I can't…" Ruth replied, coughing.

Gently, Julia and Elsa raised Ruth up. Her skin was hot and dry. She coughed again and again, expectorating a gob of thick gray sputum.

"Ruth, you have pneumonia. And you're dehydrated. You must drink. We have to get you out of the sun."

Behind her a voice said, "I'll take her." It was Chaska. Carefully he lifted Ruth and carried her to the shade offered by a small grove of maple trees. Gently he lowered her onto a bed of brush and leaves. He left and soon returned with a water bag.

Handing it to Julia, he said, "Have her drink this. It has salt."

Julia touched his hand. "Thank you," she said softly. Elsa nodded, "Yes, thank you…thank you for your kindness." Both women would remember their words.

Rifle fire exploded from the west. Chaska left to investigate. The firing continued for several minutes and stopped as abruptly as it had begun. The prisoners wondered what it was. Were they about to be rescued? Or were they to be slaughtered after the torture and hardship of the past two weeks? After an hour of consternation and worry, Chaska returned.

"You'll be staying here, at least for tonight," he told Julia and Elsa. "Chief Red Iron and the Sisseton will not allow Little Crow to pass their villages. They said if they did, the white army will attack them. The Sisseton never wanted this war."

That evening, Chaska brought them pemmican, which was quite tasty, and dried corn. Elsa used the pemmican to boil a broth for Ruth, who was able to sip it slowly. The least activity triggered Ruth's cough. After the meal, Julia positioned Ruth so that her lungs could drain more easily. It was a blessing that they were going stay put, at least for the night. Ruth—indeed all of them—needed sleep.

Every hour or so during the night Julia awoke to check on Ruth. Around two o'clock, she had to urinate and squatted behind a honeysuckle bush. As she stood, a powerful calloused hand clamped over her mouth, and a thick arm encircled her waist. The foul fishy smell of an unwashed body enveloped her as she was thrown facedown to the ground.

A hand under her dress pawed at her crotch. Her assailant began to grunt. She struggled to scream but her jaw was in a viselike grip. As she squirmed beneath him, his erect penis stabbed at her vagina and anus without penetrating her. He pressed down on her tailbone with his left hand, immobilizing her pelvis. His knees kept her legs spread. Now he could enter her.

Suddenly he was off her, as if uprooted by a tornado. Exhausted by the assault, Julia gathered her knees beneath her and turned to the sounds of a violent struggle. She heard a gurgle, followed by silence. A face appeared out of the darkness.

Once again, a hand pressed her mouth, only this time it was gentle and the scent unmistakable. Kind arms embraced her. It was Elliot.

"Shh…shh…" he whispered. "Carl and I are here. We're going to cross the river. Our horses are over there. We must hurry."

"I can't swim," Julia whispered. "And Elsa and Ruth are with me."

"I know. I know."

"Ruth has pneumonia. She's very weak…"

"Älskling, I know. We have no choice. We have to go…now." Elliot helped Julia to her feet. She gasped at the sight of her attacker's lifeless body. Elliot took her hand and led her to the riverbank. "We don't want to wake the other hostages."

Carl had Ruth on his back; she had her arms around his neck. Thankfully, her coughing had subsided. Elsa stood next to them. No one spoke. Silence was critical if they were to escape. Elsa pointed to the river and shook her head, mouthing the words, "I can't swim."

A figure appeared out of the shadows. Elliot drew his knife, and Carl clutched his tomahawk. It was Chaska. Julia placed her hands on Elliot's chest. "He's a friend."

Chaska extended his hands, palms outward, a sign of supplication. Carefully Chaska approached Julia and spoke softly.

"I will take you to where the river is shallow. You can cross there."

An hour later, they were on the south bank of the Minnesota River. Chaska watched as they disappeared into the early morning gloom. He told them to recross the river at a ford above the Yellow Medicine Agency and head east toward Renville. They should travel at night and stay off roads and marked trails. With luck, they should make it to Hutchinson.

Bareheaded and barefoot, the white captives trudged past the Upper Agency buildings. There were more than a hundred women and children and a few old men. Many wore hand-me-down native clothes because the Indian women had taken their dresses, and the Indian men proudly wore their bonnets.

Watching them pass were a group of twenty-one Christian Dakota and Sisseton and Wahpeton Sioux. Among them was Little Paul Mazakutermani and Gabriel Renville who were appalled by Little Crow's treatment of these pathetic human beings. Gabriel Renville was the son of mixed-blood parents who had a 3,000-acre farm and modern home near La qui Parle. He thought something had to be done for the captives.

Among the captives were Sarah Wakefield and her two children. Lucy was tied to her back and James walked beside her. Chaska and his mother followed on a horse. They were part of a wide five-mile-long caravan heading north. In it were hundreds of Mdewakanton Dakotas who were overloaded with all sorts of stolen goods, including furniture, household items, clothing, jewelry, and ornaments.

Wagons, carriages, and buggies were stuffed and piled high with pillaged property. As they bounced along, these carelessly loaded conveyances frequently tipped or toppled, dumping their contents onto the ground. When this happened, the mules brayed their discontent, and startled horses whinnied and reared in their harnesses. The cacophony was punctuated by random rifle shots, cracking whips, and screaming children.

Little Crow rode over to Little Paul and Gabriel Renville. "You should leave here. We're going to burn these buildings," he said. "Come, go with us!"

Little Paul and Renville shook their heads. "No, chief, we're staying." They were joined by Red Iron, Akipa, Samuel Brown, and the Crawfords, who also refused to leave.

Little Crow raised his lance and shouted, "We must join together to defeat Sibley's army! We must drive the white man from our land! If we don't come together all Dakota Sioux will suffer terribly." His appeal was met with silence, and their body language was unmistaken: he and his mostly Mdewakanton Dakota warriors were on their own. It was a profoundly depressing moment. His goal of uniting all Dakota Sioux was moving beyond his grasp.

Renville's small group followed Little Crow's column of a thousand warriors, and their families and captives. Staying at the Upper Agency was somewhat risky since Sibley's army would be on move, and they could be trapped between combatants.

After two miles, Little Crow made camp, raising three hundred wigwams by nightfall. Gabriel Renville's group passed through the camp and once again were appalled by the captives' pathetic state. They continued on to Hazelwood where Renville proposed they invite Little Crow to a council where they would demand he release the captives and allow them to return home.

The council occurred the following day. Little Crow refused to free the captives.

Chief Walking Iron, who had participated in the treaty negotiations of 1851 and 1858, rose and asked bitterly, "Can it be possible that Little Crow has many white prisoners because he intends to make Sissetons and Wahpetons his prisoners too?"

Red Iron, a Sisseton chief, sent messengers to the northern Sisseton and Wahpeton villages asking for reinforcements to confront Little Crow and the Mdewakanton. The following day hundreds arrived, and a large gathering took place. It was a fateful meeting of a thousand Dakota Sioux. Clearly there were two opposing factions: those who wished to continue the war, and those who vehemently opposed it and wanted peace.

Speaking for those who opposed the war, Little Paul in his elegant way said, "If we had known you were going to kill white settlers, we would have kept you from it. You have done our people a great injustice. To right this terrible wrong, you must turn over the white captives."

Iron Gourd, a young Mdewakanton warrior retorted, "Do you think the whites will spare you because you turned over the captives. You speak like a child!"

The ranks of those advocating continuing the war began to shrink. The group desiring peace grew every day, and it welcomed all whites who were able to escape their captors or sought refuge. Little Crow was losing influence. He, more than anyone, knew that the looming battle with Sibley's army would be decisive---for his young soldier warriors and for him personally. What he did not know was a defeat would imperil every Dakota Sioux in Minnesota, regardless of guilt or innocence, age, or gender.

Chapter 9

Abraham Lincoln sat at his scarred mahogany desk on the second floor of the White House. It was Friday morning, August 29, 1862. The windows were open, and the pungent smell of fetid waste pervaded the second-floor office. The tall, bearded president was accustomed to the stench emanating from the nearby Washington City Canal that no longer carried barge traffic and was an open sewer.

Military maps covered the floor, except for the space under the long table where the cabinet met. Additional maps of all sizes hung on the walls or were rolled and stuffed into cubbyholes. Sheaves of correspondence, files, and papers were stacked on every horizontal surface. It appeared to be an office in chaos, except that Lincoln or one of his secretaries---John Nicolay or John Hay---could readily locate any document.

The edge of a large, unfolded map rested on Lincoln's left leg. Its focal point was northern Virginia, where General John Pope's Union forces stood between the Army of Northern Virginia and Washington, D.C. Manassas Junction was just 26 miles from the Capital, a fact foremost in the President's thoughts.

After defeating General George McClellan's Army of the Potomac during the Seven Days Battles around Richmond, General Robert E. Lee had skillfully pivoted his army north, and now there was no doubt in Lincoln's mind that the Confederates were headed for Manassas and the Capital. Lincoln feared the Civil War could come to a calamitous end, and right quick.

A general officer entered Lincoln's office. It was Henry Halleck, who recently succeeded McClellan as general-in-chief. He was 47-years-old, a graduate of West Point, and was known in the army as 'Old Brains' for his scholarly treatises on military science. Prior to the war, he was a successful businessman in California. A skilled organizer, from 1861–62 he commanded the western department that included the armies of generals Ulysses S. Grant and Don Carlos Buell, who won major victories in Tennessee and Mississippi.

Halleck was credited with these successes, and in July 1862 he was promoted to lead all Union armies. Lincoln thought his new generalissimo knew how to win. Halleck was, however, Robert E. Lee's opposite: uninspiring, risk-averse, and much more comfortable behind a desk than commanding troops in battle. Worse still, he was never in a hurry; his gears were low and lower.

"Good morning, General," Lincoln said, as he draped a lanky leg over a nearby chair. "You have news?"

Halleck remained standing, his eyes bulging.

"Yes, sir," he replied, nervously rubbing his elbows. "The Confederates attacked Pope yesterday afternoon. South of Bull Run, and northwest of Manassas."

Lincoln stood and placed the map on the long table. "Show me where, General."

"Here, Mister President," Halleck said, pointing to the Warrenton Turnpike south of Bull Run. "General Pope believes its Jackson's corps that attacked him. Gibbon and Doubleday were engaged. That's all we know." He blotted his high forehead with a handkerchief.

"Where's Longstreet?" Lincoln asked.

Halleck replied, "Pope thinks Longstreet is east of the Bull Run Mountains, preparing to join Jackson. Lee is probably with him."

"You mean Lee has divided his army? Isn't that reason for Pope to attack him?" Lincoln asked.

Halleck rubbed his elbows again, uncomfortable in the President's gaze. "That opportunity, Mister President—if it were ever present—is probably gone now. Pope's priority must be the security of the Capital—until the entire Army of the Potomac arrives."

"I agree with that, General. When can we expect the Army of the Potomac to be in position?"

"As you know, sir, General McClellan's V Army Corps landed here at Aquia Creek northeast of Fredericksburg last week and is marching to the Rappahannock. And III Corps is moving down from Alexandria. Pope should have seventy-thousand men, with more on the way."

Lincoln was weary. He had slept only a few hours the previous night, a pattern he had been following for weeks. Mrs. Lincoln pleaded with him to rest, but any opportunity to revive his mind and body would have to wait until Lee no longer threatened the Capital.

Lincoln said, "We ordered McClellan to move his army north on August 3. Nineteen days passed before his first contingents reached the upper Potomac. Now we're being attacked thirty miles from here, Washington is threatened, and we're still waiting for the rest of his army to be brought up! Why the delay?"

Halleck tugged at his collar and cleared his throat.

"It's a complicated business, Mister President. The logistics involved simply took time to organize. And of course, the Confederates could attack our base at Harrison's Landing at any time. Withdrawing such a large force in the face of the enemy is risky, and it must be done deliberately, carefully."

"General, we know it is far more than simply logistics. McClellan's headquarters believes that the real enemy is this administration. And McClellan is sulking. He is preoccupied with his position in the army after his failures in front of Richmond."

"He is letting known his dissatisfaction with his superiors—namely me, Secretary Stanton, and you. He does not know the meaning of the word 'subordinate'. He views orders as suggestions, options to be considered rather than obeyed. We've overlooked his insubordinate behavior in the past. No longer. We can't afford to. The Union won't survive."

The President appointed Halleck general-in-chief because he needed both a capable military advisor and a buffer that stood between him and his political enemies, especially the War Democrats who supported McClellan. Halleck would be his lighting rod whenever it was necessary to change commanders or shift strategic priorities.

Halleck would sign the orders, while Lincoln remained in the background, his fingerprints on nothing. One of Halleck's first acts as general-in-chief was to order McClellan to move his entire army out of the Peninsula to northern Virginia.

"I agree completely, Mr. President," Halleck replied. "And I will see to it that General McClellan understands our concerns."

"Thank you, General. I am pleased we agree. Kindly, keep me informed."

Lincoln took a paper from his desk.

"Before you go, General, I received a telegram from Governor Ramsey of Minnesota several days ago. As you may know the Dakota Sioux are on the warpath in that state, and the Governor wants to delay the draft in Minnesota by one month. Secretary Stanton has denied that request."

Lincoln read from Ramsey's telegram, "'Half the population of the State are fugitives', and so on…and then he asks for a one-month delay on recruitment. What is your view?"

Halleck cleared his throat and said, "We can't afford to lose those troops, especially now, with Lee in northern Virginia."

Lincoln nodded. "I replied to the Governor that he needs to deal with the Indians. I told him that necessity knows no law. He must do what he has to do to bring this emergency to an end."

Halleck stood.

"That's quite clear, Mr. President, but I'm concerned that the Confederates are behind this uprising. We may wish to confront the situation in Minnesota directly."

"Perhaps, but first we must stop Lee, and protect the Capital. This trouble in Minnesota could not have come at a worse time."

John Pope was a Kentucky-born West Pointer who was decorated for gallantry in the Mexican American War. In 1861, he was appointed brigadier general of volunteers and attracted Lincoln's attention by defeating a large Confederate force on Island Number Ten in the Mississippi River and then seizing Corinth, a large rebel city.

For these accomplishments, he was brought east and given command of the newly formed Union Army of Virginia. His opponents were Lee and his lieutenants, Generals James Longstreet and Thomas 'Stonewall' Jackson. His primary mission was to protect Washington while McClellan redeployed the one-hundred-twenty-thousand soldiers of the Army of the Potomac from Harrison's Landing on the James River to northern Virginia. This redeployment, however, was taking time and Lee seized the opportunity to attack Pope before he could be reinforced.

When the gruff, cigar-smoking Pope arrived at his new command in late June, he proceeded to alienate his officers and those in the Army of the Potomac by publicly chastising them for their passivity.

He told them, "Let us understand each other, I have come to you from the west, where we have always seen the backs of our enemies, from an army whose business it has been to seek the adversary and beat him when he is found."

His pomposity would have doomed most officers, but Pope was well-connected. His father had been a circuit court judge in Illinois and had received lawyer Lincoln in his courtroom on many occasions. Then too his wife's father was Congressman Valentine Horton, a close friend of Secretary of Treasury Salmon Chase.

His cousin was married to the sister of Mary Todd Lincoln. And he was selected as one of four army officers to escort president-elect Abraham Lincoln on his train trip from Illinois to his inauguration in Washington, D.C.

Many in Washington and the Lincoln administration admired Pope for his stance against slavery and for introducing the hard edge of war to the Southern people. He permitted his soldiers to forage on Southern land and take whatever they needed from farms and shops without payment.

Unlike McClellan, he severely punished rebel civilian saboteurs and trespassers. The initial civility and deference shown the Southern people and their property no longer applied. The nature of the war was changing, a shift that Lincoln favored, and it was Pope who initiated it. Soon the rebellion would become an unlimited war, an all-out struggle without mercy, until one side or the other gave up.

On August 18, Pope received a report captured from a courier for General J.E.B. Stuart, Lee's chief of cavalry. It revealed that Lee intended to attack the Union left. Learning this, Pope immediately ordered a pullback to the north bank of the Rappahannock River between Rappahannock Station and Kelly's Ford. The move placed him in a more defensible position and on the same side of the river as General Ambrose Burnside's Union forces at Fredericksburg.

While Pope repositioned his army, Lee conceived an audacious plan. He was determined to bring Pope to battle before McClellan arrived with reinforcements. Early on August 25, he ordered Jackson to march his twenty-four-thousand men in a northern arc past Pope's right flank to the town of Salem.

The next day he would follow the Manassas Gap railroad east through Thoroughfare Gap to Manassas Junction where the Union had the bulk of its supplies. This Jackson did with alacrity—he marched fifty miles in forty hours—and on August 27 Jackson's cavalry under Stuart seized the junction, cutting off Pope from his base.

Pope knew of Jackson's march north on August 25, but he incorrectly deduced that Stonewall was headed to the Shenandoah Valley. Worse still, he failed to understand that Lee was now moving with lightning speed, that he no longer had the initiative, and that his army was in a precarious position.

General McDowell entered Pope's headquarters tent. A year earlier, in July 1861, he had been defeated at the First Battle of Bull Run and was promptly replaced by McClellan. Now he was the III corps commander in Pope's army.

"Good evening, general!" McDowell said jubilantly. "We have been presented with a great opportunity to thrash the rebels and bring this war to an end!"

"Indeed, general," Pope replied from behind his portable writing desk. "Kindly explain."

McDowell strode to the map table and pointed to Manassas Junction.

"Jackson's army is here, at Manassas, and our cavalry has found Longstreet south of White Plains, 30 or so miles west of Jackson."

Jaw thrust forward and gesturing with closed fists, he said emphatically, "Sir, Lee's army is split, utterly divided. We can attack them, one at a time! It's the chance every military man prays for!"

McDowell stepped back and saluted. "I await your orders, sir!"

Neither man particularly liked the other, but this was no time for petty feelings. Cigar in hand, Pope leaned over the map and pondered it for several minutes. Then he pointed to Bristoe Station on the Orange and Alexandria railroad five miles south of Manassas Junction.

"We know elements of Jackson's corps is here, at Bristoe Station. We will attack them there, then move north to Manassas. The army will concentrate on Jackson and smash him."

"And what of Longstreet's corps?" McDowell asked.

"He's west of Thoroughfare Gap, beyond the Bull Run mountains," Pope replied. "Rickett's division will block him, or at least slow him down. Once we've bagged Jackson, we'll move on Longstreet. The war could be over before the leaves turn."

McDowell was uneasy. "General, we should be certain Longstreet does not link up with Jackson."

"I agree, General McDowell, and I'll leave that to you, for now at least." Pope extended his hand. "Good hunting, general. Keep me informed. I will meet you at Bristoe Station."

When Pope arrived at Bristoe Station, he found Jackson was gone. Jackson had also abandoned Manassas Junction, leaving behind the smoldering remnants of Union supplies that his men had joyfully set aflame after feasting on captured rations and filling their rucksacks. Perplexed, Pope assumed Jackson was trying to escape, and he set about trying to find him.

The problem was Jackson's divisions took three different routes northwest to their destination, a wooded ridge just west and south of the old Bull Run battlefield behind an unfinished railroad. Reports reached Pope that the rebels initially were at Centreville, then south along the Bull Run river, and finally on the Warrenton Turnpike.

All three reports were correct, but rather than sort through the confusion, Pope marched and counter-marched his infantry without result, exhausting his soldiers, and forgetting that Longstreet was just over the horizon. Lee was counting on Pope to make mistakes, and this was the first. The Union Army of Virginia was thrashing about, its commander muddled, and much of McClellan's army was not in position to help.

On August 28, one of McDowell's III Corps divisions under General Rufus King was ordered to march on the Warrenton Turnpike to join Pope at Centreville. King, however, suffered from epilepsy and for a week he had been commanding his division from an ambulance. As his four brigades moved out, King suffered a severe seizure and, unbeknownst to his brigade commanders, would be incommunicado during the critical hours ahead. The division would be leaderless when close coordination was most needed.

Late in the afternoon, the brigade under General John Gibbon was tramping east near the town of Groveton when a shrill screeching sound erupted from hundreds of rebel throats.

"Yee-haw! Yee-haw! Yee-haw!" The yell came from a wooded hill to their left. Next, they saw parallel columns of Jackson's infantry form a line of battle as Confederate artillery opened up. The Union soldiers, mostly volunteers from Wisconsin, had never been in a fight before, but they did not panic. Later they would be renowned as the Iron Brigade.

Gibbon formed them into line of battle until the two sides faced each other, no more than sixty or seventy yards apart. Both sides discharged their weapons nearly simultaneously, creating a thunderous roar and plumes of acrid smoke. They continued to fire at each other at close range.

Jackson sent in more troops in a frontal assault, but the outnumbered Federals hung on. General Abner Doubleday's brigade plugged a gap in Gibbon's line. The fight became a stalemate, and remained so until sunset, when the two lines gradually drifted apart, leaving over two thousand dead and wounded on the battlefield.

Nearly one of every three men engaged on both sides was shot. That night, fearing an overwhelming attack by Jackson in the morning, Gibbon and Doubleday's brigades joined the rest of King's division and withdrew southeast toward Manassas Junction.

Pope watched the battle from his position eight miles away near Bull Run. That night he learned of the fight's intensity, and irrationally concluded that King had Jackson in his grasp. All he needed to do, Pope surmised, was to box Jackson in and deliver a final crushing blow.

However, Pope did not know that King's division had departed the battlefield, together with General James Rickett's division that had retreated from Thoroughfare Gap after a brief engagement with Longstreet's lead brigade. King's and Rickett's divisions were in McDowell's III Corps, but no one had heard from the commanding general for over twelve hours. Eventually he and his staff reappeared after wandering lost in some backwater for the better part of the day.

All Pope needed to do on the morning of August 29 was strengthen his defensive position at Centreville and wait for reinforcements from the Army of the Potomac. The rationale for doing so was the preservation of his weary and discombobulated army, and the protection of the nation's Capital. But he did not see it that way.

After all, he had been placed in command to deal a lethal blow to the rebels and, being a man of action, that was precisely what he intended to do. The fog and vicissitudes of war be damned.

As he declared to his army upon taking command, his policy was to attack, not defend, because, as he said, "Success and glory are in the advance."

Pope hastily conceived a two-pronged advance to overtake Jackson. One pincer, under General Philip Kearney, would advance down the Warrenton Turnpike from Centreville, and the second under General Franz Sigel would strike up the road from Manassas to Gainesville.

This plan was based on two serious misconceptions and a persistent blind spot. First, many elements of his army were not where he thought they were.

Second, Jackson was not trying to get away; he occupied a strong position on the unfinished railroad north of the Warrenton Turnpike, and his men were rested and ready to resume the fight.

Contrary to Pope's belief, Jackson was preparing to pounce, not run, and somehow the Union general had forgotten about Longstreet, whose corps of thirty-thousand men was about to join Jackson. Together the two corps would have fifty-four-thousand battle-hardened veterans, and they would be led by Robert. E. Lee.

Halleck was handed a telegram when he returned to his headquarters from the White House. It was sent by Pope around mid-morning. The general was convinced he had cornered Jackson and was concentrating the Army of Virginia. Already Sigel was attacking, and Kearney was coming up.

Halleck waved the telegram at his staff and said, "Where is Longstreet? Where is Lee?" His questions were met with silence and blank expressions.

"I see," Halleck groaned. "Once again, we are in the dark about the rebels' whereabouts, much less their intentions. Tell General Pope I want to know where Lee and Longstreet are by the end of the day!"

Longstreet's corps passed through Thoroughfare Gap during the morning, raising clouds of dust visible to Jackson. Stonewall sent Stuart's cavalry to guide Longstreet to tactically strong positions on his right flank. Meanwhile Jackson's divisions were occupied with Sigel's nine-thousand men who at dawn plowed into Jackson's center and left.

The fighting spanned a two-mile front and involved many federal German-American units that fought bravely and stubbornly. But Jackson's line held, buttressed by aggressive and accurate artillery fire. Unfortunately, Kearney was late—he had ignored Pope's order to march before dawn—and by the time he arrived at the vanguard of Heintzelman's III Corps the battle had devolved into clusters of individual melees rather than the intended coordinated Union assault.

The last gaggle of office seekers and afternoon visitors left Lincoln's reception room. The President absently massaged his right hand that ached after being clutched by so many overeager and passionate hands. His face concealed the cloud of weariness that often overtook him this time of day.

One visitor had struck a note of lingering sadness. Widow Esther Machamer came to the White House to thank the President for defending the

Republic; her only son, Private Henry Machamer, was killed the previous month at Malvern Hill.

Through tears, she whispered, "Mister President, I know how difficult it must be for you to see so many young men die. I hope you can take comfort in the fact that Henry's family prays for you every day."

Her eyes met his, and then she left, before he could reply. Lincoln knew he would think of her that night, when he tried to sleep, without success, until his brain succumbed.

Halleck was waiting for him when Lincoln returned to his office.

"Encouraging news from Sigel, Mister President," Halleck said, rubbing his elbows. "He attacked the rebel line this morning and his men are making good progress against Jackson's line. Heintzelman has joined the battle and Porter is moving up on the left flank. General Pope is confident of victory."

"Excellent, General," Lincoln said as he leaned on the cabinet table and studied the map. "Please, show me the army's position."

"It's here, sir, along the Warrenton Turnpike south of Bull Run. There is an unfinished railroad where Jackson's men fortified themselves—with little success, I might add."

"And what of Lee and Longstreet?" Lincoln asked.

"We believe Lee is with Longstreet's corps at Thoroughfare Gap, sir."

Lincoln asked, "I would expect them to join the battle, wouldn't you?"

"Yes, Mister President. For that reason, General Pope has deployed infantry to block Longstreet while he attends to Jackson. Then he—together with McClellan and the Army of the Potomac—will deal with Longstreet."

Lincoln paused and stroked his beard.

"Let's be certain McClellan understands his role and objectives." His worn expression appeared hopeful, a rarity. "We have reason to be optimistic. Is that correct, general?"

"Yes, Mister President. This could be the success we have sought for the past year."

Lincoln nodded and sat at his desk. He turned and looked up at Halleck, who was mopping his brow.

"I'll be dining with Mrs. Lincoln this evening. You and I will meet in the morning. Until then, keep me apprised."

At 10 a.m. Friday morning, General John Bell Hood's division of Longstreet's Corps intersected the Warrenton Turnpike after overcoming weak

Union opposition and marching through Thoroughfare Gap. The dust-covered Texans were in a hurry. They swung left and advanced toward the thunderous sounds of battle erupting from Jackson's right flank. Soon they were skirmishing with Union troops from General John Reynold's infantry division.

All but one of Longstreet's remaining divisions deployed to Hood's right, across the Warrenton Pike south of Groveton and facing the Federal left flank. General Richard Anderson's South Carolina division would arrive early the next morning.

By late afternoon, Lee had Pope in the jaws of the Army of Northern Virginia, and he was ready to clamp down. But the careful Longstreet demurred. He was not ready: not all his units were in place, and he wanted to reconnoiter the ground. Actually, there was no need to rush. Jackson was holding his line, and Stuart had identified a large Union force moving up from the south on the Manassas-Gainesville Road.

These were two veteran Army of the Potomac divisions under General Fitz-John Porter; they were accompanied by McDowell with Rickett's division. Recognizing the threat to Longstreet's right flank, Stuart deceived Porter and McDowell by dragging tree branches up and down the road, creating clouds of swirling dust, as if a large hostile force was bearing down on the Federals.

Already Porter was prone to deception. Cautious by nature, he was confused and frustrated by an order Pope wrote that morning instructing him to link up with Sigel, Heintzelman, and Reno on the Warrenton Turnpike. That was clear enough, but Pope went on to say that the whole Union command should halt and be prepared to fall back behind Bull Run that night if it needed supplies.

Pope concluded the order with a further obfuscation: "If any considerable advantages are to be gained by departing from this order, it will not be strictly carried out."

The order also reassigned King's old division to McDowell, who promptly left Porter and moved north to join Sigel and Reynolds. Before he left, though, McDowell received information from Buford's cavalry that Longstreet's corps had been observed crossing the Warrenton Turnpike at 9 a.m.

Inexplicably, McDowell did not pass this information along to Pope, who remained unaware of Longstreet's presence. But he shared the news with Porter, who decided the dust cloud swirling in front of him must be the leading spear of Longstreet's corps. Porter decided not to advance as ordered; rather, he dispatched a skirmish line and stayed put.

Late in the afternoon Pope urged Porter to advance against the right and rear of Jackson's line. When Porter objected, stating he was facing a large rebel force, Pope dismissed the assertion as fanciful and shifted Porter's divisions to the main line. Once again, Pope missed an opportunity to learn of Longstreet's presence and the lurking threat to his army.

At dusk, Longstreet sent Hood's division on a reconnaissance in force up the Warrenton Turnpike. They encountered the recently arrived McDowell, and the two sides got so intertwined that one disoriented Union major was captured as he attempted to lead a rebel regiment from Mississippi. In the twilight, and with everyone covered in dust, it soon became impossible to discern friend from foe. Finally, Longstreet withdrew Hood from the fight, which had accomplished nothing except that Lee realized it was fortunate he had not ordered a full out assault that day.

Pope was in an ebullient mood the following morning, Saturday, August 30. In his mind, he had Jackson cornered, and by noon he was convinced that the Confederates were retreating. Once again, his sanguine nature allowed him to interpret information as he wanted it to be, rather than how it actually was or could be.

He learned the previous night that Hood had attacked his left but then withdrew. *'That was encouraging,'* he thought. Better yet, this morning rebel wagons were seen heading away from the battlefield. Pope concluded that these two events meant Jackson was whipped and pulling out. He ordered his commanders to block Jackson's escape.

Jackson was not running away. During the night he pulled his men off the line for rest and resupply, leaving a skeleton force on the unfinished railroad to sound the alarm in case the Federals resumed the attack. The wagons the Federals saw moving away were ambulances carrying Confederate wounded.

On Stonewall's right, Longstreet waited, having learned that Pope was massing his army for another attack on Jackson's lines. Pope ordered the assault despite a reliable report that Confederate forces were present in substantial numbers on his exposed and undermanned left flank.

Pope dismissed the warning, absently uttering, "Oh, I guess not."

His Union troops would charge across Longstreet's front, from right to left, into the jaws of the trap Lee had set for them. Longstreet's artillery was positioned on a ridge at the angle of the jaws. There were eighteen batteries in all, and they could sweep the open ground with exploding shells and cannister when Pope's infantry advanced into the killing field.

While Longstreet patiently awaited Pope's assault, Abraham Lincoln and his assistant private secretary, John Hay, were riding their horses from the Soldiers' Home to the White House. Lincoln much preferred the cool fresh air and quiet of the Soldier's Home, and he and his family spent much time there during the summer.

The three-mile ride would occupy most of the hour.

On the way, the President said, "I sent telegrams to Banks, Burnside, and McClellan this morning, asking if they had any news of Pope. They did not, but McClellan wrote back that we had two choices, either to help Pope with all available forces or, and I quote, 'Leave Pope to get out of his scrape and at once use all our means to make the capital perfectly safe'. I replied that I would prefer to concentrate all our forces to open communications with Pope, but that such a decision was up to General Halleck."

Lincoln halted his horse and continued, "John, I think McClellan wants Pope to lose. That sounds illogical, but I'll wager that his feeling is shared by quite a few officers in the Army of the Potomac. Recall that Pope talked down to them when he arrived here last month, and now perhaps McClellan and his officers are hoping he'll get his comeuppance."

John Hay was a poet by inclination and a lawyer by training.

"I believe General McClellan is most concerned about his status. He is constantly inquiring about his position and command. Frankly, Mister President, I think he is very low—in the mind, that is—and can't see the woods for the trees."

Lincoln nudged his horse, "I'll say this, though, McClellan had his army looking parade ground smart before he took it down to the Peninsula. And he cut quite a figure during those big reviews: tall in the saddle, as though he was born a centaur. Put on a fine show, too, especially for the dozens of fine ladies and gentlemen who brought their picnic baskets and sipped champagne while our troops sweated in their fresh new uniforms."

The President tipped his hat to two ladies out for a stroll.

He continued, "A year ago McClellan told me the idea was to crush the rebellion at one blow, terminate the war in one campaign, crush it at its very heart. But instead of seeking battle, he sought a larger and larger army, saying the Confederates far outnumbered him. Ben Wade said he was like the boy who wanted to learn how to swim without getting wet. Of course, being a Democrat didn't help the general's standing with the Radicals."

It was a sunny day, thickly humid, as Washington was in August. Hay looked at Lincoln and chuckled. "Remember last November when we went to McClellan's quarters on Lafayette Square, and he was at a wedding?"

"I do," Lincoln replied, smiling thinly. "We waited nearly an hour. When he returned, instead of meeting with us, he went up to bed and took a nap. As I recall, John, you were rather upset. Said his insolence was unparalleled."

"Indeed, Mister President. Then he contracted typhoid in January, and everything stopped…"

"At a very inconvenient time," Lincoln interrupted, "when Congress and the public were angry with the army's inaction."

Lincoln paused, as he always did, to view the iconic red sandstone Smithsonian Castle off in the distance. Next to it was the unfinished Washington Monument.

"Classic architecture, John, but isolated from the city. We should attend to that when this rebellion is over…create a mall with the Capital at one end and something inspiring at the other."

"On another subject, Mister President, we are receiving very detailed reports from Governor Ramsey in Minnesota. It seems the Indians have murdered over five hundred people along the Minnesota River valley, and up north, too. He wants federal help."

"I know," Lincoln replied. "Halleck has kept the 6th Minnesota there instead of moving it down to Tennessee. Apparently, the former governor, Henry Sibley, is in command. Not a professional soldier, and he's had some conflicts of interest regarding Indian matters in the past. We may have to send them a seasoned commander. Trouble is, I'm having the devil's time finding one myself."

General James Longstreet watched the blue waves of Porter's Federal infantry cross the plain toward Stonewall's defenders. A courier rode up and handed him a message. It was from Lee, ordering him to send a division to reinforce Jackson's right flank.

He returned the courier's salute and said, "My compliments to General Lee, and I will do as ordered. But the Federal's attack will be broken long before those troops are in position." At that, he gave the signal for his artillery to fire.

The Confederate gunners were ready. The artillery exploded with a thunderous crash, expectorating clouds of billowing white smoke that floated in the hot, humid air. The devastation in the Union ranks would be remembered forever by those who survived the battle.

Headless torsos, serrated loops of bowel, and scarlet lipomatous clumps of human flesh were everywhere. Many Federal combat units simply disintegrated. Others tried to carry on, but most fell back, their formations in chaos, fragmented and isolated in the thick underbrush.

As the cannonading tapered off—the caissons were nearly empty—Longstreet ordered the twenty-five-thousand men in his five infantry divisions to advance from their shielded positions. In the lead was Hood's Texans who overran a New York regiment of nattily uniformed Zouaves in tasseled fezzes, blue jackets, baggy red trousers, and white spats; a quarter of these four-hundred-ninety volunteers were dead within minutes, a horrific mortality that would not befall any other unit during the war.

The other jaw—Jackson's corps—recognized the Union's sudden vulnerability and moved forward, driving back the Federal infantry. Abruptly, Pope's ill-led army was in retreat, not as frantic as it was during the first battle of Bull Run the previous year, but nonetheless an astonishing reverse.

The following morning Lincoln entered John Hay's bedroom around eight o'clock. His secretary was dressing.

"Well, John," he said, "we are whipped again, I'm afraid. The enemy reinforced on Pope and drove back his left wing and he has retired to Centreville where he said he will be able to hold his men. I don't like that expression. I don't like to hear him admit his men need holding."

The Union men did not need holding; they had fought well, surely as bravely as the rebels. What they needed was skilled leadership: generals in charge who knew their trade. The difference between the Federal and Confederate armies were Lee, Jackson, Longstreet, and subordinate commanders like Hood, Hill, and Stuart.

In the span of three months, they had driven McClellan from Richmond's doorstep, compelled the Army of the Potomac to retreat back north, and completely befuddle and outmaneuver Pope. Now they could almost see the dome of the Capital in Washington.

Pope had left Washington in July confident that he would teach the easterners how to fight and put down the rebellion. Six weeks later, he was exhausted, demoralized, and withdrawn, a man who had no stuffing left. Halleck placed Pope under the command of McClellan when the Army of Virginia retreated from Bull Run to the fortifications around the Capital. A few days later Lincoln reorganized the army under McClellan, and on September 6 ordered Pope to report to the Secretary of War Stanton for assignment.

To Pope's surprise, Stanton informed him that he was to proceed immediately to Minnesota as commander of the newly formed Department of the Northwest.

"The Indian hostilities now prevailing," Stanton said, "require the attention of a military officer of high rank, in whose ability and vigor the government has confidence, and you therefore have been selected for this important command."

Pope was devastated. He was being exiled to a frontier outpost. His career was in shambles. Resignation was an option, but he was not a quitter. On September 9, he boarded a train for Minnesota.

Chapter 10

Hutchinson was an armed and vigilant community when the five Swedes descended the hill and crossed the South Fork Crow River into town. They had traveled off roads and kept well north of the Minnesota River valley before turning south, encountering no one after escaping the Dakota encampment.
Their only nemeses were gnats and mosquitoes. Elliot and Carl led the two horses carrying Ruth and Elsa, who were much too weak to walk. Julia was on foot behind them; she was sore and terribly tired but buoyed by the knowledge that she was carrying their baby.

A familiar voice shouted at them from the small blockhouse on the stockade. It was Robert. Moments later he was embracing the women.

"My god, I didn't think we would ever see you again! My god…! What happened?"

Elliot described how he and Carl found the women, their escape across the river, and the four-day trek to Hutchinson.

"Where's Gustav?" Elliot asked.

"Somewhere with the army," Robert replied. "He thought it would be the best way to find you."

"And William and Ester?" Julia exclaimed, grabbing Robert's hand.

"Safe and healthy. They're staying with Mrs. Harrington."

Julia sank to her knees and quietly sobbed. Carl lifted Ruth and Elsa from their horses, and the two women joined Julia on the ground. They were a pathetic sight, faces covered with dirt and insect bites, dresses filthy and torn, and bodies utterly drained, like corn stalks in a drought. But they were alive, and they would heal.

For three years, since becoming the first Episcopal Bishop of Minnesota, Henry Benjamin Whipple had sought to rescue the Dakota and Ojibwe from the 'stupendous piece of wickedness' that he thought characterized the U.S. Indian administration.

He had complained first to President James Buchanan without result and now, in September 1862, he was about to meet with President Lincoln at the White House to explain why hundreds of white men, women, and children lay dead and mostly unburied in Minnesota, the tragic victims of a war that should never have happened.

The bishop was accompanied this day by General Henry Halleck, his cousin, who arranged the meeting. Lincoln was all too familiar with visits by religious leaders. Almost invariably they had a message for the President that came to them from God. Lincoln sometimes wondered why God would not speak as directly to him, the President, as he did to men and women of the cloth. Today he would find Whipple to be a different sort: he had a message, except that he did not claim it was God's.

Lincoln stood when Whipple and Halleck entered his office. He and the tall youthful bishop were nearly the same height. Whipple's right hand was bandaged, the result of an infection that developed after he accidentally pierced his palm with a needle while suturing a wound suffered by a farmer during the battle of New Ulm.

They greeted each other by grasping the other's left hand and sat at the table in the center of the room where the cabinet met. Halleck remained standing until the President asked him to be seated.

"I regret the civilian casualties in your state," Lincoln began. "Over eight hundred, I believe. Men, women, and children. More civilian deaths than we have seen in this Civil War."

"Yes, Mister President," Whipple replied, "and the non-combatant casualties—including innocent Indians—are likely to rise, considerably."

Lincoln nodded. "Bishop, I understand you have deep knowledge of the native situation in Minnesota. If that is true, perhaps you can enlighten me. I do have time for this and wish to understand your views."

Whipple was slightly taken aback by Lincoln's willingness to hear him out. Everyone knew the country was in crisis: At this moment, the bishop's friend, General George McClellan, was about to challenge Robert E. Lee's army north of the Potamic near Antietam. The Union was facing defeat and dissolution, and yet this President was clearly concerned.

"Mister President, the current tragedy in Minnesota is rooted in our treatment of the Indians from the time the United States became a nation. Firstly, our system is based on a falsehood. We recognize Indian tribes as independent nations and make and ratify treaties with them as we do with any foreign power. We do this with the full knowledge that they send no representatives to us, and we none to them. We do this knowing that they have no power to compel us to comply with a treaty's provisions, and that we can—and in fact do—unilaterally modify treaties whenever the government finds it convenient.

"In this way, we have taken millions of acres of native land for our purposes in exchange for absurdly small sums of money and modest annuities that most Indians never see, and that enrich the traders and scoundrels that sell them whiskey and shoddy goods. Worse still, we force them into debt, so that they are compelled to surrender even more land in order to feed their families. It is a corrupt system; it has always been a corrupt system.

"This year, the annuity payment was very late. Already the Dakota Sioux were near starvation. Many died last winter after their dogs were eaten. There was no game to speak of, and those that farm usually consume what they grow. Furthermore, this year's crops were not ready for harvest. At the Lower Agency, the government Indian agent refused them food that was available in storage, and the traders would sell them no food on credit. The suffering was visible to the most casual observer, and the native unrest, particularly among the young men, was obvious to those of us who know them.

"An incident occurred in August that incited the Indian's attack on the Lower Agency at Redwood. Thereafter, all Hell was unleashed on defenseless people, and no white man, white woman or white child was spared. The culprits were a minority group of mostly Mdewakanton Sioux under Little Crow. They committed almost every atrocity known to man: torture, decapitation, immolation, and rape. Whole families were slaughtered. Women were taken captive, abused, and held for ransom.

"It should be no surprise that everyone in the State of Minnesota—and many elsewhere—are demanding Sioux blood. General Pope is mounting a campaign to bring Little Crow to battle and hopefully end this awful war..."

"Mister President," Halleck interrupted, "Pope has dispatched Colonel Sibley and over twelve hundred troops up the Minnesota River valley. Our scouts tell us Little Crow has fewer than a thousand warriors. Pope expects victory by the end of the month."

Lincoln was indifferent to such optimistic predictions by his field commanders, and especially from Pope. He turned to Whipple. "It appears the federal government could have averted this tragedy. Is that your view?"

"Yes, Mister President," Whipple replied. "Indeed, yes. This war could have been avoided had the annuity payment been on time and if the Indian agent—Thomas Galbraith—had released food from storage at the Lower Agency. However, had the outbreak not occurred this summer, it would have happened eventually—and it may happen again unless the present system is reformed."

Lincoln said, "You seem to suggest that the root or roots of the problem go deeper than one late annuity payment or the poor judgement of a particular Indian agent. I was told—actually warned—early this year that corruption was rampant in our Indian Affairs Department."

"Special Commissioner George E.H. Day—a government official who was dispatched to Minnesota last year—sent me a report. I would like to read it to you."

Lincoln retrieved a letter from his desk. "On the first of January, Commissioner Day wrote, 'I have discovered numerous violations of law and many frauds committed by past agents and a superintendent. I think I can establish frauds to the amount from twenty to a hundred thousand dollars and satisfy any reasonable intelligent man that the Indians whom I have visited in this state and Wisconsin have been defrauded of more than a hundred thousand dollars in or during the four years past…

"The whole system is defective and must be revised or your red children, as they call themselves, will continue to be wronged and outraged and the just vengeance of heaven continue to be poured out and visited upon this nation for its abuses and cruelty to the Indian'."

The President returned the letter to his desk and picked up another.

"Two months after Commissioner Day's warning, I received your letter, Bishop. I referred it to the Department of Interior. I regret doing so, particularly since Day had recently alerted me to the Indian situation. I should have treated your letter differently than I did. Of course, I was occupied with this rebellion, but that does not excuse my deficiency. I am the chief executive of the country, and it is my duty to attend to the kind of issues you raised."

Lincoln continued, "Bishop Whipple, I quote from your letter: 'The first thing needed is honesty. There has been a marked deterioration in Indian affairs since the office has become one of mere political favoritism…Every employee ought to be a man of purity, temperance, industry, and unquestioned integrity. Those selected to teach in any department must be men of peculiar fitness—patient, with quick perceptions, enlarged ideas, and men who love their work. They must be something better than so many drudges fed at the public crib'."

Lincoln held out the letter, and said, "I agree, of course. But I fear such perfection is a grail difficult to find, even though it may be earnestly sought."

"I concur, Mister President," Whipple sighed. "I believe, however, that there are good men in our country who could make a difference."

Whipple stood and faced Lincoln. His youthful face was clean-shaven, and his long hair was combed back and fell onto his shoulders.

"My heart aches for these poor wronged people. They should be treated as wards of the government rather than people of a sovereign nation. They cannot live without law. In sight of my mission, an Indian woman was violated by brutal white men with such cruelty that she died. No one was punished and no investigation was made.

"An old chief once answered my plea against Indian drunkenness and adultery by saying, 'My father, it is your people, who you say follow the Bible, that bring us the whiskey. It is your white men who corrupt our daughters. Go teach them to do right, and then come to us, and I will believe you.'"

John Nicolay entered the room and stood silently by the door. Lincoln looked up and acknowledged his presence.

"Bishop, my secretary signals our time together is ending. Thank you for your insights and recommendations. My only promise to you is that I will do all in my power to see that justice is observed in this…I was going to say 'war' but in fact I consider it a rebellion, an uprising…I will strive to see that the guilty are punished and the innocent absolved. Major reforms are needed, I agree, but my first priority is the preservation of the Union. All else is subordinate and must wait."

Chapter 11

The dark cloud of depression embraced Little Crow. He was exhausted, spent. Nowhere did he see a glimmer of light in the black tunnel of despair he was traveling. The deer stew Mina had set on the plate before him was untouched. No one was allowed in his tepee. No one except Mina whose lover White Eagle was captured when the soldiers killed her father Running Bear, and her mother Weayaya.

Running Bear was Little Crow's boyhood friend, and Weayaya was his cousin. They were peaceful, traditional people, who were upset with Little Crow's involvement in the attacks on white communities.

"This will not end until all Dakota men are dead," Running Bear told Little Crow when their paths crossed west of Hutchinson, "all of us, all Dakota men and women, old and young, will suffer terribly. You have done a terrible thing."

On September 12, Little Crow wrote to Sibley. He reminded the colonel that he had one-hundred fifty prisoners, whites and mixed bloods, who were well treated. Then he asked quite simply how he could make peace for his people. By the time Sibley received the letter, he knew Little Crow's influence with his warriors was waning or gone completely.

The failures at Fort Ridgely and Hutchinson were partly responsible, but also the young men sensed Little Crow's growing passivity; they doubted his resolve to fight to the end. When Running Bear's daughter appeared and Little Crow took her into his tepee, the warriors were convinced he had joined the peace seekers. A few of them plotted his death.

The Dakota Sioux were hopelessly divided. The peace seekers and the war party under Little Crow occupied two separate camps on the upper Minnesota River. A growing number of Dakota vocally opposed the war, and they looked to Little Crow to make peace. A rumor spread among the peace seekers that Sibley would not punish anyone who had not killed civilians. Yet the young warriors wanted the war to continue until all white men were driven from their land. They told the peace seekers that all Dakota, warriors and peace seekers alike, would die if the war was lost.

Little Crow began preparations for one more battle. It had to succeed, or he and his tribe would perish.

Fifty miles southwest of Hutchinson, Gustav Lindquist finished dressing an open thigh wound sustained by a young Minnesota volunteer during the second battle of Fort Ridgely. "The wound is clean—no pus or corruption—but it has to heal from inside out. That's why it needs to drain. Understand?"

"Yes, thank you," the soldier said.

"I want to see you the day after tomorrow. Find me if you're feverish or chilled."

Three men entered the Fort Ridgely dormitory that had been converted to a surgery and clinic. The taller one wore the insignia of a colonel. It was Henry Sibley. He walked over to Gustav and his patient.

"Good morning, doctor," he said. "Thank you for caring for this soldier. I see you have many others waiting."

"Yes, uh…?" Gustav asked.

"Sibley, Colonel Henry Sibley. And you, sir?"

"Doctor Gustav Lindquist. I'm here primarily because the Indians kidnapped my sister-in-law."

"Sorry to hear, Doctor. Where?"

"She was taken at Hutchinson—during the battle. My brother and cousin are tracking them. I thought I'd follow the army in the hope you'd find them. I've been helping with the wounded."

Sibley stroked his beard.

"Doctor, you are welcome to accompany us. We believe Little Crow has many captives, perhaps hundreds. We could use your skills. The army will be moving out soon, now that the rain has ended and the road is decent."

Gustav wiped his hands with a towel, stood, and faced Sibley.

"Colonel, why has it taken the government so long to help us here?"

Sibley had heard the question uncounted times during the past weeks.

"We're fighting two wars, the rebellion in the South, and this one. There have been major battles in Virginia the past month, and it's been difficult getting through to the War Department. But now Lincoln has appointed

General Pope to take command here. And the third Minnesota regiment is back from Tennessee."

"My family came from Sweden," Gustav said. "A month ago, there were seventeen of us on three good farms north of Hutchinson. The Indians killed ten, including my mother, father, two brothers, my cousins and their parents." Pointing to the bandages on his face, he continued, "They cut me and my brother in Hutchinson, and took my sister-in-law. God knows what they've done to her. We want them to hang."

"I assure you, Doctor," Sibley replied, "all will hang."

Major General John Pope arrived in St. Paul on September 19 after a lengthy train ride from Washington that included stops in Cincinnati and Chicago. He was met by a terrified and angry populace and a ferocious Governor Ramsey, who declared, "The Sioux Indians must be exterminated or driven forever beyond the borders of this state."

The state capital was crowded with hundreds of terrified Minnesota families who had fled their farms and towns when Indians from both the lower and upper agencies rampaged throughout the state. For them, too, retribution was foremost in their minds.

Pope reviewed Sibley's actions since he took command. There was no question Sibley was confronted with many challenges, including lack of trained troops, rations, and essential equipment. Moreover, initially he had no cavalry or horses, but relied on mounted citizen volunteers who often ignored Sibley or failed to follow basic military principles. The catastrophe at Birch Coulee was, in part, the result of such conduct.

Despite these handicaps, though, Sibley did appear to be overly cautious. Was it fear of failure, or lack of physical courage, or something else? Pope did not know but he assured Sibley that he would 'push forward everything to your assistance as fast as possible', and reminded him that he was now officially an officer in the U.S. Army and no longer a member of the state militia. Pope, not Governor Ramsey, was his superior and Sibley was to report directly to him and to act only on his orders.

To his superiors in the War Department, Pope told of the 'wide, universal, and uncontrollable panic everywhere' in the northwest.

"Over five hundred people have been murdered in Minnesota alone and three hundred women and children are now in captivity…children nailed alive to trees and houses, women violated and then disemboweled—everything that horrible ingenuity could devise."

But Stanton and Halleck had no time for the tribulations in Minnesota. Although McClellan had stopped the Confederates at bloody Antietam, Lee continued to be a threat to Washington, and the rebels were advancing toward the Ohio River in northern Kentucky. The Union needed every soldier and resource for its defense. In short, Pope would have to do with what he had.

After being delayed two days by more drenching rains, Sibley departed Fort Ridgely on September 19 with sixteen hundred men. Included were two-hundred seventy experienced infantrymen of the Third Minnesota who had been paroled after being surrendered by their officers at the battle of Murfreesboro in July 1861.

Also, present were thirty-eight mounted men of the Renville Rangers, sixteen citizen artillerists, and the lead scout, John Other Day, who the previous month had bravely guided sixty-two people at Yellow Medicine to safety. Gustav rode in one of the wagons assigned to the Third Minnesota; he did not know that Julia and his surviving family members were safe in Hutchinson.

The four-mile-long column advanced on the government road up the southwest side of the Minnesota River valley toward the Upper Agency forty miles distant. Sibley was cautious, and progress was slow. At four o'clock in the afternoon, he stopped and made camp near the Lower Agency.

The troops dug rifle pits and built barricades to protect the camp. Nearby they found and buried the body of Philander Prescott, a sixty-one-year-old trader and interpreter, who was long married to a Dakota woman; he was killed by Little Crow's men during the August 18 attack.

The slow march continued for the next two days. Each afternoon they stopped and fortified their camp. Often they spotted distant Indian riders tracking the column's progress.

On September 22, Sibley ordered a halt for the night at Lone Tree Lake, about three miles east of Wood Lake. A stream exited Lone Tree Lake through a ravine and wandered east. Tall bluestem grass covered the gently rolling ground surrounding the lake.

They made camp on the south bank, with the Third, Sixth, and Seventh Minnesota regiments each forming the side of a triangle. Pickets were posted at the border of the camp but not beyond. Sibley did not think he would encounter Little Crow's army for another day or two.

That night, Little Crow quietly concealed his warriors in the deep grass along the road. He had about nine hundred men but decided against a night attack. Rather, he would wait until morning and ambush Sibley's long column on the road, breaking it into small parts that could be destroyed one by one. A victory was critical, for both the cause and for him personally.

If Sibley's army was annihilated, it would be months, perhaps years before the Federal government, preoccupied as it was with the Civil War, could mount another campaign. It would give him time to build a Sioux powerhouse that included tribes that so far had not joined his crusade to evict the white man from their ancestral lands. If he lost this battle, the Sioux peace factions would prevail, and they would likely kill him.

Gustav slept fitfully. His back ached more than usual, a result of the constant jolting it received in the wagon on the rain-rutted road. Around 5 a.m. he gave up and joined three soldiers boiling coffee.

"Morning, doc," one of them said. "Want some joe?"

"Yes, thank you," Gustav replied. The soldier handed him a tin cup and filled it with steaming brew.

"Anyone know what the plan is for today?" Gustav asked.

A voice from behind said, "We'll follow the road to Yellow Medicine." Gustav turned to face Lieutenant Joyce, a liaison officer from General Pope's staff.

"What's there?" a soldier asked.

"Not sure," Joyce replied. "We've heard Little Crow is there with about twelve hundred men. And hundreds of prisoners, mostly women and children."

"So, there's going to be a battle today," Gustave observed.

"Hope so, doctor. Time to bring this business to an end." The lieutenant left to inspect the pickets.

A soldier filled Gustav's cup.

"Have another, doc, you may be real busy soon."

When the sun rose at 7 a.m., a small contingent of hungry troops from the Third Minnesota regiment hitched up four wagons. They left the road and headed north to get potatoes at a farm near the Upper Sioux Agency three miles away. These men were unhappy with their rations and were acting on their own, a disciplinary breech by veteran soldiers who should have known better.

As the wagons emerged from the camp, Little Crow immediately recognized the danger: they would run over or expose his warriors who were concealed in the grass about two hundred yards from the road. Yet there was nothing he could do, except load his Sharps carbine and prepare to fight. Before the first wagon had gone very far, it flushed an Indian who rose up and discharged his musket. The shot triggered a flurry of rifle fire from the wagons.

Immediately, the alerted camp formed firings lines and brought up the howitzers. The two-hundred-seventy disciplined veterans of the Third Regiment advanced and delivered a volley that devasted the exposed Indians, killing and wounding dozens. The artillerists took a terrible toll with canister shot; their howitzer became monster shotguns, spraying attackers on the right and in the ravine with lead balls and metal shards.

Chief Mankato, who had fought bravely at Fort Ridgely and Birch Coulee, was killed by a cannonball as he and his warriors charged the camp. Everywhere the Indians suffered casualties without making any headway against the firepower of disciplined infantry and accurate artillery.

Little Crow had deployed less than half his force before he was compelled to order a retreat. It was pointless—suicidal—to continue to engage a superior and better armed foe when the outcome was certain defeat. He had counted on surprise and speed to offset their inferior numbers and weaponry. How ironic it was that a few maverick soldiers, intent on filling their bellies, accidentally exposed Little Crow's warriors and thwarted what could have been a strategic victory.

Gradually the Indians withdrew, leaving dozens of their dead and wounded on the rolling prairie. This would be the last battle. The Dakota Sioux war was at an end; that is, there would be no more battles, but the killing and suffering was only beginning.

The following day Little Crow gathered the men who had survived and returned to his camp.

"I am ashamed to call myself a Dakota," he told them. "We should have whipped them because they fight like women. But they outnumbered us and had big guns. Perhaps we were betrayed. The reasons do not matter. Now we must leave this valley, our home, and scatter over the plains like the buffalo and wolves."

The survivors of the Lindquist and Eriksson families except for Gustav returned to their farms from Hutchinson. All structures except the original Lindquist cabin had been burned to the ground and the contents taken or destroyed. The livestock had been slaughtered or stolen. The most consequential losses were the draft horses and oxen that were needed to do just about everything important during spring planting and at harvest time.

They knew the next few years would challenge their intellect, stamina, and faith. But they believed God had preserved them for some reason, and they would dedicate their lives to fulfilling the dreams that brought their families to this land. In the land, they would find solace, purpose, and recompence.

The leaves were turning, and there was a morning chill, reminding everyone that another Minnesota winter was only weeks away. Surviving until spring would be a challenge as great as any they faced during the past three weeks. The first priority was adequate shelter.

Elliot went to Oskar Nilsa's farm and borrowed the tools they would need to rebuild. Oskar said his sons were serving in the 5th Minnesota at Fort Abercrombie in North Dakota.

"I'll be up to help you as soon as I can," Oskar promised. "After I get the crops in."

Meanwhile, Robert rode east to Minneapolis and bought two sturdy Percheron draft horses and arranged to purchase a pair of oxen in the spring. He met with John Pillsbury and assured him that, despite the calamity and their losses, the family would strive to satisfy its financial obligations.

Pillsbury appreciated the commitment and offered to extend additional credit. He asked if Robert would be willing accompany him to St. Paul to meet Governor Ramsey and relate what had happened to his family.

"Many families have lost relatives," Pillsbury said, "but I've not heard of a worse tragedy than yours. I'm sure the governor would like to hear it first-hand." Robert agreed; he wanted to show his appreciation for Pillsbury's patience and generosity.

The following day at noon they were received by Alexander Ramsey in his office at the state capital.

The governor appeared harried, so Pillsbury got right to the point, "Governor, I thought you should meet this young man because he is one of seven survivors of a family of seventeen that immigrated just last year from Sweden. The rest were massacred by the Indians. They torched their farms north of Hutchinson and stole everything, everything including horses and livestock. A terrible tragedy, Governor, the worst I've heard."

Ramsey stood from his chair and walked around the desk. He grasped Robert's hand. "Please accept my condolences, Mr. Eriksson. I can assure you that the Indians will be exterminated or driven from our state. I just received word that Colonel Sibley has won a big victory near Wood Lake, just south of the Minnesota River. He's killed many Sioux warriors, and he knows where the captive women and children are."

"That is excellent news, Governor," Pillsbury said. He paused, then, "We know how busy you are…"

"Nonsense, please sit," Ramsey replied, gesturing to a leather couch.

"I want to hear more from Mr. Eriksson. Tell me what happened to your family."

Robert described in detail the massacres and destruction at their farms, the battle at Hutchinson, and the rescue of Julia, Ruth, and Elsa. He ended by saying, "I'm not sure how we're going to do it, but we will rebuild and put our crops in next year." He gestured to Pillsbury and continued, "We are indebted to Mr. Pillsbury—he's been very generous—and we want to repay him."

Ramsey turned to his secretary, Miles Berry, "Get someone from the St. Paul Daily Press over here. Mr. Eriksson's experience will be of great interest to our citizens—and to the legislature. The Indians have done terrible, terrible things and the people should read about the horrors directly from the victims."

Rising from his chair, the governor turned to Robert and said, "The state militia is going to help your family. Major Dickson is my aide. He'll arrange a shipment of supplies to help you through the winter."

Robert replied, "Thank you, sir. I have one request. My cousin, Dr. Gustav Lindquist is with Colonel Sibley's army. Would it be possible to let him know that his relatives, Julia Lindquist and Ruth and Elsa Eriksson were rescued and are safe at home?"

"By all means," Ramsey replied. "Major Dickson will see to it."

"Thank you, Governor," Robert said, "my family is most grateful."

The governor said, "John, thank you for bringing Mr. Eriksson to see me. And Mr. Eriksson, Miles here will show you to the anteroom where the reporter will interview you, and then Major Dickson will make arrangements for some supplies."

Pillsbury had been impressed with Robert Eriksson since the first day they met three years ago; this Swede had surprising sagacity for a man his age, and he was tough and energetic despite his spare frame.

As they left the Capital, Pillsbury said, "Robert, I'd like you to come to my home and meet my wife. We'll have dinner, and you can stay overnight in our spare room. What do you say?"

Robert readily agreed. He had not had a decent meal or slept in a bed for a month.

John Pillsbury was born in New Hampshire of Puritan stock. His family arrived in North America in 1640. On April 19, 1775, four Pillsbury men were among the colonial militiamen who confronted the British on Lexington Green. As a teenager, John clerked in his brother's country store and then engaged in the business of merchant tailoring for four years.

He moved to Minnesota in 1855, settled in St. Anthony, and entered the hardware business. His business continued to grow despite the financial crash of 1857 and a costly warehouse fire. Now he was branching out into lumber and flour-milling. In 1856, he married another New Hampshirite, Mahala Fisk.

The two-story frame house stood on a broad irregular lot in a well-maintained neighborhood. Pillsbury unhitched the Belgian from the buggy and put him in the stable. They found Mrs. Pillsbury in the small sitting room near the front door. She was doing needlepoint. At her feet preening a doll was their adopted daughter, Addie, who would soon be three years old.

"Hello, Mahala, I brought a dinner guest," John said. "This is Mr. Robert Eriksson, a gentleman I met three years ago. Most of his family were massacred by the Indians near Hutchinson. A terrible tragedy."

Mahala stood and enclosed Robert's right hand in both of hers. Her Victorian hairstyle framed an attractive face with kind eyes and a finely shaped nose and mouth.

"Welcome, Mr. Eriksson. I'm so sorry to hear about your family. How many perished?"

"Ten," Robert replied, "including my mother and father."

"Please accept my sympathies," Mahala said as she picked up Addie. "A terrible loss. We heard many children have been killed."

"Their farms were burned, too," John said. "We just visited the governor. He will provide some assistance for Robert's family, as we will too."

"Hundreds of refugees from the west are arriving in our city every day," Mahala said. "Our church—the First Congregational Church—is offering as much assistance as it can. We are doing a fundraiser tomorrow. John, I hope you can attend."

John replied, "Of course." He turned to Robert. "I serve in the church's 'society', a finance group as it were."

John spotted a rifle standing in a corner. Certainly, it was out of place in the parlor.

"What's this rifle doing here, Mahala?"

"I'm learning to fire it," Mahala replied, "with you gone most of the day and often at night, I want to be able to defend our home in case those Indians find their way here."

"But...but, Mahala, they are a hundred miles away...," John sputtered.

"That may be true. In any case, I'll be prepared."

John began to speak but stopped: he knew it was no use.

At dinner that evening, Robert was introduced to Astrid Hansen, a lovely young Norwegian woman who had escaped death on August 19 when her family and neighbors were fleeing their farms.

"We were on the road to Hutchinson when the Indians attacked us," she said. "I hid in a ditch covered with grass and listened to the screams...helpless..." She paused. Mahala touched her hand.

"My family...all of them...were killed...brutally, without mercy. I will never forget one particular Indian. He rode a black horse with a white face."

"I know him!" Robert said, sitting upright, absently dropping his knife and fork on the plate. "He killed three of my cousins and took my aunt and cousin captive. Thank heaven, they've been rescued." Robert's gaze fixed onto her oval blude eyes and said, "I'm sorry, Miss Hansen. That Indian's name is White Eagle."

The table was silent until Mahala said, "I met Astrid at the Nicollet Hotel after she managed to make her way from St. Peter to Minneapolis. She was trying to convince the doorman to allow her into the lobby. I saw how frayed and terribly stressed she was and told the doorman I would vouch for her."

Astrid turned to Mahala, "You were very kind, Mrs. Pillsbury. I was so desperate."

"I learned Astrid was multilingual—is it five languages, Astrid?" Mahala asked.

"Yes, I speak English and Norwegian, of course, and Swedish, German, and Dakota. I understand French, but don't speak it yet."

John said, "Astrid is working in our store now as a translator. Very helpful."

"And I'm hoping we can find her a position teaching languages," Mahala said.

Mahala stood to go to the kitchen. Astrid rose to follow her.

"She is staying with us until she finds a place of her own."

John said, "Robert and I will be in the parlor. Please, join us when you're finished."

The large stone fireplace held a stack of wood and kindling that John lighted with a match.

"I thought our meeting with Governor Ramsey went quite well," John said, directing Robert to a maroon Victorian leather chair by the fire.

"The interview with the Daily Press was an excellent idea. Ramsey is hell bent on whipping up public sentiment against the Indians. I won't be surprised if we see swift justice and punishment."

Robert leaned forward, "That Indian who killed Astrid's family and mine should be the first to hang. I would like to release the trapdoor myself. They should all hang. Every one of them."

"Yes, of course," John said, as he sat opposite Robert. "I suspect they will be tried by a military court. The Army won't waste time."

"On another subject," John continued, "would you be interested in coming to work for me? I need someone like you who knows farming and has a good business sense. My company is growing rapidly. Supplying the army is a major part of that, but this Civil War will end—hopefully soon—and we can resume normal commerce. When that happens, I want to be ready. Being first is always the best strategy. Would you be interested?"

"I'm grateful," Robert replied. "But I have no qualifications. I was home schooled. I know nothing of financial transactions, purchase orders, ledgers…"

John interrupted, "First of all, you're qualified because I say you are. As to the other stuff, you'll learn, I assure you. Robert, there's an explosion of migrants coming to this state, and they are reproducing like rabbits. Big families, with big appetites."

"They need to be fed and housed. They need meat, flour, hardware, and lumber. Farming will be profitable but processing the crops, making food out of wheat and corn is where the big opportunities are. That's what my nephew, Charles, and I want to do. You can be part of it if you want."

"Mister Pillsbury, I'm interested. But my family has more land now than we can farm, what with just three men to do all the work. My cousin is a doctor and can't do physical labor anyway because he broke his back. And we have to rebuild—cabins, barns…"

"I understand, Robert. Look, you won't be doing much of anything during the winter. Spend it here, in St. Anthony, learning the business. Then tend to your land in the spring, rebuild during the summer, and come back here after the harvest."

"What are you offering, exactly, Mister Pillsbury?" Robert asked.

"You'll work with me in the office and clerk in the store and warehouse. Learn about markets, suppliers, logistics, and finance. There are some farm and forest properties I'll want you to visit when the weather allows. I'll need help running the business. I'll pay you twenty-five dollars a month to start. You can live in the warehouse. Recall that you and your cousins stayed there when you first arrived in Minneapolis."

"I do, but I have a different question—and I don't mean to pry or snoop, Mister Pillsbury—but why do you need me now?"

John stood, grasped a poker, and jabbed at a smoldering log in the fireplace. "Confidentially, Robert, I have other interests, and want to spend more time pursuing them. One in particular is the University of Minnesota. Our state must have an institution of higher learning, but the University is deep in debt and closed. Congress this year passed a land-grant bill that will donate land to endow colleges."

"Our University doesn't qualify because it's not functioning, and it won't resume teaching until it gets out of debt and can hire faculty. I think there's a way to raise money, retire the debt, and reopen the University. But I must have the time to do it. That's one reason I need you—and frankly others—to help with the business."

Robert uncrossed his legs and sat up, "I see. I'm sure it's important." He paused. "One other question: will I be able to invest in the business?"

"You mean ownership? Equity?" John replied.

"Yes."

"I'll think about that. Perhaps new ventures would be most appropriate—such as the flour mill we want to build."

Robert stood. "I'll need a couple of months on the farm. If the family agrees, I'll be here the first of December." If not, I'll let you know by the end of the month.

Chapter 12

The enormity of the defeat at Lone Tree Lake weighed heavily on Little Crow. He was paralyzed by despair. A black cloud had been descending on him gradually since the repulses at Fort Ridgely and Hutchinson. Now he was completely in its grasp. Life now was only about survival. The killing had to stop, and a way had to be found to peacefully surrender the white captives to Sibley.

Fortunately, the vast majority of these mostly white and mixed-blood women and children were in the village near the mouth of the Chippewa River that was home to the growing number of Dakota Sioux who wanted peace. Already these peace seekers were fortifying the village to repel any attempt by Little Crow's soldiers to reclaim the captives.

Little Crow wanted to avoid a tribal civil war. He resolved to leave this place, to remove his family and warrior followers from Yellow Medicine and the Minnesota River valley forever. He would never see his homeland again. The good times with friends and relatives would be gone forever. All that inspired and sustained him for fifty-two years had to be left behind. Or he and his men would surely hang.

But before he headed north, Little Crow wanted to see his cousin, Antoine Joseph Campbell. They had known each other for decades and shared many experiences. Campbell's grandfather was a Scottish-born trader and interpreter who married a Dakota woman; they had son, Scott, who married Margaret Menagre, a mixed-race woman, who became a trusted advisor to Little Crow.

Antoine was the son of Scott and Margaret, and he served Little Crow as an interpreter, secretary, and go-between with Colonel Sibley. Unbeknownst to Little Crow, it was Antoine who helped the Dakota Sioux peacekeepers remove most of the white captives to their village while Little Crow was engaging Sibley's troops at Lone Tree Lake. Over forty captives still remained prisoners in Little Crow's camp.

A bolt of fear struck Antoine when he was summoned to Little Crow's tepee. Did the chief know of his role in protecting the captives? Was he aware of his recent communications with Sibley? He did not know.

Antoine found Little Crow by the fire with Mina, wrapped in a blanket.

"Come in, my cousin," Little Crow said in a friendly tone. "There is a chill this morning. Here, sit by me and enjoy the fire's warmth." Mina stood to leave.

"Mina," Antoine said. "White Eagle is alive. He was captured when your father and mother were killed by the soldiers."

Mina asked, "Where is he?"

"I think he's a prisoner at Redwood—the Lower Sioux Agency. But I'm not sure."

"Thank you for telling me," Mina said, and left the two men alone. She paused outside the tepee, thinking perhaps Antoine could get a message to White Eagle that she could be carrying his child. *'No,'* she thought, *'it is probably better for him not to know.'*

Sitting across from Little Crow, Antoine asked, "Where are you going?"

"I see your wives are packing."

"We'll move north and west, until we find a suitable place to winter," Little Crow replied.

"We leave tomorrow." He paused to draw the blanket over his shoulders.

"Before we go, I want to thank you for all that you have done for me and the Mdewakanton. You have been a true friend. We have done much together. As boys we hunted deer along the St. Croix and speared beaver and muskrat. You were my interpreter at Mendota and Washington. And these past weeks you have been at my side despite the danger. I ask, is there anything I can do for you before I leave tomorrow?"

"Have you considered surrendering to Sibley?" Antoine asked.

Little Crow scoffed, "He'd have a noose around my neck before sunset."

"They've never hung anyone before," Antoine replied.

"I know the trader Sibley, my gentle cousin, and I've heard what Governor Ramsey has been saying in the newspapers. Blood revenge is what they seek—what all whites will demand. We will be hunted like rabbits. You may be lucky and escape their anger because you have European blood and a white man's name. But no Dakota will be spared. If they surrender, they'll hang, and the women will become slaves."

Antoine cleared his throat and said, "Then you must release all the white captives still in your camp. Turn them over to the other village where they will be safe."

"I'll do that, as a parting gift and an expression of my affection for you. But I should tell you that some of my warriors will want to keep their white women. They may not agree to release them, and I can do nothing about it. But I will try…I will try."

"Thank you, cousin," Antoine said and left the tepee, mounted his horse, and headed for the Dakota village at the mouth of the Chippewa River.

His victory at Lone Tree Lake did not lessen Henry Sibley's caution. He failed to pursue Little Crow's defeated warriors, stating that he did not have the necessary cavalry. Besides, he was worried that a vigorous pursuit could spark a massacre of the white captives. Instead, he remained at the lake to care for the wounded and consider his next move.

Antoine Campbell rode into Sibley's camp on the second day after the battle. He had been sent by the upper and lower Dakota Sioux chiefs who had opposed Little Crow and who wanted peace and an end to hostilities. Their village at the Chippewa River held over two-hundred-fifty prisoners. The chiefs wanted Sibley to know that the prisoners were safe, and that Little Crow and his warriors had left the valley and were headed north.

"The road to the village is secure," Antoine told Sibley.

"Wabasha, Red Iron, Little Paul, and Taopi are there and ask that you come and receive the captives."

Sibley studied Antoine. Was he to be trusted? His expression was inscrutable.

"Did you speak with Little Crow, as I asked?"

"I did, Colonel, and I told him he should turn himself in to you. He laughed. He said the day he surrendered to you would be his last on earth."

"I expected that," Sibley replied. "We'll find him—eventually. I want you to take a message to Wabasha and the other chiefs."

Sibley sat at his portable desk and wrote:

Today I learned from Antoine Joseph Campbell that you desire peace and wish to turn over the captives in your village. I urge you to keep them safe. I will be at your village soon with my army. Have a white flag displayed so that my soldiers do not fire on you. You will be held accountable for any hostile acts or harm that befalls the captives. We will shake hands with those of you who remained friendly during the past moon and did not join Little Crow.

"Deliver this letter," Sibley told Antoine. "Read it to them. Be certain they understand it. I'll see that you are rewarded when this unpleasantness is over."

Sibley's army broke camp the next day. The long column could have closed on the village in a day, but instead the ever-prudent Sibley stopped in the afternoon after covering only ten miles and built a fortified camp, complete with entrenchments.

The same routine was repeated the following day. Meanwhile the captives in the village, who had heard rumors that they were about to be rescued, became increasingly anxious as two days and two nights passed without any sign of Sibley's liberating army.

Finally, at noon on the third day, Sibley arrived and built a fortified camp five hundred yards from the village. It would be known as Camp Release. The sight of their rescuers evoked cheers from the captives, many of whom felt such joy that they sobbed, some hysterically, and a few even fainted.

Their joy became utter ecstasy when the troops paraded before them. The bayonets gleamed in the autumn sun and flags fluttered luxuriously as color bearers raised them high in the westerly breeze. The spectacle peaked when the fifes and drums played Yankee Doodle.

The Indians looked on with awe and fear. The young troopers marched with precision; they wore new Union Army uniforms and appeared smart and robust. In contrast, even the young Dakota men and women were thin, disheveled, and subdued.

Many of them wore a piece of white cloth on their arm or chest, signifying their passivity and submission. White flags of surrender sprouted from tepees. One Dakota man placed a white blanket on his black horse and wrapped himself in an American flag.

Already Gustav Lindquist was frantically searching the village for Julia, Ruth, and Elsa. They were nowhere to be found. One after another he questioned the captives huddled in the center of the village awaiting rescue. Only a few were willing to talk to him. The others feared to speak because they did not want to jeopardize being freed after weeks of terror and suffering.

Finally, an elderly woman motioned for him to sit by her. She whispered that three women disappeared from the camp one night nearly two weeks ago.

No one knew what had befallen them. Were they killed, taken by Little Crow's men, or did they simply escape? She had no idea. Gustav described them. The woman wasn't positive, but she thought those three women fit Gustav's descriptions.

Around 2 o'clock in the afternoon, Sibley, his officers, and two companies of infantry entered the village. They were met by an assembly of Dakota leaders who listened as Sibley condemned the acts of terror committed by the Dakota Sioux and demanded deliverance of the captives to his care. One by one, the chiefs spoke of their innocence, and stepped forward to shake hands.

One of them, Little Paul Mazakutemani, was particularly articulate. Little Paul, as he was known, was a farmer and a converted Christian. During the past month he served as a proponent and spokesman for the Dakota Peace Party.

He said to Sibley, "I have grown up like a child of yours. With what is yours, you have caused me to grow, and now I take your hand as a child takes the hand of his father…I have regarded all white people as my friends, and from this I understand this blessing has come…This is good work we do today…Yes, before the great God I am glad."

Sibley was impressed by Little Paul's words and demeanor, and said, "Indeed this is good. From now on, I would like you to be in my service."

When the speeches ended, the captives swarmed Sibley and his officers. Altogether there were two-hundred sixty-nine of them, including one-hundred seven mostly white women and children and one-hundred sixty-two mixed-bloods. They were a pathetic lot.

Later Sibley wrote, "Some seemed stolid, as if their minds had been strained to madness and reaction had brought vacant gloom, indifference, and despair. They gazed with a sad stare. Others acted differently. The great body of the poor creatures rushed wildly to the spot where I was standing with my brave officers, pressing as close to us as possible, grasping our hands and clinging to our limbs, as if fearful that the Red Devils might yet reclaim their victims."

When Chaska learned that Sibley's army was approaching, he feared being arrested and told Sarah Wakefield he was leaving the village with his mother. She pleaded with him to stay, arguing that Sibley would not punish any Dakota who helped white people. Reluctantly, Chaska agreed.

Now it was time for Sarah to join the other captives surrounding Sibley and his officers. She bid a tearful farewell to Chaska's mother, who gave her a piece of her shawl. Then she placed a hand on Chaska's arm.

He said, "You are a good woman, you must talk to your white people, or they will hang me. You know I am a good Christian and did not shoot Mr. Gleason. I saved your life. If I had been a bad man, I would have gone with Little Crow and those bad chiefs."

Carrying little Lucy, Sarah took her son by the hand and made her way through the crowd until she stood before Sibley and Reverend Stephen Riggs, the expedition's chaplain.

After introducing herself, she said, "My children and I were saved by a Dakota man and his mother. His name is Chaska. He protected us on many occasions when we were threatened with death. I would not be alive and standing before you if it were not for him."

Sibley said, "Please, Mrs. Wakefield, we would like to meet this man."

Sarah turned and waved at Chaska, motioning for him to join them. Reluctantly, he came forward. Sibley shook his hand.

"Thank you very much for aiding Mrs. Wakefield and her children," Sibley said. "You were very brave to do so." He grasped Chaska's hand and raised their arms together in a gesture of triumph.

Facing the two infantry companies, Sibley shouted, "Three cheers for Chaska!" The troops had no idea why they were cheering this Indian, but they did so anyway. "Huzzah! Huzzah! Huzzah!"

Sibley asked two officers to look after Sarah and her children and together with Reverend Stephen Riggs set out for his camp.

On the way, Riggs said, "I know Chaska quite well. He is a Christian and often reads the Bible with me and my wife on the Sabbath." Sibley acknowledged the Reverend's comment with an absentminded grunt. His thoughts were totally focused on hanging every Dakota even remotely associated this war.

In St. Paul, General Pope divided his time between writing angry letters to General Halleck and Secretary Stanton and organizing his department. The former was a concerted effort to reverse his dismissal and banishment to the northwest following the defeat at Bull Run, while the latter was necessary to end the Dakota war and ensure that the atrocities suffered by the people of Minnesota would never happen again.

On September 28, Pope sent a letter to Sibley admonishing him for reporting his victory directly to Governor Ramsey. "While the dispatch was very satisfactory in relation to your operations, I beg to remind you that it was improperly addressed to the Governor, who no longer has any control over military operations in this State. All dispatches or requisitions for any troops whatever serving in this department are to be addressed to these headquarters…"

The next paragraph of the letter was as chilling as any written by a United States Army commander: "The horrible massacres of women and children and the outrageous abuse of female prisoners, still alive, call for punishment beyond human power to inflict. There will be no peace in this region by virtue of treaties and Indian faith."

"It is my purpose utterly to exterminate the Sioux if I have the power to do so and even if it requires a campaign lasting the whole of next year. Destroy everything belonging to them and force them out to the plains, unless, as I suggest, you can capture them. They are to be treated as maniacs or wild beasts, and by no means as people with whom treaties or compromises can be made."

Pope's venomous words reflected the bombast being spewed from the mouths of nearly every government official or public voice in Minnesota. They did not differentiate between men, women, or children.

The celebratory atmosphere at Camp Release was replaced by the stern business of taking Dakota men into custody. The day after cheering Chaska's kindness to Mrs. Wakefield, Sibley had him arrested, manacled, and chained. Sarah Wakefield's hysterical protests were ignored. The same fate befell other men in the camp, including many peace seekers.

Over the next two weeks, Sibley sent mixed-bloods into the countryside to spread the word that anyone who surrendered would be treated as a prisoner of war and fed and housed during the coming winter. That brought in hundreds of Dakota Sioux men, woman, and children who otherwise faced starvation. Most of the men were arrested and chained together in pairs, while the women and children were confined in a separate camp.

Still not satisfied that he had all the possible murderers in custody, Sibley devised a ruse with the cooperation of the Indian agent, Thomas Galbraith. He announced that the annual annuity would be paid despite the uprising. However, no payments would be made unless all the men appeared for roll call at the Upper Sioux Agency.

The next day over a thousand Dakota lined up as they always did at eight o'clock in the morning on payment day. The women and children were told to go through one door, while the men were instructed to check their weapons at a second door and proceed through to collect their annuity payment plus a bonus. One by one the disarmed men went through the door and were promptly manacled and chained.

At last, Brigadier General Sibley thought he had all the culprits he could collect. Never mind that many, if not most, of the actual murderers and rapists had escaped before his army arrived too late to arrest them.

Chapter 13

My paramount object in this struggle is to save the Union, and it is not either to save or destroy slavery. If I could save the Union without freeing any slave, I would do it, and if I could save it by freeing any slave, I would do it; and if I could save it by freeing some and leaving others alone, I would also do that.

What I do about slavery, and the colored race, I do because I believe it helps to save the Union. I shall do less whenever I shall believe what I am doing hurts the cause, and I shall do more whenever I shall believe doing more will help the cause. I shall try to correct errors when shown to be errors; and I shall adopt new views, so fast as they shall appear to be true views.

I have here stated my purpose according to my view of official duty; and I intend no modification of my oft-expressed personal wish that all men everywhere could be free.

Abraham Lincoln
Letter to Horace Greeley
August 22, 1862

The day before the last battle of the Dakota Sioux war, Lincoln met with the cabinet and unveiled his Emancipation Proclamation. He had been working on it since July, and kept it locked in his desk drawer awaiting a significant Union victory in the east. That had happened on September 17 when McClellan fought Lee to a standstill at Antietam Creek in Maryland. The Union had suffered grievous losses, but it forced Lee to take his army back to Virginia, ending his campaign to defeat the Army of the Potomac on northern soil.

The proclamation would be published in preliminary form, and a key paragraph stated:

That on the first day of January in the year of our Lord, one thousand eight hundred and sixty-three, all persons held as slaves within any State, or designated part of a State, the people whereof shall then be in rebellion against the United States shall be then, thenceforward, and forever free; and the executive government of the United States, including the military and naval authority thereof, will recognize and maintain the freedom of such persons, and will do no act or acts to repress such persons, or any of them, in any efforts they may make for their actual freedom.

Lincoln sought comments from his cabinet and chose to open the meeting with quotes from the humorist Artemas Ward. He held the book up for all to see, and then read from the first of several earmarked pages, "'Trouble will come soon enough, and when he does come receive him as pleasantly as possible. The more amiably you greet him, the sooner he will go away'."

Lincoln chuckled, as did a few of his listeners while others merely stared at him, perplexed. Secretary Stanton, in particular, appeared chagrined, wondering why the President was behaving this way on such a momentous day.

Turning to the next page, Lincoln continued, "'I am not a politician, and my other habits are good, also'." Again, he laughed, but the quote was received with polite silence. Lincoln closed the book and set it aside.

"Gentlemen, I sense your solemnity. That is as it should be." He folded his hands on the table, as if in prayer, and said, "I made a covenant with God that should we achieve a victory over Lee I would, by executive order, free the slaves where they can practicably be freed. Lee has been driven back to Virginia, an evident victory. I believe it is therefore God's will that the slaves be freed. That is, freed to the extent possible during this struggle."

"I confess that I made the covenant with God even though it was not always entirely clear to me what was in the best interest of the Union."

Lincoln paused.

"Mr. President," Montgomery Blair said, "I'm concerned that this Proclamation could drive the border states to secession." Blair was the Postmaster General and the lawyer who represented Dred Scott when the black slave lost his fight for freedom before the Supreme Court in 1857.

Lincoln continued, "I've thought about the border state problem. We have discussed it many times here, in this room, around this table. I have overruled antislavery pronouncements in the past for fear of losing the border states. But they refuse to listen to any proposal, including compensated emancipation. They will not change. For the good of the Union, it is presently more dangerous for this administration not to act than it is to act."

"On a single day, over two thousand of our soldiers were killed at Antietam, over ten thousand were wounded. This struggle is no longer a rebellion that can be put down and life resumed as before. What comes out of this war, no one can predict. But I know whatever comes out of this war will be different, and slavery will not be part of it. Today, I am proclaiming freedom for all, thenceforward and forever."

The lawyer in Lincoln knew that the Proclamation was a fragile document, its stipulations neither definitive nor permanent. Proclaiming freedom for the enslaved was one thing but guaranteeing it, and enabling it, for all black men and women would be a labor for generations.

Lincoln worried that the high command of the Army of the Potomac would disavow the Proclamation and compromise its enforcement. Certainly, McClellan and others in high command were aligned with Lincoln's political opposition. The President was concerned that there was a subversive creed circulating in McClellan's headquarters that espoused passive resistance to his conduct of the war. He sensed it during the Peninsula campaign and at the Second Battle of Bull Run when McClellan wondered if he should 'leave Pope to get out of his scrape'.

Lincoln's concern became acute when he was informed that Major John J. Key, a member of Halleck's staff and brother of McClellan's aide, was quoted as saying the defeat of the Confederate army on the battlefield was not the Union objective.

"That is not the game," he told a fellow officer. "The object is that neither army shall get much advantage of the other; that both shall be kept in the field till they are exhausted, when we will make a compromise and save slavery."

In other words, a Union military victory that doomed slavery was not 'the game'.

On September 27, Lincoln ordered Key to appear before him at the White House. Major Key acknowledged that he had been quoted accurately.

Whereupon the President immediately dismissed him from the Army, writing, "In my view, it is wholly inadmissible for any gentleman holding a military commission from the Unites States to utter such sentiments." The message was clear: Lincoln would not tolerate insubordinate behavior from any officer.

A week later, McClellan issued a general order that it was the army's duty to enforce the Emancipation Proclamation. He was stating the obvious, but apparently felt it was something that had to be said, and that he needed to say it.

At midday, the three men left their scythes in the wheat field and walked the quarter mile to the cabin. They were hungry and would eat quickly because the October days were growing shorter. Elsa and Ruth had prepared their meal of vegetable beef soup and wheat bread.

They ate in silence until Elliot said, "I figure we have about another three days of work in that field. What do you think?"

"Yea," Robert replied, "if you don't count putting it up."

Carl ladled another helping of soup into his bowl and broke off a hunk of bread. "Maybe one of us should work fulltime on the new room. It could snow soon, and we should get it closed up."

"Good idea," Elliot said to Carl. "You're the better carpenter. Robert and I can finish the wheat. Start tomorrow?"

Carl nodded and mopped his soup bowl dry with more bread. He looked at Elsa who was standing by the fire.

"Your bread is the best, Aunt Elsa. Always has been." She smiled.

Robert said, "Elliot, it was smart to expand this cabin rather than try to rebuild your place before winter."

"Ya, for sure," Carl said. "It's going to be crowded in here but having all of us under one roof is simpler—and safer."

Robert had been waiting for an appropriate opportunity to discuss Pillbury's offer with his brother and Elliot. He began to speak, "There is something…"

The cabin door opened. It was Julia. "Look who I found on the road from Hutchinson!" It was Gustav. They all stood and one by one embraced him. "Welcome home, brother!" Elliot exclaimed. "Where have you been?"

Gustav ignored the question and went to Elsa and Ruth.

"Thank God, you're safe!" He hugged both. "I was with Sibley at Yellowstone when a message arrived from the governor that you had been rescued. But I don't know how. Tell me. Please."

Julia related the details of their rescue by Elliot and Carl and the arduous journey to Hutchinson. Then she asked, "Gustav, the cuts on your face seem to be healing."

Gustav touched both his cheeks.

"Yes. Miss Thompson sutured them. She works with Dr. Mayo in Le Seur. They've heard of you, Julia, and want to meet you."

"Gustav, we have to get back to the field," Elliot said. "We'll talk at dinner."

That evening the eight family members sat around the table after dinner and discussed the future. Thanks to the supplies sent by Ramsey and Pillsbury, they had enough food to get them through the winter and well into spring. The decision was made to rebuild Elliot and Julia's cabin and Gustav's clinic and cabin after the planting was finished in April or May.

The present cabin would then be home to Carl, Robert, Elsa, and Ruth. They would gradually replenish the livestock, including dairy cows and beef cattle. As to crops, they had plenty of seed and would decide in March what to plant and the number of acres for each.

Little William was asleep on Julia's lap. She laid him down in his bed and returned to the table.

"I have some news," she said, blushing slightly. "I'm…I'm expecting."

All of them cheered. Elliot took her hand. It was the first beam of sunshine in their lives since August.

Carl gently slapped Elliot's back, "Hello, Father!" Gustav and Robert shook his hand.

As the celebration ebbed, Robert said, "I have news too, but it is of a different kind."

He paused, as everyone stopped talking and looked his way.

"When I was in Minneapolis, I stayed one night with the Pillsburys. As you know Mister Pillsbury—John Pillsbury—loaned us money three years ago, and I wanted to reassure him that we intend to repay the loan as agreed—despite the present difficulties. He was appreciative and said we could rearrange the terms if necessary."

"Then he asked if I might be interested in working for him. Frankly, I was taken aback, and didn't know what to say. He went on to explain his vision for commerce after the Civil War. And, he said he wanted time away from the business to help the University of Minnesota get out of debt. He wants to train me so he will be able to help the University."

"What did you tell him?" Elliot asked, a slight edge in his voice.

"I told him I would discuss it with you," Robert replied as his eyes met the gazes of each member of his family. "And I've been giving it a lot of thought."

"Well?" Carl asked, a little impatient.

Robert shifted in his chair, "I think I should accept his offer—at least during the winter when I would be missed here the least."

"What will you do? What's the job?" Gustav asked.

"He's going to teach me the business, primarily hardware but he's also thinking about flour milling and lumber. Minnesota is growing rapidly. So is the entire country, particularly west of the Mississippi. People need food and building materials, and he wants to be a supplier of these necessities—a good strategy, I think. Simple and logical."

Julia said, "Robert, it sounds to me like you'll be leaving us—maybe not right away, but eventually. Am I wrong?"

"The answer is yes and no. Let me explain what I think we should do—as a family." Robert placed both arms on the table and folded his hands. "Pillsbury will pay me twenty-five dollars a month to start. That's a good amount of money, right?" Everyone nodded.

"I propose we put that money into our company…"

"What company?" Elliot interrupted.

"The one I hope we're going to form. Let's just call it the Company for now. We put everything we own into the Company—land, buildings, tools, and livestock. Exclude personal things. Any money we bring in goes into one pot from which we pay our business expenses, and our salaries. Each year, before we decide how much to pay ourselves, we decide if we want to invest in more land, tools, equipment—or something else. For example, I saw a McCormick reaper in Whitesboro. It's impressive, does the work of ten men. None of us could afford to buy one for our individual farms, but we could pool our money and use it on all our land."

"The point is: all of us will be partners in the Company. Instead of each of us operating three separate farms and a medical practice, we do it as one enterprise. We grow together, prosper together—and suffer together when things don't go well."

The cabin was silent. Robert waited for everyone to ponder what he was proposing.

After several minutes when no one spoke, he said, "I know. It's a lot to think about."

"Actually, Robert, it's not all that complicated," Julia said. "I like the idea, but I'm not a farmer. What do you think, dear?" She looked up at Elliot, who was standing by the fireplace.

"I wonder what Andreas, Olaf, and A. P. would think," Elliot said.

"I believe A.P. would like it," Elsa said, her voice cracking slightly.

"So would my father," Carl observed. "Olaf often said we were always in this together, as one family."

Gustav ran a hand through his reddish-brown hair and said, "I'm not sure I'll be able to contribute as much as everyone else. Julia may be able to, but maybe not me. That's a problem…"

"It's not Gus," Robert said kindly. "You and Elliot are the heirs to Andreas' land. So, your land would be in the Company. And with the population growing I'm sure you'll be a busy doctor."

"I agree with Robert," Elliot said. "Crops have good and bad years, but your work—and Julia's too—will always be there." He placed a foot on the bench next to the table and continued, "Robert, tell us more about your role, as you see it, if we decide to do this Company."

"I'm good with numbers and money. I'll keep the books and work the farm as you do, but perhaps not as much. In the longer term, I would like us to get us into grain distribution. We would not only produce grain but store it—keep it dry—until the price is right and then ship it to the best market. We could build a granary and store our neighbors' grain, too."

"By working for Pillsbury, I'll learn business practices, particularly transactions. I'll meet people, just as I met the governor two weeks ago. That's how I got the message to you, Gus, about Elsa and Ruth."

"My brother is always thinking," Carl said. "I do like his idea, though."

Julia said, "Before we decide, I suggest we write down precisely what the Company is and how it's going to be run."

It was late. The sun had set hours before, and everyone was tired. Elliot scanned the faces of his family. They had experienced a lifetime of sorrow during the past month. Remarkably, though, they were thinking about the future, just as Andreas and Britta had more than five years ago in Sweden.

Now his parents were buried on the land they sought for their children. Doubtless it was up to him and his brother and cousins to secure that land for future generations of Lindquists and Erikssons. How to do that was the question. Tonight, however, he was certain of one thing: they should do it together.

"I agree with Julia," Elliot said. "Robert, it's your idea. Will you do that—put the Company on paper?"

"Yes," Robert replied. "I will. I gather everyone agrees that I should accept Pillsbury's offer?"

Everyone nodded, except Elliot. He replied, speaking for everyone, "It's fine with us. If something unexpected comes up, though, you may have to come back."

"I know," Robert replied. "Our land is the first priority."

Chapter 14

The authority to prosecute and punish the Indians was never in doubt, at least in the minds of Sibley, Pope, Ramsey, and most Minnesotans. Sibley assembled a Military Commission and told Pope, "If found guilty, they will be immediately executed, although I am somewhat in doubt whether my authority extends quite so far. An example is, however, imperatively necessary, and I trust you will approve the act, should it happen that some real criminals have been seized and promptly disposed of."

General Pope read the remainder of Sibley's letter and turned to his adjutant, Major Stanley Meeks.

"Sibley has appointed a military commission to try the Indians. I'm aware of some precedent for this. Do you recall the details?"

Meeks was a staff officer who spent two years reading the law with John Todd Stuart, Lincoln's former law partner in Illinois. He was commissioned after Fort Sumter and assigned to Pope's staff following the Second Battle of Bull Run. Army life agreed with him, and he hoped to be a career officer. Like Pope, he wanted to finish this assignment quickly and return east where the opportunities for advancement were far more favorable.

"I've reviewed them, sir, and prepared a memorandum on military commissions for your review," Meeks replied. He handed Pope a paper. "I can summarize, if you wish."

Impressed, Pope took the paper.

"Please continue, Major."

"During the Mexican War," Meeks began, "General Winfield Scott appointed military commissions to try Mexican civilians and his own troops for certain crimes, such as murder, assault and battery, and robbery. These commissions replaced civilian courts in hostile occupied territory after a declaration of martial law. Subsequently, the Supreme Court confirmed that the President had the authority to appoint such commissions, but lower courts ruled that they were inappropriate once hostilities had ceased or when there was no demonstrable military necessity…"

"Spare me the details, Major," Pope interrupted, "can Sibley proceed with a military commission or not?"

"I think the answer is 'yes', but…"

Pope cut him off, "Good. Is there anything else?"

Clearly discomfited, Meeks said, "General, there is another issue. The United States has always treated Indian nations as sovereign entities. This was the basis for entering into the various treaties that allowed our government to acquire their lands…"

Abruptly Pope threw his cigar on the floor.

"What the fuck does that have to do with what we're talking about? Don't waste my time, Major! For god's sake what's the point?"

"The point being this Indian war may be considered a war between nations and as such the Dakota Sioux prisoners are legally prisoners of war and not subject to punishment for the killing or the destruction they did as part of their war effort."

Exasperated, Pope hissed, "Are you saying they should go free—now that the war is over? That's pure bullshit!"

Meeks retreated. "General, I am not advocating for one approach over another, simply explaining the possibilities. Even if they were considered prisoners of war, they could be punished for acts violating the laws of war, such as murder, or killing unarmed civilians or their captives."

Pope was nearly apoplectic. "Sibley's military commission will proceed. Every goddamn Indian will hang if convicted."

Impassive, Meeks stood, saluted, and calmly said, "Yes, sir."

The morning was cool and damp. The five members of the Military Commission that Sibley convened sat at a short table in the cramped tipi-like army tent. They were joined by Adjutant Isaac Heard who would serve as Recorder; he was a bookish, unprepossessing lawyer from St. Paul and a member of Sibley's staff.

Lieutenant-Colonel William Marshall, a prominent Republican, nodded to Lieutenant Olin, the Judge Advocate, to begin. This was the Commission's first day of trials. It would meet continuously for the next month, and pass judgment on three-hundred-ninety-three Indians, most of whom understood little English and had no idea that they were on trial for their lives. None were provided with counsel. Due process was summarily denied.

The first defendant was not an Indian. Joseph Godfrey was the thirty-two-year-old son of a Black woman and French-Canadian voyageur. His mother was a slave by the name of Courtney who around 1830 was brought to Fort Snelling by an army officer and sold to Alexis Bailly, a successful mixed-blood fur trader.

Godfrey therefore was born into slavery, and as a young boy he ran errands for Henry Sibley who lived with Bailly during the winter of 1834–35. Sibley's cook and servant was Joe Robinson, a mulatto, whom Godfrey knew. Almost certainly Robinson was a slave since at that time few Blacks in Minnesota were free men. Sibley may not have owned Robinson, but in the midst of the Civil War he did not want anyone to learn what Godfrey might know, namely that Sibley once had a servant who was a slave.

The prisoner Godfrey was conducted into the tent by a guard. His appearance was anything but that of a ruthless killer. He was short, bearded, a little stout, and he wore a coat and shirt buttoned to the top. On his head was a plush cap with turned-up earflaps that covered his curly hair except for unruly strands that jutted out on either side. His trousers concealed the manacle on his ankle. On his feet were moccasins, the only item of Indian dress. Adjutant Heard thought he was younger than thirty-two and perhaps a little cross-eyed.

Holding a document, Lieutenant Olin read, "Charge: Murder. Specification first: In this that the said Godfrey, a colored man, did at or near New Ulm, Minnesota, on or about the 19th day of August 1862, join a war party of the Sioux tribe of Indians against citizens of the United States and did with his own hand murder seven white men and women and children, more or less peaceable citizens of the United States."

"Specification second: In this that the said Godfrey, a colored man, did at various times and places between the 19th day of August 1862 and the 28th day of September 1862 join and participate in the murders and massacres committed by the Sioux Indians on the Minnesota frontier."

After placing the document on the table, Olin faced Godfrey and asked, "Joseph Godfrey, how do you plead, guilty or not?"

In a soft, sweet voice, Godfrey ignored the question and replied, "I am thirty-two years old. I was born at Mendota. My father was a Canadian Frenchman and my mother a colored woman. At the time of the outbreak, I was married to a Dakota woman and lived on the Reservation on the south side of the Minnesota River, between the Lower Agency and New Ulm, about twenty miles below the agency and eight miles above New Ulm."

Godfrey removed his cap and clutched it with both hands to his chest. Already the members of the Commission were spellbound by his halting speech and gentle manner: a listener was instantly attentive and sympathetic. No one thought to ask him to declare his guilt or innocence.

He continued, "The first time I heard of the trouble I was mowing hay. About noon an Indian was making hay near me. I went to help him. He was to lend me his oxen. I helped him load some hay, and as we took it to his place, we heard halooing and saw an Indian on horseback, with a gun in one hand."

"When he saw me, he drew his gun up and cocked it. I asked what the matter was. He said all the white people at the agency had been killed by Indians. He said I had to choose which side I was on, the whites or the Indians. I knew if I said whites, he would kill me. So, I went to my house and took off my pants and put on a breechcloth."

He paused, cleared his throat, and said, "I went with the Indian toward New Ulm, and we met a lot of Indians at the creek, about a mile from my house. They were all painted for war and said I must be painted. They then painted me. I was afraid to refuse. We then started down the road and saw two wagons with people coming toward us."

"There was a house nearby. The Indians told me to wait by the road and tell them when the wagons got close. Half the Indians went to the house and shot two girls and a man. I think they were Dutch. Then they came back to the road and killed two men in one of the wagons. I didn't see who was killed in the other wagon."

Everyone in the tent was mesmerized by Godfrey's testimony. He named the Indians who did the killings, described how and where they did it, and underscored their cruelty and utter ruthlessness. In all this, he purported to be an innocent and reluctant observer.

"I got into the wagon," Godfrey sighed, as if reliving the moment.

"We went toward New Ulm. When we got near to a house, the Indians all got out and ran ahead of the wagons, and two or three went to each house, and in that way they killed all the people along the road. I think the town was Milford. I stayed in the wagon and did not see people killed. They killed the people of six or eight houses—all before we got to the Travelers' Home."

"There I saw an old woman with two children—one in each hand—running away across the yard. Muzzabomadu shot the old woman and jumped over and kicked the children down with his feet. The old woman fell down as if dead. I turned my head and did not see if the children were killed. After that, I heard a shot behind the barn but did not see who was shot."

General Sibley entered the tent and stood behind Godfrey. The Judge Advocate began to stand but Sibley gestured for him remain seated.

Meanwhile, Godfrey continued, "Then the Indians got in the wagon and told me to start down the road. We got to a house where a man lived named Schilling—an old German man. They told me to jump out. I jumped out and they gave me a hatchet and said I should kill the people in the house."

"There was an old man, his wife, and son, and a boy and another man. They were at dinner. The door was open and the Indians were right behind me and pushed me in. I struck the old man with the flat of the hatchet. Then the Indians ran in and commenced to shoot all of them. Later I saw the man I hit shot dead in the road."

Sibley shook his head in disgust, turned, and left the tent. Godfrey's vivid testimony went on for another forty-five minutes. His descriptions were those of a keen observer rather than a participant. He incriminated his father-in-law who he said shot a sick woman in her bed and set the house on fire. Next, he described his participation in the battles at Fort Ridgely, New Ulm, Birch Coulee, and Woodlake (Lone Tree Lake). He presented himself as a reluctant warrior who could either go along or be killed.

When Godfrey finished, Lieutenant Olin asked, "Godfrey, did you ever brag about how many people you killed?"

"No, sir," Godfrey replied, shaking his head, "I never boasted I killed white people."

The Lieutenant looked briefly at a document.

"Then how did you acquire the Dakota name O-ta-kle. It means Many Kills. They named you Many Kills. How did that come about, Godfrey, if you killed no one?"

It was pointed question.

All eyes were on Godfrey, who replied, "They gave me my name on account of many being killed where I struck the old man with the hatchet."

"I suppose that's plausible, Godfrey," the Lieutenant observed, "but we have witnesses to hear. If the court has no questions for the defendant, I will call the first witness, Mrs. Mary Woodbury."

"Proceed, Lieutenant," Lieutenant-Colonel Marshall said.

A mixed-blood woman was ushered into the tent and stood facing the Commission. She glanced briefly at Godfrey.

Lieutenant Olin asked, "Mrs. Woodbury, do you recognize this man, Thomas Godfrey?"

She nodded.

"Let the record show that Mrs. Woodbury replied in the affirmative. Now, Mrs. Woodbury, did you see this man at any time during the fight at the Lower Agency?"

Mary was tired and disheveled, but she spoke firmly with a trace of a New England accent. "I was taken by the Indians the day of the fight on Monday." Pointing to Godfrey, she said, "I saw him first at Little Crow's village two or three days subsequently. He painted his legs and face for a war party and put on his breechcloth. They said they were going to New Ulm. He started off with them—he was willing to go, he was whooping around."

"He was very happy with the Indians. He appeared to be as willing to go as any of the Indians and took a prominent part. When they came back, there was a Wahpeton named Kunckkatrinme who said the Negro was the bravest of all—that he led them into the house and clubbed them with a hatchet. I was standing in the prisoners' tent and the Indians asked him how many he killed, and he said only seven."

Marshall asked, "Mrs. Woodbury, did you ever see the defendant kill or harm anyone?"

"No, sir," she replied.

"Then, what you are telling us is just hearsay. Is that correct?"

"Well yes, but…"

Marshall interrupted her, "Thank you, Mrs. Woodbury. Lieutenant, please call the next witness."

The next two witnesses, Mary Schwandt and Mattie Williams, testified that they did not see Godfrey hurt anyone, though he appeared to be with the Indians willingly.

Mary said, "Never saw him treat anyone harshly. In fact, a week ago, before the army arrived, he said I should run away, that the Indians would never know." Mattie suggested that Godfrey actually was kind to her: he had reassured her that, "We are not going to kill you."

The last three witnesses were three mixed-blood men: David Faribault Jr, his father David Faribault Sr., and Bernard Labatte. Only the senior Faribault's testimony was damaging.

"I know Godfrey," he said. "He told me he was in war parties with the Sioux. He said he had killed seven men. This was in the beginning, he said he had killed them this side of New Ulm in the road. He said he killed them with the tomahawk."

"Did you ever see the prisoner Godfrey kill or harm anyone?" Marshall asked.

"I saw him in four battles, with a rifle and a bow and arrow. I saw him shooting with the rest of them…"

Impatient, Marshall pressed harder.

"But you never saw him directly kill or wound anyone, is that your testimony?"

"Yes, I suppose so," Faribault replied.

Marshall stood. "The witnesses are excused. Remove the prisoner. The court will reconvene in thirty minutes."

The Commission did not resume its deliberations until noon. In addition to Marshall and Olin, its members included Colonel William Crooks, a West Point graduate and commander of the 6th Minnesota; Captain Hiram Grant, who fought at Birch Coulee and whom Sarah Wakefield threatened to shoot if he hanged Chaska; and Captain Hiram S. Bailey, a Fillmore County farmer who enlisted as a private with the Second Minnesota Infantry and soon after was commissioned.

Crooks opened the discussion. "I must confess, gentlemen, I don't know what to think about Godfrey. He does not strike me as a bloodthirsty murderer. Yet the witnesses, particularly the older Faribault, saw him in action, as if he were a willing participant in the fighting—and the killing."

Marshall lighted a cigar and said, "No one saw him kill or wound anyone. He went along with the Indians because he feared for his life. Still, I suspect he was more involved than he led us to believe. I don't think we have enough to hang him, or to let him go. I believe we should wait. See what we learn from the other defendants." He turned to Grant and Bailey, "Captains, what say you?"

Bailey spoke first.

"I believe we should defer any decision. Godfrey could be very helpful to the court. He could implicate many. Save us time. Let's see how he does."

Grant was less perplexed than the others.

"I think he's an actor, a real performer, and a liar. I'd hang him tomorrow. Waiting, though, has some advantages."

"Right, then, we agree. Our decision is deferring judgment until a future date." Marshall turned to Olin, "The next defendant, Lieutenant."

"Beg your pardon, sir," Olin said, "but I believe General Sibley will be unhappy with any delay in sentencing Godfrey."

"Oh, how so?" Marshall asked. "Why the hurry?"

"I don't know, sir," Olin replied. "He wanted to be certain we put Godfrey on trial first. He never said why."

Marshall puffed on his cigar, thinking, then said, "I'll speak to the General this evening, after dinner. Who is the next defendant? We have to pick up our pace, gentlemen, or we'll be here 'til next summer."

While the trials continued, Sibley ordered patrols to search the countryside for victims and survivors needing help. This morning Lieutenant Martin Van Buren Scott led ten members of his patrol southeast toward Fort Ridgely. The previous day they found the bodies of three Dutch farmers who were shot dead while working in their fields.

Nearby were the corpses of two women and a small boy; they had been hacked to death and thrown into a creek. Scott ordered them buried and their graves marked. Then he read from the Bible that his mother gave him when he graduated from Hamline University in Red Wing:

The sky was blue and cloudless, a crisp fall day with a cool breeze from the northwest. By mid-morning, Lieutenant Scott's patrol crossed into Renville County north of the Minnesota River. It was home to many Scandinavian and German families that had recently immigrated. So many, in fact, that it was common for neighbors not to know each other. They rode up to a cabin near Beaver Creek. It was quiet and there was no sign of life. Oddly, the door was slightly ajar.

Scott ordered Sergeant Hadley to dismount and investigate. Hadley was a big man with a full reddish-brown beard, and he was one of the few regular army non-commissioned officers in Sibley's command.

He pointed to Private Roebuck, "You, come with me," he barked.

The two men held their rifles at ready and approached the cabin. Hadley kicked the door fully open, and both soldiers entered. There, before them, lying on a torn feather bed stained with blood, urine, and feces was the emaciated body of a woman. Next to her was the skeletal form of a child. They were breathing.

"Good God," Hadley murmured. "They're alive."

The woman groaned and tried to sit up but was too weak. In a barely audible whisper, she said, "Please kill me, but not my daughter. Please…please." Her eyes were open, but her vision was so clouded that she saw only the vague outlines of two figures standing over her. She thought they were Indians.

A veteran of two wars, Sergeant Hadley thought he had seen everything humans could suffer and endure. Yet he had never seen anything like this poor woman and her child. Their starved bodies were devoid of normal tissue: fat and muscle had been metabolized to keep them alive. Yellow, parchment-thin skin clung to their skeletons and defined their abdominal organs. Their hair was infested with ticks, and their faces, arms, and legs were speckled with bruises and insect bites.

Hadley kneeled and touched the woman's shoulder.

He said, "Madame, we are Union soldiers. You are safe. We will take care of you and your daughter."

The woman raised herself up on an elbow and touched his face.

"Oh, thank you. Danke, danke." She fell back and took her child's hand, who tried to speak but could only whimper.

Tears formed in Hadley's eyes and drizzled down his cheeks, wetting his beard.

"What's your name, madame?" he asked, his voice cracking.

"Justina Boelter," the woman replied hoarsely. She had a German accent. "Mrs. Justina Boelter. This is my daughter, Ottile. My oldest daughter—Amelia—died days ago. I left her in the woods. My baby Julius was taken by my husband's brother. I hope they are safe. I believe my husband and his father were killed."

Exhausted, she laid back.

Justina Wendland Boelter was born in Prussia and married John Boelter after emigrating to America. They, together with their three children and the families of John's father and brother, moved from Wisconsin to Renville

County in June 1862. Two months later, on August 18, the first day of the Dakota Sioux War, the Indians killed John while he was tending his cattle and John's father who was haying.

Justina was baking when her brother-in-law, Michael, ran to her cabin and told her to flee because Indians had just shot and killed their neighbors. Michael took baby Julius and ran east toward Fort Ridgely more than twenty miles away.

Burdened with two daughters, Justina was unable to keep up with Michael. She turned and saw that the Indians for some reason were no longer following her. A dense wood next to the Minnesota River offered cover and concealment. She burrowed into a thicket and remained there with her two children for two days without food or water. At night, she could hear the Indians talking across the river.

When Amelia became feverish, Justina obtained water from Beaver Creek and raw potatoes from her plundered home. After staying in a new hiding place for three days, she went to her mother-in-law's house and found her lying on the floor, partially decapitated. It was a terrifying sight. She fled in panic, without looking for food.

Justina and her two children remained hidden in the woods, subsisting on a few raw potatoes and cucumbers. She nursed two-year-old Ottile from her breast.

Later, she recalled, "At the end of five weeks the elder of the two children—Amelia—died of starvation, and I had become too weak to get about, except with great difficulty. The night before Amelia died, she asked piteously for water; but it was dark, and I was, in my weak condition, unable to get her water."

"I told her to wait until morning, when I could see, and she should have some water. But the dear little sufferer never saw the morning. She died during the night, and a chilly, dark rainy, and dismal night it was."

Justina was too weak to move away from her dead child. Her breast milk failed. She and Ottile ate grape leaves until a killing frost destroyed them.

Desperate, she decided to seek food at her brother-in-law's farm: "After long labor I reached the field, a quarter of a mile distant, and found a few potatoes and a small pumpkin. Unable to carry both, I carried the potatoes a short distance, and then returned for the pumpkin. Finally, I succeeded in getting both to the place where Ottile was."

A week later, Justina was so weak and cold that she was certain death was near: "I concluded to return to my own home, and, if I must die, to die at my own home. And yet I had hope that mercy was in store for one who had suffered so much. Trusting in Him who is stronger than man, and who is always better to us than our fears, I took up my child, and by the aid of a stick, used as a cane, I finally reached my once dear but now desolate and cheerless home. I gathered the scattered feathers into a bed on the floor, and laid Ottile down, as near dead as alive, and as white as alabaster. I laid down with her and slept in my own house, after an absence of nearly nine weeks."

Hadley looked up at Private Roebuck, who was wiping away tears he could not stop.

"Private, ask the Lieutenant to come in here."

When Lieutenant Scott entered the cabin, he too was overwhelmed by the human tragedy before him. The Sergeant introduced Justina and described what had happened to her and her family.

Scott said, "We'll take them to Camp Release. First, though, we should feed them. I don't think they will find our rations agreeable. There were chickens at that last farm we visited. Get one or two and make a broth. Then find a wagon." He removed his coat and spread it on Justina and her daughter.

Bishop Whipple paced outside Governor Ramsey's office in St. Paul. He was anxious to meet with the Governor to express his concern that many innocent Dakota Sioux were being targeted for punishment simply because they were living on the Reservation when the war erupted.

The door to the Governor's office swung open and the secretary, Miles Berry, said, "Your Grace, the Governor will see you momentarily. It may be several minutes. You are welcome to be seated."

"Thank you kindly," the Bishop replied. He was about to sit when a familiar face emerged from the Governor's office. It was Captain Charles Flandrau, the defender of New Ulm, and a prominent lawyer in civilian life.

Smiling and extending his good hand, Whipple said, "Good to see you, Captain. It's been a month since we were together in Mankato."

"The pleasure is mine, sir," Flandrau replied. "And thank you again for helping care for the sick and wounded from New Ulm. You and the supplies you provided were a godsend. What, may I ask, brings you to the Capitol?"

"I arrived last evening from New York. My purpose is to appeal to the Governor to restrain General Sibley's military commission from punishing innocent Indians!"

"I think Sibley is doing exactly what many of us want and expect," Flandrau said evenly. "I didn't see any innocent Indians at New Ulm."

The Bishop placed his left hand over his heart in a gesture of supplication, "Captain, the Dakota who waged war and committed the atrocities were a renegade band of thieves and malcontents under Little Crow, a discredited former chief. They should be tried and held to account. But not the peaceful Dakotas who were in the majority. They never wanted war, and they committed no crimes. Surely, they should not suffer as a result."

Flandrau put on his military overcoat and hat.

"Bishop Whipple," he said, "you are the most successful worker among the Indians of Minnesota. I doubt anyone will ever surpass you in that regard. I applaud you for that. Still, my advice is to allow our system of justice to play out. If it does, I doubt anyone will be treated unfairly."

Miles Berry stood in the door of the Governor's office, "Your Grace, the Governor will see you now."

The Bishop said, "Captain, perhaps we can continue this conversation another time."

"Yes, indeed, I look forward to it." He paused and touched Whipple's arm. "A word of caution: you will find Governor Ramsey and I share similar views."

Berry held the door as Whipple entered the office.

Smiling broadly, the Governor rose from his chair and shook his hand. "Sorry to keep you waiting, Bishop Whipple," Ramsey said, "but I'm running behind, as usual." He was medium height, clean shaven, and sported modest sideburns that complimented his high forehead.

"Captain Flandrau told me how kind you were to the people of New Ulm after the battle. Thank you, on behalf of the State. Please, be seated."

"I appreciate your kind words, Governor and your willingness to see me on such short notice. I am here on an urgent matter involving the Military Commission that General Sibley has convened at Camp Release, and the roundup and imprisonment of hundreds of Mdewakanton Dakota…"

Ramsey interrupted, "What, specifically, are your concerns, Bishop Whipple?"

"First and foremost, Governor, I am concerned about the innocent women, children, and elderly men who are being held at Camp Release and Fort Snelling. They are not warriors and had nothing to do with the war—neither the atrocities nor the destruction. They are starving and many are sick. It is a human tragedy on a vast scale that will only get worse as winter approaches. I beg you to have mercy and provide them relief and shelter."

Ramsey asked, "Did you read or hear what I said to the legislature a few weeks ago?"

"Yes," the Bishop replied. "If I recall correctly you said, 'the Sioux Indians of Minnesota must be exterminated or driven forever beyond the borders of the state'. Surely, sir, that was hyperbole—an exaggeration. You can't truly intend that."

"I meant every word, Bishop. And further, every warrior who had anything to do with the war will go to the gallows or face a firing squad. That is my promise to the people who were murdered, to the women who were raped, to the families who lost their homes and possessions, and to the brave soldiers who died defending our State. Not one Dakota Sioux will remain in Minnesota unless he or she is dead. I guarantee it."

The Governor's words and tone triggered a massive discharge from Whipple's sympathetic nervous system, over which he had no control. The adrenaline surge stimulated a million cells. His skin crawled and heart raced. He fought an impulse to flee. While the room was cool, he flushed, a reaction the Governor quickly noted.

"I know you empathize with the Indians' situation," Ramsey said, "I admit that the government in Washington has at times mismanaged its treaty obligations, however, that is no justification for mass murder, torture, or senseless destruction. We cannot expect people to return to their towns and farms if the Indians remain in the State."

"No settlers or businessmen will come here. Our economic development will be set back decades. This is a reality, Bishop Whipple, and not something I can simply dismiss because it could affect a few Indians who may be innocent of wrongdoing. We have to be pragmatic about this, and that is exactly what I intend to be."

Whipple leaned forward in his chair and said, "Your position is quite clear, Governor. Please understand mine. These Indians are members of my diocese, my flock, and I am compelled by my oaths and beliefs to act in their best interests, whether spiritual or physical. I have witnessed their decline for three years now. Their annuities went first to the traders who cheated them, and then refused to issue credit when they were desperate and starving…"

Ramsey raised both hands. "Bishop Whipple," he interrupted, "we have discussed this before. I am well aware of these allegations. Even if they are completely true—which by the way I do not believe—Little Crow and his band of murderers have no right to do what they did, and…"

"I completely agree, Governor, but spare the innocent! Please, spare the innocent! Do not punish those Dakota who were not only peaceful but also risked their lives to save the white women and children held captive. Chiefs like Taopi, Anawangmani, Mazakutemani, Tiwakan and Wabasha founded the Dakota Peace Party. They and their followers rescued over two-hundred white captives from Little Crow's camp and protected them until Sibley's army arrived. They—and others—deserve to be recognized for their bravery and loyalty, and they should be treated fairly."

Ramsey stood and said, "A few weeks ago, John Pillsbury brought a young farmer to meet me to describe what happened to his family during the first week of the war. Seventeen of them immigrated from Sweden a year and a half ago and settled on land north of Hutchinson."

"The day after the slaughter at the Lower Agency, the Indians murdered ten members of his family and kidnapped his aunt and her daughter. The five survivors then fought in the Hutchinson battle. Two of them were wounded and the wife of one, a midwife, was captured and taken to Little Crow's camp where she was sexually assaulted. Fortunately, the three women were rescued by two very courageous members of her family. The survivors are now trying to rebuild their farms."

Ramsey sat on the edge of his desk. "Bishop Whipple, I suggest you speak with that family. They may provide you with a different perspective."

"Governor," Whipple said softly, "I fully commiserate with that family and every family who lost a loved one or suffered in any way. That is not the point I am trying to make. My point is there are good, law-abiding Dakota Sioux that do not deserve to be punished or disadvantaged. Many have abandoned their native ways, adopted our dress, and built homes and farms."

"They practice our faith and send their children to our schools. Gradually the Indians are being assimilated into our communities. Just as we hoped they would. To exile them now will be tragic and, I believe, a mistake that will have long-term consequences for our state and indeed for the whole nation."

Whipple paused, sighed, and said softly, almost in a whisper, "I met President Lincoln last month. I think he understands my concerns."

Ramsey smiled thinly. "The President is a fair man. He is also a politician. The war with the Confederacy is not going particularly well. This is a Republican state, one that voted for Lincoln in 1860, and he needs Minnesota now in the mid-term elections. I seriously doubt he will feel obliged or inclined to intervene on behalf of the Indians."

It was a glorious autumn. The air was crisp and fragrant. The leaves of maple trees were turning red as their chlorophyll waned, revealing the ever-present red pigment. Silvery dogwoods sprouted crimson red berries that attracted hundreds of birds preparing for migration or the long Minnesota winter. An evening chill hinted of the bitter cold to come.

Isaac Heard barely noticed these earthly phenomena. The trials were weighing heavily on him. As the Commission's Recorder, he tried to capture the details of each witness's testimony. Every night he slept fitfully, disturbed and often awakened by nightmarish images of violent death and destruction.

This evening he was meeting with Reverend Stephen R. Riggs, who was a vital intermediary between the Dakota prisoners and the court. Most of the prisoners knew and respected Riggs. He was a Christian missionary fluent in the Dakota language, and for decades he, like Bishop Whipple, worked to assimilate the Dakota people into American society.

When the Dakota war broke out, Riggs and his family fled southeast from Hazelwood on a harrowing journey that took them near embattled Fort Ridgely and New Ulm. After securing his family in St. Paul, Riggs joined Sibley's army as military chaplain and interpreter.

"Good evening, Reverend," Heard said as he opened the flap to Riggs' tent. "A bit chilly tonight. I think it might rain."

"I'd offer you coffee or tea, Isaac, but my supplies are nil. I'm happy we will be leaving in a day or two. Please sit over there if you like."

"Yes, I too will be happy to leave this place," Heard replied. "I hope the Lower Sioux Agency has a building where we can continue the trials. The tent we're using now is much too cramped and it's beginning to stink."

Riggs sat opposite Heard and said, "I understand General Sibley has ordered more haste in the Commission's proceedings. He wants the trials completed this month?"

Heard replied, "That's right. We've tried ninety-six, and there are about three hundred to go. I might add that your assistance is much appreciated. In many ways, you are serving as a one-man grand jury. The Indians are very candid with you. So you're able to identify those who are likely guilty and should be arraigned."

"At trial, many of them have openly admitted they participated in various battles or were present when people were murdered. When that happens, there is no need for witnesses. It takes only minutes to find them guilty and sentence them to death. Very, very efficient."

"Dakota culture stresses honesty. That's why so many prisoners are incriminating themselves." Riggs paused and scratched his head. "They believe that telling the truth will benefit them. I don't think they understand the seriousness of these trials. In fact, I know they don't."

Heard looked away and said wistfully, "They've received…they've received no due process."

"How do you mean?" Riggs asked.

"No legal counsel. And we have not informed them that what they say to the court may result in their conviction and the death penalty."

Riggs wrapped himself in a blanket and said, "From what I've read in the few newspapers we get here, the entire state is calling for their execution. I'm afraid it has become a terrible necessity. I do hope, though, that we do not punish those who opposed the war, and particularly those who helped people escape to safety."

Heard buttoned the fur collar of his overcoat.

"Agreed. By the way, that mulatto Godfrey has been very helpful. He has fingered a dozen or so who were claiming no involvement. His observations and memory are remarkably detailed. Not the least thing seemed to escape his eye or ear. This Indian had a double-barreled shotgun, another a single-barreled, another a long one, another a short one, another a lance, and another one nothing at all."

"Just incredible recall! One Indian said he was nowhere near any fight, but Godfrey claimed he saw him and his sons painting themselves green and red for battle. Most of those he identified will hang. We should give Godfrey some consideration for that. He's been sentenced to die, but I would favor locking him up instead."

"Don't you think he's conflicted? I mean as a witness?" Riggs asked.

"Sure, that's possible," Heard replied, "but so too is Thomas Robertson and Charles Crawford and David Faribault. All of them may be serving their self-interest, trying to save their necks. I don't blame them for that. But they do come across as credible—quite believable, in fact."

"They're mixed-bloods, Isaac," Riggs said. "Mixed-bloods often get the benefit of the doubt when at the same time a full-blooded Indian is not believed."

Heard nodded in agreement. The two men fell silent, as if in reflection.

Finally, Riggs asked, "Anything of particular interest tomorrow?"

"First case is that Indian, Chaska," Heard replied. "He's accused of killing George Gleason, the man who was taking Mrs. Wakefield to Fort Ridgely."

"Oh, yes," Riggs said, "I was with Sibley when Mrs. Wakefield told him that Chaska had saved her life. Sibley cheered the Indian. I know Chaska quite well. He's a devout Christian, taught the Bible at Hazelwood, and lives with his mother and sister on their farm. There is absolutely no chance he harmed anyone or participated in the violence in any way. Why is he being tried?"

Heard replied, "Because he was with that Indian—Hapa, I believe—who shot and killed Gleason. He may not have committed the crime himself, but it's enough that he was present when the killing was done. The same applies to every other defendant."

"If you were at the scene of a battle, you're guilty and you will hang. If you were there when a white man, white woman, or white child was killed, you are guilty and you will hang even though you did not do the killing yourself, or even if you tried to stop the killing. It's quite simple, really."

"Is it? Is it that simple?"

"Yes, Reverend, it is. And I'm off to bed. Another long day tomorrow."

The morning dreariness was depressing and made worse by the lack of tea and bread for breakfast. Sibley ordered preparations be made to depart Camp Release on the morrow. The trials would resume at the Lower Sioux Agency sixty miles southeast. The Army and its prisoners would march at daylight. Today, however, the Commission would hear as many cases as possible, beginning with the defendant Chaska.

Already the trial tent was stuffy and reeking with the distinctive odor of unwashed bodies. Sarah Wakefield sat on a bench with other witnesses. Her face reflected the anxiety gripping her.

She was terribly unhappy, thinking to herself, '*I must do everything in my power to save Chaska. No other captive whom he protected will step forward, particularly that woman from Forest City who often combed his hair and arranged his clothing. She curried his favor nearly every day, practically throwing herself at him. And then she abused him terribly after he was arrested. Such duplicity!*'

The Commissioners entered the tent and took their places at the small table. Isaac Heard removed a sheath of papers from a worn leather satchel. He placed a glass inkwell on the table and began to write with a quill pen.

The adjutant said, "Bring in the defendant."

Chaska wore a green jacket over a gray shirt. He was tall, slightly bent, and he was manacled at the ankle. Sarah noticed that he was trembling, more likely from fear than the cold.

"Chaska," the adjutant asked, "were you present when George Gleason was killed?"

Chaska appeared confused. Riggs repeated the question, and Chaska nodded.

"Let the record show that the defendant Chaska answered, 'Yes'," the adjutant said. "He was present when Gleason was murdered. We now call the witness, Mrs. Sarah Wakefield."

Sarah rose and stood next to Chaska facing the Commissioners.

She held up her hands as if in prayer and said, "This man saved my life and the lives of my two children. He protected us in his tepee, together with his mother, for six weeks, until the army arrived and freed us. Chaska should not be on trial for his life! Hapa killed George Gleason, and he would have killed me and my children if Chaska had not stopped him. Please, I beg you, release him."

She sobbed, covering her face with her hands, and collapsed in Riggs' arms.

The expressions on the faces of the Commissioners ranged from sympathy to incredulity to suspicion. Later, several of them would voice the opinion that Wakefield was in love with Chaska, that she perhaps had intercourse with him, a detestable act, they said, by a white woman.

The Commissioners looked at one another and signaled their verdict. The adjutant rose and said, "It is the judgment of the court that the defendant Chaska is guilty of murder, and he is sentenced to death by hanging."

Sarah screamed, crying, "No! No! This is not justice! Do you not believe me! He saved my life! This is terrible!" She clenched both fists and thrust them forward, "Damn you! Damn you!"

Riggs tried to calm her, but she continued to rant, accusing the court of prejudice and calumny. Finally, she collapsed on the ground, curling up her knees in a fetal position. Through all this, Chaska remained impassive. The adjutant ordered two guards to remove her. Chaska was led away and another prisoner brought in.

During the next six hours, twenty-three Indians were found guilty and sentenced to hang. They were the last prisoners tried at the Upper Agency. A fierce cold northwest wind was blowing, and Sibley needed supplies and shelter. It was time to depart this unhappy place. The trials would resume at the Lower Sioux Agency.

Early the following morning, Sibley and his army departed Camp Release. The wagon train held the prisoners, who were chained to each other, and the white captives who would be returned to their farms or towns. Many would find empty homes and deserted cabins because their families had been slaughtered or fled east to safety.

Some of the former captives were left at Fort Ridgely, where they received medical attention. Two of them were Justina Boelter and her daughter, Ottile. Eventually they would be reunited with Michael Boelter and Justina's baby son, Julius, in St. Paul. Three generations and nine members of their family were dead and lying unburied on their farmland.

Chapter 15

Members of the Cabinet entered Lincoln's office and took their seats around the long table. It was October 14, 1862, and the President was attending to the many matters brought to his attention daily. Many were trivial but often important because his administration was facing a Congressional midterm election that could reverse or seriously erode the Republican majority in the House of Representatives.

The North had expected the Civil War to be won quickly. But it was nearly lost at the Second Battle of Bull Run and, despite the narrow Union victory at Antietam, many disappointed and disgruntled folks were pointing fingers at the Lincoln administration. Then too the war was expensive, and new taxes were being levied to pay for it.

Conscription, the suspension of habeas corpus, and other government intrusions were anathema to citizens who were used to a small federal government whose activities were generally confined to post offices, custom houses, and a few military outposts on the coast and in the wilderness.

"Mister President," Secretary of War Edwin Stanton began, "we're very concerned about Pennsylvania, Ohio, and Minnesota. Our agents say the Republican party and you in particular are being attacked by nearly every newspaper in those states, and that we could lose half our Congressional seats in this election." He turned to Gideon Wells, Secretary of the Navy, and asked, "Am I exaggerating?"

"Not in the least," Wells replied, absently stroking his abundant beard. "The situation is very acute, I fear. There may be little we can do about it now, but we should avoid irritating the voters further."

At this, Lincoln tossed the papers he was reading onto the table, and said, "I understand your concerns, gentlemen, but I do only what, in my judgment, has to be done for the survival of our Republic. Just six weeks ago Lee and his rebel army were on the doorstep to the Capital, less than ten leagues from where we are sitting."

Lincoln stood and went to the window. Surrounding the White House were hundreds of army tents with kettles cooking over campfires. Soldiers were being drilled. Officers and sergeants were barking orders. Dozens of wagons bounced and clanked over ruts and potholes. It was organized chaos.

He returned to his seat and said, "Washington has become a vast military encampment. Tens of thousands of soldiers who have to be fed and clothed and armed. Then, they must be transported, resupplied, and tended for their wounds and ills. Gentlemen, we had no choice but to expand the federal government and, yes, take steps not one of us would have chosen to do in normal times."

Wells cleared his throat and said, "I think we are only saying, Mister President, that the administration should avoid actions that may offend our supporters, without jeopardizing the war effort."

Lincoln returned to his seat and scanned the faces at the table. "Such as?"

The Secretary of the Interior, Caleb Blood Smith, waited for someone else to speak, cleared his throat, and responded, "The situation in Minnesota, for example, Mister President."

"You're referring to the Dakota Sioux uprising?" Lincoln asked.

"Yes, sir," Smith replied. "The fighting is over. The Dakota Sioux have been defeated. I suggest we allow General Pope and Governor Ramsey determine what punishment is to be dealt the Indians. Interference by the federal government will not be received well by the public—and particularly the voters—in Minnesota, and likely elsewhere."

"I'm not following you, Mister Secretary," Lincoln said apologetically.

"Perhaps I can elaborate, Mister President," Stanton offered.

Lincoln leaned back in his chair and said, "Please do."

"Three or four days ago," Stanton began, "I received two letters from General Pope. In them, he stated that the Indian trouble in Minnesota was no longer an acute military problem. The outrages against white settlers had stopped, and Little Crow's warriors have been decisively defeated by Sibley's army. The Dakota Sioux war, Pope proclaimed, was effectively at an end. What ordinarily would have been cause for celebration, however, was muted by Pope's statement, and I quote: 'many of the fifteen hundred Dakota Sioux prisoners are being tried by a Military Commission for being connected to the recent horrible outrages and will be executed'."

"I see," Lincoln said. "No doubt this Military Commission consists of officers who participated in recent battles and were attacked by the same Indians on whom they are now passing judgment. And you suggest we stand aside and allow Pope and this Military Commission to pass judgment and administer punishment?"

"I'm not suggesting anything, Mister President. But in the last election Minnesota voted overwhelmingly for Republicans—and for you, sir. We should simply keep that in mind."

Lincoln sighed and looked down at his folded hands. Then he looked first at Smith and then directly at Stanton. "As Commander-in-Chief, I am directly responsible for any action taken by a Military Commission. The Militia Act that was passed only three months ago specifically requires me to review and approve or disapprove all executions ordered by a military tribunal. Pleases tell—order—General Pope that there will be no executions without my written consent."

Stanton rose from his chair and replied, "I will telegraph General Pope immediately."

After Stanton left, Gideon Wells said, "I am having difficulty understanding how the Indian massacre in Minnesota can be considered a war, as if it were combat between two sovereign nations. There was no formal declaration of war on either side. The Indians attacked mostly farms and homes, rather than government troops or facilities. We know that many Sioux did not participate in or condone the violence in any way. Isn't this more correctly a rebellion by a group of disaffected Indians under that scoundrel Little Crow?"

The former governor of New York and current Secretary of State, Henry Seward, chuckled and said, "What difference does it make? They committed criminal acts and should be held to account."

Wells replied, "If indeed it was a war between two sovereign states or nations, then the captive Indians should be held as prisoners of war and subject to criminal trial only if they are accused of war crimes. Otherwise, they should be paroled at the end of hostilities and allowed to return to their villages."

"Good grief!" Secretary Smith blurted. "We'll have another rebellion on our hands if we parole a single Indian who participated in these massacres. I just spent two weeks in Minnesota. Feelings are boiling in St. Paul, gentlemen. The people are outraged. They seek—indeed demand—retribution for the atrocities committed against innocent civilians—many of whom only recently arrived in that state and were unaware of tensions between the traders and the Indians. I favor letting Governor Ramsey and General Pope and his commander in the field, Brigadier Sibley, handle this matter as they see fit."

The room was silent as everyone at the table anticipated the President's response. A minute passed.

Finally, Lincoln said, "The country has erred in the treatment of our native peoples. It began with the British, and we continued their policies with little modification. The rebellion in Minnesota—it was a rebellion, as Secretary Wells indicated, not a war—was a consequence of our belief in this country's manifest destiny."

"We wanted the land where they lived and hunted, and we managed to acquire it through a series of treaties, some of which were of questionable legitimacy, and then we created and tolerated an Indian system that has spawned corruption so widespread and endemic that many in government fail to recognize it for what it is—a permanent stain on our government and the country."

Lincoln rose from the table and went to his desk.

He returned holding a document written in his hand, and said, "I reviewed Chief Justice Marshall's opinion in *Cherokee Nation vs Georgia*. I'm sure all of you are familiar with that case. Marshall wrote and I quote, 'Though the Indians are acknowledged to have an unquestionable, and, heretofore, unquestioned right to the lands they occupy, until that right shall be extinguished by a voluntary cession to our government; yet it may well be doubted whether those tribes which reside within the acknowledged boundaries of the United States can, with strict accuracy, be denominated foreign nations. They may, more correctly, perhaps, be denominated domestic dependent nations'…"

Lincoln paused, raised his right hand for emphasis, and continued, "And these are Marshall's words that spoke most loudly to me, 'Meanwhile they—the Indians—are in a state of pupilage. Their relation to the United States resembles that of a ward to his guardian. They look to our government for protection; rely upon its kindness and its power; appeal to it for relief to their wants; and address the president as their Great Father'."

Seconds passed before Secretary Smith looked around the table and asked, "How does Marshall's opinion apply to what we are talking about, Mr. President? I refer to the situation in Minnesota?"

"The situation in Minnesota is now in my hands, Mr. Secretary. General Pope, Governor Ramsey, and Brigadier Sibley must await my judgment. I hope I can act with the kind of wisdom Justice Marshall displayed thirty years ago." He paused, squinted at Secretary Smith not unkindly, and said, "I will not hang men for votes."

Salmonella typhi is a bacterium responsible for typhoid fever. It invaded eleven-year-old Willie Lincoln's body in early 1862, most likely from water in a nearby canal contaminated with infected fecal matter. He died in the White House on February 20, and was embalmed in the Green Room, which his mother had recently redecorated.

When Elizabeth Keckley, Mrs. Lincoln's dressmaker, was preparing Willie's body for burial, Lincoln entered the room and said, "My poor boy, he was too good for this earth. God has called him home. I know he is much better off in Heaven, but then we loved him so. It's hard, hard to have him die." And then the President broke down and cried.

After the Cabinet adjourned, Lincoln went to his wife's bedroom. Mary Todd Lincoln was lying on the bed, dressed in black, as she had been since Willie's death. Next to her was Tad, their nine-year-old son who was recovering from the typhoid he contracted at the same time Willie was taken ill.

"Molly," Lincoln whispered, using the nickname he had used in his love letters to her. "It's Father. I'm sorry for not coming earlier." He sat on the bed and touched her hand.

Mary's eyes fluttered. She looked up and studied her husband.

"Ah, Mister Lincoln," she said softly, "you're tired. I can see the weariness in your mouth."

"How are you?" Lincoln asked softly.

"The same as your Molly has been since Willie died," she replied. "What crisis—or emergency—did you have to handle today?"

"No crisis today. But the Cabinet devoted an hour to the situation in Minnesota. The fighting is over, but there's a clamor to punish—indeed hang—the Indians."

"That doesn't surprise you, does it?" Mary rose up and sat next to her husband. Tad squealed and thrust his head between the two of them. Lincoln stroked his cheek tenderly.

"No, it's not a surprise. Yet I find myself more concerned than I expected, considering everything else."

He stood and walked to the window, glanced out briefly, and continued, "I'll say this to you, and do not wish it repeated…" Lincoln hesitated.

"Good heavens, what were you going to say?" Mary asked, a little impatient.

Abruptly Tad leaped from the bed and ran in circles before the fireplace, shouting, "Yea! Yea! Yea!" and collapsed giggling on the oriental rug.

Lincoln smiled and knelt next to his son. Tad jumped onto his father's chest and hugged him.

"What were you going to say?" Marry asked. "Please, tell me."

Smiling, Lincoln enfolded Tad in his long arms and replied, "It can wait 'til later. I want to hold my boy."

Mary joined them before the fire, and said, "Will there ever be a later." It was not a question.

A uniformed rider dismounted in front of the Swede's cabin and knocked on the door. When there was no answer, he walked toward the sound of hammering. Carl was finishing the roof over the new room.

The rider shouted, "I have a letter from the Governor!"

Carl set the hammer aside and climbed down the ladder. "Say again?"

"I have a letter from Governor Ramsey for the Lindquist and Eriksson families. Are you one of them?" the rider asked.

Carl grunted and said, "I'm Carl Eriksson."

The rider reached into his saddlebag and handed Carl an envelope. "I was ordered to wait for your reply."

The day was cloudy and the afternoon light was dim. Carl sat on a log and opened the envelope. He squinted. The letter was drafted by an accomplished calligrapher and addressed to the Lindquist and Eriksson families:

I wish to express the sorrow I feel in my heart for the tragic deaths of your family members who perished at the hands of the murderous Dakota Sioux Indians under Little Crow. Please know that all Minnesota feels your pain and offers condolences. Our State is determined to punish every Indian even remotely associated with these criminal acts. Soon the Military Commission will reconvene at the Lower Sioux Agency. I respectfully request that you travel there and appear as witnesses to describe what you saw and experienced. Your family's catastrophe is unequaled anywhere.

Lieutenant Henriksen will await your decision. If you agree, he will accompany you there tomorrow. I know this is a difficult time, but I trust you want justice for your departed loved ones.

Sincerely,
Alexander Ramsey, Governor of Minnesota.

Carl folded the letter and returned it to the envelope.

"Most of the family should be home soon. We'll discuss the Governor's request and let you know tonight. You may join us for supper if you wish."

"Thank you, but I don't want to interfere with your discussion of the Governor's request,"

Already Carl had one foot on the ladder.

"I don't think there'll be much discussion. We'll go with you tomorrow. At least my cousin, his wife, and me. Maybe the doctor too." Halfway up the ladder, Carl said, "By the way you can bed down in the new room tonight. No one has moved in there yet."

The journey southeast to the Lower Sioux Agency took nearly two days. Julia and Gustav rode in the covered wagon drawn by the two young Percherons that Robert purchased in Minneapolis. Carl, Elliot, and Lieutenant Henriksen rode ahead on their mounts whose lineage was unclear though their compactness hinted at Morgan ancestry.

They arrived in the late afternoon and were immediately welcomed by Brigadier General Sibley in his headquarters tent.

"Thank you for coming. I realize how difficult and inconvenient it is for you to travel after such a terrible loss and so much suffering. I understand that several of you were wounded at Hutchinson?"

Gesturing toward Gustav, Elliot said, "My brother and I got cut, but our wounds are healing fine."

Sibley studied Gustav and asked, "We've met before, I believe at Fort Ridgely?"

"Yes, General, I joined your army at Fort Ridgely and stayed with you until the victory at Lone Tree Lake. I went home after helping with the wounded."

"We're grateful for your assistance, Doctor," Sibley said as he motioned to chairs around an unfinished white pine table.

"All of you, please, be seated. Would you like coffee, or perhaps something stronger? I have an excellent whiskey."

Only Carl replied, "I'd appreciate a whiskey, General."

Sibley sat at the head of the table and began, "We are at the end the trials. Over the past month we have sentenced three-hundred-two Dakota Sioux Indians to death for their participation in the massacres. We intend to hang all of them, hopefully before the end of the month. Tomorrow is the last trial."

"I asked Governor Ramsey to facilitate your testimony because the defendant is a warrior by the name of White Eagle. Based on our interrogation of a number of witnesses, we believe this White Eagle and his accomplices were responsible for the deaths of your family members, and the destruction and theft of your property. At his trial tomorrow, we simply want the four of you to describe, for the record, what you saw, heard, and felt during those terrible days." He paused before asking, "Do you have any questions?"

"Yes, General," Elliot replied, "just one. Will our testimony actually make a difference? It sounds as if you have all the evidence you need." He paused and said, "I'm not sure why we are here."

Sibley shifted uncomfortably in his chair. "Yes, well, that's a reasonable question. You see, the four of you have lost family, your homes have been destroyed, you fought at Hutchinson, and two of you were wounded. You bravely rescued Mrs. Lindquist and Mrs. Eriksson and her daughter from their captivity. So, your experience spans the entire tragedy of this war, and speaks to the imperative to punish the guilty. We want it to be part of the commission's official record."

After moments of silence, Julia said. "General, during my captivity I was helped greatly by a Christian Dakota Sioux named Chaska. He clothed and fed me, and helped us escape when Elliot and Carl found me. I—we—owe our lives to him. I want to find and thank him. Might he be among the prisoners here?"

Sibley coughed, glanced at his aide, Lieutenant Chambers, and replied, "We have several prisoners here by that name. Chaska means first-born son in the native language. So, there are a few Chaskas among them."

"May I see if the Chaska who helped me is in your custody?" Julia asked.

Sibley stood. "Yes, of course. Lieutenant Chambers will see to it tomorrow—after your testimony. Now, if you'll pardon me, I have duties to attend to. You will be shown to your tents. I look forward to seeing you in the morning."

That evening, in their tent, Julia said, "There's something strange about this…"

"How do you mean?" Elliot asked.

"Robert was interviewed by the newspaper when he visited the governor. The details of our family's tragedy, the loss of our buildings and livestock, the battle in Hutchinson, my captivity and rescue. Everything was in the newspaper. There is nothing we can add to what they must already know. And I had the sense during our meeting with General Sibley that we're here more for decoration than giving new testimony."

Elliot said, "Strange or not, I want to do everything I can to see White Eagle hang. That is all I want out of this. It will be hard for me to be in the same room with that son of a bitch."

In his tent after dinner, Sibley sat as a portable desk and wrote to General Pope:

The last trial will take place tomorrow. We have moved expeditiously since arriving at the Lower Sioux Agency. In compliance with your order, we have convicted defendants of capital crimes who were complicit in any manner. The process has been further expedited by trying four to six of them at a time. Many trials have taken no more than ten minutes.

Today the four Swedes arrived at the behest of Governor Ramsey to testify before the Commission. Their testimony tomorrow will become part of the permanent record and it will provide a vivid first-hand description of the vicious crimes committed by these villains. The idea to bring them here was brilliant.

I understand the President has ordered a review of every capital case. We are preparing the records, and they will be forwarded to you within a fortnight, if not sooner.

The morning sun had just risen when a male voice outside their tent said, "Mister and Mrs. Lindquist, the Commission requests your presence in an hour." It was Lieutenant Hendriksen.

"Your breakfast will be here shortly."

Elliot opened the tent's flap and said, "We'll be ready, Lieutenant. Where do we go?"

"Over there," he replied, pointing to a small wooden building that once served as a summer kitchen for one of the traders, Francois LaBathe, who was killed on the first day of the war. "It's the only building still standing."

Elliot closed the flap and turned to Julia, who was wearing an ankle-length black dress and gray bonnet. "You look very nice, dear," he said. "All I have are my work clothes."

"You look fine," Julia said absently as she sat at a small table.

"Still worried about Chaska?" Elliot asked.

"Yes. He must be one of the condemned. He has to be here…"

"We should go…they'll be waiting for us."

The former cookhouse was crowded with the Commissioners, witnesses, and observers, including a reporter from the St. Paul Daily Press who had arrived at the Lower Sioux Agency the previous evening. Members of the Commission sat at a long table facing the defendant, two witnesses, and a dozen spectators.

Lieutenant Olin stood and said, "Bring the defendant White Eagle."

A soldier positioned the manacled Indian in front of the Commission. White Eagle's face was impassive, reflecting none of the hate roiling his gut. He would give no hint of regret or contrition. *'This was a warrior's fate,'* he thought, *'and he would confront it with courage and resolve.'* Let the farmer Indians and Christian Dakotas cower in obedience to these evil white men who infected his land like locusts.

Lieutenant Olin held up a document and read, "White Eagle, you are charged with the murder of innocent men, women, and children in their homes and on their farms. Specifically, you are charged with the deaths of a woman giving birth and her husband while in Dr. Lindquist's clinic north of Hutchinson."

"Afterward you burned the clinic and Dr. Lindquist's home. You then murdered A.P., Rolf, and Gunnar Eriksson while they were working on their farm, burned the family cabin and barn, and kidnapped Elsa and Ruth Eriksson.

In addition, you took part in Little Crow's assault on the Lower Sioux Agency where you killed Andrew Myrick, a trader." He paused, then asked, "How do you plead, guilty or not guilty?"

Stephen Riggs translated the charges and told White Eagle to say either guilty or not guilty. White Eagle refused to enter a plea, and Olin said, "Let the record state that White Eagle entered a plea of not guilty. We call the first witness, Mr. Elliot Lindquist."

At the rear of the room, Brigadier General Sibley rose from his chair and said, "May I suggest the Commission at this time hear the uninterrupted testimonies of Mr. Elliot Lindquist, Dr. Gustav Lindquist, Mr. Carl Eriksson, and finally Mrs. Julia Lindquist. Such an approach would not only save time, but it would also provide a complete and clear picture of what actually transpired during that first terrible week of the war."

Colonel Marshall scanned the faces of the other four Commissioners. All appeared to concur with Sibley's suggestion. "That is an excellent idea, General. Lieutenant Olin, please proceed. And have the defendant face the witnesses."

During the next forty-five minutes, Elliot, Gustav and Carl described their experiences in graphic detail, including the attacks on their families and farms, the battle at Hutchinson, and the rescue of Julia, Elsa, and Ruth. They identified White Eagle as the leader of the band of killers, but acknowledged that they did not witness the actual killings. Members of the Commission listened and asked a few questions, mostly for clarification. Then it was Julia's turn.

She stood, glanced at White Eagle, and faced the Commission directly.

"I agree with everything my husband, Dr. Lindquist, and Mr. Erikson said. I have nothing to add. But I want to say, for the record, that while in captivity I was often treated with kindness by the many Dakota Sioux who never wanted this war. One man in particular quite literally saved my life. He gave me water and food at times when my body was exhausted and I had given up any hope of surviving and returning home to my family."

"This man's name is Chaska. I understand Chaska is a common name, but I respectfully request that I be given the opportunity to see if this particular Chaska is among the prisoners in your custody. If he is a prisoner, I would like to appeal to the authorities to pardon him or at least re-consider his case. I would bear witness to his innocence and indeed to his goodness."

The room was dead quiet. The reporter from the St. Paul Daily Press was writing furiously.

Elliot stood next to Julia and said, "I too would like to find this man Chaska. Without his help, we would not have escaped from Little Crow's camp—we'd be dead now. Simple as that."

Carl stepped forward.

"I agree." He pointed to the door. "Let us see if he's in that stockade out there."

Once again, Sibley rose from his chair in the back of the room.

"I told the witnesses last evening that they can visit the stockade after today's proceedings are closed. May I suggest the Commission conclude the case against the defendant, and bring these proceedings—these trials—to a close."

Without debate or discussion, the Commission found White Eagle guilty, and sentenced him to death by hanging. This being the last trial, Sibley dismissed the Commission and ordered its members to report to their units.

Julia, Elliot, Gustav, and Carl were ushered out of the *ad hoc* courtroom by Lieutenant Chambers, who said, "General Sibley has asked that I take you to the stockade where the convicted prisoners are being held. There are over three hundred of them. I will ask the guards to parade them by you. Tell me if you see the one you're looking for, and I'll have him pulled out of line."

The prisoners were a sullen and pathetic lot. All were thin, filthy, and dressed in an assortment of tattered native and white man's clothing. Many were shoeless, while others wore well-worn moccasins or leather boots. Most of them were sitting outside in the cool fall air, doing nothing except occasionally talking.

Inside one of the thirty-two teepees enclosed by the stockade was Chaska, sitting cross-legged in a circle of twelve men. Sunlight shined through the opening for the lodge poles and illuminated every face; each was turned toward Chaska, who was reading to them from the Bible.

"Today," Chaska said, "we learn of Lazarus from the Gospel according to John. Lazarus was the brother of Mary, who washed Jesus' feet with oil…"

A soldier stepped into the tepee and shouted, "Fall out! All of you! Out!" Chaska stood, translated the soldier's order, and followed the last man out of the tepee.

Outside he squinted in the sunlight, using the Bible to shield his eyes. A squad of soldiers were lining the prisoners up and directing them to walk past a small group of white people standing at the gate. Who were they? What could they want? Retribution? Everyone here is sentenced to death. Will we be tortured first, he wondered?

One by one the prisoners passed by Elliot, Julia, Gustav, and Carl. The Indians appeared resigned to their fate, indifferent to the abrupt change in the monotonous routine they endured every day.

White Eagle was among the first dozen, but he was the only recognizable face until Elliot suddenly shouted and pointed to an Indian wearing a blue wool jacket, "That one! In the blue jacket. He was one of the war party who killed Olaf and Britta!" It was Lazy Dog, who had crushed Britta's skull with a tomahawk after Olaf was shot and while Elliott lay unconscious in the corn field. Julia grasped Elliot's arm as he stepped forward as if to attack Lazy Dog.

Gustav said, "He's going to hang, brother. You can't do anything worse to him." Reluctantly Elliot relaxed.

A half hour went by as two-hundred-eighty prisoners tramped before them.

The last group was in line when Julia exclaimed, "That's him! That's Chaska. Please, I would like to speak with him!"

Lieutenant Chambers said, "Very well. Sergeant, bring that prisoner over here,"

The four Swedes surrounded Chaska as if to shield him from harm. Julia said, "Oh, Chaska, we want them to release you. You are innocent. You should not, must not die for something you did not do!"

Chaska said, "I'm grateful—to all of you." He held up his hands in prayer. "I appreciate your efforts on my behalf. Most of the prisoners here are innocent of any violence against your people. Nearly everyone here should be freed, not just me. Every day, I pray to God that this will happen."

"That's wishful thinking, Chaska," Elliot said. "I believe we might be able to secure your freedom. Our family has suffered terrible losses. Surely our plea for your release will carry a lot of weight with the authorities."

"Perhaps," Chaska replied. "Right now, I am preparing myself and my fellow prisoners for the day when we will be executed." He held up his Bible. "I am teaching them about Jesus Christ and the Gospels. Over a hundred of these men are attending my classes."

Gustav asked, "Are they converting to Christianity?"

"Some," Chaska replied. "More of them every day. Nearly fifty were Christians when the war began. I've been a Christian for many seasons."

Lieutenant Chambers stepped forward. "This must be the man you were looking for?" he asked.

"Yes," Julia replied. "And we request a meeting with General Sibley. We wish this prisoner, Chaska, to be released. Today, if possible, before we return home."

Chambers turned to a sergeant. "Dismiss the prisoners. Close the gate." He motioned for the Swedes to follow him, "I will take you to the General's adjutant."

The headquarters tent was a beehive of activity. Sibley stood behind his desk reading documents and signing orders. The adjutant announced them, "The lady and the gentlemen have a request, General."

"Please, come in," Sibley said pleasantly. "Have a seat, if you wish. Did you find this Chaska?"

"Yes, we found him," Julia began. "We request he be released—pardoned is perhaps the correct term. General, Chaska is not a murderer. Hapa killed Mr. Gleason. Chaska tried to prevent it. I believe Mrs. Wakefield's testimony before the Commission supports his innocence. We ask that you free him."

Sibley tossed the papers he was holding onto the desk and said, "What happens to Chaska is no longer the charge or concern of the Army. President Lincoln has assumed responsibility for the 303 condemned prisoners. He is reviewing all capital cases and he alone will decide if anyone, including Chaska is to be pardoned. So, there is nothing I can do. It's out of my hands."

There was a moment of silence. Sibley resumed his paperwork. Looking up, he asked, "Is there anything else? I'm quite busy, as you can see."

Julia asked, "Is there anyone else we should speak to…?"

Sibley smiled thinly, "You could appeal to the White House directly. The President has requested the Commission's records. He will receive them in the next few days by special courier."

Elliot nodded and said, "Thank you for meeting with us, General."

"You're welcome. Now, if you'll excuse me." Sibley turned his back.

They left the headquarters tent and walked in silence toward their wagon. Finally Carl said, "We can get halfway home by nightfall if we leave now."

Julia stopped walking. The three men turned, and Elliot asked, "What are you doing, dear?"

"I won't being going with you," Julia replied. "I'm going to Washington, to see the President, at the White House."

As Elliot glared at Julia, Carl said, "Gustav and I will meet you at the wagon. I'll get the horses ready."

The two of them stood facing each other.

Julia said, "I'm not giving up. We owe it to Chaska—and, by the way, to ourselves. To meekly accept his execution as inevitable is spineless. I am not spineless. You know that. You knew that when you married me…"

"Julia, we have to get ready for the winter. There's a lot to do…"

"Elliot, you don't have to go with me. Go home with Carl and Gustav. I can take care of myself. You know that, too."

Elliot reached out and took her hand. "These are dangerous times. It's not safe for a woman—especially an expectant mother—to travel so far alone. I'll go with you. Promise me, though, that whatever happens in Washington will be the end of this…this terrible trouble."

Julia replied, "I promise. Afterwards, no matter the outcome, we will go home."

In every town in Minnesota, and particularly in the capital St. Paul, angry voices demanded the immediate execution of the prisoners. Emotions were further stoked by the wrathful rhetoric emanating from Governor Ramsey and other elected leaders, including U.S. senator Morton Wilkinson and Congressman Cyrus Aldrich.

Newspaper editorialists further fueled the public clamor for a mass hanging. One in particular, the Stillwater Messenger, threatened mob action: "if these convicted murderers are dealt with more leniently than other murderers, the people of the State will take law and vengeance into their own hands, and woe to any member of the hated race that shall be found within our borders."

On November 6, the New York Times published an editorial entitled 'Mercy to the Sioux' based on information that must have been leaked to the newspaper by someone close to the White House.

"We are glad to learn," the editorial announced, "that it is not the purpose of the Government to deal in a sanguinary manner with the lately belligerent red men of Minnesota. The large number of 'big Injuns' of all grades and dignities, and with all sorts of unpronounceable names, who had been condemned to the gallows, will be respited…" Was Lincoln thinking of reducing the sentences? The revelation prompted General Pope to order the prisoners transported southeast to Mankato for execution.

The three-hundred and three condemned Dakota Sioux were shackled two-by-two and loaded into thirty wagons for the sixty-mile journey to Camp Lincoln on the Blue Earth River in Mankato. Accompanying them were two regiments of General Sibley's command and native women, including Mina, who would serve as cooks and laundresses. They would pass through the same country where Little Crow's warriors had committed many of the uprising's worst atrocities. In their path was Fort Ridgely and the devastated town of New Ulm.

Chaska and White Eagle were chained together in the second to last wagon. Mina and the other native women walked behind as the column wound its way on the government road along the south bank of the Minnesota River. The first night Sibley camped within view of Fort Ridgely that was visible on a plateau above the north bank. The prisoners were given water and venison but remained shackled in the wagons. The night was cold with a brisk westerly wind and only a few prisoners were able to sleep as they sat shivering in the dark.

Around midnight, Chaska asked White Eagle, "Do you go to church?"

"No," White Eagle replied. "Why do you ask?"

Chaska said, "We are going to die soon. Jesus Christ died for us so we may enter heaven. You may want to be baptized, so you can unite with Jesus in heaven."

"I don't know about heaven," White Eagle said dismissively.

Chaska waited. A few minutes passed before he said, "In heaven, those saved by God will have new bodies without the curse of sin. There will be no one who is blind, deaf or lame in heaven. God is in heaven, and he will remain with us until he creates a new earth for us."

White Eagle whispered, "I don't think your God will want me. I have killed many people, and stolen, and burned." He paused and added, "I did not violate women."

"You may enter heaven if you confess the wrongs you have done—the sins you have committed. We have all sinned. If we confess our sins, God is faithful and will forgive us."

A soldier on guard duty rapped the wagon with the butt of his rifle.

"No talking," he growled.

The next day, Sibley's column entered the outskirts of New Ulm. Its citizens were just returning after the battles in August resulted in the deaths of fifteen defenders and civilians and the virtual destruction of the town. They were cleaning up and beginning to rebuild the more than one hundred dwellings that had been burned to the ground.

As Sibley approached, Sheriff Charles Roos boldly rode up to Sibley and demanded he turn over any prisoner who had participated in the attacks on New Ulm. Sibley refused, but agreed to divert his train around rather than through the town. Sensing danger, he deployed troops to protect the prisoners and native women.

Emma Eifert, a thirty-four-year-old woman and mother of two boys, was re-interring her husband who was killed during the second battle and hastily buried before New Ulm was abandoned. She joined a mob of men, women, and children running toward the wagons holding the prisoners. They wielded an assortment of weapons.

Eifert had a pickaxe. Screaming Dutch epithets and shouting, "Moordenaar! Moordenaar!" she dodged a soldier trying to block her path, leaped onto a wagon, and buried the pick in the back of a prisoner. Before she could deliver another blow, a trooper grabbed her skirt and yanked her out of the wagon. Undeterred, she climbed into Chaska's wagon and furiously pummeled him and White Eagle with her fists and feet. Two soldiers wrestled her off the wagon and pinned her to the ground. Later, Sibley would refer to her as the 'Dutch tigress'.

The New Ulm mob was driven back by a Sibley-led bayonet charge but not before more prisoners and soldiers sustained injuries from clubs, knives, and rocks. Chaska and White Eagle were unharmed, but two wounded prisoners later died.

While Sibley continued on to Mankato, a second column of seventeen hundred Dakota Sioux non-combatants—women, children, and elderly—and members of the Dakota Peace Party were traveling overland to Fort Snelling where they would be held until the Department of the Interior decided what to do with them.

In command was Lieutenant Colonel Marshall, a member of the Military Commission, who anticipated trouble enroute from angry settlers and local militias.

He declared to the newspapers that, "I would risk my life for the protection of these helpless beings…I want the settlers in the valley to know that they are not the guilty Indians."

After crossing to the north bank of the Minnesota River, Marshall's overfilled train slowly moved east. In its path was the town of Henderson where many settlers had fled when the war broke out. The townspeople, including many refugees, were all too aware of the savage outrages committed by Little Crow's soldiers.

Despite Marshall's announcement that these Indians were innocent of wrongdoing, his train was met by an armed, angry multitude. One white woman grabbed a nursing baby from its Dakota mother and bashed it on the ground; the baby died and was buried that night. Eventually, Marshall and his men drove off the mob and continued their slow march to Fort Snelling.

When Sibley reached Mankato, the prisoners were housed at Camp Lincoln, a name given to it by someone whose identify has been lost to history. There they would await news from Washington. By now, everyone knew the fate of the prisoners would be decided by President Lincoln. Sibley departed for St. Paul, and would not return.

Chapter 16

On November 11, Secretary of the Interior Caleb Smith received a letter from the Commissioner of Indian Affairs, William P. Dole, who was in Minnesota. Smith promptly forwarded the letter to President Lincoln. In it, Dole wrote:

"My attention has been called to a statement in the newspapers to the effect that some three hundred Sioux Indians have been tried by Court Martial and condemned to be hanged for murders committed during the late outbreak in Minnesota, and that the execution of the sentence only awaits the approval of the President...I cannot reconcile it to my sense of duty to remain silent while measures of the character indicated in the statement above mentioned are being executed. I am fully aware, that in the prosecution of their hostilities, these Indians perpetrated most horrible and atrocious crimes, and were guilty of barbarities which shock every feeling of humanity, and are only known in Indian warfare. The whole country is justly incensed and exasperated by their conduct, but, notwithstanding this, it seems to me that an indiscriminate punishment of men who have laid down their arms and surrendered themselves as prisoners, partakes more of the character of revenge than the infliction of deserved punishment; that it is contrary to the spirit of the age, and our character as a great, magnanimous and Christian people...their sentence may be modified by the President, and for the reasons above imperfectly and hastily set forth. I trust you will lay the subject before him, together with this letter and, if possible, prevent the consummation of an act which I cannot believe would be otherwise than a stain upon our national character, and a source of future regret."

Lincoln read and reread Dole's letter and handed it to John Hay.

"It's my fault. All of it," Lincoln said. "I started to tell Mrs. Lincoln how I felt, but thought better of it. Willie's death still lies heavily on her. But I will tell you, John."

"You may recall early this year I received a report from Special Commissioner George Day describing the fraud committed by Indian agents. It was outright thievery—no other way to characterize it. Soon after, I received another letter, this one from Bishop Whipple, warning me of a marked deterioration in Indian affairs. But on both occasions, I failed to act. I simply got it off my desk."

"And the upshot is hundreds of innocent dead people, mostly farmers and their families, many of them immigrants who struggled and sacrificed to come to this country. Now, there are three-hundred and three Indians and mixed-bloods awaiting hanging, and an enraged citizenry that will accept nothing less than a mass execution and the exile of every Indian in the State of Minnesota."

"Mr. President," Hay began, "you make difficult decisions every day. Last week you replaced McClellan with General Burnside…"

"I know, John," Lincoln interrupted. "Precisely. I make decisions. That's my job—the President's responsibility. In the case of this Minnesota Indian calamity, I did not do my job. I referred it to someone else, and failed to follow-up." He paused, randomly selected a document from his desk, glanced at it and tossed it back on the pile.

"Kindly inform Attorney General Bates that I will need his services. We are going to thoroughly review every single capital case, all three-hundred and three of them. No Indian—no man—is going to hang unless there is evidence he has committed murder or rape."

Lincoln picked up Commissioner Dole's letter.

"I will tell Dole that I admire his thinking and particularly the statement, 'I cannot reconcile it to my sense of duty to remain silent'. I—the country—need more men like him."

Attorney General Edward Bates was the oldest member of Lincoln's cabinet and the least busy. He occupied the office before the creation of the Department of Justice, and he had no authority over U.S. attorneys. His main function was to generate legal opinions for Lincoln and the cabinet, but they were seldom requested because the President and many members of his cabinet were lawyers themselves.

So the Attorney General had time to spare, and Bates immediately immersed himself in the trial records of the Dakota Sioux prisoners awaiting execution.

Julia and Elliot boarded the steamboat *Antelope* at Redwood and cruised down the Minnesota River to St. Paul, where they took the first of three trains to Washington. Shortly after they boarded the train from Philadelphia to Washington, the conductor entered their car and announced that a young expectant mother was in labor and asked if any of the passengers was a doctor or midwife.

Julia raised her hand, and the conductor ushered her to a car in the rear of the train. It was a special car similar to the one P.T. Barnum had built for Jenny Lind's singing tour in 1851. The car had a parlor, bedroom, bathroom, and galley.

Two men were in the parlor. The tallest was Bishop Henry Whipple who was traveling from New York to Washington to see President Lincoln. The other was his friend, George Wingate Parks III, heir to a shipping fortune, whose wife was suffering labor pains in the bedroom.

The conductor said, "Mr. Parks, this lady is a midwife and may be able to help Mrs. Parks."

Parks bowed slightly to Julia and said, "Excellent, and you are?"

"I'm Mrs. Julia Lindquist. I am a midwife. Where is the expectant mother?"

"In here," Parks replied, opening a door. Julia entered the narrow bedroom. Lying on the bed was a pretty young woman drenched in perspiration and moaning unintelligibly. An anxious older woman in a maid's uniform was standing at the head of the bed.

"Excuse me," Julia said, as she sat down and felt the young woman's pulse. It was fast and thready. "What's your name?" Julia asked.

"Martha, Martha Parks," she replied.

"Martha, I am a midwife. I have delivered hundreds of babies. I will help you deliver yours. Is this your first?"

"Yes, and thank you for coming," Martha replied, as another contraction began.

Ninety minutes later Julia emerged from the bedroom and said, "Congratulations, Mr. Parks, you are the father of a very healthy boy. Martha is doing fine."

Bishop Whipple stepped forward and patted Parks on the shoulder and shook his hand. "Wonderful, Ben. Congratulations."

Parks asked, "Mrs. Lindquist, can you stay with us for a while—until we know Martha is recovering?"

"Yes, of course," Julia replied, "but could you send someone for my husband, Elliot Lindquist. He's in the third or fourth car, I believe. The conductor knows who he is."

After Elliot arrived, the four of them sat in the parlor sipping tea while Martha slept. Bishop Whipple learned that the Lindquists were members of the unfortunate Swedish farm family that was reported in the St. Paul Press.

"So tragic," Whipple said. "I suppose you are looking forward to the executions. By the way, may I inquire why you are traveling to Washington?"

Elliot turned to Julia, who explained, "We're hoping to see the President and ask that he pardon one of the Indians. And Bishop Whipple, may I say that we are not 'looking forward to the executions' as you put it. Ten members of my husband's family were murdered ruthlessly. We do expect their killers to hang."

Whipple reached out and took Julia's hand. "Mrs. Lindquist, I did not intend to imply you were bloodthirsty. I simply meant you wanted justice for your departed relatives." Julia nodded.

Whipple then asked, "May I inquire who is the Indian you will ask the President to pardon?"

"His name is Chaska," Julia replied. "He saved our lives, mine in particular." She proceeded to describe the events in detail and Sibley's refusal to pardon Chaska. "The general said it was no longer in his power to do so, and he sarcastically told us to take it up with President Lincoln. That is the reason we are traveling to Washington."

Whipple smiled and said, "Of course, Sibley never thought you would actually try to see the President."

Smiling, Elliot said, "No doubt, but then he doesn't know my wife."

"Mrs. Lindquist," Whipple said, "as you probably know, there are quite a few Indians who go by the name of Chaska. I know of at least three. Can you tell me more about this particular Chaska?"

Julia replied, "He is a Christian Dakota Sioux who lives at Hazelwood..."

Whipple raised his hand. "Pardon the interruption. I know him, or I should say I know of him. His Dakota name is Tawachi and he teaches the First

Testament at the Hazelwood School. Reverend Stephen Riggs speaks highly of him. What was he found guilty of?"

Elliot replied, "He was present when another Indian shot a trader, a fellow named Gleason. That was sufficient reason for the Military Commission to find him guilty of murder and sentence him to death."

Whipple stood and paced the small room for a minute.

"I have an appointment with President Lincoln the day after tomorrow. I am asking him to pardon any Indian not directly responsible for a death or rape. You can accompany me, if you choose, and present Chaska's case."

Julia responded. "Yes, that would be wonderful, thank you." A healthy baby's cry from the bedroom prompted smiles from everyone.

The nation's capital was choked with people, mostly military and camp followers but also a growing number of government workers and vendors. The city's population had doubled during the year and a half since the beginning of the Civil War. The rapid expansion strained sanitary facilities, and newcomers brought diseases such as measles and smallpox.

Being November, the wagons of the express companies were loaded with turkeys and chickens. The prevailing street chatter was about McClellan's dismissal and the likelihood that General Ambrose Burnside could secure a Union victory over Robert E. Lee before Christmas.

After spending the night as guests of the Parks family, the Lindquists met Bishop Whipple outside the White House at 11 o'clock in the morning. They took the graveled pathway past the statue of Thomas Jefferson to the North Front entrance.

"I must warn you," Whipple said, "there will be dozens of people in here hoping to see the President. We will make our way single file past them, and up the stairs to his second-floor office. Mrs. Lindquist, I will take you by the hand, and Mr. Lindquist you will follow close behind your wife."

They made their way through the throng of people occupying nearly every square foot of floor space from the doorway to the staircase. The air was stuffy and polluted with cigar smoke and stale smells. Whipple's clerical collar and commanding physical presence persuaded the crowd to give way, and soon they were standing outside Lincoln's office where they were met by John Hay.

"Good morning, Bishop, the President will be with you shortly. He is meeting with the Attorney General. May I inquire who are with you?"

Whipple introduced the Lindquists and the reason they were accompanying him.

"I'm sure the President will be interested," Hay said. "He often mentions your last meeting with him in September. It touched him deeply."

The door opened and an elderly gentleman emerged holding a stack of papers. It was Edward Bates.

He thrust the papers into Hay's hands and said, "John, these are the case reviews for the Indians awaiting execution in Minnesota. The President asked me to give them to you so he might refer to them as needed." Hay thanked him, and Bates plunged into the mass of people lining the stairway.

Lincoln appeared in the doorway. "Bishop, a pleasure to see you again. Please come in."

"Thank you, Mr. President, and may I introduce Mr. and Mrs. Lindquist from Minnesota. They lost most of their family during the recent Indian uprising. They have a special request regarding one of the convicted Indians."

"I see," Lincoln replied, as he gestured for them to be seated. "But first I should tell you in complete confidence that we have nearly finished our review of the three-hundred and three capital cases."

"I was anxious to not act with so much clemency as to encourage another outbreak on one hand, nor with so much severity as to be real cruelty on the other. And as you suggested, Bishop, we attempted to distinguish between those who participated in massacres from those who took part in battles. We found evidence that only two Indians were actually guilty of rape, a much smaller number than alleged during the trials."

Years later, Julia and Elliot would recall their meeting with Abraham Lincoln as if it just occurred. The feelings he engendered survived undiminished. This man was carrying the burden of the Civil War on his shoulders. Yet, in this moment and on this issue, he was completely focused on justice for a group of men who had no political or economic standing, and who could have been conveniently dispatched by allowing Governor Ramsey and General Pope determine their fate.

"Mr. President," Whipple asked, "May I ask how many of them you will pardon?"

"You may ask, Bishop, but the exact number of those to be executed is not yet known. And even if it were, I would be reluctant to say just now. I can tell you, again in confidence that the majority will not hang. That is a fact that I do not want to be public until after my message to Congress next week."

"I assure you, Mr. President, that any information you share with us today will always remain private," Whipple said. He glanced at Julia and Elliot, and both nodded their agreement.

Lincoln turned to Julia and Elliot. "Now Mr. and Mrs. Lindquist, you have a request. First, though, tell me about your family's tragedy."

When Elliot finished, Lincoln said, "Mrs. Lincoln and I are deeply sorry for your loss and offer our condolences to you and your family. I know of other families in Minnesota who are grieving murdered relatives, but none of such magnitude as yours." He paused and glanced at Bishop Whipple.

Whipple took the cue and said, "Julia, kindly tell the President about Chaska."

"Mr. President," Julia began, "I was captured at Hutchinson, stripped of my clothing, and taken by the Indians to their camp on the Minnesota River. During the night, which was quite cool, a Christian Dakota named Chaska gave me clothing and food. He continued to look after me and other captives until Elliot and his brother found us. By us, I mean myself and two of Elliot's cousins who were also captives. Chaska helped us escape by directing us to a shallow place in the river where we could cross safely. And, he told us how to avoid being recaptured as we made our way back to Hutchinson."

"I have since heard that Chaska helped other women captives like me. He risked his life for us, and asked for nothing in return. I knew him only briefly, but I cannot conceive of him harming anyone, much less committing murder. We told this to General Sibley and asked him to pardon Chaska, but he said the decision was now yours. That is why we are here. We ask simply that he be pardoned and set free."

Lincoln retrieved a letter from his desk. "Last week I received this letter from Mrs. Sarah Wakefield. In it, she too asked for a pardon for Chaska and recounted how he protected her during the weeks of her captivity. Apparently she and her two children lived in his wigwam for nearly a month. She also said Chaska was present when another Indian—Hapa was his name—shot and killed the man who was driving Mrs. Wakefield and her children to safety. I asked Attorney General Bates to inquire about Mrs. Wakefield, and his sources in Minnesota seemed to indicate Chaska and Mrs. Wakefield may have been romantically involved. Do you know anything about this?"

"No, I don't, Mr. President," Julia replied. "I did meet Mrs. Wakefield and her children while I was a captive. I can't imagine them being lovers. But I can't positively say they were not."

"It's not relevant, is it?" Lincoln said, not expecting a reply.

He sighed and smiled. "Mr. and Mrs. Lindquist, thank you for bringing Chaska to my attention. I will review his case personally." Lincoln smiled and stood, "I wish you a safe trip home to Minnesota."

Wistfully, he added, "One day I hope to visit Minnesota. I would like to see your land and meet your family. And Bishop Whipple, it is always a pleasure visiting with you."

Crowds of angry men gathered in the river towns of New Ulm, St. Peter, and Mankato. The topic was Lincoln's long-awaited announcement of how many Dakota Sioux prisoners would be hanged and how many would be pardoned and released. The newspapers reported the President's December 1 message to Congress. In regard to the Dakota Sioux uprising, he said:

"The State of Minnesota has suffered great injury from this Indian war. A large portion of her territory has been depopulated, and a severe loss has been sustained by the destruction of property. The people of that State manifest much anxiety for the removal of the tribes beyond the limits of the State as a guarantee against future hostilities…I submit for your especial consideration whether our Indian system shall not be remodeled. Many wise and good men have impressed me with the belief that this can be profitably done."

Doubtless the last sentence brought some satisfaction to Bishop Whipple, but for most Minnesotans the message was a disappointment because it contained no hint of the President's decision regarding the prisoners at Camp Lincoln. Consequently, local meeting houses, and particularly taverns in the Minnesota River valley were scenes of secret plotting and planning. Various schemes were hatched and the universal goal was death to the Indians and anyone who tried to interfere.

The prisoners at Camp Lincoln had little shelter from the bitter cold. They huddled together in the frigid December weather. After a heavy snowfall, the temperature dropped further, and they set fire to their straw bedding to keep warm.

The officer in charge was Colonel Stephen Miller who fought at Bull Run and other battles before returning to Minnesota when the uprising began. Since taking command, his primary concern were rumors of a large lynch mob heading for Camp Lincoln. After collecting reinforcements and more cavalry, he confronted the mob of two hundred or so men on the night of December 4.

They were from St. Peter and Traverse des Sioux. A contingent from New Ulm had turned back after learning well-armed soldiers were waiting for them. The mounted Miller and his troopers surrounded the mob as it approached the camp.

Miller hollered, "Who comes there?"

Someone replied, "We have come to take the Indians and kill them!"

Miller barked, "You will do nothing of the kind!"

And that ended it. Miller arrested a few and the rest retreated, a sensible course of action given the sub-zero temperature. No conspirator was prosecuted because no public official in Minnesota would bring charges, and regardless no local jury would have found any one of them guilty.

The following day, Miller transferred the condemned Indians to a new log prison constructed in the middle of Mankato. The heavily guarded transfer of chained prisoners from Camp Lincoln to the center of Mankato was uneventful, primarily because its citizens did not expect any one of them to leave town alive.

A week later, Sibley received the transcription of a handwritten document from the President:

"Ordered that of the Indians and Half-breeds sentenced to be hanged by the military commission, composed of Colonel Crooks, Lt. Colonel Marshall, Captain Grant, Captain Bailey, and Lieutenant Olin, and lately sitting in Minnesota, you cause to be executed on Friday the nineteenth day of December, instant, the following names, to wit 39 names listed by case number…The other condemned prisoners you will hold subject to further orders, taking care that they neither escape, nor are subjected to any unlawful violence. Abraham Lincoln, President of the United States."

Thus Lincoln reduced the number to be executed from three hundred-three to thirty-nine. This was the result of a careful review by two government lawyers, George C. Whiting and Francis Ruggles, who carefully reviewed every case. They found no evidence that two hundred-sixty-four prisoners took part in a 'massacre' or committed rape.

In one case, that of ex-slave Joseph Godfrey, Lincoln conducted his own review. This occurred because General Sibley and the Military Commission disagreed. Sibley favored execution, while the Commission thought a lesser penalty was appropriate since Godfrey had been a very cooperative witness. Lincoln, who wanted to reduce the number executed, sided with the Commission and commuted Godfrey's sentence to ten years in prison.

On the list of thirty-nine was eighteen-year-old Wahcoota. He was the first son of a Mdewakanton chief, and thus called Chaska by members of his family and village. Joseph Godfrey testified that Wahcoota participated in the Milford massacre. When he was sentenced to hang by the Military Commission, his name was entered as Chaska Wahcoota on the court record that was forwarded to Lincoln. Not on the list was Chaska Tawachi, whom Lincoln pardoned, with the concurrence of Whiting and Ruggles, after the Lindquist's visit to the White House.

The two Chaskas met at Camp Lincoln when White Eagle introduced them on the day they arrived in the new Mankato prison.

"Godfrey lied," White Eagle said. "Wahcoota was not at Milford. He was at Birch Coulee, but he had no weapon and did not fight."

"Still, he might be on the White Father's list to hang." Chaska said.

Wahcoota nodded. He was tall for an Indian and muscular. His chiseled features belied an inner kindness.

"Yes, but that's not why I wanted to meet you. White Eagle spoke of your God and Heaven. I would like to know more. You are a Christian?"

"I am, since I was young," Chaska replied. "We Christians and those who are learning like White Eagle meet twice a day—in the morning and late afternoon We read from the Bible and talk. You are welcome to join us. We were meeting in the bark wigwam at Camp Lincoln. Here we will meet by the straw bales, over there, in the corner."

Colonel Miller read of the bloody battle at Fredericksburg in the St. Paul Pioneer. On December 11, Burnside crossed the Rappahannock River in eastern Virginia with one hundred thousand men of the Army of the Potomac and entered Fredericksburg. They were three weeks late. As so often happened in this army, someone had screwed up.

The portable pontoon bridges were still in Washington when Burnside arrived on the riverbanks opposite Fredericksburg in late November. During these three critical weeks, Lee was able to assemble his army and occupy a strong defensive position above the town. So strong, in fact, that Lee thought Burnside would not assault it, and was likely planning an attack downstream. Except that Burnside was the most incompetent general ever placed in command of an army.

The following day, incredibly, Burnside ordered General Sumner to make a frontal assault on Marye's Heights where James Longstreet was entrenched in force. At the same time, General Franklin attempted to turn Lee's right flank that was solidly anchored by Stonewall Jackson.

The outcome was a bloody Union defeat with the Army of the Potomac suffering over twelve thousand casualties. Wave after wave of brave young men were slaughtered in the meat grinder of Confederate bullets and cannonballs. The ordinary soldier's heroism could not overcome their commanding general's stupidity.

Miller tossed the newspaper aside and said to his adjutant, Lieutenant D. K. Arnold, "Another licking, I'm afraid. Cashiering McClellan was a mistake."

He stood, went to the window, and looked down on the site where the gallows would be built. It was near the river and opposite the log prison. Already the execution date had been postponed a week from December 19 to the day after Christmas. The delay was due to the lack of enough rope to hang the thirty-nine Indians.

Already Mankato was filling up with people who wanted to view the hangings. They were coming from everywhere. From St. Paul and Minneapolis on stagecoaches and steamboats, and from the Minnesota River towns in wagons and on horseback. The weather warmed, melting the late November snow and turning roads into tracks of tenacious mud that fouled wheels, clung to axles, and sucked shoes off horses. Soon all the rooms for rent were taken. Many visitors pitched tents, slept in their wagons, or resorted to staying in neighboring towns.

Chaska's twice daily Bible readings were attracting an increasing number of prisoners. So much so that they were constantly shifting the straw bales to create more space. Wahcoota became his most astute and devoted pupil. The young man's memory was astounding. He could recite verses after hearing them once. He asked insightful questions, some of which Chaska found difficult to answer. After a week, Chaska asked Wahcoota if he would like to lead one of readings. This he did on Sunday morning, December 21.

Forty-four prisoners were seated on the floor and more were standing behind them. All were thin, cold, and weary. Hopelessness had overtaken them. The only sound was the occasional clinking of a shackle.

"I will read from the Book of John," Wahcoota began in a bold deep voice.

"John said 'For God so loved the world, that he gave his only begotten Son, that whosoever believeth in Him should not perish, but have everlasting life'."

Lifting Chaska's Bible high so all could see it, Wahcoota said, "Now, together, let us recite what John said."

Wahcoota then repeated the verse, word by word, and waited for his listeners to echo each phrase. They did so, subdued at first, but with growing conviction.

Wahcoota continued, "All you need to know about God is in the words of John. 'God loves you so much that he gave his only Son. And if you believe in Him you will not perish'."

A prisoner stood and shouted, "If he loves us, Wahcoota, why doesn't he free us from these chains?"

Chaska feared Wahcoota would not be able to answer the question; he was about to respond for him when Wahcoota said, "God loves you. God created you. But he cannot live your life. If you have sinned and if you confess your sins and accept God into your life, he will forgive you, and you will go to Heaven and be with God and the Lord Jesus."

The prisoner sat down, and another arose. "Are we all to die here?" he asked. "Or will this God save us?"

Chaska was no longer concerned about Wahcoota's ability to answer.

"All of us have two lives," Wahcoota began. "The life here on earth, and our spiritual life. We may leave the earth, but if we believe in God our spiritual life goes on forever and all of us will meet again in Heaven."

"That is, provided we accept God and Jesus and confess our sins. So yes, our bodies may die here, but all of us have the opportunity to live again in Heaven. It is up to you to decide if you want to cleanse your spirit and be saved."

Wahcoota paused and scanned his audience. His handsome face expressed compassion. He held up the Bible and said, "If you want to be saved, come forward and touch the Book. Please, come forward and touch this Book. I will wait while you decide." He folded his arms and bowed his head.

No one moved. A minute passed. Slowly, the prisoner who asked about death stood and came forward. Wahcoota offered the Bible. The prisoner grasped it with both hands and pressed his face against it. Another prisoner did the same, and another, until more than half the group touched the Book. It was a deeply spiritual moment, even for many who did not come forward.

Chaska realized this young Dakota man was unique, a natural preacher. He had been born with a God given gift. It must not be wasted.

The following morning nearly a hundred prisoners showed up for the meeting. Chaska was reading from the Gospel of Luke when Colonel Miller appeared leading a platoon of soldiers. His adjutant, Lieutenant Arnold shouted in Dakota, "When I call your name, step forward!"

The perceptive Chaska deduced that Arnold was calling the names of the Indians who would be executed. Construction of the gallows had begun that morning. It was logical that Miller would segregate the condemned prisoners in preparation for hanging.

As the first names were being called, Chaska took Wahcoota by the arm and whispered, "If he calls your name, I will step forward."

Perplexed, Wahcoota asked, "But why?"

Chaska replied, "Do as I say. And take the Bible."

"What if you are also on the list?"

"I know I'm not. Don't ask me how I know, but I do." Chaska said firmly.

Arnold continued to read from the list. "White Eagle!"

Then, after eleven more names were read, "Chaska Wahcoota!"

As Chaska stepped forward, White Eagle gave him a quizzical look. A faint murmuring emanated from the other prisoners.

"Silence!" Arnold barked.

After Arnold read the last name, Miller ordered the thirty-nine prisoners to be removed to the first floor of an adjoining three story stone warehouse known as the Leech Building. Once there each man would be chained to the floor.

Chapter 17

The skeleton of the massive gallows was taking shape. It was a square structure measuring twenty-four feet on a side, fourteen feet high, and it was constructed of freshly cut oak. Each of the four top beams was notched to accommodate ten nooses. The condemned men would stand on a single platform that was suspended by a series of ropes tethered to a central rope. Once the nooses were tightened around their necks, the central rope would be cut, releasing the platform, and all thirty-nine men would drop and hang at once.

After the condemned men were secured in the Leech Building, Lieutenant Arnold informed them, for the first time, that they had been found guilty of a capital crime and would be executed in four days, on the day after Christmas. Colonel Miller advised them to spend their remaining time on earth seeking redemption, and said each man would have the opportunity to speak with a minister or priest. The pronouncements provoked no visible emotion.

Later that day, when they were alone, White Eagle asked Chaska, "Why did you step forward when he called for Chaska Wahcoota? I don't understand."

"White Eagle," Chaska responded, "why I did it is between me and God. I ask that you keep it to yourself, and to tell no one."

"No one needs to know. Especially these white devils. I would just like to know for myself."

Chaska said nothing and waved to a middle-aged man in a clergy's cassock. It was Monsignor Augustin Ravoux, a French Jesuit priest who had served the Dakota as a missionary for twenty years. Miller had arranged for Ravoux, Stephen Riggs, and John Williamson to provide spiritual support for the thirty-nine men.

"Father Ravoux," Chaska said, "I would like a Bible to use for the next few days. Is that possible?"

"Yes, of course," Ravoux replied. "I don't believe we've met. You are…?"

"Chaska Wahcoota," Chaska lied.

The priest studied Chaska and said, "I know the name but I can't connect it with your face."

Chaska smiled and raised his hands in a gesture of futility.

"Yes, of course," Ravoux said, "It is unimportant considering the circumstances. I will find a Bible for you. Is there anything else you need?"

"Yes, Father, I wish to be baptized before I die. I believe others here also want to be baptized."

Late in the afternoon Chaska spotted Stephen Riggs talking to several prisoners. Certainly Riggs would know he was not Wahcoota. There was a nook in the wall behind him where he could hide but the chain to his ankle was too short. Instead, he sat cross-legged and pulled the blanket over his head as if sleeping. A few minutes later he heard Riggs speaking with someone nearby.

"I am Reverend Stephen Riggs. I want to help you prepare your soul for salvation."

Silence was followed by, "Tell your sleeping friend over there I can help him, too." Chaska waited several minutes, and looked up. Riggs was gone.

Father Ravoux returned that evening with a Bible bound in dark maroon leather. He told Chaska he wanted it returned on Christmas day following the worship service and baptisms.

Chaska spoke to the entire group after their first decent meal since arriving in Mankato. The prisoners were sitting, swathed in their blankets. A few were smoking pipes or cigars. Most of them were attentive as Chaska stood holding the Bible.

"Death is the one certainty in life," he began. "Everyone will die sometime. We here will die four days from now. That is a fact, a certainty. Our time on this earth will end in four days. I say to you now that we should use our remaining time on this earth to prepare for life after death. Because there is life after death, a life that can be better and more fulfilling than the one we have lived here, on this land of ours."

"You may think there is no life after death. That is your decision and you may be right. Consider this, though, what if you are wrong, and there is in fact a life in Heaven, an eternal life with God and Jesus Christ? What if you fail to prepare yourself for that life while you are still here on earth? Would it not be wiser for you to give your spirit to God and Jesus Christ if there is just a chance Heaven awaits you?"

The only sounds were from a few ankle chains and firewood crackling in the stove.

Chaska continued, "To prepare, you must first learn about Jesus Christ and his relationship to God. Jesus was born to Mary, a virgin, and her husband Joseph, who had not lain with her before the birth of Jesus."

Chaska opened the Bible and said, "I read from the Gospel according to Saint Matthew, *'And Jesus, when he was baptized, went up straightaway out of the water, and the heavens were opened unto him and he saw the Spirit of God descending like a bird and lighting upon him. And a voice from Heaven said: This is my beloved Son'*."

He described the life of Jesus as a carpenter, preacher, and healer. He told of the miracles, the sermon on the mount and beatitudes, and the crucifixion and resurrection. Tomorrow we will learn how Jesus sent his eleven disciples to teach and baptize all men from all tribes.

"I leave you with this to think about tonight. It is from the Gospel According to John."

Chaska paused briefly and continued, "Jesus said to Martha, Mary's sister, *'I am the resurrection and the life: he that believes in me, though he were dead, yet shall he live. And whoever lives and believes in me shall never die'*."

Again, he paused, his head bent as if in prayer. Looking up, he scanned the motionless men. "Sleep on those words tonight, and find me in the morning."

Meanwhile, Colonel Miller was becoming increasingly concerned a riot could break out and interfere with the executions. A bunch of ruffians and rowdy toughs appeared in Mankato on December 18. They were heavy into beer and liquor, and many locals complained these undesirables were committing petty crimes and disturbances.

Finally, Miller appealed to Sibley for more troops, and he imposed a ban on the sale and consumption of alcohol. During the week before Christmas, Miller received over a thousand troops and cavalry from various regiments in the state.

Mina was allowed to visit White Eagle. They had not seen each other since Mina's family was killed and White Eagle captured. She was four and a half months pregnant, and it showed.

"You are with child," White Eagle whispered when he saw her. They clasped hands and sat on the floor.

"Yes," Mina said. "I will have him when the snow melts in the spring."

"Him, you say. How do you know it's a boy?"

"I just know," Mina replied. "I want to name him Running Bear, after my father."

"That is good." He grimaced. "I will never see him. We die in three days."

Tears flowed down Mina's cheeks.

"I know," she sobbed. He squeezed her hands.

"What will happen to you?" White Eagle asked.

"They are sending us to Fort Snelling. I was allowed to follow the prisoners here to cook and do laundry."

They sat together in silence until White Eagle said, "I've become a Christian." Pointing to Chaska, he continued, "That man has taught me about God and Jesus Christ. You too should become a Christian, so we can meet again in Heaven, and you can tell me about our son."

"What do I have to do?" Mina asked.

"Confess your sins, as I did. Mina, I did terrible things. I killed people. I killed women and children and dishonored their bodies. I deserve to die. I've asked God to forgive me."

A soldier signaled Mina. It was time to leave. White Eagle removed a woven leather necklace and handed it to her.

"Give this to our son when he becomes a young man. Tell him his father wants him to be a proud Dakota, and to follow God's teachings."

The following morning Lieutenant Arnold transferred the prisoner Tatemima from the Leech Building back to the log prison. It was discovered that he had been misidentified as the killer of a German woman. The list of those to be executed now numbered thirty-eight.

By Christmas day, thirty-six of the condemned prisoners chose to be baptized. Father Ravoux and John Williamson conducted the ceremony following the worship service. Afterwards, Chaska went to Father Ravoux and handed him the Bible he had borrowed.

"My son," Ravoux said, "keep the Bible. You have done God's work with these men, in a very short time. I find it difficult to believe you killed anyone, or harmed anyone. And I still cannot connect your name—Chaska Wahcoota—to your face."

Chaska knelt, and looking up said, "Father, this Book will comfort us tonight. We are very grateful."

The priest touched his forehead, "God bless you, Chaska Wahcoota—or whoever you are."

Later, Father Ravoux wrote: "Christmas day, I remained with the condemned from one o'clock in the afternoon until one o'clock at night…I delighted in praying with the poor fellows and conversing with them in a group together, or with each in private…In the moments of confidence we spoke of the things of God…I considered myself happy in being able to prepare them for the great journey to eternity. It was easy to see in the serenity of their countenances, the great calm that possessed their souls. And when they assured me that death had no terrors for them, I found no difficulty in believing them."

The work on the gallows continued until sundown on Christmas day when the thirty-eight nooses were finally in place.

The next morning dawned at 7:18 a.m. The sky was clear blue and the temperature was above freezing. At eight o'clock, the prisoners were given fresh Indian attire, war paint, and beads. The majority covered their faces and bodies with red iron oxide.

Although most of them had been baptized, they remembered what the medicine men had always told them: upon death, only those painted red would be allowed to pass over the river into paradise. Chaska was one of the few who wore a shirt and trousers and no paint; he had no doubt where he was going.

Outside, surrounding the gallows, were one thousand infantry and five hundred cavalry formed in an open square facing the Leech Building. The soldiers were there primarily to intercept any attempt by a mob to attack the prisoners. Around them were thousands of spectators who occupied every empty space on the ground, roofs, and hilltops. A few watched from a sandbar in the river.

At ten o'clock, the thirty-eight men were lined up in a column two by two. Their manacles were removed, and their elbows were tied behind their backs. They continued to talk with the guards, reporters, and clergy. Some of the Indians were joking, others simply chatting, and a few were content to be silent.

Chaska was at the end of the line. He would be the last to mount the gallows. White Eagle was next to him.

"You are going to die in white man's clothes?" White Eagle asked, frowning.

"No," Chaska replied, "I'm going to die in the clothes I have worn since I was a boy at Hazelwood." They shook hands.

"Thank you for all you have done for me," White Eagle said. "I wish I had known you before…" His word trailed off. "You understand…"

"I do," Chaska replied. "Soon we will be in a better place."

Someone tapped Chaska's shoulder. He turned. It was Stephen Riggs.

"Chaska!" he exclaimed, "what are you doing here? The President pardoned you!"

The door to the prison opened and the captain of the guard ordered the prisoners to march. The column began exiting the Leech Building onto Main Street where the mammoth gallows awaited them.

Chaska began walking while Riggs strode next to him.

"I don't understand, Chaska, why are you doing this? There is no reason for you to die…"

It was difficult to hear because the prisoners were singing a Dakota song.

Chaska handed his Bible to Riggs and said, "Reverend, read The Good Shepherd in the Gospel According to John."

Riggs took the Bible and watched as Chaska ascended the gallows. A guard placed a white muslin hood over his head, and adjusted the noose around his neck.

The thirty-eight men continued to sing. They stood on the gallows, holding hands, waiting.

The drum beats began. The rope was cut. Abruptly the platform dropped away. Suddenly there was silence.

Afterward, Riggs opened the Bible to John 10: 1–21, and began reading.

Epilogue

A month after the hangings, Whipple received a letter that Chaska wrote to him from prison. In it, he described Wahcoota's devotion to the Christian faith and the young man's unique qualities as a student and communicator. "Bishop Whipple," Chaska wrote, "I believe God is in him like no other man I have known. I pray you will seek his release from prison and admit him to your faith and trust."

With the assistance of William Huntington Reed, the rector of All Saints Church in Massachusetts, Whipple secured Wahcoota's release from Fort Snelling and brought him to Faribault. For two years, Wahcoota accompanied Whipple as the Bishop traveled about Minnesota. He learned the Episcopal Church's history and polity, and liturgy and theology.

Now, they were traveling west to the Dakota Territory where Wahcoota would establish a mission.

Whipple and Wahcoota arrived at the Lindquist farm.

Elliot and Julia welcomed the Bishop.

"So good to see you again, Bishop," Elliot said.

Smiling, Whipple removed his dusty hat.

"Thank you for allowing us to visit. I hope you received my letter."

"Yes, yes we did," Julia replied.

"Allow me to introduce my colleague, Wahcoota. He was highly recommended to me by Chaska, before his death. Wahcoota is working toward becoming a deacon in the Episcopal Church."

Wahcoota stepped forward when Julia offered her hand. His dark hair was cut short and he wore a black dickie with a white clerical collar, linen trousers, and a black frock coat.

"Mr. and Mrs. Lindquist, I understand you were responsible for obtaining Chaska's pardon from President Lincoln. I want to thank you. Chaska introduced me to Christ. He saved my life."

The day was hot and ravenous mosquitoes were gathering in the twilight.

Elliot said, "Please come in out of the sun. We still have a little ice that I cut from the lake last winter."

The four of them sat around the dinner table sipping cool water.

A child squealed and crawled into the room followed by a tow-headed boy.

Julia said, "These are our children, William and Rachel. William is six and Rachel just turned two." William sat on Julia's lap and Elliot picked up Rachel and kissed her cherry red cheek.

"How is the rest of your family?" Whipple asked. "They suffered such a loss."

"They're healthy, thank you. We replaced the log cabins with frame houses and rebuilt the barns. Put crops in at all four farms this spring. Right now, the harvest looks good. We created a company, so to speak, to handle all our financial affairs. We share the risks of farming and invest in equipment none of us could afford alone."

"My cousin, Robert, married a woman he met at Pillsbury's hardware store in Minneapolis where he works during the winter. Gustav is courting a midwife in Le Suer where he spends a fair amount of time working with Dr. Mayo. And my other cousin, Carl, lives with his aunt and her daughter. So, I would say we're doing fairly well. Except like you, Wahcoota, we owe so much to the people we've lost. The most important thing we can do is, make sure we are worth the sacrifices our family made for us."

Whipple said, "Now that the Civil War is over, I expect we're going to see more people moving here."

Elliot replied, "Already the land that people abandoned during the uprising is being re-settled."

"Did you hear Little Crow was killed in Hutchinson last month? He was picking raspberries. A farmer and his son shot him."

"Yes, we heard," Elliot replied, "the militia was called out briefly, but there was no disturbance."

Julia said, "Bishop Whipple, we are anxious to hear what happened to Chaska. Why did they hang him? His name did not appear on the list the President sent to General Sibley. How could—how did this happen?"

Whipple turned to Wahcoota.

"Perhaps you should explain, Wahcoota. You were there."

Wahcoota related how Chaska had taken his place when the condemned men were segregated from the other prisoners. "Mr. and Mrs. Lindquist, at the time I didn't know why he did it…" His voice cracked. "We know from Father Roux, a Catholic priest, and Reverend Riggs, that Chaska was responsible for converting nearly all of the men to Christianity before they were executed. He converted over a hundred other prisoners as well. He was greatly admired, and respected, even by the guards. A month or so after the executions, Reverend Riggs met with Bishop Whipple in St. Paul." He paused and looked to Whipple.

Whipple began, "Reverend Riggs saw Chaska in the prison just as he and the others were being taken to the gallows. He pleaded with Chaska not to go. Whereupon Chaska handed his Bible to Riggs and told him to read The Good Shepherd in the Gospel According to John. I have the Bible, here."

Whipple removed the maroon leather-bound Bible from his saddle bag. "Chaska underlined certain passages in John, chapter ten. The one most relevant, I believe is this." Whipple adjusted his spectacles and read slowly, "*I am the good shepherd: the good shepherd giveth his life for the sheep.*"

"You see, I was one of his flock," Wahcoota whispered, his words thick with feeling. "And so, too, were the other prisoners."

The room was quiet.

Finally, Whipple said, "Indeed, Chaska considered them his sheep."

He continued to read from John, "*I am the good shepherd, and know my sheep…and other sheep I have, which are not of this fold: them also I must bring, and they shall hear my voice; and there shall be onefold and one shepherd.*"

Julia said, "He sacrificed himself so you, Wahcoota, could live, and so others could be comforted and prepare for death."

"Yes, that is true, Mrs. Lindquist. Like a good shepherd, he showed them the way to redemption. Someday, I hope to write about him. More than anything, I want to live a life that justifies what he did for me."

The following morning Bishop Whipple and Wahcoota climbed into their wagon and headed west. They would travel through land that for a thousand years was home to indigenous Native Americans. Now the land was divided into parcels and sold to mostly well-intentioned people who would use the earth for their purposes, rarely share it with anyone, and do little to conserve it.

Ahead of them was a barren reservation created to hold an exiled people, the Dakota Sioux. Among its struggling occupants were Mina and her two-year-old son, Running Bear. Further west were other native peoples who would be despoiled, disenfranchised, and their land taken.

Manifest destiny was exerting itself in ways no one, not even Thomas Jefferson, could have anticipated. If he had lived, Abraham Lincoln would have reformed the system and enforced the law. However, his successors did not share his devotion to decency or the Constitution of the United States.